Cyclones and Daggers

Powerful Pawns Book Two

Rauri Rose

Book cover by Olivia at fiverr.com/oliviaprodesign

Map Designed on Inkarnate by X

Print ISBN: 979-8-9922776-3-0

E-book ISBN: 979-8-9922776-2-3

1st Edition 2025

Contents

FOREST OUTSIDE

OLVARIA

For those ready to take their life back...

CHAPTER ONE

The Red Band

Alaceandra

I f I get knocked out one more time, I swear to Ptheryeth, someone is
getting kicked in the balls. This blunt force trauma cannot be good
for my brain.

Where am I? I attempt not to gag as the smell of mildew and linen
assaults my senses. I know I am laying down somewhere. *But where?*

My head pounds as I struggle to open my eyes. They feel as if they are
permanently glued shut. I will my body to move, but it aches as if it has
been trampled by stampeding horses and I do my best not to cry out in
agony.

What the fuck happened? I finally muster the strength to peel each eye-
lid open, but only darkness greets me. *Great. All that effort for nothing.*
I blink rapidly before trying to run my fingers over the material beneath
me to get some bearing on my surroundings. Thankfully, I manage to get
one of my hands to twitch at my command with only the barest twinges
of pain. The other arm remains unresponsive. Wincing, I try to move the
other one again, but still it remains immobile.

Do not panic right now, Lace. Figure out what is going on. Panic later.
Taking a small breath, I allow the fingers of my responsive hand to trace

the linen beneath me. The fabric is smooth and silky, like a comforter spun from the finest threads. Now that I think of it, whatever I am laying on is quite soft. Which means, although my body is aching, it does not seem to be because of poor sleeping conditions.

Well that is nice at least... I think to myself sarcastically.

Laughter rings out from somewhere beside me and I try to lift my body to find the source, but my muscles reject the attempt. Instead, an oppressing weight forces me further into the mattress beneath me. If someone were to tell me that boulders were just stacked on top of me, I would believe them. *Remember to stay calm, Lace.*

"Easy," A terrifyingly familiar voice whispers disturbingly close to my face. "The spell is not fully complete yet. Once it finishes, you should feel a lot lighter. Then you may move."

"Spell?" I croak. My voice is raspy and I cough. The faint taste of something metallic—*blood?*— dances along my taste buds. Threads of panic weave themselves tighter around my heart. I fight against the invading force that I now recognize to be a spell with more fervor. More boulders stack on top of me making it almost impossible to move.

The man sighs. "Do not worry yourself. It should be settled in just a minute. Be patient." I feel a hand brush over my hair and I try to jerk away at the contact, but I find my body only feebly twitching. Nonetheless, once his hand disappears, so does the pain. The aches and weakness in my body slowly melt away until it is only the weight above me that stops my movement. My heart is racing, but I do my best to keep the panic out of my voice. *This man is powerful. Is he the reason why I am here?*

"Where..." A small tickle remains in my voice and I clear my throat to get rid of it. "Where am I?"

"You will learn soon enough."

I grit my teeth. "Is there something in the way of telling me now?"

"Hmm," is his only reply. I try to place his voice, but as soon as my mind latches on to the idea of someone, the memory floats away.

I grunt in frustration and I hear him chuckle in return. After another minute the weight on top of me lifts and so does the darkness. I shut my eyes against the light of the room. Although it is not overly bright, compared to the utter darkness of before, it feels blinding. While my eyes adjust, I clench the hand that only a moment ago was paralyzed. It complies without hesitation. *He is powerful indeed.* When I can finally see without squinting, I glance up and study the stranger warily. In front of me stands a man. A man who is far too close for comfort. Since I am now in control of my limbs, I scoot away from him hastily.

"There she is." The man chuckles before kneeling in front of me. He has white hair and red rimmed eyes with eyelashes tipped in black. He blinks them slowly at me, observing me like I am in some sort of exhibit.

I look away from him. "Who are you?" Maybe in another world I might think the man attractive, but his eyes are unnerving. They are voids of darkness that seem to lack a soul. I blink at a wall, trying to discard the image from my brain. The walls are made of brown and white stone with small etchings of winged creatures alongside fires and tattered buildings. When I turn my head, the carvings shimmer with some kind of red and gold powder, and I find myself a bit mesmerized at the sight.

"My name is Sydon." His voice jolts my attention away from the carvings and I swing my gaze back to him, biting my cheek so as to not react. "I met you once before. In a cave." He waits for a reaction, but I give him none. "Ah, I see you do not remember," he mutters to himself before smirking. "Either way, it is nice to make your acquaintance once again."

Cave? I wrinkle my brow. *What cave could he be...? Fuck. Was he one of the men that abducted me when I first arrived in the Dark Lands? Is*

3

that why he sounds so familiar? No. I would have remembered his face. I wonder if Sorin would recognize him... Memories crash into me of the past few weeks. I gasp, tears welling into my eyes. "Where is Sorin?" *He was stabbed, was he not? Is he... No, do not think like that, Alaceandra.* Pinpricks of heat start to well on my skin as I jump from the bed and start towards the door. *He has to be here too. He was with me in the woods. They would not have just left him, would they?*

A loud voice rings out in my head. *Stop. Go back to bed, Alaceandra.* My eyes widen as I feel my body mechanically make its way back to the bed at the center of the room and sit on the edge of the mattress. The heat that had started to burn along my form died in an instant the moment the voice entered my head. I shoot panicked eyes to Sydon.

He gives me a solemn nod. "I would not recommend you try to escape. You will find your efforts futile." He motions towards my arm.

I look down. On the wrist opposite of the bracelet Mandi gave me sits a new burgundy band made of some kind of stone. The skin around the band is red and raised. I touch the stone. As my fingers make contact, a zing of pain travels up my arm, and I tear my hand away.

"I would not recommend trying to rid yourself of that either," Sydon whispers.

"Why? Why am I here?" I stare down at the shackle, my shoulders slumping as tears start to fall from my eyes.

Sydon squats in front of me, capturing my gaze. "I think you know."

The prophecy that lay in that exact same cave, where Sydon claims to have first laid eyes on me, echoes in my brain.

Before her twenty-fifth birthday is upon her, this shall come to pass.
Catastrophe will strike those who wish to mar her skin.
Demoni shall roam the land in which she once called home.
Every creature shall know her name.

Fear will strike those with the most might.

Giants will pass away.

Hark, you who do not wish to hear this warning!

Ignorance will not save you from her bloody fists!

Justice will soon rule this land again.

Kindle her fire, make it worth her while and maybe her flames will not scorch those she loved so fiercely (though her flames are strong and grow hotter with her age, do not worry about their effect on you, they will not last too long—do not be afraid of her or yourself in this journey—we are counting on you to show her the true way to salvation, a way not lined with bodies, loss, and despair, but instead alight with the truth of the meaning behind her sparks—you are the only one who can achieve this, S, you are our only hope, please bring her back to us).

It has to be that damned prophecy, I think to myself, before I once again tear my gaze from the strange man.

"I will leave you to get adjusted," Sydon says, before standing and walking towards the door.

"Wait!" I call out.

"That man I was with... Is..." I swallow against my rising emotions. "Is he...?" I cannot bear to speak the words into existence.

Sydon's expression goes blank. "I will be back to sort your schedule soon," he says. Then he leaves, shutting the door behind him with a loud bang.

CHAPTER TWO

The Blast

The Prince

Hours ago...

My father is here. My muscles jerk from what can only be the residual power of one of the King of Helomasi's totems. I clench my fists against the pain ravaging my body. *I cannot let him control me. Not now. There is too much at stake.* Scanning the wreckage of the attack, I block another sword hurtling towards my head. Sending a stream of slicing wind at the attacker's arm, I watch as the limb gets severed from its owner and wrinkle my nose. *Gross.* Spinning on my heel, I search the remains for any sign of Alaceandra or the other two men. Once my father activated my totem, I lost sight of Alaceandra and her guard, who I once thought was named Credour, but have only come to learn in our journey is named Sorin. Who knew the little dove had her own tricks up her sleeve? *I must find them.* The idiotic soldier tries to swing at me once again with the arm not currently severed from his body, interrupting my thoughts. I kick out, causing the man to stumble and fall into a stack of bodies littering the ground. *How annoying.*

My eyes catch on movement towards the border. *There you are.* I watch Sorin sprint away from Fadres— or I guess Sam— with the princess close at his side. Suddenly, a burst of darkness explodes from Sam's form covering soldier after soldier in a sheen of darkness before they drop to the ground—dead. My eyes widen. *Well, isn't that impressive?* Using the breeze to boost my speed, I dodge the fallen corpses and make my way towards Sam, who is now fully immersed in whatever dark power he holds. The soldiers who remain try to grab at my clothing, but I deftly avoid their grip until I make it to Sam's side.

"Need some help over here?" I ask Sam in a dry tone.

He only grunts at me in response, throwing another beam of blackness at a soldier behind me.

I duck and glare at him. "Okay then." I form a sword of cutting wind and swing it at an armored man to Sam's left, causing Sam to jerk to the right.

He swings his gaze towards me, his eyes filled with ice. Wisps of darkness hug his head like a helmet and I cannot help but find this skill of his just a tad bit imposing. "This is not the time for games." His voice comes out in an icy growl and I back up a step.

"I didn't think it was. You are usually the one who plays them anyway." I dodge another soldier's club before it slams me in the face.

"Not when it comes to Lace, idiot." He throws a bit of... *death magick maybe?* at another armored man causing him to writhe on the ground in agony.

"If you say so." From where I'm standing that is the main thing he's doing, *but what do I know?* We all have our own games with Alaceandra. At least I can own up to mine.

"What the fuck is that supposed to mean?" Sam's voice is cold. Deadly. I would be more intimidated, but we are in the middle of a pretty intense battle and I have definitely lost sight of the little dove for a bit longer than I am comfortable with given the circumstances.

"Nothing. Look. Do you think you can hold them back with your magick? We should probably follow—"

Abruptly, a blast of energy knocks me forward and I spin around, only to realize it is coming from the woods outside the village. *The same woods the little dove ran into just moments ago.*

"What was that?" I whisper.

What is left of the soldiers in the village and the elvisera in the sky all turn toward where the energy emanated and rush in its direction, leaving the remaining villagers, Sam, and me in their wake.

"Alaceandra," Sam says, before following the retreating forms of the attackers.

"Fuck," I reply, then sprint after him. *Please let her be okay.*

CHAPTER THREE

Ashes

The Prince

As we make our way into the trees, the voices whispering through the wind start to get louder and louder.

Once I capture—

—blood spilling over—

—for dinner—

—should be easy to—

—happened here?

I grit my teeth against the pain of the noise and will the voices to quiet as we tread on light feet towards the center of the forest. Unfortunately, it seems the invaders' short head start was enough for them to make it to the energy's center first. We quickly lose sight of them upon entry into the overgrown thicket of trees outside of Olvaria. A clawing energy gnaws at the pit of my stomach. I push the wind beneath us, making our steps lighter and faster as we race through the woods. *We have to make it. We just have to go a little faster.* Suddenly, the gnawing transforms into a stabbing pain resonating through my body, and I collapse to the ground, coughing up blood. Sam pauses in his steps.

"Go!" I gasp out. "You have to get to her."

Sam growls. "I am not just going to leave you here."

"I will be fine." I cough, and more blood pours from my mouth. "I only need a moment. I will catch up. We cannot let them have her."

"It is dangerous out here for you in this condition," Sam says stubbornly. Hauling me to my feet, Sam half-drags, half-carries me closer to the center of the forest. "If you are not recovered by the time we get there I will drop you near a tree, but I will not leave you. As annoying as you are, Alaceandra would never forgive me if I let something happen to you," Sam grumbles. "What is going on with you anyway?"

I grit my teeth in exasperation. "My father is here," I say simply.

Sam's eyebrows scrunch together. The pain from the totem starts to diminish and I yank my body away from Sam's, forcing myself to endure the aftershocks of pain from the totem I know will soon follow. Manipulating the air around us, I convince it to lend us more of its strength, resuming our speed. Although the pain of the totem is debilitating in the moment, its effects tend to wear off quickly, unless the user of the totem can maintain prolonged concentration and connection with the tool. Lucky for me, my father has never been so disciplined as to learn how to maintain this control, so the pain of the magickal weapon has never lasted long. Unfortunately, he instead prefers to use this weapon of choice in short bursts to weaken his victims before using his minions to control them by other means. *Ptheryeth forbid the man got his hands dirty himself.* I suppress a shiver. *I will get my revenge. I must.*

"What does your father have to do with—"

"I will tell you later." *I will have to if he has any part in this.* "For now, we need to find Alaceandra."

"Fine, but you will tell me. We cannot have you collapsing like that out on the battlefield."

"I'll try not to make a habit of it," I reply sarcastically.

A loud caw sounds in the distance, and the invading elvisera start to soar away from the forest. One by one, the voices in my head begin to dissipate. *No, no, no. Why are they leaving? Are they tracking Alaceandra? Or worse, did they find her?* Sam's and my pace quickens even further.

We finally make it to a clearing in the woods. Lavender invades my vision causing me to stop abruptly. *What the-?* The blackened branches and foliage of the forest are layered with a thick gray substance. *Ash.* Everything within the clearing is caked with a thick coating of ash. It glitters in the sunlight and chokes the air around us. *It's everywhere.* I look around and notice there is only one place that seems untouched by the heavy haze of soot. The ground at the edge of the clearing opposite us. Instead of that grass being covered with the thin gray powder, it is instead soaked with blood. Blood that seems to have all come from one body that used to lie at the clearing's edge, but is now nowhere to be seen. *Losing that much blood is sure to be fatal. I hope whoever died there did so quickly.* I don't allow myself to think that it could've been Alaceandra. *No, I would know if it was her. I am sure of it.*

"What happened here?" I echo one of the thoughts that invaded my brain not so long ago.

"Death," Sam hisses out.

I shoot him a sideways glance. "There are no bodies."

He looks at me, annoyed. "The ash is the bodies."

"Oh." My eyes are once again drawn to the blood-soaked spot on the forest floor. The injury must have been brutal. The deep red stains shine starkly against the gray coating surrounding them. The blood looks fresh. It is still wet, the liquid not completely soaked into the ground yet. Although I have seen a lot of gore today, something about this picture has dread clawing at my throat. Alarm bells ring in my head as I continue to stare, but no matter how much I try, I can't pinpoint why. I gesture to the morbid scene. "That one must have died before the blast, then."

"Or was injured before, but yes."

I turn my head in his direction. "There is no way someone loses that much blood and doesn't die."

Sam shrugs. "Either way, this looks like there was a fight here of some sort. Seeing as Alaceandra's strongest ability is fire at the moment. I have to think it was involving her."

"Do you think Sorin is still with her?"

Sam's eyes trace over the blood-soaked ground. "I have to," he whispers.

I nod. "I do not sense anyone else around here. I think all the rest of the invaders have left." I point towards a retreating elvisera in the distance. "Do you think that means...?"

The darkness floating around Sam's form grows more intense, more restless. He gestures to our surroundings. "With all this ash? Either parum bellator fried these assholes and escaped." He meets my eyes. "Or they have her." Sam turns his gaze to the retreating elvisera. It has now flown so far that is barely visible in the sky. "Unfortunately, the fact that they are retreating does not tell me that she escaped. I think they would still be scouting the woods searching for her if that were the case. No, they got what they wanted." He looks back at me, his eyes swirling with blackness and turmoil. "Now we just have to get her back."

"We will," I say with certainty. *We have to.*

...assholes! Always leaving me behind...

A man's voice causes me to jerk my head towards the woods. *Ah, so they have not all left.* For the first time in my life, I smile at the invading noise. "And I know just who to question first." I stalk in the direction of the sound. Sam, for the first time in our encounters with each other, follows me without question.

CHAPTER FOUR

The Incident

Alaceandra

Present...

I search the room for anything I can use as a weapon. Although I would not say my short stint in Olvaria has made me an expert in survival, I have learned enough in my training with the men, *and the battle that landed me in this place,* to know that I very likely need something to help me go against the leaders here if I am to escape. The room I am in is somewhat small. The most notable aspects are the carvings in the walls and the floor which glitters of a familiar red stone. I pause my search and crouch down to study the flooring more closely. The stone is strangely reminiscent of what was woven into the armor of the men that attacked us. *How curious.* I store that detail in the back of my brain for later.

A creaking jars me from my thoughts. My eyes dart around quickly to see if I can find something, *anything* that can work as a weapon for the time being, but this room seems completely bereft of sharp objects. As I am about to give up all hope, my eyes catch on a small golden pin stuck between the foot of the bed and the floor. *Probably will not help with much, but better than nothing I suppose.* Reaching, I catch the edge of it with my nail and pull it towards me. Quickly, I weave the small pin into the waistline of my clothing as I scramble to stand upright. As soon as it is completely hidden, the door opens. I lick my lips nervously and try to move carefully to not stab myself as I turn to see who has entered my new prison.

My father stands in the doorway, face red, his hands clenched at his sides. He stares daggers at me as his breath saws in and out of him and his body vibrates as if it is taking everything in him to stay where he is. He is wearing bronze robes but they are slightly tattered. A twig is still half attached to the bottom of his cape and dirt is smudged on his face and hands. I would laugh at his state if his murderous glare was not fully directed at me.

My heart stops. I take a step back. "King Nikoli." My voice is shaking.

"Insolent brat."

He advances on me, the soft scrape of the blackened twig trailing after him. "I warned you not to make a fool of me and what do you do?" Suddenly, he grabs me by the throat; his eyes are crazed, unfocused. "The first chance you get you go running off with my trusted advisors and the prince from the other kingdom? I will not be made a fool twice, Alaceandra. You will behave this time or I swear to all of Ptheryeth I will—" Shocked, I claw at his fingers. I am about to reach for the pin I had just armed myself with when a throat clears from the hall.

"Now King Nikoli, we are not to harm the princess, at least not so soon. Please meet the other kings in the grand hall for discussions. I need to inform the princess of her schedule."

Sydon stands just on the other side of the threshold, a cold, calculating look on his face.

My father releases me and I gasp for air. My father backs up a couple steps and I clench my fists to stop myself from retaliating. *You will get your revenge soon enough,* a sweet, sickly voice rings out in the back of my head. My eyes widen at the sound. I had heard it once before. My stomach turns at yet another reminder that I have no idea where Sorin is or if he is okay.

"You heard my warning," my father grunts. *I did, but you did not hear mine. Do not worry, dear father, even warnings not heard can be delivered.* That same voice giggles in my head as I track my father's progress as he leaves the room, pushing past Sydon and disappearing down the corridor. I suppress a shudder.

Sydon watches King Nikoli exit the hall before looking back at me and sighing. "He was not supposed to be in here."

I shoot him a confused look.

"What?"

He walks towards me slowly shutting the door behind him.

"He was supposed to see you with the others. Not alone. I was not going to have him see you yet."

I back away from him. "What authority do you have over that?"

"Don't worry about that for now."

He cannot be serious. I let out a small groan.

He widens his eyes at me before chuckling. "I can see you are frustrated. I am only approaching you to heal that wound on your neck before it worsens. You are to meet the others soon and we do not want bruises around your neck when that happens. I also would like to hand you your schedule for the next week. Please do not be startled."

"This is ridiculous." I continue to move away from him. "I do not want to be *healed* by you. If you and my father are so concerned about his image he should not have laid his hands on me. You can put the paper

16

by the door. Just because I am a prisoner does not mean I need to play by your rules." *Not this time.* "Now please. Leave." I cross my arms.

Sydon rolls his eyes. "If you wish." He walks back to the threshold and places the paper on the floor by the door. Before he closes the door, he pauses. "You will be here for quite a while, Alaceandra. It will be a lot easier if you comply with the words on that paper." He points to the rolled up parchment. "The harder you make it for us, the harder things will be for you and for the fate of Ptheryeth. For all of our sakes, please make the right decision. You have ten minutes, then you must meet me outside this room." He shuts the door with finality.

I grab the pillow on the bed and throw it after him. It smacks the door with an unsatisfactory thud before falling to the ground. I hold back tears and touch my throat. *I hope everyone is okay.*

CHAPTER FIVE

The Schedule

Alaceandra

A fter giving myself another minute to breathe, I stomp over to the door and snatch up the schedule that Sydon placed there. Unraveling the ornate scroll, I see a simple list of events laid out in neat handwriting.

> *For the Princess~*
> *Upon Waking- Retrieval and Breakfast*
> *Then- Skill of the Day*
> *After- Meal*
> *Then- Manners*
> *Final- Dine and Rest*

I turn the paper over in my hands, but it remains empty other than those few words. The paper is surprisingly soft, its silkiness more reminiscent of linen rather than the pulp of any wood I had felt before, but the pleasing texture does not soothe the anxiety that wells up in my stomach. *What the fuck?* There were no times associated with the schedule. Nor were there any explanations. Just tasks and when those tasks were associated with the previous ones. Ptheryeth knows an explanation would have been the least my abductors could have given me after, well... abducting me. *What does manners even mean? Do these asshats really mean to teach me how to be polite? As if father has not been drilling those very same lessons into me ever since I could learn to sit up properly? What a joke.* I roll the scroll back up and push the pillow away from the door with my toe, sighing. *I guess the only way to get answers to this mystery is to venture out of my fortress, even if that does mean running back to my captors.* I slowly pull the door open. Although I hate that I am leaving before my supposed ten minutes are up, I would hate to have someone other than Sydon, *someone like my father,* come retrieve me. At the moment, Sydon is the evil I know. An evil that has not caused me harm... yet. I take a deep breath and cross my arms over my chest.

"Now what?"

Sydon lounges against the opposing wall but straightens as he spots me.

"Come on." Sydon walks towards me, gesturing for me to step out of my room. I keep my feet planted firmly on my side of the door. "The kings are waiting. If I keep you away from them for any longer, then we will have another one wandering this way, and I do hate how much trouble they get into on their own." He sighs.

I cross my arms. "I would prefer not to meet with them."

"It is not in your best interest to go about preferring at the moment, princess."

"Even so," I mutter, rubbing my neck.

"You should let me heal that."

"That would mean you would have to touch me and as you were definitely one of the ones who abducted me I think that is a firm no," I say, taking a step back.

He gives me a hard stare. "Let's go." He turns and walks down the corridor.

Biting the inside of my bottom lip, I follow him. When I finally catch up, I decide to ask him another question. Although I do not think he is a safe person to be dealing with here, he does seem like the most open one I will be able to talk to. Especially if the options are him or the kings. I wonder what his place is in all of this. *Is he a servant? No. He seems to hold some kind of sway here. But what?*

"Where is the man I was with?" I ask again.

Sydon gives me a sideways glance.

I grit my teeth. *Okay, guess we still are not getting anywhere with that question.* "What is the schedule for?" I blurt out next instead.

"What do you mean?" *Ah ha.*

I sigh. "On the scroll. You said it would be easier to comply with the things on that paper. It was just a simple schedule. What was it for? It seemed... I do not know. Vague."

"Hmm.... I would read over it again. Maybe you missed something." He reaches grand redwood doors with tiny golden vein patterns running through them that sparkle delicately in the light. They would be impressive if my eyes were not glued to the back of Sydon's head in disbelief.

"...read it again?"

He nods decisively before moving forward and pushing a small knob that almost blends in with the golden patterns on the door.

"There is nothing more to read! I looked at both sides of the paper."

He does not look my way, instead he continues turning the knob as he sighs. "That is what you think you did, but you were not truly looking were you? Either way, it *is* best to comply with what the scroll states. For all of our sakes." Finally, he glances back at me. I continue looking at him with wide, imploring eyes, *because what is he talking about?*

He interrupts my panicked thoughts with a flourish of his hands, his task with the doorknob finally complete. The door is now shimmering, the golden veins lighting up in pretty zigzag patterns up and down the doorway. "We are here. I advise that if you know how to mask your emotions, you do so now and do your best to stay quiet. The men in this room are out for blood. Yours, to be exact. Your running away from Helomasi did not earn you any favors with the rulers of Ptheryeth... or at least not with this group of them anyway." He mutters the last part. "If they can blame it on the men you were with rather than yourself, then you might find this prison more hospitable." He turns away.

I study him for a moment. "Why are you being helpful?" I whisper. "I do not know you and truly I see no reason why other than to keep me in line. What is your angle?"

"Trust me, princess." Sydon says darkly. "I am not here to help you, but I do know you. More than you know." With that, he opens the doors.

CHAPTER SIX

The Kings

Alaceandra

"**W**elcome," a deep, bored voice booms through the large room.

The room around me is made of some kind of white marbled stone. Streaks of black and red feather themselves throughout, staining the otherwise pristine slabs with delicate patterns. In front of me stands four large daises made of the same material. On each sits a man dressed in fine clothing. *Well, three men in fine clothing,* I think to myself bitterly. On the fourth is my father. His clothing is still torn and streaked in filth, as it was when I saw him earlier. I try not to smile at the picture of him looking so out of place next to the other men, but then I remember that I am the one that is here against my will, not him, and the urge falls away as quickly as it came. Gritting my teeth, I push my toes into the floor trying to ground myself.

Studying each of the men's faces, I realize I recognize only one other man up on the stands in front of me. *King Demetrius. Why am I not surprised? But who are the others?*

Maybe you should ask. The sickly sweet voice is invading my mind once again. *It might be nice to know the names of the ones I am to destroy.*

22

My heart rate doubles. *Just ignore it. Maybe it will go away if you ignore it.*

"Respond to the kings when they welcome you, brat," My father snaps, pulling me away from my inner monologue.

Right. Big scary room. Big scary men. I blink. *So they are all kings, but from which kingdoms?*

"Why am I here?" I ask instead.

The king who welcomed me smirks. "To fulfill your duty, princess."

I furrow my brows. "And that is?"

The other king gives my father a sideways glance. "Did you not educate your daughter on what she is to do?"

"Why should I have? She is not to question me, only to listen and do as she is told when it is relevant to do so. She needs no prior knowledge," my father retorts.

"It seems her ignorance is what got us in this situation now. If she knew what she was supposed to do we would not be in this mess. How is she supposed to open the portal if—" The other king bites back, but is quickly cut off.

What portal? I have not been able to open any portal.

"She knew what she was supposed to do. Marry Demetrius' son." He points to the king in question, who glares at him. "He could not keep her in his kingdom. It is he who—" My father snaps.

King Demetrius' face goes red. "If your daughter were not so rebellious, it would have not been—"

"My daughter? Your own son is gone too. Need I remind you?!"

I watch the kings squabble with interest, but try to keep my expression blank. Only a couple of months ago I would not have been so keen to notice such a blatant struggle for power in a room, but if Sorin, Sam, and the prince taught me anything in our time together it is the importance of gathering information. My heart sinks when I think of the men once again. *I really hope they are alright.* Wiggling my toes in my shoes, I try to refocus on the kings in front of me. It seems that although these men stand united in wanting me here, there does not seem to be a strong leader among the four. *That could be dangerous.*

"Enough!" Sydon's voice booms from behind me.

I startle at Sydon's voice and have to stop myself from reacting audibly. Surprisingly, the kings begrudgingly stop their bickering. *Well, I do not like that.* My eyes dart between the kings and the man now standing at my side.

"I have presented you with the princess," Sydon continues casually. "If she is to be trained properly here before fulfilling her duty, she must know who she is dealing with. Now please introduce yourselves." Each word Sydon says is measured and I find myself wanting to put more space between us the more he speaks. Instead I stay still, pressing my feet firmly into the stone beneath me, and take a small breath trying to calm myself. It does not work, but I try to pretend like it does.

"Right," the man who apparently believes in my education says, standing. He stares at Sydon though when he speaks. "I am Telvonius." His eyes flick briefly to me before they once again make contact with Sydon. He arches a quick brow before the expression drops. "King of Unduli," he finishes, a small smirk on his face. Finally he looks at me, "Pleasure to meet you, Princess Alaceandra." He sits.

The next man who I now recognize to be the one who originally welcomed me in— *if you can call it that*— opts to introduce himself from a seated position. "Mirksyl." He looks at me with bored eyes. "King of what you all would call the 'Dead Lands.'" He waves his hand at me and yawns.

"You've met the others," Sydon says.

King Demetrius and my father glower at me.

"So I have," I whisper.

"You have been called here so we can all meet you. Your time here will not be long but it will be arduous. Do not think of rebellion as you did before. It will not be met without punishment, and trust me when I say that punishment will be severe. This is your final opportunity to make things right before the solstice," King Demetrius says. "Do not make a fool of yourself." He turns his attention back to Sydon. "Has she been given her schedule?"

"She has," Sydon replies.

"As it should be," he mutters. "Have her back after breakfast. We will decide on the skill then. We need to discuss."

"Understood," Sydon says. Turning back to the grand doors he starts to walk towards them. "Come, princess."

I stay still. Staring into my father's eyes I ask the one question that has been burning in my brain since I passed out and found myself here.

"Where is Sorin?"

A slow, sinister smile curves itself across my father's features. "I knew one of my trusted guards would not aid in your disobedience, but with the state of the man we found I could not be sure. Now I have a name to his face. Sorin. That insolent guard who always seemed to pull you from your quarters. I knew I should have killed him when the spell spoke of his last indiscretions, but good wine does cause for a lack of proper judgment."

"What are you on about?" Another king snaps.

I stop listening. Instead, my stomach knots, the room seeming to grow heavier with each second that passes. *He did not know. Fuck, that damned cloaking spell! I had forgotten that Sam had disguised Sorin's features and now I have given his identity away.* I clench my hands at my sides.

Turning, I stalk from the men and walk towards the other danger lurking on the outskirts of the grand double doors. Sydon.

What an idiotic move! I silently curse myself. *I should not have said anything. He is sure to use this information against me.* Right before I exit the room, a whisper of wind carrying my father's voice reaches me. "See you soon, dear daughter."

CHAPTER SEVEN

Gales of Darkness

The Prince

Hours Ago...

S am pushed past me as soon as we entered the wood line and now I find myself trying to keep up with him as we race through the forest towards the man's voice. The task is surprisingly difficult. A forest as dead as this one makes for a lot of noisy fallen branches which prove themselves unhelpful when trying to be stealthy. I urge the wind to sweep them away as they come across my path. In only a blink, Sam seems to disappear into the shadows of the trees before re-materializing further away. As much as I hate to admit it, I would have a hard time keeping up with the man if it were not for the winds aiding me.

Who are you, Sam? I cannot imagine a simple guard possessing so much power. I had questioned this very same thing when we were forced to rely on each other in the woods as we looked for the little dove the first time together only a couple months ago, but it seems I had only seen a fraction of his abilities. Now though, those shadows that lurked when he pushed away the beast attacking him are much more pronounced. They cling to him like armor, only wisps of them escaping as he moves through the forest. The sight is unsettling.

I wonder how he gained skill so quickly. I cannot imagine he would have hidden power so immense, especially since doing so would have risked his own injury while we were looking for Alaceandra and Sorin. Unless, of course, he allowed himself to be injured purposefully? Very curious. Fortunately for him, this newfound power of his is quite useful to me right now, so I will not question him about it too much. Yet. Once we get the little dove back in our sights though, she will have a lot of explaining to do.

Worry snakes a trail up my spine and I do my best to push it away. *She will be fine. She has to be.* As much as I will enjoy persuading the little dove to explain all these newfound secrets, I can only do so if we can get to her and retrieve her safely. *Which we will do. No matter what we must go through to accomplish it.* I still have plans for her and, although actually meeting the Tikilium princess has complicated those plans, they must remain. *For now.* Shaking those thoughts away, I refocus on the man in front of me.

Gathering the threads of wind to push my form with more force, I finally catch up to Sam. He holds a hand out and turns to me, placing a single finger over his lips. I urge the gusts of wind to quiet and I feel some kind of magick click into place around us. *Ah yes, Sam has blocked sound from traveling. At least this skill of his I am familiar with.* Glancing around Sam, I see our target. Slowly, we follow behind the soldier as he stomps down the trail, listening in as he mumbles to himself.

"It's not like I wanted to be out in these blasted woods to begin with. It's scary as fuck out here." The man clenches his fists. "Stupid mom. 'Join the king's' guard. It will give your life purpose.' Not sure if being lost in the fucking forest is what she meant, but sure."

The man continues to talk, but from our vantage point it does not look like he is speaking to anyone but himself. He looks to be young and scrawny, with the beginnings of a beard and hair that looks slightly greasy in the low light. I do not recall him from our battle earlier, but that does not mean he was not one of the men that invaded the village. He wore the same black and burgundy armor as those we fought, but seemed otherwise weaponless.

"The commander is going to kill me," he grumbles. "Or maybe I can pretend to have died out here and start a new life?" He scoffs, dragging his feet as he walks along the path. "Yeah right..."

"This is pitiful to listen to," I mumble to Sam.

He gives me a dry look before refocusing back on the man. "We can grant his wish... Only I am not really in the mood for a game of pretend," Sam says, darkly before laughing. "At the very least we can teach him a lesson. The man's grievances are leaving him completely oblivious to his surroundings, it would be best if we try to capture him now." Sam's voice sinks to a low, smoky tone. Darkness starts to congeal into an inky mass around Sam's form. I squint at the man. He feels my eyes on him and looks back, raising a brow. "Can you pull his attention over there?" Sam turns back to the soldier and nods towards a tree to the man's left.

"Of course I can," I say, rolling my eyes. Gathering up the threads of wind around me, I push a burst of air into the tree. It shakes violently and tiny orange fruits tumble from its blackened branches. One smacks the soldier's arm causing him to turn towards the disturbance.

"What the fuck?" The man grumbles.

Suddenly, Sam's darkness rushes towards the man and spreads out over the field, leaving only a shimmering shadow to hover around Sam. I narrow my eyes. *Yes, it looks as if Sam has become much more advanced. Hopefully that will not prove an issue later on.*

29

The target's scream pulls my attention away from Sam. The soldier now lies on the forest floor at the base of the tree, his head in his hands as he rolls back and forth.

Sam snorts. "Maybe that was too much." Sam breathes and as he inhales, the forest brightens, but only slightly. The darkness once again solidifies itself around Sam like armor. The soldier's body relaxes enough for him to let go of his head and scurry back towards the tree that was shaking only moments before.

Sam speaks without looking at me, his voice a rumble. "Advance on him from the left, I will do so from here. The more he feels trapped, the greater the chances are he will talk." The darkness shielding Sam grows to cover him before receding back completely. In a blink it is gone and in front of me stands a man that looks nothing like the man before. His hair is now a dark black with streaks of silver, his eyes are a haunting blue, and he looks older and weathered. Sam grabs my arm and I feel his magick curl around me as well. I look down at my hands and they also appear to have transformed. They are paler and well-used. I arch a brow at Sam.

"I have disguised us into those he fears." His eyes have a far-off look. "This will help us."

"How do you know who he fears?"

His eyes lock on mine. "Don't worry about that."

I grit my teeth. "You will be questioned on your secrets."

He smirks. "I am sure I will, but that will be only around the time you are ready to reveal yours." He turns away from me, physically dismissing me. "Go take your place. We do not want to lose this one."

His eyes harbor challenge, and if it were not for the fact that working with this man is the only way that we are going to get the little dove back, I might have hit him. If I am honest with myself, the little dove's fondness for this infuriating so-called guard is also a main contributor, but I find that I am not much one for being honest with myself at the moment. I take in a slow breath and let it out. "Fine." Turning away, I walk deeper into the forest to the left of the target, positioning myself inline.

"Follow my lead," Sam mouths to me.

It is my turn to shoot Sam a dry look, but I nod at him all the same. As one, we advance.

CHAPTER EIGHT

The Soldier

The Prince

We approach the soldier as he cowers at the base of the tree. He catches sight of me first, and his face pales before his eyes flicker over to Sam and he promptly loses all color. Desperately, he scrambles to his feet and clings to the tree behind him like it is some sort of lifeline grown to save him. *Unfortunately for him, it is not.*

"What do we have here?" Sam says, looking at me. "Looks like an errant soldier to me, what do you think? Do we have a deserter on our hands?" Sam looks to me.

"Seems to be that way," I say. *Let's hope Sam knows what he is doing.* "What shall be done about that?" I tap my finger against my chin dramatically.

"I guess we will have to figure it out... unless, of course, you think we should just report it to the commander?"

Okay so...neither one of us is the commander. Good to know...

"Huh, maybe we should." I turn to the man trembling against the big oapik. "What do you think? Shall we report your offense?"

"N-n-no," he whispers, doing his best to become one with the tree. "Y-you c-can't b-be h-here. Y-you left with e-everyone else." He is trembling as his eyes dart back and forth.

"And yet here we are," I say flatly. Sam walks closer to the soldier and I do too, until we have trapped him against the tree he is frantically pushing his body into.

"H-how?"

"Worry not about that," Sam says with the same flat tone and the man flinches. "Tell me. Why are you hiding this time?" Sam tilts his head.

"I-I'm not!"

Sam takes another step forward. The man screams.

"Shh," I soothe as Sam advances. "We aren't going to hurt you... unless...?"

Sam's eyes sharpen as he watches the soldier.

The man gulps. "U-unless what?"

"Unless you keep from us what we are searching for. We came back to find it. Are you going to tell us what we want to know?" Sam finishes my statement.

The man swallows hard. "W-what if the commander finds out?"

"He won't." It is now Sam's turn to soothe the man.

"What do you want to know?" The man asks, his voice small.

"Where is the girl going?" I growl. As fun as toying with this man is, his only significance here is to get us back to my little dove. I would prefer him to be hasty about it.

Sam gives me a sharp look, and the man pushing himself against the tree pauses to look at me in confusion before his eyes lose focus and dart back to Sam.

Sam sighs. "You heard him. Where is she being taken?"

"Y-you should know where-" The man looks from me to Sam; sweat begins to bead on his forehead.

"As should you, but that is not what I asked. Consider this a test— answer the question," Sam says firmly, grabbing the man by the front of his armor and pulling him to his feet only to push him harder against the tree.

"Sydon says we cannot hurt her," The man whimpers.

"Who said anything about hurting her?" I snap. The man flinches in Sam's grasp.

"No one! I just—"

"Where is she?" Sam growls.

The man closes his eyes and darkness gathers around his head. He screams, trying to pull away from Sam but finding himself unable. "Sorry- sorry!" The man looks at Sam once again. "They are going to the mountains! The palace in the mountains!"

Sam stares at the man blankly for a moment, whatever he sees in his eyes causes him to hesitate. Abruptly, he blinks and smiles, dropping the man back onto the ground. The darkness that was lingering around his form starts to dissipate into the trees surrounding us. The soldier does not seem to notice. "Thank you. You passed." Sam claps his hands together and turns away from him like he didn't just scare the shit out of the man. He motions for me to do the same. I do.

"I-is that all?" The man asks, his voice filled with hesitation.

"Yep," Sam says still not facing the man. We start to make our way back to the forest. "Continue on your way back to your duty post. If I catch you out here again, I will not be so forgiving."

"Y-yes sir. Thank you." The man quickly pulls himself from the base of the tree and turns to scurry away from us back onto the path he was following before. As soon as his foot makes contact with the dirt of the small path he passes out. His face hits the soil with a hard thud.

"He will be fine," Sam says, returning to his normal form, his shoulders slumping slightly. I feel a tingle as his magick leaves me as well. Sam looks exhausted. "We should find a place to rest for the night away from him." He tilts his head at the soldier. "We will need to start on the path in a couple hours."

"Why are we waiting? And are we just going to leave him there? Won't he just run and tell his commander once he gets back to them?" *Why would Sam leave an obvious threat behind? Even if said threat is passed out at the moment, there is no telling what he will say when he awakens.*

"Yes, we are leaving him. He will not be an issue. Of that I am sure. Would you want to bring back up to your commander that someone caught you deserting your duties in the woods? Seems like a pretty deplorable thing to want to admit."

"Unless he thinks we are just going to report this incident anyway. He might want to cover his tracks."

Sam sighs. "That will not happen."

"You can't be sure of that!" I take a breath. "Another thing to consider is if he discusses this encounter with the forms we were inhabiting. What if he wants to apologize to these forms again in order to ensure they don't further punish him? Then they will know someone is out there impersonating them. It would ruin your disguise in the future."

Sam raises a brow. "He can't."

"Why not?"

"I killed them."

"Oh," I sigh. *At least that is two less pieces to worry about...* "Well, either way... he is a loose thread if we leave him behind. He can completely ruin our chances of getting back to Alaceandra."

"He won't. Trust me. That nap of his will make sure of that."

How could a nap...? I tilt my head. "Are you saying he will forget?"

Sam shrugs. "I am saying he will not want to remember."

"How can you be so sure?"

"That is for me to know."

I grit my teeth. "I do not like being kept in the dark."

"Neither do I. How does it feel?" Sam laughs, but that quickly turns into a cough. "Fuck..." Sam mutters.

"What is it?"

Sam grows more pale. He grits his teeth and sighs. "Today's battle coupled with my deciding not to put the dimwit out of his misery," he replies, motioning towards the man now snoring face down on the forest floor. "It seems I might have overdone it a little with that last disguise. I would like not to discuss it. Now, let's go," Sam says firmly before walking along the path.

Always with the name calling... At least he has decided on a new target. I pause thinking about what he just said. *Why would not killing the soldier have any effect on Sam's current state?* I watch as Sam starts to disappear behind the clusters of blackened bushes and trees. *Unfortunately, it seems I will not be able to figure it out standing here.* With a sigh, I follow.

CHAPTER NINE

To Be Powerless

Alaceandra

Present...

"I told you to stay silent," Sydon growls as he moves swiftly down the hall. "I understand you are worried for your friend, but they need not know that. You unveiling that will do you no favors in the future. You need to follow my orders."

I follow behind him. "And risk losing my place as the only one here who does not take orders from you?" I mumble. "I will pass."

He stops and I almost bump into him. "What is that supposed to mean?" He says without turning towards me.

I roll my eyes. "Nothing." I sigh. "I am aware I made a mistake, but you cannot blame me for doing so. No one here— including you— is willing to tell me where my... guard... is." I nibble my lower lip. "I will keep asking around until I find out, whether it puts me in danger or not."

"And why is that?" He asks, turning towards me. "Does the man mean that much to you?"

I narrow my gaze at him. "He has saved my life on countless occasions. It is only natural for me to be concerned about his well-being."

"He was one of the ones who helped ferry you away from your duties, princess. Someone who is willing to do such a thing knows little about safety," he shoots back.

"What if that very duty is what means to cause me harm?"

"There are bigger things at stake than your individual safety."

"For you, maybe," I whisper. "For whatever agenda you are pushing forth, but I find that only happens to be the case when the one behind such agendas is not the one in harm's way. When their own individual safety is not on the line; much like with you. You cannot convince me that you hold no stake in whatever is going on here, which is why you seem to find so much joy in monitoring my actions."

"You have no idea what you are talking about, Alaceandra."

He turns fully towards me, and I only now realize how much the man towers over me. Instead of cowering though, I straighten my stance, balling my fists at my side in defiance.

"Do I not? I might have been naive to these political ploys only a few months ago, but it is quite plain to see that you have some sway here. Those kings listened to your words, Sydon." I spit out his name. "Your commands even! If you want to convince me that you are as powerless here as I am, then you will have to try a lot harder than that."

"Who says my aim is to convince you of anything?"

I roll my eyes. "Nice deflection."

He advances on me, and I back up. One hand going to the little pin still tucked neatly in my dress. My back hits the stone wall and tiny firelight dances across my skin before being sucked towards the red bangle at my wrist. I watch as the light circles the bracelet before disappearing.

"Do you want the truth then, princess?" The word 'truth' echoes in my ears before fading away and my gaze whips from my bracelet and back to Sydon in confusion. His eyes almost seem to glow crimson with some unknown power, and I do my best not to react to their intensity. "The truth is that the fate of this world lies on your shoulders and if you do not do your part to shape up and learn what the reality of that fact means, then whether you or I have so-called 'power' or not will mean shit."

My eyebrows raise at his use of language, but I try to disguise this surprise by casting him a bored look. "Is this some tactic of intimidation?" I ask, trying to keep my voice steady, but I can feel my hand shaking slightly around my tiny pin.

I need him to step away. I may not be able to do much with this pin, but I can at least make the man bleed a little before I go down if I need to.

"I am aware of the prophecy, Sydon. What I am not aware of is why everyone thinks that having me in their possession will help them gain control over the outcome of it."

Slowly, I push Sydon away and step to the side. His eyes follow me but he allows me to escape. *Good.* I keep the pin clutched in my palm.

"Either way, while that power may not mean a thing when the game is over, it means the world at the moment. I am the captured party here, am I not? I am the one being closely monitored. I am the one out of the circle of knowledge. I am the one they apparently need to open whatever Ptheryeth-forsaken portal they were talking about back there!" I watch Sydon's face for a reaction, but he gives me none. My next words come out quieter, more measured. "I am the one whose individual safety is at risk. Not you. Whether you value that freedom or not is not what is important here. What is important is that you have it and I lost it. All so you and," I point back down the hall, "those kings can try their hand at deciding fate."

Sydon sighs and looks away from me. After a moment of silence, he shakes his head and restarts his path down the hall. I stare after him in disbelief before angrily following behind him, doing my best to keep up with his quick pace. The silence between us drags on, and I briefly wonder how much damage my little pin can do to the back of his neck. Before I can luxuriate in the thought too much, he speaks again. "I understand you are frustrated, Alaceandra."

I scoff.

He ignores me and continues on. "But you will understand why all this is soon enough. When that time comes, you will do well to remember this conversation. You might have a different perspective on who truly holds the power then."

I doubt it. I reply internally, but outwardly I stay silent and continue to follow behind him, because what really is there to say? Hard as I try, Sydon does not seem like he will give me any answers. Even worse, it seems I have found yet another man who loves to speak in riddles. *Just my luck.* I slip the pin back into my clothing and rub a finger over where I know the little vine lives on my thigh. *I will find you soon, Sorin. I promise.* I send the thought out to him, hoping beyond hope that somehow he will know that I am thinking of him.

We walk in silence, both deep in thought. Finally, I notice that we are not heading back to my room. Instead we find ourselves walking down a hall filled with blue sparkly lights. The rocks seem smoother here, like many people have walked this path, whereas the walls to my rooms seem more rugged as if they were only recently carved out. I wonder at the difference. Trying my luck, I decide to ask my prison guard.

"Where are we going exactly?" I inquire.

He turns his once again red-rimmed eyes in my direction before continuing forward at a slower pace, allowing me to catch up to him. After a moment, he answers me. "Breakfast."

CHAPTER TEN

Breakfast

Alaceandra

The breakfast hall is massive. I crane my neck up to see where the ceiling of the room ends, but cannot make it out completely. The only impressions I can see are the same glittering blue rocks that are in the hallway. They reflect the light of the room and sparkle in the dark ceiling like stars in the distance. The walls of this room are decorated with little globes of firelight that brighten the room only enough that it can be seen, but not enough for the light to strain the eye. The floor is made out of the same shimmering material as the wall, but the rocks are arranged neatly in designs along the floor. There is an alcove in the back of the hall where I can hear the clang of pots and pans and the room smells slightly of some kind of savory meat.

The hall itself is filled with tables with five chair clusters around the room. The chairs are gold with intricate swirls decorating the metal and blue fluffy cushions on the backs and seats of them. The tables are a matching gold with blue marbled tops. At the very center of the room sits a raised platform with a larger rectangular table that holds six chairs. Instead of these tables and chairs mimicking the blue and gold of the others, the metal of the pieces are a pitch black and the cushions and table top sparkle a brilliant crimson. I would think the room more beautiful if I were not trapped within it.

Sydon closes the door behind us with a heavy clang and I sigh. Other than the noise in the back of the room, the hall is completely devoid of people. The abundance of chairs and tables does tell me that there are more people here than just the kings and Sydon. *Not a good sign.* The fact that I have not seen them though must mean that this place is expansive. *Or they are good at hiding their army.* I can feel my heart sink at the thought. *Which means it will likely be hard to find Sorin without detection. I will need a plan.*

As we near the large rectangular table, I can see there is already a bowl set at its center filled with what looks to be a sweet milk, grains, fruit and some kind of tan, creamy paste. Beside it sits a little plate of meats and cheeses and a tall glass of clear liquid. As appetizing as it looks, the thought of food at the moment makes my stomach turn.

"Is that my breakfast?" I ask Sydon.

He nods.

"Where is yours?"

"I have already eaten. It is closer to midday now. Your meeting with the kings has us slightly off schedule."

"Oh."

"Go. Eat." He starts to guide me up the platform, but I shake him off. Taking a deep breath, I make my hesitant ascent up the stairs and stand in front of the place setting that bears my breakfast. Sydon follows behind me and sits in the chair to the right of me. Hesitantly, I take a seat.

"Must I eat on this platform? It is quite odd especially because this room is so... empty." My eyes dart around the space and a sense of unease fills me.

"It is the king's request. You will get used to it."

"I hope not," I whisper.

Sydon sighs. "Look, princess. You still have training later today. You must eat, and we do not have enough time to talk while you do it."

Rude. "What kind of training?" I ask.

"You will know when we arrive."

Asshole.

I eye the food suspiciously, remembering one of the reasons I was captured in the first place. "How do I know you have not done something to the food?" I pick at the bowl of milk with my spoon, swishing the little grains and fruit from one side to the other. My stomach turns at the memory of Sorin, Sam, the prince, and me being unable to move after Sylvie poisoned our dinner. Fire starts to sparkle along my skin as the memory brings on another of Sylvie covered in Sorin's blood. Her hands clutching the knife she used to stab—

"You do not, but it is your only option at the moment," Sydon's voice breaks through my rising panic.

The fire is once again sucked into the bracelet at my wrist, and I clench my hand into a fist. *What all is this bracelet capable of?*

"Is that your way of saying something has been done to it?" I snap at him, trying to ground myself to the present.

"Must you ask so many questions? Usually prisoners are much more quiet."

"Doubtful," I say, stabbing a piece of meat. "Good to know I am not your first prisoner, though."

He looks up to the sky before pinning me with a glare. I return his look with a scowl. "Eat your food, princess. Nothing has been done to it." He picks up a piece of meat from my plate and tosses it into his mouth, chewing it and then swallowing it all while maintaining that same glare. "See?"

"What about this?" I pull out a fruit from the bowl gesturing at him to take it. I watch him grit his teeth, but he takes it and tosses it into his mouth, chewing and swallowing before once again raising a brow at me.

"Now, will you eat?"

"Since you asked so nicely," I mutter, hesitantly taking a bite of one of the cubes of meat in front of me. The silence of the room is grating, but I try to tune it out as I eat my breakfast. Instead, I allow my mind to wander outside of this room. The hall was well worn, which was much different than the more jagged edges of rock that were present outside of where they are keeping me. This could mean that they only built the chambers that I am staying in recently or that not many people within this cavern travel to my rooms. Which would only make sense seeing as I assume the kings mean to keep me away from as many people as possible. It would stand to reason that they would want the same for Sorin.

Maybe if I try to find more halls like my own I can find where they are keeping him? I have to try something, and soon. Who knows what they have done to him if they do have him. I have to know he is okay. A slight tremor goes through my body. *I do not know what I would do if he was not.*

Sydon's eyes flash crimson before he looks away from me, his shoulders tense. "You have twenty minutes," he says, his voice a low rumble.

Twenty minutes to come up with a plan. I will find Sorin tonight.

CHAPTER ELEVEN

Dead Foes

Alaceandra

The rest of breakfast is thankfully uneventful. I was more hungry than I had first thought, likely due to the fact that my last meal was before the annihilation of a small village. I cross my arms over my chest in discomfort. That village served as a great aid to us when we needed shelter. Although Sylvie may have betrayed us, the other townsfolk did not. At least not to my knowledge. They did not deserve such atrocities. I hope they are able to rebuild without any more loss.

"We are running behind. Walk faster," Sydon snaps me out of the haze of my thoughts. The path we are walking on has the same worn quality as the one to the dining hall. The rocks this way are smooth and sink towards the middle of the path. *Must be where people walk the most.* Excitement builds at the base of my spine. *There has to be something to that. Hopefully the newer paths are not too difficult to find.* The only difference between the stones around the dining hall and these rocks is that these do not hold the same blue gems. Instead, the rock is empty of any ornamentation and is a smoky gray color. *I wonder if the glowing gems have any meaning.*

"You will begin your training today," Sydon says. "We will skip all other lessons and allow you to rest after this, but your routine will be far less flexible tomorrow. We have a tight schedule." He turns to me. "Do not make me regret that decision. I am aware this is an... abrupt... change for you, but the more you comply the better the transition will be. I am hopeful some extra sleep will jar you out of this combative mood of yours."

Do not get your hopes too high. "Answers would be better than rest."

Sydon sighs. "Come."

As strange as it is that they are aiming to train me—*whatever that means*— only a day after their kidnapping, I cannot help but be a bit excited by the prospect. Strengthening me means giving me more tools to escape. If I can have better control over my abilities and even greater combat training than what Sam and the other men have taught me over these past few weeks, next time I will not be so easily captured. *I will make sure of it.* I decide that I will go with this weird schedule of theirs *for now*, but when the time comes to get out of here, I will show them how detrimental underestimating me can be. Squaring my shoulders I continue to follow Sydon.

He arrives at a plain wooden door and glances at me before opening it. A cacophony awaits us on the other side. Men and women in matching shorts and shirts of black, teal, bronze, and silver fill the space all talking excitedly. When they spot me, the room goes quiet. My heart skitters in my chest as my eyes catch on familiar faces in bronze. Some of the soldiers I had seen hanging around my father before I had left the palace stand in small groups around the space leering at me.

I pull my eyes away. *Okay, so Tikilium soldiers are present. That must mean that the other men in uniform are soldiers from different kingdoms. Likely all hailing from one of the kings I met this morning.* My eyes skate over the men in teal. *Those men are likely from Helomasi.* My gaze falls over the men in black. *Are these the men that attacked us?* One of the soldiers smirks at me. I wrinkle my nose and look to the last group of soldiers in silver. One of the women tilts their head at me, their body language screaming curiosity, rather than hostility. *Seems I might be safest with that group then... but where are they from?*

A man walks in with a scrawny man dressed in the same burgundy and black armor as the men from yesterday.

"What were you doing outside? Go get dressed. You are late." He throws the man towards the back of the room.

"Yes, sir," the man says shakily before practically running towards an alcove in the back of the room. The hairs on my arm stand on end and I rub them, surprised when they shock me. I look around and notice that a couple of others have the same affliction, but they look more annoyed than surprised. *Must be normal then.* I continue to take in my surroundings.

The room itself is quite impressive. It is large. On one side sits some kind of equipment. I can make out balls of different sizes and stacks of plates of metal, but the rest I do not recognize. The walls are lined with wooden and metal weapons, ropes, and small containers full of some kind of gem that is brightening the room. *I wonder what it is all for? Am I going to use it all? And why even train me to begin with? What battle do they think I will help them fight?* My mind fills with question after question that I know I will not be given the answers to anytime soon.

The scrawny man runs out from the back alcove with a fresh set of black clothing and makes his way towards a group of men in matching attire. His legs and arms have bruises and he has a small gash over his right eyebrow. *Where did he come from?*

"You need to get changed," Sydon says. I will myself not to jump at the sound of his voice. I had forgotten he was behind me.

I turn to glance at him. "Into what?"

"There is clothing for you in that back room." He points to another little alcove in the corner. "No other trainees are allowed back there so do not worry about your privacy. I will ensure you are safe while you change. Come." He starts to walk back to the room.

I follow him. "Why would you need to ensure that? Are people going to attempt something here?"

He shrugs. "It is always best to stay on your guard."

I duck into the little alcove and find a set of blood red clothing sitting on a wooden bench. *Well, that won't make me stand out.* I think to myself sarcastically. Begrudgingly, I change out of my old clothing. Grabbing the strip of blood red fabric next to the shorts and shirt, I use it to bind my breasts in place. Picking up my tiny pin from my other set of clothing, I weave it into the fabric under my arm. I do not know why I feel the need to hold onto it at all times, but I do. This day has already been unbearably long, and I will take comfort where I can get it. I slip into the shorts and top and leave my discarded clothing neatly folded on the bench.

Slowly, I scour the area, using what little time I have to scout for any more weapons I can use. The room appears empty aside from the bench. I scan the walls to see if there are any hidden doors or windows present, but again come up empty. Finally, I eye the flickering little candles. Climbing on the bench, I reach for one. *These might be heavy. I could hit someone with it with enough force to knock them out, maybe?* My fingers brush one of them and a searing pain rips through my wrist, causing me to crumple onto the bench.

Ow! I stare down at the red shackle on my wrist and notice it is glowing. The skin around the band is also now inflamed. *I guess there is more than one reason they attached you to me,* I grumble internally down at the bracelet. Glancing back up at the flickering candle, I decide to give up for the time being. *I cannot take too long. Casting too much suspicion this early will only lead to problems in my escape.*

Taking a breath, I step down from the bench and make my way back towards the door to the gym, rubbing my wrist to try to quell the remaining sting. Walking out of the room, I almost bump into Sydon's back.

"You are not allowed through that door. Step back or I will make you step back." The anger present in Sydon's voice causes my hair to stand on end.

A trainee, as Sydon calls them, in bronze I recognize as one of my father's close friends- *What was his name?... Huermold or Jalune? -* is standing with his fists clenched on the other side of Sydon. We make eye contact and he smirks.

"Looks like I won't need to go in there. The princess has come out to face me herself."

"She has not. She is here to train. You would do well to remember your place here, Huermond."

Ah, Huermond! Right.

Huermond's eyes flash with anger. "You would do well to remember yours! You would not even have her if it were not for us." Huermond turns his attention to me. "Where are Fadres and Credour?" He growls. "I know they left with you. We all saw it. What did you do with them?"

"I-" I stutter. *Last I knew, in the grave. I am pretty sure in the ground if what Sam told me held any weight, but I do not think it is wise to volunteer that information. Especially not to this man, who seems like he would have my neck in his hands if it were not for Sydon blocking his way.* "I do not-"

"Trainees! Get in formation. Now!" A tall, muscular, bald man commands from the middle of the room.

Huermond growls a bit and pins me with his gaze. Sydon steps in front of me blocking his view.

"You heard the commander. Go."

"This is not over," I hear Huermond say before his thudding footsteps signal his departure.

"Where are those men?" Sydon asks in a bored tone.

"I am pretty sure they are dead," I whisper.

"By you?" Sydon asks in a surprised tone. He finally looks at me. I watch his gaze quickly flick over my form, pausing a bit longer on my reddened wrist, but he does not comment.

I sigh, slowly placing my arms behind my back. "No. Unfortunately not."

"By the men you were with then?"

He is not your friend, Alaceandra. I practically shout to myself. *He likely is asking these questions to gain more knowledge of those who are hopefully trying to rescue you. Do not humor him. You will regret it.*

"Answers come with a price, Sydon," I snap at him instead. "If you want to hear my stories you better have some to tell too."

Sydon laughs. "Fine, but it is probably best if you stay away from him. He does not seem the type to let go of things easily." He watches Huermond's departure warily. "We cannot have a trainee going against us. It would only cause issues. I will keep an eye on him."

I nod in agreeance. Without access to my abilities or my men, I will need to be more careful around here. It seems not all my enemies are on the same page when it comes to me. My mind wanders to the last soldier that lost his friend at my hand in the caves and I shiver. *Very careful.*

"Let us go. The commander is not one to be left waiting."

I swallow before nodding again, and we make our way to the middle of the room.

CHAPTER TWELVE

The Strand

Alaceandra

"Fire," the tall, muscular, bald man's voice rings through the room. "A deadly but powerful weapon." The man makes eye contact with me. "And a skill that some of you possess." He nods at me. "Today we will be working on how to use it in combat. During our training today, we are joined by Sydon and Tikilium's princess Alaceandra." He starts to pace slowly at the front of the room. "The kings' eyes are on you." He stops and sweeps his gaze across the room. "Do not make a fool of yourselves." I feel the men around us straighten and all eyes turn on in our direction. The man at the front of the room continues his pacing. "Split your groups in two. Half on this side and half on the other." He returns his gaze to me and Sydon. "You two remain. I will brief everyone on the exercise once you are in position." He pauses and raises his brows. "Move!"

"Yes, sir!" The men and women around us shout and then scramble to find their place on either side of the gym.

The man at the front of the room then approaches us. "Sydon," he says.

"Rafton," Sydon replies.

I see them smirk at one another and then clap their hands together and hug quickly giving each other a pat on the back in the process.

"Are you joining us today for training?" Rafton asks.

"Today and in the future. The kings request that Alaceandra's powers and combat be mastered before the solstice."

Rafton raises a brow. "That is quite the feat."

"You can do it."

Rafton nods. "I can, but why? Is it not ill-advised to have her stronger before—"

Sydon shoots Rafton a look and I glare at the side of Sydon's face. The only nice thing about people talking about you like you are not there is that it allows you to gain insight if they do not watch what they say. Sydon's acknowledgment of my presence ruins that advantage.

"Whether it is advised or not," Sydon says, "makes little difference. She needs to be trained. I can count on you, yes?"

"Of course," Rafton says before taking a step back. Shifting his attention to me, he speaks. "When soldiers enter this room they lose rank. It helps maintain balance," he explains. "All who are here are trainees, including you, princess. I can't wait to see what you are capable of." Turning dismissively, he walks away.

Sydon turns to me. "Show me that cuff." He points to the red bracelet on my arm.

"Why?" I ask.

He sighs. "I need to adjust it."

"Adjust it how?" I take a step away from him.

"To allow it to let you use your powers within this room."

My ears perk at that. "Why would you allow me to use my powers at all after taking them only this morning?" *My powers can give me a good advantage in my escape. If I can now use them, maybe I could—*

"Would you like access to them or not?"

I glare at Sydon. *Dick.* Reluctantly, I stick out my arm.

"As I thought." He grabs my wrist and my body tingles as he does *something* to the band. Red and yellow sparkles encircle the bracelet, causing me to shiver. I hear something click. Suddenly, tiny sparkles of fire start to erupt over my skin causing Sydon to release me. "If you try to use your powers outside of this room that band will ensure you lose access to them for a while. If you would prefer that not happen, keep the magick usage to training."

The fire surrounding my body grows a fraction. "Fine," I say.

"Good, now— do you know how to make that disappear?" He asks, eyeing my flames warily.

I roll my eyes. "Yes," I reply. I close my eyes and focus in on the tiny strings of energy. A thin string connects each flame to my skin, and I do my best to pull them back to myself. I pause, noticing a much thicker strand connected to the smaller string that seems to span much farther away than the ones on my body. I tug at it, but the energy does not release itself back into me. *What is this connected to?*

"Are you two finished?" Rafton asks from the left side of the room. "We need to begin."

My eyes shoot open, and I stop tugging at the strand. Fortunately, all the fire has disappeared from my body.

"Yes," I say.

Sydon gives me a curious look, but nods. "Let us start."

Rafton claps his hands together. "Alaceandra, to your left. Sydon, with me."

Sydon joins Rafton at the corner of the room, and they start to discuss something. I move over to the left side of the room to stand between the woman in silver who tilted her head at me when I first arrived and the scrawny man who arrived late.

"I'm Lylane," the woman says. "You are the Tikilium princess." She smiles excitedly at me.

"Um, yes," I reply.

The scrawny man sighs. "So you are the one they were searching for? And you need to be trained? Does not seem very impressive to me."

"Jaq! Do not be rude!" The lady in silver- Lylane—swats at the scrawny man- Jaq causing him to almost fall over. "You are one to talk. You show up here late and covered in bruises. Doesn't seem so impressive to me."

"Jeez," Jaq says. "I was just saying..." he mumbles, rubbing his arm.

"Well, keep your sayings to yourself. She is to be the ruler, after all, show some respect."

"Whatever," Jaq says.

"Ignore him," Lylane says, rolling her eyes. "It is great to meet you."

I scrunch my nose in confusion. *Why is she being so nice? Is she not here to keep me prisoner?*

"Attention!" All eyes turn towards Rafton. "For today's training, this half," he motions to the right side of the room. "You will be the attackers and this half," He motions towards the left side of the room. "You will be the protectors. We will start with battle sequence B." He stares at each trainee then turns his gaze to me. "Alaceandra, this will be a test of your abilities. You will have to try to circle each trainee in front of you in a ring of fire. They will be doing their best to capture and subdue you by grabbing hold of your bracelet. I need to see where you are starting at to know how best to train you, so give it your all." He gives me a small smile. "In the meantime," he looks at the rest of the group. "Protectors and attackers, you will battle to subdue the other. You can get out by being encircled or by being dealt a 'killing blow.'" He regards all of us. "Does everyone understand their assignments?"

Not really. "Yes, sir!" The trainees around me yell.

"Good. May your training commence!" Rafton commands; then the room erupts into chaos.

CHAPTER THIRTEEN

Training

Alaceandra

T hree men move into a triangle formation and start running towards me while the others in the group watch them for only a moment before their eyes land on me. I watch as their bodies prime themselves for attack. Lylane steps in front of me.

"Move to the middle of the group and try to call on your fire," she says, her knees bending as she readies herself. She spares me a glance back. "Hurry."

I take a step back and the scrawny guy moves to her side. "You heard Lylane. What are you waiting for?"

What am I waiting for? I look behind me for an opening. Finding one, I quickly duck between the masses of bodies on this side and do my best to make it to the middle of the group. The trainees allow me to move, stepping to the side as soon as they realize my intentions. Once I make it to the middle of the group, I look around. Unfamiliar forms surround me. Anxiety gnaws at my gut. *This training is unlike anything Sam has done with me. How am I going to encircle so many people with fire? I have never encircled one!*

Suddenly, a pressure starts behind my eyes. *Calm down.* That sugary sweet voice echoes in my brain. It sounds quite bored. *You can take down this entire room... just let me lead.*

Dread replaces the anxiety. *No!* I reply to the voice. *You cannot.*

I can hear it sigh. *Fine, but you will fail.* I can feel the voice recede to some other place within me.

I will not, I grumble back to it, but I get the sense it cannot hear me— whatever *it* is. *Okay, ignore the creepy voice. All I have to do is make fire. I can do that, right?* I close my eyes. I can hear the sounds of combat raging on in front of me. The noise makes my heart race as images from yesterday filter through my brain. *Bodies everywhere. Discarded clothes. Buildings crumbled to the ground. Blood.... Sorin's blood.* I feel tears start to well in my eyes and urge them to stay back. Suddenly, I am shoved back and my eyes shoot open.

"It is not time for a nap," a woman in bronze snaps at me.

"Yeah," a man in teal echoes. "You are going to make us lose the exercise!" He whines.

"Sorry," I mutter. I watch as one of the trainees from the opposing team grabs another man's arm and twists it back, almost to the point of fracture before tripping him and making him face plant on the mats beneath us. Once he is down, the trainee kneels on his back and places a hand on his throat. The downed trainee taps the mat before he is then released. The attacking trainee stands and the downed trainee walks over to the edge of the wall— defeated.

We all take a step back as another wave of trainees crashes into us. I take a deep breath and try to summon my fire, but I only see that one thick strand in front of me. *Come on.* Frustrated, I tug at the strand. It resists. I tug at it again. It resists again. Grinding my teeth in annoyance, I visualize grabbing onto the strand with both hands and pulling with all my body weight. It still does not budge, but this time I feel a surge of energy run down the line. *Woah,* I think as I watch tiny green sparkles rush into my hands and transform into red and gold shimmers. *Beautiful.* The shimmers sparkle around me before latching onto my skin, creating tiny threads of magick. *Success!*

Opening my eyes, I see that there is now tiny flames dancing over my skin. Those around me step back as to not be burned.

"She has it!" Someone yells, and the crowd starts to part in preparation.

"Remember!" Rafton yells. "Once you are encircled, you are out. Do not move from the circle until you are dismissed."

I hear grunts of confirmation. A thin path is made between myself and the opposing team, and I move forward within it until I am just out of reach from the other trainees. A hand on my shoulder almost breaks my concentration.

"Have you ever done this before?" Sydon stands behind me. I did not even see him leave the corner of the room.

I shake my head no but keep my gaze locked on a teal trainee.

"It's relatively simple," he whispers so only I can hear. "How do you visualize your power?"

"What do you mean?" I ask.

"How do you see your power connected to you? What does it look like?"

"Is that important?" I ask, narrowing my gaze on the teal soldier as he kicks a woman in black. She blocks and uses his leg to throw him off balance, but he uses the momentum to throw her to the ground. She taps. He laughs.

Sydon sighs. "At the moment, yes."

The trainee in teal looks around for his next target.

Reluctantly, I answer Sydon. "A thread. I see it as a thread."

"Interesting," he mutters.

The teal trainee locks eyes with me and smirks, moving in my direction. I glare at him. "How so?" I say through gritted teeth, gathering my flames. The trainee's smirk transforms into an all out cocky grin. He starts to run at me.

"To draw a circle around this trainee," Sydon says, ignoring my question. "Imagine gently laying your thread around them in the shape. Try this one slowly and lay a bigger circle so they cannot escape before it is closed," Sydon directs.

I blow out a breath in acknowledgment. Concentrating on the ball of fire in my hands, I pull at one of the strings attached to them. As I pull the thread lengthens into more of a string, then a thin rope. I imagine throwing the rope at the teal trainee's feet. The man steps back from the fire, startled, his smile dropping. Snapping the rope of fire, I imagine pulling it around his body and gently laying it around him. As the rope touches the ground, fire starts to appear, until the trainee is entrapped in the flames. *Or should I say surrounded by candlelight?* The flames are miniature. Barely tall enough to overtake the trainee's shoe. *And the circle itself?* It is barely a circle, more like the shape of a large puddle, its sides more wavy than perfectly round. As pitiful as the circle itself looks, the act of throwing it has taken the wind out of me. My body shakes as I try to make the flames grow around him. No matter how hard I try the flames remain small and nonthreatening. I growl in frustration. The teal trainee, that cocky smile once again on his face, raises a brow at me and attempts to step over the flames.

"Iyan! You are out. Get to the sidelines," Rafton yells.

"But sir, this flame would not hold in a—"

"Are you defying an order?" Rafton snaps.

"No, sir," Iyan replies. Glaring at me, he makes a point of stepping out of the circle before stalking to the edge of the room.

"Nice attempt," Sydon says, stealing my attention back to him. I can feel myself sweating with exertion. "Let us try again. Can you pull that back?" He points to the tiny flames still burning, that everyone is now battling around.

"Yes." I grab the small rope in my mind's eye and pull. It snaps back into my hands, allowing flames to once again dance along my skin. My heart is racing. As good as I had felt this morning, I am not fully recovered from yesterday's events, and my body is making that fact known. Ignoring the feeling, I allow my gaze to rake over the dwindling crowd until my eyes lock on a woman in bronze tossing a man, who I recognize from my team, over her shoulder. Gathering my flames again, I try to force them to grow. They comply. This time I toss slightly larger flames in a small circle around the woman. This circle is a bit neater, its sides slightly less wavy. I smile at the accomplishment. The woman glances up from staring at the flames around her to give me a gentle thumbs up. The flames are up to her knees, so I pull them back and she exits the circle, jogging towards the wall.

"Better," Sydon says. "Next—"

"I have it," I say.

"Good," Sydon says, his tone hard. I feel his heat leave my back, but I do not glance in his direction. *He is your captor.* I remind myself. *He was helping you to use you further, not out of any kindness. Finish this exercise. Find Sorin. Get out of here.*

I feel like my body is almost at the point of collapse, but the number of trainees around us is dwindling fast. There looks to be around five left on the opposing team and three left on mine. Those three are me, Lylane, and Jaq. On the opposing? One silver trainee, two black, one teal, and

Huermond. Lylane takes down one of the silver trainees and they smile at each other as they part ways. Jaq is dealing with a teal trainee and a black. *I am a little surprised he is still in...* I think to myself as Jaq ducks under a punch and trips the trainee in black, before rolling away from them. *He is quick.*

"Princess!" Huermond taunts. My eyes whip in his direction right before the ground seems to vibrate weakly beneath me. *What was..?*

"Trying to stop me with those embarrassing flames of yours?" He jeers.

"That is the exercise," I toss back weakly.

"You look like you can barely stand. Do you think you will win this?"

I do my best to throw the flames around Huermond's feet. They sparkle around him, but do not spark to life. *I am drained. Fuck.* Although fire still glitters around my form, it refuses to be thrown, its threads sticking and melting into me. Looking around, I notice that Sydon seems to have disappeared completely.

The other trainee in black grabs me from behind and I yell, burning him with the fire still gathered in my hands. He screams, but does not release me. Rafton looks on, but does not move to help. *Probably because this is the point of this stupid exercise. Fuck, fuck, fuck. What do I do?*

"The truth of the matter is," Huermond continues, "I know the real reason why you are here." His smile is predatory. His voice is now barely above a whisper. "A deserter will never be my ruler. If you do not tell me where you left Fadres and Credour, you can consider yourself as good as dead."

I try to gather more fire in my hands, but it seems as though all the threads are now frayed, and as I try to pull more flames to me the threads snap away, leaving the power just out of my reach. I do my best to wiggle free from the other trainee but his grip is too strong. *Think, Alaceandra, think.* Right as Huermond is about to place his hand across my throat in his 'killing blow,' I hit the ground— hard.

"And a shit talker does not make a good soldier," Lylane says from behind me, striking her own 'killing blow' on the soldier in black.

"Yeah, they are not very observant," Jaq says, his hand against Huermond's throat.

Rafton blows a shell, and a high pitched noise fills the room. "End of exercise!" He yells.

Huermond stomps off with the trainee dressed in black.

"Thanks," I say to them.

"Don't mention it," Jaq grumbles. "We just wanted to win the exercise." With that, he walks off.

"He might have, but I cannot stand a bully." Lylane laughs. She has a cut on her arm but seems otherwise unharmed. "Come on. We should clean up." She extends a hand.

I hesitate but accept her hand. *If she cannot stand a bully, why is she working with the kings?* She pulls me up a little too forcefully, and I almost continue my upward motion back to the floor.

"Fuck! Sorry," She says, steadying me.

"It is fine," I reply, patting her hand. As I stand, I notice I am barely able to hold my body weight and start to crumble back to the floor.

"Woah!" With surprising strength, Lylane stops me from falling and maneuvers herself to help me stand. "On second thought, maybe we get you to the infirmary."

"I am okay," I say, my voice wispy.

"Bullshit," She says and starts to lead me to the door. I get the feeling she is allowing me to follow next to her instead of carrying me herself. This girl seems quite strong, but looks to be attempting to conceal it. *Odd.*

"I have her," Sydon's voice suddenly booms from behind us.

"Oh.. um okay," Lylane says, shooting me a wide glance. Sydon takes me from her, scooping me up in his arms. I attempt to fight him, but my attempts are weak, and my eyes start to fall shut from exhaustion.

"Get cleaned up, Lylane," I hear him say.

"Yes, sir," she replies, before her footsteps echo away. I think I am watching her, but realize that my eyes have closed some time ago.

"Where did you go?" I ask Sydon dreamily, my voice barely a whisper.

"Go to sleep, princess. Your body needs to recover," he responds.

I want to fight the sleep clawing to claim my consciousness. I resist its call with every last once of energy left in me, but in the end it is no use. I succumb to its inky black depths.

CHAPTER FOURTEEN

The Palace

The Prince

Hours Ago...

W e had fallen asleep farther up the trail where the tracks of the other soldiers disappeared into the woods.

"We will wait here for the man we spoke with to wake up and continue on the path," Sam said. "Following him is probably our best option to finding where they are keeping Alaceandra. Unless you have knowledge of a palace in the mountains?"

"I do not."

"As I thought." Sam coughed then. "Let's rest here."

I worried that Sam would not recover in time and I would have to go without him. *I would have gone without him. My little dove had only just gained her wings. I know that my father means to clip them. I cannot let that happen. Not only because I need her at full power for my plans to work, but also because I... care for her. At least so much as to not want her dead, which I know is what will happen if everything works in his favor. If anyone is going to ensure her downfall it is me, not some king who has to rely on totems in order to keep his kingdom under control. Although I hope it does not come to that.*

When I awoke the next morning, Sam was nowhere to be seen, but when I searched the surrounding forests he seemed to appear from thin air. He looked a lot better. So much so that it would have been hard to tell that he had even been in a battle less than twenty four hours ago.

"There he is," Sam whispers pulling me from my thoughts. "Come on."

The soldier we encountered yesterday is now racing down the path in front of us. I use the wind around us to lighten our steps and encourage any noisy branches and leaves, *of which there are many,* to move out of the way as we follow the man through the forest. He darts and weaves through the trees and underbrush. Surprisingly, it is more challenging then expected to keep up with him. The man is fast.

We travel like this all morning. The man seems frantic and does not slow his pace, nor does he stop for food, water, or even to use the bathroom. We keep up with him, and I do my best to remember the paths we are taking. *It will make it easier to escape in the future if we know where we went.* Finally, after the sun has hit its highest point, we arrive at the side of a giant mountain. It is so large that when we look up we cannot see the top of it. The rocks on the mountain range from a deep black to dark greens, browns, and yellows depending on the way the light shines on it. The mountain would be beautiful if not for the fact that it is keeping my little dove captive.

A small door opens at the bottom of it and a man walks out.

"Why are you out here? Did you just make it back from the mission?"

"Yes, sir. I ran into some... complications on the way back."

"What kind of complications?"

The scrawny man looks around, and I can feel Sam's magick tingle over my skin as he cloaks us deeper in the woods.

"Be careful. If you overdo it again I am leaving you here," I whisper.

"Watch it," Sam whispers back. "That was a one time thing."

"If you say so."

"Nothing major, just got turned around," the scrawny man says, bringing our attention back to them.

"You are lucky I am the one at this door and not any of the other guards," The man at the door grumbles.

"I know," the scrawny man says cheerily.

The other man sighs. "Come on in then, you are late for training. If you move quickly enough maybe Rafton won't notice." He smirks.

"I doubt that," the scrawny man says scurrying past him. The other man sighs and turns to follow.

"Come on, maybe we can catch the door," Sam says, sprinting towards the quickly shutting mountain door. Grabbing a rock, Sam tosses it towards the opening of the door as he runs. I push the rock to move faster, and it wedges itself in the door frame. The door shuts before we make it, but a tiny sparkle of light peaking from the opening means the rock did its job of making sure it did not close completely.

I grab the edge of the door to try to pry it open, but it doesn't budge. *Now what?*

"Sam, help me with this."

He nods and grabs the door as well, but doesn't pull. Instead he closes his eyes and sighs.

"What is it?" I ask.

"If we open this door, they will know we are here."

"Why is that?" I ask, exasperated.

"It is spelled."

"How do you even-?"

Sam glares at me.

I sigh. "What do we do?" *Never thought I would be asking Sam for direction, but here I am working with my enemy. He will hate me soon and wish he hadn't worked with me to get her back, but until then I guess our motives are aligned.*

Sam runs his fingers through his hair. "It would be more of a problem if I am caught. If we can somehow sneak you in, though..."

That would be ideal, but... "Why would it be a problem if you were caught more than me? My father is in that building. Or at least I think he is. I felt his totem on the battlefield. If I am caught, especially if he thinks that I am working with you all, then he will surely kill me."

Sam's eyes widen and he grabs my shoulders. "Totem?"

I look skyward. "It's the king of Helomasi's gift. He controls people with totems. This is old news."

"You did not inform-"

"Can we move on?" I cut in, acting bored. *I guess it is good for him to know the information. The issue is I did not mean to share it. Hopefully that does not come back to haunt me later.*

"This is important information," Sam growls. "If he has that gift and was on the battlefield, that means he is one of the ones who abducted Alaceandra. What if he is using it against her? What do the totems do?"

I had not considered that. "He does not have the discipline to use it outside of short bursts or certain distances. Mine only causes me pain when I step out of line, but there are others..." I look around. "We need to come up with a plan to get in there. The door guard can come back at any moment. Can you not disguise us as those men again?"

A worried look crosses over Sam's features. "I am afraid it will not work on who we are up against if I use my powers on us both, I am..."

annoyance flashes in his eyes, "too weak," he spits out the words. "After our battle. I need to have more time to recharge." He lets out a sharp breath. "But," he continues, "if we can get you in there and reconnected with Alaceandra, hopefully you both will find Sorin, and you can let me in in a couple days. I should feel a bit better by then."

"Why are you trusting me right now?" I ask, genuinely curious. Our first go around these lands together was... hostile, to say the least. The fact that he is actually trusting me with a mission right now is surprising.

"I don't have a choice," he says.

"Ah," I say. "So a truce for now then."

"If that is what it takes, asshole." He smirks at me.

Always with the names. "Okay then, this is what we will do."

About an hour later, Sam is using his abilities to help pry the door open. Strangely, we did not re-encounter the door guard. *He was probably preoccupied with whatever the scrawny man was up to. A mistake on their part.* Once the door is completely opened, a tremor goes through the mountain, and I have to hold on to the side of the door to stay upright.

"What was that?" I ask Sam.

"Their alarm. Subtle, right?" He rolls his eyes.

"Yeah."

"Are you set for the plan?"

"I am."

He nods his head, thoughtfully. "Great. I will see you in one week."

"One week it is."

In a blink, Sam disappears into the shadows, and I make my way into the castle.

CHAPTER FIFTEEN

The Sacrifice

The Prince

I walk into the building and down the hall until I reach a large room filled with black rock and shiny yellow gemstones. It is not long before I am spotted.

"Hey you!" A man in bronze armor yells. "How did you get in here?"

Well at least they recognize an intruder. I was about to be really offended that we lost to this group of soldiers. Although this one has different armor. Very interesting.

A man grabs at me, but I avoid his grasp, shoving wind in his direction to make him lose his footing. With a grunt he hits the ground. I do my best not to laugh. More men start streaming out of the halls around us until I am surrounded. Many sharp objects are pointed in my direction, and I raise a brow at their wielders. Lazily, I raise my arms.

"I am here to speak with my father," I say my tone bored.

"And who is he?" One man in bronze spits at me.

"My prince?" A soldier in teal armor lowers her weapon. "Is that you?"

"It is."

Her hands flex on her weapon. "But I thought that you abandoned the cause to be with that girl?" She narrows her eyes at me.

"Does that really seem like something I would do?" I shoot her a admonishing look.

"Well, no but..."

"Get him an audience with the king," another woman in teal armor shouts. "I would like to hear his explanation. I would assume his father would be quite interested as well." She sneers at me.

A murmuring rumbles over the crowd.

"Fine," A man in bronze armor says. "We will take him, but do not lower your weapons."

I see a couple nods of agreement.

The second woman in teal armor peels away from the crowd and grabs my arm roughly. "This way."

I follow her down one of the large halls while around ten of the other soldiers in teal take up the rear, weapons at the ready, leaving the other soldiers in armor of silver, black, and bronze behind. *So not all of them followed. That is another point in their favor then.* The winding and turns of the halls seems to be purposefully disorienting, but I keep a sense of where I am going despite that. I had a lot of time wandering the halls of Helomasi's castle. It is going to take more than a bit of misdirection to leave me unaware of my surroundings. We arrive at a large redwood door with golden veins running through it. *Pretty.* I think to myself sarcastically. The woman turns the knobs in a couple different patterns before the lock finally releases and I am nudged into the room.

"Son." My father, King Demetrius of Helomasi, sits on a pedestal in the middle of the room. "Are you here to embarrass our family once again?"

"What do you mean embarrass our family?" I ask, nonchalantly.

Anger causes my father's face to turn red. "Slap the boy," he commands one of the soldiers. Suddenly, I am grabbed and slapped viciously by the woman who escorted me. I lick my teeth and sigh in response, but dare not to rub at my cheek. Instead, I turn back to my father to stare at him.

"Was that really necessary?"

"You ran off with that girl! Of course it was necessary! Why should I not have them sever you limb from limb at this very moment?"

"I went after the girl," I start calmly. "To stop her from escaping. I saw her and her guards leave under the cover of the night and did not want them to get away. So I followed. I was in the process of figuring out how to get back to our kingdom when the raid happened on that village."

"The soldiers reported you fought back," my father says through gritted teeth. "You would not have done so if—"

I take a leap of faith and cut him off. "The soldiers wearing armor of black, father?" I arch a brow at him. "Why would I allow some other kingdom to capture our prize? I was doing my duty by fighting back. Last I checked our soldiers wore armor only in teal." I narrow my gaze on him. "Should I ask why you are working with these other armies? Does that not go against—" *his plans to destroy them.*

"You may not," he cuts me off grasping that blasted totem in his hand. I crouch down as pain rushes through my system. Fisting my hands in annoyance, I endure. Finally he releases it, and I can breath again. He smiles. "So you did not abandon your kingdom."

"For Tikilium scum? Never." *At least not that you should know of yet.*

"How can I be sure you can be trusted?"

"You cannot, not now," I try. "But I will prove my loyalty." *Not to you of course, but that is not what is important here. Your day of doom shall come, father, and it will come soon. I can only hope that you are unprepared for it as I was unprepared for your cruelty for all these years. Helomasi will prove a better kingdom without you.*

"Good." He drops the totem on the table in front of him. "It would be good to get more eyes on the girl. I will talk to the others about you resuming your duty with the girl, maybe she will trust you more as you were with her on your..." he narrows his eyes, "side quest," he finishes. "But you will be closely monitored. The minute it looks like you are at risk of endangering the mission you will be punished. Severely. Do not test me. I cannot have my son making a mockery of Helomasi. The other kings have already been at my throat due to your past indiscretions."

"Understood," I say, barely paying any attention to his ramblings. *If everything goes to plan he should be dead by next week. His threats are of little consequence.* As nonchalant as I am attempting to appear, I know not to take my eyes off the king. I have found it is much easier to get away with little acts of rebellion as long as he thinks he will be able to detect them. He has always toted that he is good at reading people's eyes. That is how he makes most of his decisions on who to trust in the kingdom. I have always found he is incorrect in that opinion of himself. His arrogance has always been a flaw of his.

He nods. "The soldiers will lead you to a safe place to wait before you are reintroduced to the princess."

"Do you have her guards here as well?" I ask, cautiously.

His body tenses. "Why do you ask?"

"They were a bit of competition for her attention. I was just wondering if I had need to separate them."

"Interesting..." He taps his fingers against the table. "But you need not worry about them. One has been handled and the other was reported to have disappeared in combat." He narrows his eyes at me. "Get to your room. I need to discuss your being here now before they find out from someone other than me."

Handled? "Understood."

"At ease, soldiers." The soldiers only now drop their weapons from my back. "Please show him his rooms.

The woman beside me casts me a suspicious look before returning her gaze to my father. "Yes, sir." Her tone is one of anger.

"Are you upset soldier?" My father asks, his tone deceptively concerned. "This is joyous news. My son has returned. I am now no longer a fool in the eyes of the other kingdoms. Are you not feeling celebratory?"

The air in the room grows tense, deadly. The other soldiers shift slightly in discomfort. The woman's eyes widen. "Apologies, my king. Yes, I am very happy. This is great cause for celebration," she says earnestly.

"Hmm... good." He stands from his chair and turns away from us. "Lead my son out," he commands.

With another annoyed glare, the soldier walks out the door. I, of course, follow.

CHAPTER SIXTEEN

Dreams

Alaceandra

Present...

I stand in a field of purple-tipped grass. Behind me sits a small cabin that has smoke billowing up from its chimney. The sun is setting and there is a chill in the air. I am barefoot in a yellow dress and Addie, my elvisera, lays sleeping on the ground next to me. I run my fingers over her feathered head and smile. The world around me smells of pink duncicule flowers, fresh air, and a faint metallic scent that I do my best not to think about. Everything but the breeze is calm. That whips around me, wildly, as if it is playing with the hem of my skirt. I let out a short laugh as pure joy fills my senses.

Quickly, the sun disappears and the world grows dark. The joy that filled me before now sinks into dread as the breeze, that once danced along my skirt, turns violent and frigid. I cross my arms trying to warm myself, but try as I might the chill continues to invade my senses. I spin around to try and get to Addie, but she has disappeared. In her place stands the shadow *of a man. I squint trying to make out who it might be, but the wind whips over my eyes making it hard to see.*

"Hello?" I shout, but I can tell my voice too is lost to the ferocious winds around us. I start to turn and try to run towards the cabin behind me when I am stopped by a noise.

"Alaceandra..." That voice. The one that has been haunting my dreams. It floats to me on the breeze, its tone coaxing me to try and find it. I turn around once again and peer through the violent winds, but only see the shadow of the man still standing at the same place I had left him. Instead of trying to approach the man, I turn away once more, doing my best to run against the wind and reach the small cabin. All of its lights are now on. The smoke that once billowed gently from it is now blown away as soon as it escapes the small opening of the chimney. I have the feeling that if I can just reach it, then I will be safe from whatever storm is raging in these fields.

"Do not veer too far away. Your visitors await you..."

I wake up in a cold sweat. *No, no, no! That man is back in my dreams.* Panic fills me as I recall the contents of the dream. *Why does he keep showing up? Does this mean he found me?* Disoriented, I look around, but no shadowy figures lurk in the room around me. In fact, I seem to be back in the room I was assigned when I first arrived here. *He must have been the shadowy figure. Why else would there have been those winds? And what did he mean my visitors await me? What visitors?* I rack my brain to see if I can come up with some meaning for the dream, but the more I focus on the details the harder they are to hold on to. I grow frustrated and squeeze the blankets beneath me. *I will have to figure out the weird dream later.*

No light filters in from under my door, nor does any sound meet my ears no matter how hard I strain to hear it. *What time is it? It must be late.* I have no idea how long I have been sleeping for. *Sleeping?* I was not supposed to be sleeping. I need to search the property tonight, find Sorin, and come up with a plan to escape this place. *Why was I asleep?*

Memories of training filter through, further replacing the memories of the dream. The chaos of fighting around me. Rafton yelling at trainees when they were defeated. The fire circles I threw at people's feet. That strange thread within me. *Shit. I passed out after overusing my powers.* I close my eyes to recheck on that strange thread that I saw, but when I try to access that place inside of me, a wall stands in the place the threads should be. *So the bracelet really is blocking me. That is not good.* I inspect the wrist with the red band still attached and notice that the inflammation has thankfully gone away, leaving my wrist unmarred. *Well there is at least that.*

Checking my body for any other injuries, I realize that other than the sense of tiredness I feel, I am completely fine. I, thankfully, have no scrapes, bruises, or broken bones from that training session today. *Or was it yesterday? I really need to figure out the time.* I also seem to be in the same red clothing. *Not the best color for sneaking about, but maybe I still have enough time to search this place. It does not look like it is morning quite yet. Now I just need to figure out how to get out of here.* Slowly, I make my way from my bed and towards the door. The room itself has been really quiet, and I did not hear any noise coming through the door from the hall so hopefully...? I push my ear to the door to listen further. *Quiet. Hopefully that means no one is watching the door at the moment.*

First, I try the most obvious thing... the door handle and almost jump back when the door opens smoothly. *Why would they leave the door unlocked? Has it been this whole time?* I did not take my abductors as people dumb enough to not lock a door, which is why I had not tried using it earlier. *But father was able to get into my room really easily...*

79

Why keep it unlocked? They must have some other way of ensuring I stay here if they are not relying solely on the door to my room. I glance down at my bracelet remembering the pain I felt earlier from it and sigh. *Probably a tracker as much as it is a shackle. That would only make sense.* Gritting my teeth, I slowly emerge from the room. No burning sensation accompanies my escape. *Okay, good to know I will not have to worry about that.... for now.* Staying close to the edge of the wall, I walk down the rugged hallway, doing my best to stick to the shadows. *Just because they are not guarding against me getting out, does not mean that they will be okay with me wondering around trying to find Sorin. I still have to be careful.* I remind myself. When I reach a path that looks like it could go in multiple directions, I choose the path that looks the least used— opting for pathways with jagged rocks over those that look smoothed out. *If I am correct about my theory, they want to keep us both in low traffic areas.*

As I walk my dread grows, but I ignore the feeling. Instead, my gaze darts around looking for anyone who could be watching me, but nothing catches my eye. *Come to think of it, no one is around at all. Where has everyone gone?* A warm tingling sensation from the tattoo in my thigh throws all other thoughts from my mind. I place a hand over the mark, my eyes widening. *Sorin?* I race down the paths, using the sensation as a compass. The farther I go the more my tattoo warms causing my heart to race. After what feels like forever, I reach a plain wooden door, much like that of the gym from earlier. Urgently, I push at the door, but it does not budge. *Fuck, so they decided to lock this one? Great.*

"Found what you wanted?" A familiar voice whispers from behind me. I almost jump out of my skin. Grabbing at the pin in my binding strap, I spin around and swipe at the person behind me. I just barely miss him *because of course I do.*

Sydon leans back. A smirk on his face. Tilting his head, he motions to the pin in my grip. "Where did you get that?"

"How long have you been following me?" I shoot back.

He arches a brow. "The entire time. Did you think you could leave the room without anyone knowing?"

I tense. "Not particularly," I grit out.

"Then why are you surprised?"

"Why did you not say something sooner?" My eyes dart around him looking for anyone else who might have accompanied him, but I still spot no one.

"I wanted to see where you were going. Now. Are you going to go back to your room, or are you going to force me to bring you there myself?" He starts to move towards me, but I back away and he stops, a curious look on his face.

"What is behind this door?" I motion to it. The tingling in my thigh is going haywire at this point, and I do my best not to touch Sorin's vine. The last thing I would want to do is bring Sydon's attention to it.

Sydon's brow furrows. "That is none of your concern."

"I beg to differ." I glare at him.

"Alaceandra, do not mistake my patience with you as any indication that you do not have to follow orders."

"Do not mistake my compliance with the day so far for submission. Now tell me what is behind that door."

"Would you like to know the truth, princess?" His eyes have turned red and his voice has taken on that strange echo quality that I vaguely recognize. He continues to approach me until he is within breathing distance before stopping and looking down at me, his face full of curiosity.

I force my hesitation away. "That would be preferable," I grit out.

"Fine then. Let's make a deal." His voice continues to echo in my ears, his tone lilting. "I will show you what is within this room, but in exchange you will return to your room and inform no person within this palace what you have seen within it."

"Will you answer any questions about what I see? Can I discuss whatever this is with you?" I ask skeptically.

"I will answer what I must," he replies simply. "As far as discussion... I will remain outside of the deal itself. You may discuss with me, but I may not reply to all that you seek to know."

Cryptic, but who else would I discuss my findings with? Those who can help are still outside of these walls. I am on my own until I can escape or am found. "Deal," I say, reluctantly. I feel magick click into place around me, and I cannot help but feel like I may have made a mistake. *Does not matter. I can feel something beyond that door. I cannot pass up the chance that it might be Sorin. Whether he is alive or... not. I need to know where he is. He must leave with me when I escape. Besides worse case is that I cannot tell any guards or kings what I have seen behind those doors. Truly, why would I even want to tell them? I lost all loyalty to my own father the minute he shipped me away. Not that I had much to begin with.*

"As you wish then, princess." His eyes fade back to their red-rimmed state, and he moves around me to place his hand on the door. It glows slightly before something clicks. Sydon opens the door slowly. "Come then, see what is inside."

CHAPTER SEVENTEEN

Vines

Alaceandra

I dart into the room before Sydon can block the entrance. The tingle in my thigh is now burning and my heart is racing in my chest. The room is simple. The floors are lined with wooden planks and outfitted with ornate rugs. There are a couple of chests and tables scattered around. In the corner is a small lamp, but what really grabs my attention sits in the farthest corner. A large bed made of black metal is tucked neatly against it. On the bed lays a man. A man wrapped in vines.

"Sorin?" I whisper. My feet take me to him before my brain can stop them. I find myself falling to my knees at his bedside. His eyes are closed, his lashes fanning softly across his cheeks. He looks to be sleeping, but he is too still. *Why is he so still?* Tears threaten my eyes as I see that his vines have woven themselves tightly around his form as if they are trying to forge some kind of armor and protect him. His skin is pale, paler than any natural tint. "Is he...?" *Dead?* My voice is the barest of whispers, but I do not dare to speak the words, too afraid of their consequence. Tears start to fall from my eyes freely. I lift my hand shakily to touch Sorin's cheek, but Sydon's voice stops me.

"I would not touch him."

My hand curls into a fist. "Why not?" I ask, my voice still low. I keep my eyes on Sorin. Not one muscle on his body even so much as twitches. *What has been done to you?*

"You do not know how it will affect him."

Affect him? "It could affect him? Is he... alive?" I try to hide the hope from my voice, but I fail miserably. *Please be alive.*

"He is in a... between state," Sydon says. "Neither living nor dead." Sydon sighs. "He lost a lot of blood when we found him in the woods outside of Olvaria. "Luckily, the stab wound in his stomach was cauterized but... a lot of blood is a lot of blood. I tried to revive him, but—"

"You tried to save him?" *Why would they try to save him?*

"For information purposes," Sydon says, his tone a bit annoyed. "He was one of your guards when you were with your father. We wanted to know how he made his way to the Dark Lands... and to you." I can feel his eyes on my back, but I do not answer. "Unfortunately, healing him only brought on the vines. He has been like this ever since my attempt. His heart is beating, but there have been no signs of consciousness. It is clear he is important to you somehow, but if he becomes a problem to the kings when it comes to you completing what they want you to—"

"He is not the reason I left Helomasi," I say. "If he winds up dead because they think him a threat, they will regret it." Anger overtakes me at the thought that they would kill Sorin, especially with him in such a vulnerable state. *Cowards. They would kill him over being a threat, but not see the very threat so blatantly in front of them. They hid your Sorin away. They could have used his life to keep you in line, but they wanted you to suffer. Wanted you to think he was dead. They need to be punished. We will have our revenge, Alaceandra.* That sickly, sweet voice is loud in my head. *We will paint this castle red with the blood of our enemies and burn it down. Just let me take care of it...* My body starts to glow with fire, but as the embers spark to life on my body, they get sucked into the bracelet and fizzle out. I growl in frustration. A hand on my shoulder has me spinning around.

"Alaceandra, calm yourself."

"Why should I? If it were not for whatever schemes you and those kings have concocted, Sorin would not have gotten injured. He would not be on the edge of death. I would not be here in this fucking prison, waiting to be slaughtered by those who are meant to protect their people." My voice starts to rise and my vision blurs as pain radiates from my wrist but I continue on anyway. "How can I be calm when all this time Sorin, someone who has served in my father's guard for years, has been kept here—"

"Kept here so that he can stay alive," Sydon cuts me off, his body tense. "You and the men you were with are considered traitors in the kings' eyes until you prove otherwise. If it were not for the prophecy, you would have been killed along with that village in the raid. You should be grateful you were not and that he," Sydon points to Sorin, "is still alive enough for you to even be upset."

"Grateful?" I laugh sardonically. "Grateful to be used against my will in a power grab I want nothing to do with? Grateful to be the one spared when all I care for are left to perish? If the kings were so upset with me and my performance of duties in Helomasi, they should have just let me be. I would rather have died out there then to be kept here, with such vile people."

Sydon smiles, but it is not one of happiness. "Vile as we may be, we are who you are stuck with at the moment. If you would like to be free from it, go ahead and try, but know you will fail. The outcome of the prophecy is outside of your understanding, but that makes it no less important. You can destroy the entirety of Ptheryeth. Or save it. Do you not understand the gravity of that?"

"No!" I practically shout. "What would destroying Ptheryeth even entail? Or for that matter saving it? Most of its rulers are corrupt, cruel men who would rather abduct a twenty-four-year-old woman than get their own shit together. Who is to say which way they even want the prophecy to go? I have been told too little about the prophecy's meaning to even decide my stance on it." The bracelet is searing into my skin, but I ignore the pain as tears fall from my eyes. Turning back to Sorin, I watch as one of my tears splash against the vines that are wrapped around him so tightly. "You cannot expect gratitude over a life that is not chosen," I whisper. *We can take back our life, Alaceandra. We can break out of here and destroy them all... Just say the word.* That sweet voice whispers to me. I feel a door within me starting to open and I allow it, but only the slightest bit. A rushing noise in my ears accompanies the feeling of numbness that fills me as it does.

I hear Sydon sigh. "We can discuss this later. You are unstable at the moment. If your power breaks free, you will cause him as much harm as everyone else in this palace. Is that what you want?"

"I want you all to pay for what you did." My voice does not go above a whisper, but my tone is deadly.

"Alaceandra," I feel the crackle of his magick move through the room behind me. "If you do not calm yourself, I will make you calm yourself."

"And how will you do that?" There is a lightness in my voice now, as if I find his threat comical, but I feel nothing.

"I have my ways." His tone is hard. Serious. He comes closer. Not wanting his magick anywhere near me, I avoid his hand as he attempts to grab me.

"I am calm." I turn to face him, my expression blank.

His eyes widen. He looks alarmed. "Alaceandra?" He reaches for me once again.

I would not do that if I were you... A smile forces itself on my face.

Right before his hand makes contact, one of Sorin's vines— the one that my tear landed on— twitches, pulling my attention away from Sydon. The door inside me slams shut with a crash as emotions *and pain* whip through me causing me to gasp and crumble to the ground.

"Shit." Sydon grabs me, before I can hit the ground.

Glancing at my wrist where the red bracelet was placed, I notice the area around is reddened and bleeding. I push Sydon away and as I do so he sees my wrist as well.

"Let me heal your wrist, princess," he says. His tone is strangely gentle, like he is talking to a wounded animal.

I pull it away from him. "Why? Is this not the purpose of your idiotic band? Pain is a great weapon in ensuring compliance, right?" I blink heavily, my energy strangely drained once again.

"No. It is not." He gently grabs my arm. His magick rushes over the wound and when he releases me, it has disappeared. "You need to go back to your room."

I dig my heels in. "But the vines moved."

"That will be monitored."

"By who?" I square my shoulders stubbornly.

"Me," he sighs. "You can visit him again at the end of the week if you comply with your schedule."

I look at him with disdain. "If you would like my compliance, it will need to be sooner than that." I waver a bit on my feet, and Sydon reaches for me. I step away.

"Tomorrow then. We can talk about the frequency after the visit, but you need to rest."

I nod. "Okay."

"Good. Get back to your room, and do not wander."

On shaky feet, I retreat to my quarters, but this time, I can feel his presence the entire way back.

CHAPTER EIGHTEEN

The Meeting

Alaceandra

Sydon comes to my room early the next morning with a set of clothing for today in his hands. I drag myself out of bed, and am caught off-guard by his presence at the door. Throwing my body behind it, I only manage to hide half of myself from his view. Switching my weight from foot to foot uncomfortably, I attempt to bend my body awkwardly away from him as not to show off too much of my nightgown and ragged state to this weird prison guard.

"I ran into the servant on my way in," he explains as he hands me a bundle of clothing. His eyes are firmly planted above my head. "You need to get dressed quickly, the kings would like to meet with you again, but we have some things to do before."

"Is this really necessary?" I ask, sleep still heavy in my voice.

"It is." He turns away. "Make sure you check your schedule before you leave. You have twenty minutes." He grabs at the door and pries it away from me to shut it firmly.

I look at the bundle in my hands. A pair of leggings and a long black dress with a red sash tied around the waist wrap themselves around a set of undergarments. I carefully fold the bundle back up and walk on too heavy legs to the bathroom in the back of the room. Showering quickly, I don my new clothes and place the old bundle on the toilet. Then I brush my teeth, fix my hair, and take a deep breath before leaving the warmth of the bathroom.

With more energy, I move over to the door to see the piece of paper bearing my schedule sitting neatly just inside. I almost roll my eyes as I scoop it up. *It is silly to look at it again, I know what the stupid schedule says. Although its message was weird and a bit cryptic it was not overtly complicated. If he thinks making me check it again will ensure I adhere to it more thoroughly, well... he can think again.* Still, I unravel the scroll and blink as a message appears on the parchment instead of the cryptic timetable from yesterday.

> *It seems the princess would like best,*
> *More flexibility, so here is her test,*
> *If she may follow these steps this morn,*
> *A reward will greet her soon,*
> *That, I have sworn.*
>
> *For today...*
> *First- Retrieval*
> *Then- Breakfast*
> *After- Training*
> *Then- The Meeting**
> *Final- Flexible*

Really, riddles? It takes all I have to not crumble the paper and chuck it at the wall. *What kind of reward could the paper be speaking of?* Instead of trashing today's schedule, I place it on my bed. *The only way to know...*

Sighing, I open the door. "Retrieval?" I say to Sydon. He is leaning against the wall, one foot propped up behind him. He turns to me and pushes away from it.

"It seems so, let us get going."

"Hmm," I hum in approval and follow him down the hall.

We walk in silence to the breakfast hall. He opens the doors to the room, and it is once again empty. I send Sydon a puzzled look.

"Why is no one ever in this room?" I ask as he leads me to the middle table.

"What do you mean?"

"I mean," I gesture around. "It seems as if this space is meant to house multiple people at once, yet these past two times it has been empty of all but us. Why?"

"It is..." he looks around, then his shoulders slump slightly. "Safer that way."

"Safer?"

"Look, princess," Sydon gives me a hard look. "Not everyone is pleased you are here."

I snort. "I can tell." There are now seven chairs at the breakfast table. I sit in the middle seat.

"Yes, well. That anger could make your eating an issue."

"How so?" I ask. In front of me now sits a scramble of some kind. A yellow, fluffy substance holds together some root vegetables, meat, and greens. I scoop a bit of the food up and hand it to Sydon.

He looks at me blankly.

"Eat this," I say, like it is not obvious.

"Are we really going through this again?" He asks.

"And for the foreseeable future," I chime in, nodding solemnly.

He sighs, dumping the food into his palm, he throws it into his mouth. Chewing with purpose, he swallows it and raises a brow. "No poison."

I wait a couple of minutes and watch him. He watches me back. After about five minutes have passed, I nod. "Good. As you were saying." I wave my hand in his direction and scoop another bite of food into my mouth. After I have swallowed and he still has not spoken I look at him. "That anger could make my eating an issue because..." I prompt.

He sighs once again. "People can tamper with your meal, or if a fight breaks out it would be a lot messier to subdue here than in the training arena."

"The gym?" I ask.

He pinches the bridge of his nose. "Yes, the gym." He watches me another moment. "Hurry with your food, we have places to be."

I glare at him and continue eating.

After some more time passes, I continue my questions. *It seems Sydon is in a sharing mood this morning.* "If I am needed for your grander purpose then why would anyone try to harm me, especially those part of an elite guard?" I ask, my plate now almost empty.

"That is the question, is it not?" Sydon says, more to himself than to me. *Well, that answer is not very helpful is it.* "Looks like you are finished," Sydon says in reference to my plate. "Come on, we do not want to be late." He stands and walks from the breakfast hall. I, of course, follow.

"We will be working on hand-to-hand combat today." Rafton takes his command at the front of the room. Sydon stands slightly behind him. "Pair up."

I have changed into another red outfit. This time a red pair of leather leggings, paired with a sleeveless top. I have no shoes on. This is to apparently help with traction. My pin is once again tucked in my waistline. Although, it has not proved itself the most useful weapon, somehow I find myself unable to part with it. Just knowing I have something I can stab someone with, small as it is, is more comforting than being completely defenseless.

"Would you like to be partners?" Lylane's voice startles me from my thoughts. "Promise to go easy on you." She smiles at me. I spot Jaq not so far behind her, he looks to be paired with a man from the bronze soldiers.

"Um... sure," I reply. *She seems like the least likely to **want** to hurt me.*

"Great!" She says excitedly. "Over here!" She leads me to a purple mat on the floor.

"Time is up!" He looks around and I do as well. Everyone looks to be paired. He smirks. "Pick who will be the aggressor and who will defend. Aggressors, your job is to get your defenders on the mat. Defenders, your job is to not end up on the mat. Each round will go for five minutes. Do you understand?"

Is that all the instruction we are getting? No, I do not— I glance at Lylane with wide eyes but she only smiles at me kindly. *Fuck.*

"Yes, sir!" The trainees scream.

"Limitations are: no infirmary visits. Is that understood?"

"Yes, sir!" All the soldiers chorus.

"Good. Start!"

Then the gym erupts once again into chaos.

Surprisingly, I emerge from the gym alive. Although the brutality of the room did get somewhat out of control— *there were actually four infirmary patients after the session, much to Rafton's displeasure—* Lylane was more interested in teaching me than taking me down. I learned a couple different methods on how to unbalance my opponent and also that those methods were not foolproof. By the end of the session, I had taken down Lylane four times. *I do not wish to discuss how many she took me down, though. Maybe a little extra training is useful...*

I bump into Sydon's back. "Ow!" I back away from him. "Why did you stop?" I ask rubbing my forehead.

"It is time we meet with the kings again." He had disappeared during training again and when he came back, he looked annoyed. His mood had not lightened since.

"Oh..." My eyes drift to the red-veined door in front of us. *Seems I was not paying much attention.*

Sydon's body tenses. "You did well in training," he grits out.

Strange of him to pay me a compliment, but... "Thanks." I stare at him.

He nods and then turns to me, and I do my best not to back up. *Something is wrong.* "This meeting with the kings... might change the way things work."

"It is not like they have been very consistent to begin-"

He glares at me. I do not finish the sentence, not because I do not want to anger him, more so because... *why does he look so enraged?* His eyes flash red then black and then back to red again. Like he barely has a handle on himself.

"That was different. The plan is changing," he mutters. "I do not like plans changing."

"Okay..." I say, looking around.

"You being here is for the good of the kingdoms, princess. For the good of Ptheryeth."

"As you have said," I say, my brow wrinkling. *Not that I believe it. Once I can find a way to get out of here with Sorin. ...*

"Listen, Alaceandra." He slams his hand against the wall.

My pulse quickens as the air thickens. *Sydon has yet to give me a reason to actually be afraid of him. Why is he acting like this now?* I clench my fist, reach for my pin, and prepare to run.

He sees my body tense and clenches his own hands. I watch as he coaxes himself to calm down. Weight lifts from my shoulders as the tension slowly drains from the air. "Listen," he takes a breath and opens his eyes. His pupils are swirled with red, but the color has not completely taken over them. "The man you are about to be met with is against truth— revels in making a mockery of it. He is using you as much as you think we are. Do not be fooled. Take my words as a warning." A breeze drifts through the air causing a familiar shiver to run through me. I look around, but cannot find where the wind might be coming from.

Refocusing on Sydon, I shake my head. "Who are you talking about?"

"You will see soon." He stares at me. "You will not come to any more harm at my hand, but I cannot promise the same for him. It would be wise to keep that in mind." *As if I could trust his word.*

"Any more harm?" I scoff. "You and your kings in there kidnapped me, Sydon; every day here is causing me harm. Every day without…" I look away as Sorin's form cloaked in vines fills my brain. "Do not try to think yourself someone of good intent now that you have your prize in your possession."

"Think that now if you wish, but my warning still holds true."

Silence spans between us for a beat before I break it.

"Are we going in now or not?" I ask, still staring at the wall.

"Yes," Sydon responds after another moment of silence. I can feel his eyes on me. "I will open the door now."

The weight of his eyes leaves me, and I hear the door's lock unravel, before light from the king's room filters into the hall.

"Come."

CHAPTER NINETEEN

❧ ❧ ❧

Welcome

The Prince

Earlier that morning...

*M*y father has left me in these chambers for an entire day. I pace the finely decorated room that is to be my prison for the evening as I wait on my father to come back with his answer from whoever he has chosen to conspire with. Inside the room sits a chest, a bed, and a golden ornate desk. In the back of the room, there is a large doorway that leads to a bathroom. Most everything in the room is black and accented gold. A rug of the same coloring covers the rock floor. The room is spacious enough, but seems to shrink in size as I continue my pacing.

This is infuriating. Finally, I sit on the bed in the corner of the room and put my head in my hands. I have not slept the entire night awaiting my father's word, leaving me utterly exhausted. I would guess it is around lunchtime of the next day now, although I cannot say for sure, time seems to drag here. *The little dove is within these walls, maybe within my grasp, and I have to wait for my father's permission to see her. This is utterly ridiculous. What is taking so long?* I only have a week before Sam comes back and the plan continues. I cannot waste my days sitting in this room. *If I am not retrieved soon, I will need to find a way out. Another plan.*

Growling, I stand and continue to pace. One more day, and I am sure I would start to wear a hole in the fancy rug on the floor. *It would serve them right.* A noise calls my attention away from my torment, and I pause and look up to see the door to my room opening. That guard from yesterday appears, her expression filled with a bored disdain. *Finally.*

"Your father is calling upon you again. Follow me," she commands.

Disgust of my own churns in my gut. "Although I understand you may not be pleased with me at the moment," I start my voice low. "I would recommend you remember that I am your prince. You don't have to like that fact nor me for that matter, but it would be wise to show respect."

"Why should I respect a prince that betrayed his kingdom?" She snaps back.

"Everything I have done has been in the best interest of my kingdom. Everything I will do is much the same. I would do your own research before taking sides in this conflict. You do not want to find yourself on the wrong end of a war."

"Are you threatening to invoke war on Helomasi?" She looks scandalized and steps back as if she is ready to flee and inform the king of my treason. I sigh internally. *Let her tell him my warnings. He likely has already heard them. Besides, he is so deluded in his power over me due to that totem of his, he would not believe me capable of his own destruction. Instead, he is likely to attribute my comment to a war in his favor— the one he plans to invoke— rather than thinking that I would dare to say anything against him. This soldier is interesting though. I will know what piece this warrior plays in my father's games soon enough. She seems to be taking a lead role in some way among the soldiers, and he trusts her enough to fetch me. How much of my father's plan is she aware of? If she knew the war he wants to bring to our kingdom, would she follow his lead so fervently?*

This time I sigh aloud. "It seems you have not heard me. I would never wage war on my own kingdom," I say instead, my tone now hitting a bored note. "I am only offering some advice. Be careful who you disrespect. Especially when you are unaware of where you lie on the board. It may only cause harm to you in the end."

She grits her teeth and takes a deep breath. "If you are done, prince, the king does request your presence. He does not like to be kept waiting."

"I am aware," I mumble to myself, before walking in her direction. "Let's go then," I say to the soldier. She nods. We walk down a couple of halls before I feel it. A breeze sweeps itself across my spine, the sensation not unpleasant. I pause in my steps.

"Prince?" The soldier turns back to see my still form. "Everything okay? We really must—"

"Quiet," I whisper.

She complies and tries to hold back a thinly veiled glare. The wind once again brushes past me and with it a chill that travels from my skull to my toes. My heart starts to race as I realize what the wind is trying to tell me.

The dove is ahead. For some reason, I know this with certainty. A smirk takes over my face. I try to track where the wind is coming from and my eyes zero in on a red veined door.

"Are we going to the room I met my father in yesterday?" I ask, pointing to the behemoth of wood peeking out from the corner.

"We are," the soldier grumbles, her thinly veiled glare turning into one not so veiled. Her tone drips with impatience. I ignore her. If she does not wish to heed my advice, I will not push it on her. Besides, I have bigger things to deal with at the moment.

I nod. "Thank you." I continue my path forward.

She gives me an odd look, but I only stare at the door ahead, willing my pace not to quicken. There is sure to be spyware hidden within these walls and until I can zero in on their location it is best not to give my father anything to work with. My excitement would only cause him to look on me with more suspicion. We finally reach those looming doors and I take a breath. Her scent lingers in the air, as if she just donned perfume before she entered, but I know she had not. No, instead, for some unknown reason, my sense of her is heightened, and I find myself pleased with the development.

I found you, little dove, and it seems we have both found ourselves in a trap. I hope you are ready for its consequences.

The soldier undoes the pattern on the doors and pushes them open. She says something, but I don't hear it. Instead my eyes find themselves transfixed on the beautiful woman in front of me.

Let the games begin.

"My son," My father's voice booms through the room. "Welcome back."

CHAPTER TWENTY

News

Alaceandra

A few minutes before...

Telvonius, Mirksyl, Demetrius, and my father take their places on the raised dais in front of me. I study each king. Telvonius regards the room with a calm composure, his face a mask of his emotions. Demetrius looks smug and self assured, his mood doing a one eighty of what it was only the day before. Mirksyl looks to be slightly annoyed by something, but when he feels my eyes on him, he drops the expression, his face mirroring the same blank calmness as Telvonius. My search pauses on my father. My father holds an expression unlike those of the other kings. Luckily a night's rest was kind to him, at least in appearances. My father now wears a pressed mantle made of rare geometric patterned fabric. It sparkles bronze and gold in the light. The beauty of the piece, though, could not disguise the sheer amount of madness in his eyes. He exudes a mixture of excitement and righteous anger. I can hear his foot tapping incessantly against the wood of the dais. When he meets my stare, my father sneers at me. I look away, quickly. *What is going on with him?*

"Alaceandra," Telvonius drags out my name. "Glad to see you made it here safely." He sizes me up with his eyes and then looks to Sydon. "We have called you here to let you know of some... news."

News? "What kind of news?" I ask. Aside from the strange appearance of my father, I am still shaken from my conversation with Sydon. I hate that he can have such an effect on me. I hate that he can allow himself such arrogance surrounding me when he and his lot of kings are the whole reason I am here in the first place. I allow myself to re-examine the room, his words ringing through my head, but confusion colors me. *There is not anyone here who was not before. No one to meet. Maybe he meant the kings in front of me make a mockery of the truth? But why would he feel the need to inform me of that? Are they all not on the same team here? And he said 'man' not men. Which could he have been referring to?*

"You will see soon enough," Demetrius says, pride brimming in his tone. "It surely has almost arrived."

Arrived? What is 'it'?

The door behind me starts to clatter as its locks start to fall out of place. Slowly the door opens causing all the eyes in the room to swing in its direction. A woman in teal armor who I barely recognize from training and a man walks in. I blink. Not just any man. *The Prince.*

"Ah, my son!" Demetrius booms. "Welcome."

"Father," the prince acknowledges but does not take his eyes away from mine until he is within grabbing distance. Only then does he look away, doing his own study of the men in the room.

The prince is here. I watch him, my heart fluttering in my chest. It has not been long since I had been captured and yet it feels like it has been years since we were in a room together. I can tell that the past hours have been rough on him as well. He looks tired. The exhaustion does not take away from his beauty though. His inky braid still tumbles silkily over his shoulder. His gray-green eyes still do their best to pierce through my very soul. His aura still calls to mine. Out of the prince and Sam, I never would have guessed it would be the prince that is standing before me as my rescuer. Nevertheless, him being here now fills me with an indescribable sense of relief.

"Alaceandra." King Demetrius calls my attention back to him. "My son has done his duty in bringing you back to your destiny. It is time you comply in fulfilling your duty as princess of Tikilium."

My heart sinks as I process his words. *Done his duty... in what?* I cannot help but snap my gaze to King Demetrius. He is smirking at me, a challenging smirk on his lips. I look back at the prince, but he is not meeting my eyes. Instead, his fists are clenched as he stares blankly at the kings in front of us. I try not to panic. I try to maintain my composure, but the betrayal slamming into me is hard to contain. *If the prince lead the kings to us... If he is the reason that all those people in the village died...* I search the prince's face, but he gives nothing away. My betrayal quickly morphs into hurt as he does not reject his father's words. *Please tell me that is not the case.* I silently will the prince's still form, but when he does not look to me, I once again look away. *It cannot be the case.*

"The solstice fast approaches us. At the end of it, your destinies will be fulfilled and we will lead Ptheryeth to a new, better future," Demetrius continues, a smirk present on his face. "Until then, you both will be kept together, under strict watch. Alaceandra," Demetrius looks at me, "I hope you so enjoyed your news." He sneers at me. "Things will not be the same as they were in Helomasi. We are all aware of your tricks now." Demetrius then looks at the prince. "Son, I trust you can keep the princess in line under your watch this time?"

"It won't be a problem," the prince says. *The prince did disappear during the raid... there could be a possibility...* Anger starts to curl low in my gut.

"Good." King Demetrius smiles excitedly. "Sydon, please escort Alaceandra back to her new rooms. I must have another word with my son in private."

Sydon nods and walks over to me. I look back at the prince, trying to gain his attention. I want to dig my heels in. Want to scream at the prince to refute what King Demetrius is saying. What he is is implying. I want him to *fucking react in some way* to his father other than blank stares and agreement, but... *now is not the time.* Not in front of these kings. *No.* I will wait until I have a moment alone with the wayward Prince of Helomasi. Then... *he will have some explaining to do, and he better hope to all of Ptheryeth that his explanations are sufficient.* With Sorin in the state he is in, I cannot afford to make any mistakes. I will be getting out of here— with Sorin— if it is the last thing I do. If his decisions make him a casualty, he will just have to consider that a life lesson. I will myself to harden my heart against him. Taking a breath, I straighten my stance.

Sydon arches a brow at me. My mind flashes through every instance that the prince told me that he was not on my side, that I was just a pawn in his games, and I can almost slap myself for starting to believe that our time in the Dark Lands would make him want anything different. With finality, my mind flashes back to Sydon's words: *The man you are about to be met with is against truth— revels in making a mockery of it. He is using you as much as you think we are.* I bite my lip and hold back tears. *Ptheryeth, please let him be wrong.*

CHAPTER TWENTY-ONE

Old Times

The Prince

I t took everything in me not to react to my father's words in front of the little dove, especially as he gripped that damned totem right when she was in reach. Not enough for me to be completely paralyzed from the pain, but enough to let me know he had it. I was not sure if his intentions were to ensure my allowance of his lies, to punish me for my actions in front of the kings, or to make me act out. Either way, in no reality would his tactic have worked. There is too much on the line. I study my father silently. *What are you up to?* For some reason, it seems that they want Alaceandra to think that she should not trust me. *Why else would they 'reveal' to her that I am on their side. Such a betrayal would only lead to resentment on her end if she believes it.* I do my best to keep my eyes off the pretty dove. *There is a bigger plan here and I intend to figure it out, but to do so I must play into their hands.* Slowly, I meet my father's eyes. The rest of the kings have exited the room along with Alaceandra. The soldier that my father commissioned to be my prison guard still stands behind me. Her eyes are hot on my back. I can tell she has been watching my interaction with the kings and Alaceandra closely.

"Our plan has commenced," my father says, lazily. He studies me from his place on the dais. He wears a teal cloak over obnoxiously fancy garb. His clothing has streaks of teal and pink denoting his Helomasian heritage. He and King Nikoli seem wildly overdressed compared to the other two kings that exited the room who were wearing simple black and silver linens respectively, and I wonder at their dynamic. *How have they found themselves working together?* The thought brings me back to Sam, Sorin, and myself. *I guess the same could be asked of the three of us.*

I realize that my father is awaiting my answer. "So it has," I respond in much the same way he did. "What are your rules for this scheme?"

He blows out a puff of breath and his eyes flick to the guard behind me. "Leave us."

She tenses. "Yes, my king." I glance behind me to see her keep herself from stomping from the room. *What is her problem?*

The door behind me bangs closed. I turn my attention back to my father.

His eyes also return to mine. It seems he has noticed the guard's mood as well. *That is not good.* "The same as they were before. You are to get close to the princess and bond with her, and we will use this connection to open the portal to Unduli. All for the greater good of Ptheryeth."

More like the greater good of Demetrius... I think to myself snidely. *The creatures that lie in that portal will only ensure Ptheryeth's demise. My father is foolish to think that he can control them.* His words sound rehearsed, as if he had to give that response a million times over. The memory of his true plans causes disgust to well in my stomach. I force my expression to remain neutral. Aloud, I respond, "If the plan is for me to get close to her, why tell her that I have been betraying her? Does that not make our plan more difficult? If Alaceandra cannot trust me, how are we meant to bond?"

"Perhaps." My father looks towards the door, thinking. "You should be able to handle that, though. It is best for her to feel on edge. Gives her less reason to... plan other ways to escape."

Frustration builds in my shoulders, but I will myself to relax. "Understood."

"Good." He claps his hands together. "To make things easier, I have you both in the same room, but do not get too excited. You will be closely monitored with her to ensure you are behaving in line with our expectations. If I find out that you have used this advantage to help her escape..." He leaves the sentence hanging.

"I was never fond of her first escape attempt, nor will I help her implement another. Although I know my being with her in Olvaria might have caused you to cast doubt on my abilities. I am, and have always been, loyal to Helomasi. I will do what I must to keep our kingdom's best interests," I reassure my father once again.

My father nods. "Do ensure that is the case." He stares at me hard, searching for something. "You know it was quite difficult to assure the other kings of your loyalty. They thought me crazy for bringing you back into the fold after your stunt. They were certain that you had abandoned your duties and your kingdom. Your appearance here was... surprising to say the least." He continues to search my face. "What happened to the other man that was a part of your party during the raid?" He asks. "Will we have to worry about him also making a surprise visit here?"

"He has been taken care of," I say ominously. "He is not to be worried about." *Yet.*

He sighs. "Good. There is a bag full of clothing for you in the room that you will have access to. We have enrolled Alaceandra in combat training for the time being. It seems her father did not properly trained her when she was in his care and now we must fix that before the solstice.

107

Although it would be beneficial to keep her weak, she will be a less powerful weapon without the proper skills. This means the princess will prove more volatile in the coming days and may try to act out with her new skill sets. I trust you will be able to handle this as well."

I nod. *Odd. Why do they want her to have more power? What all is planned for the solstice?* My mind circles as I try to decode my father's meaning.

He nods back. "Sydon will be joining you in her watch." The sentence rushes from him, as if it were an afterthought.

"Sydon?" I crinkle my brow.

"The man you saw escort the princess out."

"May I ask wh-"

"You may not." My father shuts me down with force. There is an tense energy heavy in the room. "That is one point that is not to be questioned nor negotiated." My father suddenly looks uncomfortable; his eyes skate around the room, his paranoia evident.

What is he scared of?

"Do you understand?" He snaps.

Interesting... What is this 'Sydon's importance?"Yes..." I say hesitantly. "Is he going to interfere with the plan?"

"Of course not," my father says, his body language now relaxing. "He will be keeping an eye on the both of you though."

"Got it," I say. The weird energy of the room seems to shift back to normal. "Is that all?"

"For now," King Demetrius replies. "Take your leave. My guard will be escorting you to your new room."

Great. I nod. I turn to go.

"And son?"

I turn back.

"It is good to have you back," he says softly. His expression fatherly. I cannot remember a time where he had looked at me with such softness since the plague overtook more than half of Helomasi. *Since my mother died.*

"Good to be back," I reply. I take another moment to stare at him, before finally turning back and exiting the room.

CHAPTER TWENTY-TWO

Friend or Foe?

Alaceandra

I was silent the entire walk back down the hall. *He could not possibly have been working with the kings? Could he? Is he the reason why...?* My body feels numb. My mind feels numb. *It cannot be. He told Sorin to get me out of there. He killed to get us out of there.*

He is also the first one to encourage you to follow Sam out into the fight. That sickly sweet voice enters my ears. *He could have been trying to lure you outside of Olvaria so it was easier for his father to capture you.*

That may be true, but I would have left either way. He was standing with me to ensure my protection.

Sure he was... Or was he trying to get you back to his father so that he can enact his revenge?

I argue with that internal voice of mine, annoyed at its doubt as much as I am annoyed at my own. I was supposed to know that the prince is not trustworthy. I knew he had secrets the whole time I interacted with him. Even with that knowledge, I felt that there were moments in Olvaria where he wavered in his resolve. Moments that he considered himself a part of whatever relationship we were creating. That he could put aside whatever selfish quest he had against his father to see me as more than a pawn in his game, *but maybe I was wrong. It would not have been the first time. Maybe I am wrong about so many things.*

"We have arrived." My steps stop in front of a large door. The jagged rocks around me tell me that we are still in a newer part of these caves, but the landscape around us is unfamiliar. *I should have been paying attention to where we were going.* "This is not the room I was in."

"I am aware," Sydon says. I study him. He looks tense, annoyed even. "You have been reassigned."

"Why is that?" I ask. His muscles twitch, as if he is coursing with an energy doing its best to escape him, but he is barely keeping under his control. The red in his pupils are slowly leaking in, doing their best to take over his eyes. When he blinks, the color dances around as if evading his attempts to get rid of it.

"It will be an easier transition." He takes a quick breath. "Now. Go in. I will see you later for your visit."

"Transition to what?" I try to ask, but he is already opening the door and shoving me inside. "Sydon?" He shuts the door in my face, and I hear a lock click before his footsteps disappear from the door.

What the fuck? I stare at the stone door for a couple beats before turning around. At the center of the room lays a large bed. There is a black comforter draped across silky linens and a red canopy wraps itself along the rails at the top. On one side of the room there is a door and a black desk that looks as if it has been dusted with red sparkles. On the other side of the room near another door lies two bags. One red. One teal. The room is dimly lit with the only light coming from some small candles scattered along the walls. There is also, curiously, a small window next to the bed.

I walk over to it on quick feet and peer through. Outside I can see a dark rocky landscape around me. In front of me is a pitch black forest. *So*

I am still in the Dark Lands then... why would they let me see this? A yellow winged creature flies in front of the window causing me to jump back. *An elvisera!* I think excitedly and try to see if I can find any more lurking outside. Unfortunately, I lose sight of the little birdlike being almost as quickly as I saw him. I try to tug at the window to see if I can open it, but it only pulls open about two inches before it is held firmly in place. *Definitely not enough room to fit my body through.* With a frustrated sigh, I move away from the window and look back over the space.

A chill enters the room, and I rub my arms to stay warm, glancing at the bed. As I am contemplating whether I should get underneath its blankets, something catches my eye. A ghostly white animal skitters across the floor shoving its tiny body behind the massive black desk on the other side of the room. *But, no— that cannot be.* I race over to the desk, ducking beneath it to see if I can find the creature when the door opens. I lift myself up quickly, causing me to smash my head against the underside of the desk.

"Ow!" I rub the spot on my head that is now throbbing and peak at the person who has just entered my new chambers.

A familiar face greets me. "Are you okay?" The prince says, a smirk that is clearly masking concern is evident on his face. I make eye contact with the teal guard from earlier before she shoots me a look of disgust and closes the door behind the prince. *What is her problem?*

I rub my head some more while I study my new intruder. "Yes. I am fine." I stand up, carefully. *Not dizzy. That is good at least.* "Why are you here?" I say. It comes out a little harsher than I intended, but I allow the statement to hang in the air.

"Seems we are once again sharing a room together," he says dully. His eyes flash lavender for a second, but then he glances around the room.

"My father still plans for us to be wed. I think he thinks this will make that thought more... appealing."

Hurt starts to worm itself back into my heart. "Did you know this was going to happen? Was this part of your plan?" I ask, my voice wavering slightly.

He does not meet my eyes, instead he walks deeper into the room, over to the teal bag in the corner and starts to rifle through it.

"Prince," I say, anger beginning to take hold of my tone. My skin feels as if I am being stabbed by tiny knives as fire fights to sprout on my limbs but is unsuccessful.

He continues to rifle through the bag, his body language screaming nonchalance. "It seems you have yet to come up with a nickname for me," he replies. Finally, he finds what he is looking for. Turning, I see he holds a teal pair of pants and a white undershirt. My eyes snag on the clothing he is wearing. They are the leathers he wore a few days ago. They are dirty and smeared with blood. *Has he not changed since the battle?*

He goes to walk past me, but I grab him. "Prince, answer my question." My voice is commanding, tense— angry. My grip on him causes a spark to go through me and a piece that I did not even realize was missing clicks itself back into place. I let go of him abruptly. His eyes are shining lavender. He looks... shaken. *I have never seen the prince shaken.* Movement races again somewhere from the corner of my eye, but I keep my gaze firmly fixed on the prince's. He slowly backs away from me. His lavender eyes screaming something to me that I cannot understand. When he finally reaches the door, that I now realize leads to the bathroom, he whispers something. Then he turns away and shuts it behind him.

A couple seconds later his voice reaches me. "I wish I could, little dove, I wish I could."

CHAPTER TWENTY-THREE

Furry Beast

Alaceandra

While the prince showers, I sit on the bed. *This has become even more of a clusterfuck.* I chew on my bottom lip. *Although I now know where Sorin and the prince are, it seems I cannot trust anyone to get me out of here except for myself. On top of that, I have to figure out a way to get Sorin out, and if the prince is on the Kings' side, who is to say he will not become a block in this whole situation? Sydon seems to have his eyes firmly on my movements, and Ptheryeth knows where Sam is. This is all seeming so impossible.* I do my best not to cry, but I can definitely feel the tears starting to well. *The only bright side in this is that the coach they have here seems to have a pretty good handle on training. With only two sessions, I feel that I have a little bit more knowledge on how my fire works and have a bit of a leg up on pinning someone down. Hopefully these lessons will prove useful in my escape.*

Before any of my tears can fully escape, another flash of white runs through the room aiming for the underside of the bed. Quickly, I jump from my perch and throw my body towards the creature. My fingers curl around the beast just in the nick of time. It wriggles in my grip. *Caught you!* Internally, I cheer as I pull the creature towards me and look at its face.

"Hello, Alaceandra. Took you a while." Baldar's face is staring back at me. I almost drop him in shock.

"Baldar," I whisper. His form is not quite solid. The softness of his fur seems to appear and disappear, whispering across my palms.

"Yes, it is me. You can loosen your grip," he says, continuing to wiggle.

"Are you going to run off again?" I ask, my voice still low, my tone filled with apprehension.

"No." I can hear the eye-roll in his voice. *"You caught me. I will not disappear. Not as I did before."*

"Fine." Gently, I release him. He wriggles away and sits in front of me.

"See, still here." His form seems to almost flicker in and out of focus as I stare at him, but he remains still.

"Why do you look like that?" I ask. His form refuses to stay solid. I have to hold myself back from grabbing him once again just to assure myself that he is real.

"Like what?" The prince says from behind me.

I scream. Baldar disappears completely. *Fuck.*

The prince takes a step back. "Sorry."

"Why did you sneak up on me?"

"What were you looking at?" He shoots back.

Should I tell him?

No. You cannot trust him. I remind myself.

"Nothing. Just thought there was something on the floor." I stand, my legs slightly wobble.

"Hmm..." he hums. "You are lying to me, little dove." He steps closer. So close, in fact, that I can feel his body heat radiating into me. He places a hand on my back. Tingles of *something* tear through my skin. "I don't like it when you do that," he whispers, his mouth is right next to my ear, tickling its shell, and I have to harden my heart against the sensation it causes.

Instead of melting, I freeze. My heart races its way into my throat and it takes far too long for me to back up, but I do. "T-then I guess we have the same mind when it comes to that," I blurt out lamely.

"Comes to what?" He is smiling, his head cocked to the side. He is enjoying making me flustered, I can tell, and that thought causes me to clench my fists as anger surges back through me.

"Lying," I spit out. "We both hate it."

His smile loses a fraction of its sparkle. "It would seem so." He moves to the other side of the bed.

"How did you find me here?" I ask in a small voice.

"Followed one of the men who took you," he replies simply. He tosses the clothes that he had been holding in his other hands next to the teal bag.

"Does that mean you did not know where they were going?"

He shrugs one shoulder.

I growl in frustration. "Are we really going to do this again?"

"What again?" He looks me in the eyes.

"Become all puzzles and riddles," I say in exasperation.

"I can only be what I am, little dove."

I massage my temples. "Fine. Be who you are, but do not get in my way."

"I make no promises."

"Of course you do not," I mutter. "I do not know what your or their plans are forcing us in this room together, but do not get any ideas. We might have gotten close in Olvaria, but it seems that was due to temporary insanity on my part. Keep your hands to yourself and maybe we will both get out of here in one piece."

"Is that a threat, Alaceandra?" His voice is smoky, that cocky smile of his is practically glued to his face.

"It can be," I reply. A sneer evident on my own lips. "If you make it one."

"I look forward to it." Slowly, he walks over to the red bag on the floor, picks it up and brings it to the bed. Rifling through it he selects another outfit. This time it looks to be in my size. He tosses a loose pair of red pants with a delicate pink floral trim and a white cropped shirt on the bed along with a pair of underwear. "You should shower. Looks like you had a bit of a rough morning."

My mind stalls as I remember that I am still covered in sweat from training. *What an asshole.* I snatch the clothing from the bed and stomp into the bathroom trying not to think about the fact that the prince just had his hands all over my underwear. Or that he had just picked out an entire outfit for me. *It is not like he had not had his hands all over your body only a few days ago, Lace, nothing to freak out about now.* With a huff, I slam the bathroom door behind me.

CHAPTER TWENTY-FOUR

I Spy

The Prince

*T*he dove is back in my sight.

I scrawl the words on a tiny piece of paper and hand it to one of the yellow elvisera by our window. Rubbing its little head I transfer my thoughts to the small, majestic creature. *Bring this to Sam.* I visualize his face in my mind's eye. The elvisera flaps its wings excitedly and jets off, making three quick loops in the sky before it disappears off into the wood line. Smiling at the creature's antics, I start my search of the room. Before my shower, I dug through the bathroom looking for any spyware that I knew would be present. I found three spyglasses, but they seemed not to have any audio enabled in them. Even still, the thought that these kings would have visual devices hiding out in the bathroom made anger boil within me. I snatched them up and ran them under the water of the shower to disintegrate them, before stuffing what remained in the back of the cupboard.

Now that I find myself waiting on Alaceandra to complete her own shower, I can't help but wish I had not bathed in the first place so that I could join her. It has been a long couple of nights without her, the noise of the world becoming an agitation to my ears with the lack of her presence to stop it. I have been finding odd comfort in picturing her face when the voices become too loud. Now that I have the opportunity to see it again, I cannot help but have the urge to do whatever I can to not lose it. To not lose her. I run a hand over my face. *You are being stupid.* I think to myself. *Of course you will lose her.* I sit on the bed. Unsurprisingly, even through the battle in Olvaria and her kidnapping, her headstrong determination to sniff out my secrets has become stronger than ever. I can't help but admire her for it. She is smart to do so. They could be her ruin after all.

I rub a palm over the spot on my arm that she grabbed. Feeling her fingers against me has my craving for her growing even more. I allowed the other men to take the lead these past few weeks, but I would be an idiot to not use this time I have with her wisely. Not only because I need her trust in me to ensure that my own plans are successful, but also because I have been thinking about my dove's tongue on my cock ever since she last had me in her mouth. She's an addictive presence that I can't help but fall prey to, not that I've necessarily been trying resist it. The sooner I can have my dove beneath me, on top of me, against me, the sooner I will feel whole again.

Sighing, I stand up. It will be best if I use this extra time to walk every inch of the room. My father said that there will be eyes on me. That can only mean a plethora hidden devices. *It is his specialty after all.* He can use his power to control people and objects making them into golems of sorts. He ties these golems to his underlings to cause them pain so that they will do his bidding and also to objects so that they can be his eyes and ears around the castle. *They are annoying little things.* He is not as advanced in his totems tied to people so he rarely makes them, only reserving that power to those he has special interest in. The totems tied to objects, however, he has become almost an expert in creating. He threw his spyware around Helomasi like candies at a festival, making it hard for the average person to detect every piece of it in a room. *Good thing I am not average.*

The wind guides my search as I push it through hard to see places with different strength breezes to see if I can find any resistance. The amount of spyglass I find in the room far surpasses my expectations. One hundred and twenty insect-sized gadgets were heavily spread across the room's interior. *How disgustingly excessive.* I grab each little visual device and toss it out the window. *But those are not what I am looking for...* Searching the space once more I comb through each area until I find it. *Got you.* A spyball sits precariously in the corner of the room. *Listening device.* I urge the wind to shove it off its ledge and it tumbles down into my palm. Visuals I can easily find a way to manipulate by moving or blocking, but audio is a little more troublesome.

I have plans for my little dove, and I can't have the kings listening in on them. My dove thinks that she can threaten her way away from me. Unfortunately for her, she has yet to realize that it is far too late for threats. The moment I laid eyes on her, there was no escape. I followed her into the Dark Lands. I will follow her into Unduli itself if that is what it takes. I will escape my father, and Ptheryeth willing, she will be the reason why. Her very existence is mine to shape. Her soul mine to claim. Despite her reservations, there is only one way this will end. She will submit to her fate, whether she likes it or not.

Now I just need to figure out how to balance regaining her affection without giving away my hand to those watching us.

I stare out the window and notice that more elvisera have gathered around, looking for the next letter they can deliver. *What beautiful creatures.* They were never properly appreciated in Helomasi. Father never saw their usefulness. The fact that they played such an important part in our infrastructure never impressed him, nor did their beauty. He more so saw them as useful pests. Drains on his resources. He was forever looking for ways to replace them. *That won't happen, you have my word.* I silently vow to the little creatures.

I roll the spyball in my fingers. They should know by now that I took away the visual devices. Luckily, I have never been keen on my father's spying. I think at some points in my childhood he would hide spyglass around just to see if I would find them like some kind of fucked up game of hide and seek. My finding them and ridding the room of them isn't something he would question. *No, what I need to figure out is how I want to play this.* Do I want to get rid of the audio device in the room, and with it my opportunity to sway the kings' view of our relationship, or do I want to rid the room of all spyware to protect the dove's privacy? *Options, options.*

The shower stops, and I take a breath. It is nice being around the dove again. I can see that she has done a lot of growing even over the past forty eight hours. By all means she should be terrified at the moment. She is surrounded by people whose sole purpose is not in her best interest, but instead I watched her walk into that room with a confident grace that I know she did not hold when she first stepped foot in Helomasi. *The change suits her.*

The bathroom door opens, and I continue to stand by the window as she watches me. I can tell she is studying me. I let her. I know I did my fair share of watching her over these past couple of hours. It is only fitting that she would do the same for me. *Besides...* I think, a little smugly. *The dove's eyes on me will never be something unwelcome.* Just like it always has, her presence calms my mind, making it easier for me to focus on what is in front of me. The buzz of the palace around us quiets the longer she stares, and I can feel myself relax, my grip on the little device loosening slightly. Rolling it between my fingers once more, I pull my gaze away from the window and glance towards Alaceandra. When my eyes meet hers, she looks a little startled. I hold back a smirk. Fisting the ball, I make a decision. *Better to not give these kings any more information than necessary, even if it could help me convince them of my supposed loyalty.* I push the window open the two inches it allows me. Shoving the ball outside, I turn back to Alaceandra. *Time to give the dove a proper welcome.*

CHAPTER TWENTY-FIVE

Puzzle Piece

Alaceandra

I exit the bathroom to find the prince on the other side of the room staring out the window. He stands with his profile towards me, and I take a moment to study it as I linger in the doorway. Now that he is not covered in leathers, blood, and dirt, I can plainly see his muscular form silhouetted by the sunlight. Even without his words, he carries an air of mystery and authority. I cannot help but be slightly jealous about how effortlessly royal he looks. That was something I could never quite figure out. All this to say he looks, unfortunately for me, hot as fuck. *Just my luck. He is a sexy traitor.* I roll my eyes internally. He fidgets, and I notice that he looks contemplative. His face is slightly pinched in concentration as his fingers fidget with a device in his hand. *What is that?* I try to move quietly closer to study the object, but when I take another step into the room, he glances at me before turning his attention back out the window. *Ah great, so he knew I was here watching him.*

"Welcome back, little dove. I trust you had a good shower." He stands up straighter, looking as though he decided something. Behind him, more little yellow elvisera flutter near the window panes, their heads cocking curiously as they stare back at us. He turns his body slightly. I watch as he opens the window only a crack and tosses whatever he was holding outside of the room. *What are you hiding?*

"What was that?"

"Hmm?" He is studying me.

"What did you just throw from the window?"

He glances back at the window in question. I can tell he is internally debating how much he should tell me and irritation starts to itch at my skin. Finally, after a bit of a staring contest between the two of us, he speaks. "Listening device," he says, nonchalantly.

"...what?" I do not know why I am surprised, but I am. *How many of those were probably riddled around the room they first stuck me in? Countless, I am sure.*

"It seems like that was the only one they had in here, though, so do not worry about that. At least not for the next day or so."

"So you think they will replace them." I squint my eyes at him. "Why get rid of it then? Are you not on their team?" I question.

He smirks. "Whether I am or not makes no difference. I would prefer it gone either way." He walks back towards the bathroom and closes the small pocket door, sealing the steamy room. I turn and watch him.

"That does not really answer my question."

"Some questions are meant to be figured out on one's own."

I sigh. *Fucking riddles.* "What are we to do now?" My assigned schedule denoted this time as flexible. As much as I resent that I even have a schedule in this prison, it was a bit comforting to know what to expect from the day. Besides, the sooner it is over the sooner I can go visit Sorin again.

He turns back to me. "What are we expected to do, or what are we going to do?"

"Are the answers different?"

His smirk turns into a cocky smile. "Always, dove." His nickname for me causes tiny elvisera to dance in my stomach, and I cannot help but be annoyed by the sensation. *He is dangerous, Alaceandra! Likely more so than every other asshole in here. He should not be causing you to feel giddy. He could be the whole reason why you are here!*

"What are we going to do then?" I ask, trying to refocus.

"What would you prefer to do?" He smirks at me. The question is unnecessarily suggestive, and I know he can see the moment I struggle to not react to his tone.

My breath hitches. "What do you mean?"

"I mean what I said. What would you like to do?" He takes a step towards me.

"What is there to do? We are trapped in this room until someone comes and gets us," I snap.

He pauses in his advance. "We could try to escape?"

I furrow my eyebrows. "Why would you want to escape? From what I heard from the kings, you want to be here as much as they do." *Besides I need to get Sorin out of here before I can allow myself leave. It is my fault he is here in the first place.*

He shrugs a shoulder. "Fine. Then we can sit here in silence, look out the window like proper damsels in distress— becoming perfect sad little pawns for the captors," he gestures towards the window dramatically. "Or," he takes another step forward. "We could," he tilts his head, "debrief?" He is staring at me.

Debrief? "What do you mean debrief?" My voice is shakier than I would have liked.

His eyes sparkle. "Looks like you found an interest, little dove. Let me show you." Wind enters the room. With a sudden whoosh the flickering flames keeping the room alight extinguish. Then there is silence.

125

Nervousness sneaks up my spine. "Prince...?" *What is he playing at?* My hair moves as a breeze plays with the strands. "Yes, dove?" His whispered voice comes from behind me and I jerk away.

"What are you doing?" I whisper, my eyes darting around the room. The tiniest bit of light filters in from the window, but it does not do nearly as much as it needs to brighten the space. Instead, it only casts a beam of light, its rays declining to fill more than a small fraction of the room.

"Making it so our actions can not be seen."

"And why should they not be seen?" I ask the darkness.

An arm wraps around my waist from behind, and my breath hitches as I am hauled into the prince's arms. His lips once again find themselves skirting the shell of my ear. "Because that would ruin the plan, little dove, and we don't want to do that."

The plan? I spin around in his arms and place my palms on his chest, pushing away from him. "What plan? Whose plan?" I can barely make out his face in the darkness. "The ones you have with the kings to capture me? To betray me?" I snap.

The prince grabs my hand and pulls me back towards him, then backs us both up until the light from the window brushes the side of our arms and my back is against the stone wall. "Betray you?" He whispers. "Little dove, I warned you never to trust me. Without trust there is no true betrayal." He has the arm he grabbed held against the wall. With his other hand, he caresses my hairline then my cheek and finally ends his perusal at my jawline.

My heart skitters. Stops. Then starts beating again. I do not know why I do not pull away from him. I do not know why I do not *want* to pull away from him. His grip on my arm is firm yet gentle. It should be easy to escape, but my body will not let me attempt it. I feel an uncoiling start to occur within me. That piece that had fit itself inside me finally allowing it to take residence. A sharp breath escapes me as it breaks free from whatever was binding it. "We can agree to disagree on that," I whisper through gritted teeth.

"Yes. Let's." Quicker than I can track, the prince picks me up and slams his lips against mine. If I was not already freaking out, I am now. Waves of emotions I can not begin to recognize crash into me. Part of me wants to throw him away. Kick him. Scream at him that he cannot solve this with a mere kiss. Another part of me, though, is yearning for the familiarity that he brings in this fucked up place. Another part of me is yearning for him. I allow myself a moment of weakness. Letting go of myself as I feel his soft lips caress mine in a struggle for dominance. His lips tease mine to soften, open, let him in. For a moment, I allow it. I relax in his arms as he pulls me closer. My body melting into his like it was always meant to be there. A brightness glows around us, but even its light is not enough to break us apart. With one arm, he props me up. His forearm curving deliciously under my ass so that he can ensure that he has the perfect angle to devour my lips with his. The other explores, squeezing my thigh before tracing its way up my hip to my stomach and finally skirts its way to the back of my skull. His hand grips my hair with a desperate passion.

I lick, nibble, and bite at his lips as we continue to kiss ferociously. My body heats dangerously, begging me to allow this man to take me completely. Another moan escapes me as my nipples rub against his chest causing tingles to travel straight to my core. As if in response, the prince takes his hand from my hair and uses it to massage my breast, pinching my nipple between his fingers and rolling them. I writhe beneath his touch, feeling intoxicated on both his movements and the taste of his lips. It is not until he starts to move away from the wall that I finally realize where this encounter is going. Ripping my lips away, I wriggle in his arms trying to pry myself away. He releases me, but hesitantly. His eyes are a blazing inferno of lavender lust. When my feet touch the ground, I back away from him on unsteady legs. I know my eyes mirror his own desires, but I force myself to keep my gaze attached to his.

"W-we cannot do that," I say, trying to be firm, but my voice comes out breathy, my legs now unsteady on the ground beneath me. I clear my throat. "I meant what I said," I say this time a bit stronger. "Hands to yourself." *Until I can figure out his plans and what his part was in my capture, he is far too dangerous to be playing around with. Let alone kissing. I cannot fall into the trap of the kings' making just because I cannot stay away from the prince of all people.*

"If you say so, little dove." The prince in question has a look of pure arrogance on his face. "But be warned, I will be testing that resolve of yours, and I cannot wait to see it crack."

CHAPTER TWENTY-SIX

Cracks

Alaceandra

"Unfortunately for you, prince, your supposed charms have little effect on me. I would not be so cocky." My voice is full of false bravado, and I cannot help but be proud of the strength in it.

"I think it might be beneficial to let you know you are glowing," he says nonchalantly.

"What?" It takes me a second to process his words, but when I do, I look down and notice my skin has a very subtle shine to it. "What the fuck?" I all but shriek.

He chuckles. "It seems, at the very least, my charms as you call them have some effect on that power of yours." The amusement in his tone is unmistakable.

He is such an asshole. I think grumpily as I stare at my *glowing* hand. *Why am I glowing? Is it going to stop?* I rub at my skin to see if I can wipe it off, but the subtle glow remains. I run to the bathroom and look in the mirror. The prince is right. It is like my entire form has been kissed by the sun. *Do not freak out Lace. Whatever you do, do not freak out.* My heart is in my throat. I am definitely freaking out. I walk out of the bathroom and start to pace the room. The prince stares at me, smirking. *This needs to go away. What if the kings see? Sydon? What will they do? And why? Why did I suddenly turn into a fucking moon beam? Is it because I kissed the prince?* I glance at him but his expression is completely blank. I can tell he is studying me though, searching for... something.

"Have they taught you more about your powers since you have been here?" The prince asks.

I blink at him. "What?" I have to shake my head to process what he just said. "Why are you asking? Do you not know the answer to that already?" *Is that the reason? Maybe that gym air has some kind of glow potion in it that I have been breathing in over the past forty eight hours...*

"How would I?" He asks.

I let out a frustrated breath. "You are so confusing." *So much for that. Why is he asking about my training then?*

"So I've heard." He stares at me. "So have they?" He asks again.

"Why are you asking me questions?" I snap.

He raises his palms. "Your powers seem different than the last time we.... interacted with each other. Besides you said you wanted to debrief. That does involve questions."

My hands clench into fists. "No, I said I wanted you to debrief."

"Is that not the same thing?"

"No!" My voice comes out high pitched.

"How so?"

"Because one would be me giving up more information and the other would be a fair exchange. If anyone is going to be asking questions here, it is going to be me," I say sternly. I have to stop myself from putting my hands on my hips in pure righteous anger. My skin glows a little brighter.

"Interesting..." The prince mutters.

"Prince," I warn.

He raises his hands in surrender.

A tingly sensation overtakes my body. Fast as lightning, the glow encapsulating my body races towards my clenched fists. Startled, I open my hands causing the glow to shoot into the floor. The light grows becoming almost too bright to look at before sinking deep into the rock and spreading out in a web-like pattern.

"Dove," he says, stepping forward. His eyes track the glowing light as it seeps into the rock at our feet. His eyes widen slightly before he looks back at me. "Dove, come here." He grabs my arm and pulls me closer to the bed. We both watch as the crack continues to expand to about an inch in width. It does not look like it is on the verge of stopping. A deep growl reverberates from within it.

"That does not sound good," I say. I feel frozen in place as a small clawed paws emerge. *No, no, no! Not again.*

"Fuck, fuck, fuck." A voice squeals as a albino ferret careens into the room. It had appeared suddenly in the doorway of the bathroom before racing over to us, its feet sliding against the slickness of the rock floor in its rush. *"Now you both have done it."* When it reaches us, it tries to stop itself, but its whole body slides against the ground instead— its nails fervently searching for something to grip onto— and it goes flying into my foot.

Ow! I internally yelp, the pain freeing me from my frozen state. Its claws continue scraping against me to find purchase. I yank my foot back. Finally, it reorients itself to the upright position and skitters over to the growing crack in the ground. With a quiet rumble, it pounces on the paws peaking from the crack and bites them viciously. A faint whimper could be heard from beneath us and then the paws pull their way back into the still expanding fissure.

"Alaceandra, get your ass over here and put your hand on this crack."

"Baldar?" I question.

131

"*No, it's the king of Unduli. Yes it is me, Alaceandra, I told you I was not gone. Now, move it! Before we find ourselves with more troublesome company.*"

Baldar stands poised over the crack, waiting for the next hands to poke through.

"*Now!*"

I try to take a step forward, but the prince stops me, his hand on my arm.

"We have to do something," I snap at him before removing his hand and rushing over to the place Baldar is standing. I shove my palm against the crack before I can think better of it. Warmth tingles through my fingers and surges into my body.

"Do you know what you are doing?"

The prince now stands behind me. *When did he move?*

"Not particularly," I say.

"Then why are you touching it?"

"I think I— or we rather— are the reason it is here. Do you not remember how Baldar got here? I am trying to close it."

He gives me a look of realization. "Fuck." He kneels beside me and presses his hands to the opening as well.

"What are *you* doing?"

"I assume we do not want whatever is trying to come out of here to succeed. I am blocking other points of entry. How long do you think you will need to close it?"

"I do not know! Baldar said to put my hand here so I—"

"Baldar told you?" He studies me. "When did he tell you that?"

"Just now, he—"

Baldar, who had been silently observing our interaction, cuts me off. "*Shush, Alaceandra. He cannot see me.*"

I pause. "Why?" I mumble looking at our palms barely covering the expanse of the glowing crack. The sight would be comical if not for the fact that we were trying to block other creatures from escaping it.

"I only have enough energy to reveal myself to you. The less people who know about my presence here, the better."

"Well then how am I supposed to explain to them why I am talking to myself?" I whisper, angrily.

"You do not. Talk to me in your head."

"In my head?" I repeat.

"Yes, direct your thoughts to me, and I will hear them."

"Have you always been able to do that?"

Baldar does not answer. *Of course he does not, but I guess that is an answer in itself.* I force myself not to groan aloud. So many situations could have been avoided had I known that I could just speak to the little ferret internally instead of aloud. *Why is he only informing me of this ability now?*

"Alaceandra, when did you speak to Baldar?" The prince presses.

"In Olvaria," I blurt. "He told me if this were to happen again then I need to place my hand on the crack to close the portal."

He stares at me for a moment before refocusing his attention on his hands. "I can tell you are not being fully honest with me, little dove." He presses again.

"As I said," I say, "you will receive no answers from me until you are willing to give them yourself." Then I, too, turn my attention back to the current problem.

My hand starts to burn as I feel tiny claws batting at my palm, urging it away. Hissing in pain, I try to pull back but Baldar places his little paw over mine. Small as he is, his paw has weight to it. I look up at Baldar, startled.

"Stay with it, Alaceandra. Repeat after me. Back into the portals of where you once were. Your time in this battle has yet to occur."

"Battle?" I question, but jerk as another sharp claw swipes at my palm. *Fucker!*

"Just say the words! Quickly!" Baldar all but screams at me.

In a whisper, I repeat the words Baldar said to me. The batting against my palm calms and then disappears. The hole starts to close slowly, its glow becoming duller the smaller it gets. I watch it in awe. I can feel an energy build beneath me as it is sealed. I start to back away from the hole again, but Baldar's voice stops me.

"Stay there," Baldar warns before I can once again try to remove my palm. *"Wait until the portal has closed completely."*

I do as instructed and grit my teeth as wave after wave of energy slams into me. I watch as the energy makes its way to the red band on my wrist causing it to glow softly. *How weird. I thought that I was supposed to be unable to use my magick outside of the gym...* I want to question Sydon about this development but realize the idiocy of that. *Why would he tell me anything? He is the reason the stupid band is on your wrist to begin with.* I watch as the portal completely seals itself. My palm starts to tingle once the last inch of it is sealed and pain radiates into my palm as it feels like something is slashed into it. I wince. I look at where the pain is radiating from to see a red swirl at the base of my pinky finger. *What is that?* Apparently I had projected my panic because Baldar responds to my question.

"It's the sign of a failed portal. Do not get too many of those. There are consequences." He makes his way onto my shoulder. I flinch. It seems even after his stint away he, unfortunately, still maintained his sharp nails. *Great.*

"Consequences? From who?" I ask.

"*From you,*" Baldar states. "*The marks are storing the energy of the failed portals. Too many and you won't be able to hold it all. It will come bursting out of you... one way or another.*"

I close my hand. "*That does not sound good.*" I think to myself rather than trying to project the thought to Baldar.

"*How do I stop them from happening?*" I ask the little ferret.

"*Either allow the portal to succeed— in a controlled manner— or do not make one.*" I side-eye the prince.

"*Never making one again, so that should not be a problem,*" I snap.

"*Yeah... I am not so sure,*" Baldar says. "*You both are a bunch of horn-dogs.*"

"*We are not!*" I snap.

"*Mmmhm.*" Baldar seems unconvinced. "*I will teach you how to control it and make them so only those you seek can come through, but that will take a couple days. Until then... do me a favor and pace yourselves.*"

"*Like I said. Will not be a problem.*"

"*Whatever you say, Alaceandra.*" Baldar hops off my shoulder.

I want to scream, but instead I take a deep breath.

"Dove, are you okay?" I feel the prince's hand on my shoulder.

"Yeah," I push his hand away, dizziness causes me to stumble a step but I glare at the prince, warning him with my eyes to stay away. Once I have caught my balance, I wipe away the invisible dust from my clothing. "I... I am going to take a nap."

CHAPTER TWENTY-SEVEN

Stars

Alaceandra

I am standing in a dense forest. The trees are so thick that they block out almost all the light. I can feel my hair tickling my back, which lets me know two things; my hair is loose, and my dress is backless. When I glance down, I can see the impression of a white dress decorating my body. It has sheer puffy sleeves and shimmers in the low light. Its hem skirts just above my knees. I also know that I am barefoot. The softness of the grass hugs my feet as I stand staring at the trees in front of me. There is an ominous chill in the air. I take in a deep breath. The smell of campfire smoke and warm sugar invades my senses. Somewhere behind me, leaves rustle. I am being watched.

"What are you doing?" My voice is a tad shaky, but strong.

"Observing you," A smokey, masculine voice says.

"Why?"

"To see what you do here."

"What am I meant to do here?"

"What do you think?"

"I do not know."

"Then do nothing."

Time seems to drag on and yet move all at once. I feel as if I have been standing here for hours and only seconds at the same time. Still, I look towards the trees in front of me, pondering the man's statement as the time expands and contracts around me.

"Why do you keep bringing me here? Why will you not leave me alone?"

A low sound rumbles at my back, and I feel warmth draw nearer. I do not attempt to turn towards him. I know that it is futile. I have yet to see this man's face in these dreams. I get the feeling that is the way he intends it. I straighten my shoulders, awaiting his answer.

"I cannot," the voice rumbles. "This is the best place to reveal the truth to you, princess."

"If that is the case, why do you not reveal the truth of who you are?"

A gust of wind pulls my hair forward, exposing my back to the person behind me. He delicately touches five spots on my back. With his touch comes a gentle warming sensation. The feeling is not bad, but it is also not pleasant either.

"Let these guide you to the answer. For now, it is time you wake up." He pushes me forward into the tree. I stretch my palms out ready to catch myself before I can hit the rough bark, but I feel nothing. Instead, I fall forward into darkness.

I am jolted awake. My body feels unusually cold, and a headache is starting at my temples. A hand on my arm causes me to jump. The prince shakes me gently. "You need to wake up." My heart calms. As upset as I am with the prince at the moment, I am glad he is the one waking me up. His familiarity is comforting in my haziness.

"What is going on?" I ask, feeling disoriented.

"You tell me."

I squint up at him, rubbing my head. "What do you mean?"

"You screamed."

"Oh... I, uh, had a bad dream," I say, my mind flashing over the oddness of it. Rather than the ominous man staying in the shadow like in the last dream, he decided to stay close to me. *To touch me.* I try not to shiver. I need to figure out who he is. Or if he is just a trick of my imagination. The omens he brings are dangerous.

"I don't trust your bad dreams."

"That is probably for the best," I mutter.

He tilts his head at me. "Are you okay, dove?"

No, not really. It seems that man haunting my dreams is here to stay, and on top of that, now he is giving me clues in addition to his ominous riddles. "Yes, I am fine."

A knock sounds on the door. The prince gives me a hard look before he walks over to it and pulls it open. Sydon stands on the other side.

"It is dinnertime," he states. "Please get ready quickly. I will escort the both of you down." His words are cold.

The prince nods and then shuts the door again.

Slowly, I rise from the bed. My legs feel a bit wobbly but they hold.

"You can get dressed first. I will wait out here." The prince is eyeing me cautiously.

"Okay," I reply. I move over to the little duffle in the room and grab a simple long skirt and a sleeveless top and walk over to the bathroom. Quickly, I close the door behind me and lean against it. Doing so causes a slight burning sensation to sting along my back. *Ow.* Moving away from the door, I undress in front of the large mirror. In the low light, I do my best to strain and look over my shoulder until I can see the spots on my back that are stinging with pain. My eyes widen as I spot five tiny golden stars scattered there.

My heart drops. *Those are in the same places the man touched. Why are they there?* Lifting a hand I try to reach one of the marks and touch it.

The skin is raised and warm, but not overtly painful. When my fingertips make contact, the gentle buzz of magick strums through them. *What could this mean?* I continue to stare wide eyed at the marks until I hear a knock on the bathroom door.

"Dove, that man keeps knocking. Are you almost finished in there?"

"Yes!" I say quickly. As much as I would love to show the prince, he has yet to prove himself trustworthy. I have no idea how he is here or why, nor has he thought it beneficial to share those details with me. I meant it when I said I will not give him answers until he does. I can solve this clusterfuck on my own. Shoving my new clothing on, I turn to look in the mirror quickly to make sure that the stars are covered. Seeing that they are, I open the bathroom door. The prince stands on the other side. "My apologies."

"Are you sure you are okay?"

"As much as I can be," I mutter. "You better hurry up and get ready for dinner. Sydon is an impatient prison guard." The statement is accented by another loud knock on the door.

"Yeah. I got the sense," the prince says before ducking into the bathroom and closing the door.

CHAPTER TWENTY-EIGHT

The Figurine

Alaceandra

We walk in silence towards the dining hall. I observe the two men. Sydon's posture is stiffer than usual. His back straighter and his walk less casual. The prince on the other hand seems lost in thought, unworried about whatever we are about to face. *I wonder why Sydon looks so upset.* When we finally reach the dining hall, Sydon escorts both of us inside. Unlike before, it is filled with people. Soldiers I recognize from training and some I do not mingle together at the tables around us. They all stop to look at us as we enter.

"Continue forward," Sydon urges. He guides us towards what I know to be the raised table that is in the middle of this room. Today though, the table has large curtains surrounding it blocking it from view. The curtains are a deep black with red lace lining the bottom. *Why are they keeping it from view? Is the point of the table not so that they can look down on those eating around them?* Not that I am ungrateful for the privacy. The thought of eating up there while people talk and stare around me is uncomfortable to say the least.

I see someone wave from the corner of my eye, and I look over to see Lylane and Jaq. Lylane is smiling at me, seeming excited by my presence in the room. I smile back at her. She has been so kind to me over the last few days. If it were not for the fact that she is working for the kings who captured me, I would think we were beginning to form a friendship. The reminder of the reason why I am here causes my smile to fall. I can tell when her eyes catch on the prince because a slight frown mars her brows for only a second. She quickly wipes it away though, maintaining her pleasant expression. Jaq sits beside her, his surly demeanor still ever present. He studies the three of us with interest. When he meets my eyes, he arches a brow as if to say: *Who is the new guy?*

A gentle nudge at my back, and I am walking up the stairs, behind the curtains, and sitting at the strange raised table. Three plates and four rolls of silverware are already sat at the center of it with a glass dome over top of them. It looks like dinner today is some braised meat, potatoes, and vegetables. My stomach growls slightly. Opening and closing the portal earlier ensured I had an appetite. Sydon removes the dome and grabs one of the plates, setting it and a roll of silverware in front of me. Taking another roll of silverware, he sets the dome back in place and pulls a fork out. Methodically, he carefully pulls a bite from each category of my meal and eats it. I stare at him as he chews and swallows, fighting back a blush. As much as I am glad that he is still taking his poison detection duties seriously, him preforming such duties in front of others, especially when that audience includes the prince, has me reconsidering the intimacy of such an act.

"Um, thank you."

He nods at me.

I can feel the prince's eyes boring into the side of my head. I shift in my seat.

"Food is not poisoned," I say wryly. "Or at least... mine is not." I glance at the other two plates.

"Ah," the prince muses. Nodding to himself, he retrieves a plate of food and a roll of silverware for himself. "Let's hope that is the case for all the meals."

I chew on my lower lip. My gaze flicking to the remaining plate. I turn my attention back to Sydon. "Are you going to...?" I motion to the plate.

"I have already eaten," Sydon says.

"Okay..." I scoop up some veggies and place them in my mouth. Chewing thoughtfully, I continue staring at the plate. "If it is not for you, who is it—?" A commotion in the other side of the curtain ends my sentence. Chairs squeal, and the conversation and laughter around us stops as a single set of footsteps travel through the room towards us. Another moment goes by, and two sets of hands are opening the front curtains to let King Demetrius enter the space. The prince tenses.

"Hello, son," King Demetrius greets the prince dryly.

"Hello, father." They stare at each other. The prince looks away first causing the king to smirk. He glances briefly at Sydon. "Sydon, please escort my son and his meal to the throne room."

"I am to stay with the princess at all times when she is within a king's presence," Sydon says calmly, his tone measured.

The kings smirk drops. "Yes, well I will only be a moment."

Sydon continues to stare at the king. I can tell that they are having some kind of silent battle. Sydon stands suddenly.

"You have a moment."

"That is all I need." The king nods, solemnly.

What authority does Sydon have to be challenging a king?

Sydon gestures for the prince to get up and follow him. The prince looks at me momentarily, but inevitably stands and follows Sydon out.

King Demetrius slowly makes his way over to the head of the table and sits before turning his attention to me.

"How are you enjoying your food, princess?"

I set down my fork and glare at the king of Helomasi.

He smiles. "Lovely, it seems we will get this over with quickly then." He holds up a small figurine in his hands before crushing it within his fist. White hot pain lashes through my body. It feels as if tiny razors are peeling up every layer of my skin one by one. The sensation overwhelms me to the point that I am on the verge of blacking out. I gasp, clutching at my skirt to try to ground myself in reality. "This will serve as your lesson in manners," King Demetrius says calmly. The pain starts to ebb as the king releases the little figure. I look up at him, eyes wide in shock, breathing deeply.

"What?" I ask, my brain struggling to process his words and work through what just happened to me at the same time.

Dare a man so low, whose only tools can be used against the vulnerable, attack me? The saccharine voice has awoken in my mind.

"Manners," the king states. "It seems your father neglected to teach you them, so I have been given the job, seeing as our kingdoms are to be joined soon. I do apologize, this lesson was supposed to be given day one, but plans change." He smiles and holds up the little figure. "This totem, paired with that bracelet of yours, makes for a great lesson in consequence, don't you think?" He clutches it again, continuing to smile as he watches me struggle to process the pain. My vision goes in and out and the world around me turns hazy as I try to fight against my body shutting down.

You don't have to endure this, Alaceandra, I can help you. The voice coos.

Help me how? I ask the voice.

I can take the pain away. I can make him pay. You just have to let me, the voice urges.

Another swell of agony sweeps through my system, causing the meal I just consumed only part of to attempt to escape. I whimper, causing the king to laugh.

Fine. Fine! Do it. I command the voice, my fingers turning white as I clench them into fists.

"Every time you wish to be an ungrateful blight— a disgrace on your family name, I want you to remember this pain." He clutches the little totem again and the pain amplifies, taking my breath away.

Try that again, vile king, I dare you. The voice has turned husky in her rage.

The king, blind to my inner rage, continues his tirade. "But don't worry, if you don't remember it, I will remind you during these lessons. Don't think my son's presence here will be cause for a lack of vigilance. Any display of disobedience will be met with swift punishment; the more offenses, the longer you must endure. Are we understanding each other?" He stares at me.

I do not answer, doing my best to remain conscious as the pain tears its way through my system. My disobedience has him clutching his totem harder. Shock rattles through me as suddenly I am outside the pain. My brain no longer mine, I watch as the king speaks his next words. "I said. Do. You. Understand?" His voice is tense and full of malice.

"I will show you what I understand," that voice replies for me in a whisper filled with rage. Slowly, I watch myself lift up from the table. Blackened fire dances across my hands, in an instant the curtains around us erupt into flames. The soldiers around us notice quickly, standing from their tables and hurrying out the door to escape the flames and retrieve help. My attention remains fixed on the king.

"Y-you are not supposed to be able to use your powers," the king stammers out, doing his best to clutch at his totem to incapacitate me and back away from me at the same time.

"Oh, am I not? I was not informed," the voice says dryly from my lips. I approach him bringing my palms together. The fire gathers and shoots towards the king. He dodges. The fire hits the remaining curtain behind him burning through it in an instant.

"Alaceandra..." The king says hesitantly. "Calm down."

"Calm down?" A humorless laugh leaves me. "You capture me. I stay calm. Keep me vulnerable and under your watch. Still, I stay calm. But this is downright egregious, King of Helomasi. Enacting torture on someone the moment you get them alone? The definition of uncivilized. So, dear king, I will do you a favor. I will teach you true manners. I will show you the consequences of using your power irresponsibly, because, trust me, in this situation there is nothing to be calm about." Black fire once again builds in my palms and is hurtled towards the king. He moves to the left, doing his best to get out of the way but the fire nicks him. The smell of burning flesh fills the room along with his screams. He stumbles, trying to put out the flames and trips over one of the chairs, falling off the raised platform and onto the ground. In the process, the figurine leaves his grip, falling harmlessly to the ground before rolling into one of the remaining curtains. It quickly catches fire and turns to dust in the surrounding flames. I approach the edge of the platform and look over at him, curling more fire into my palms.

The sound of someone running interrupts my haze. I glance over to the door to see Sydon standing there, his eyes wide. The prince stands behind him, a curious expression on his face. They both head towards me. Quickly turning back to King Demetrius, I hold the fireball up, ready to hurl it down on the king below me.

Stop. Now. A deep, masculine voice echoes in my skull. My body stills, unable to move. The men grow closer. Panic overtakes me at the thought of not being able to fulfill my quest. I strain against whatever is binding me. A crack reverberates throughout the room. Suddenly I am able to move once more. *Good.* The king used the time to scramble away from me. He is hobbling, doing his best to run. I redirect the ball in his direction.

Alaceandra, stop!

No! I yell back at the voice in my head. I shoot the ball. The king drops to the floor, dodging it. *Fuck.* I form a new ball of fire shooting it towards the king once again. I move quick as lightning, my power coming to me with ease.

SLEEP! The voice yells, panic lacing its tone. I watch as the fire strikes the king's chest and he fully crumples to the ground. A smile of satisfaction creeps over my face before my body seizes. Screams echo through the dining hall as I start to fall, tumbling off the platform. A harsh breeze passes me, and I land in a man's arms. Then everything goes black.

CHAPTER TWENTY-NINE

Stories

Alaceandra

My head is pounding when I wake up. *What happened?* Groaning, I squint my eyes open. Around me is an unfamiliar darkened room. I try to lift my head to orient myself, but moving only brings a wave of nausea. I lay back down, quickly breathing in through my nose and out through my mouth to encourage the swell to dissipate. I feel like I have Ptheryeth's worst case of spirits vestige, but I do not remember consuming any alcohol during dinner. *To be truthful, I do not remember much of dinner.* Instead of lifting my body, this time I opt to lift a hand to rub my face.

"You're awake," a voice that rings too loud in the quiet room calls out. I hear footsteps approach before the prince's face is leaning over me.

"What happened?" I ask. My voice slightly scratchy. Another moment later and I am being carefully lifted up. A glass of water gets shoved into my hands. I take a slow sip. *Please do not make me more nauseous.* "Why does my body hurt so much?"

"We were hoping you would be able to answer that," another voice says.

I turn my head slightly to the side to see Sydon leaning against a wall. *Great.*

What is he..? I try to remember the events of the last couple of hours. Pieces of memories start flickering to life. I remember being led down to the dining hall. Lylane and Jaq were there, and the raised table was shrouded by curtains. Then Demetrius came in. I was left alone with him. *And then...* My heart sinks to my stomach.

"Where is King Demetrius?" I ask, my voice slightly shaky.

Narrowed gazes turn my way. "Why do you ask?" Sydon inquires.

"He was there at dinner, was he not?"

"He was," the prince provides. "What happened with him?"

I lick my lips nervously, my mouth becoming strangely dry. "He wanted to talk to me, or at least that is what he said. When you both left, though, he showed me... something... he had..." I rack my brain for what he was holding, but as I try to think of what exactly it was, the thought flutters away. I grit my teeth in frustration.

"He... had something?" Sydon prompts.

"Yes," I confirm.

"What did it look like?" The prince asks.

I do my best to grasp onto the tangled thread of memories before they disappear completely. Mentally, I jump and successfully snag one before it slips away. Once I am confident it is in my hand, I tug the thread hard. A flash of an image pops in my head, and I gasp, my body remembering a pain that is no longer present.

I set down the water on a table beside the bed and rub my eyes. "There was this... figurine. I think the king called it a totem?" I whisper. *Should I be telling them this?* I ask myself, but ultimately figure there is no harm. Who knows what kind of spyware is present in that lunch hall? They were bound to figure it out sooner or later. *If they did not already.* "It...

hurt me." More memories of that pain filter through my mind's eye, and I do everything I can not to whimper aloud. Instead, I curl up on the bed hugging my legs to my chest. Just the memory of its intensity has me wanting to flee the room.

"Totem?" Sydon questions, moving off the wall to walk closer.

The prince tenses beside me. His back going ramrod straight as his eyes fill with intensity. "How did it hurt you?"

My gaze flicks between the two of them, and I am surprised to see concern marring both of their expressions. I look away, hugging my legs tighter.

"I do not know for sure really. I just know that whatever it was, when the king held onto it tightly, it hurt." I close my eyes, trying to think of anything else, but the memory is so vivid. I snap my eyes back open, trying to decide which is better or worse. *Unfortunately, it is impossible to escape one's own mind.* I think to myself bitterly before returning my gaze to the comforter on the bed. I clench my toes around the sheets beneath me, hoping that the action might ground me back into reality. It helps a little, but not nearly as much as I would like it to.

I see the prince clench his hands into fists from the corner of my eye.

"The kings are not supposed to have any other magickal implements," Sydon says, more under his breath than aloud. "I will be back." Sydon turns and walks out the door.

"Is that what caused the fire?" The prince asks once Sydon has completely left the room. Luckily, his voice brings me back to the present, and I blink up at him.

"Fire?" I echo. *I do not remember any fire.*

Worry flashes over the prince's gaze. "Yes. Fire, Alaceandra. Do... you not-"

I shake my head no.

"What is the last thing you remember?" The prince asks.

I think about it for a moment. My headache intensifies slightly as I, hesitantly, dig through my memories. "Wanting the pain to end." I do my best to recall more, but all that surfaces is that haunting voice echoing in my brain and the forever intensifying pain. I take a deep breath, trying to shy away from that train of thought. When I look back up, the prince is studying me intensely.

"I," he clears his throat. "I am sorry my father did that to you and I was not there to..." the prince's whisper trails off.

For some reason, his apology causes that fear to spark into anger within me. *Why say sorry? If I am here because of his betrayal, why would he even apologize for the consequences of it? Is this not what he wanted all along?* "To what?" I say defensively. "Join in on your father's fun? Protect me from it? Tell me, prince, what were you going to do?"

The prince's expression darkens. "Ah, It seems you have not made your decision yet."

"What?"

"About what you believe," he says simply. I watch him as he stands, body tense, and starts to walk away from me.

"You have given me no indication on what that should be, prince," I shoot back, my brain temporarily distracted from the pain of my memories.

He nods in confirmation.

I wrinkle my brow.

"That is it?"

He turns back to me, tossing his hands up. "What do you mean, Alaceandra?" His tone is one of exasperation.

"Are you not going to-?"

"What? Confirm or deny your accusatory remarks? Your belief in me has no bearing on my plans, dear little dove. If you think that I would derive pleasure from treating you the same way my father does his pawns, then you can go right ahead and believe that." The words are harsh, but they seem to be masking another emotion. *Is that...* His hands clench into fists before returning to his sides. As much as I want to feel justified in my anger over his betrayal, seeing his cloaked hurt over my words causes a pang of guilt to run through me. He continues to stalk towards the door. He reaches it swiftly, and right as his fingers touch its surface, I stop him.

"Wait!" I call out to him.

"Why?" He snaps. His fingers pausing on the wood.

Why? I ask myself. I pause a moment too long, and he starts to open the door. "I should not have said that," I blurt.

He stays quiet. I hear the door shut.

I sigh, releasing my legs and turning more towards his back before continuing.

"Look. A lot has happened over the last couple of days, and your being here is... confusing. I want to get out of here, but I cannot do that without-" I choke a little. *Right, no talking about Sorin.* I take another breath. "I cannot do that without taking care of some things first. I wanted to believe when you showed up it was to help me do just that, but..." I chew on my lower lip a little. "Now I do not know what to believe. I am not sure if you want this marriage in the way the kings want it or not. You have never been quite forthcoming with your true intentions, but because I cannot believe everything in Olvaria was fake," I swallow hard, unexpected tears rushing forward. I force them to stay at bay. I force my voice to stay strong. "I will say this. I am getting out of here. With or without your help. If you truly want revenge on your father, I can only hope you remember not to become him in the process. Since you have given me no indication that you have already become exactly that, I can at least try not to treat you like it."

He turns back to me and nods. "I hope you remember the same. We are both destined to rule, Alaceandra. Whether we do so together or alone relies solely on our present decisions."

We stare at each other for a beat.

The prince's shoulders slump slightly. "Can I tell you a story, Alaceandra?"

I tilt my head at the prince. "Sure."

"My father was not always the way he is today."

"He was not?"

"No. When my mother was alive... it was different. He was happier."

I blink at him. "I did not realize your mother-"

"Yes. She has been for a while now. Died when I was about six. Anyway, when she was alive, he was kind of nice. I don't know, but then something happened. She fell ill, or was poisoned... the doctors were never really sure, and it turned my father into a much crueler man. He had always punished me, but these punishments became much more severe. I lost my connection with him. It made me more... cold."

"Why are you telling me this?" I ask him, not seeing where his words were headed.

"I did not bring the kings to Olvaria," the prince whispers.

I stare at him. "What?"

"I did not bring them there. I did not even know they were coming. The only reason I knew my father was part of the fight was because he used his totem against me. The pain caused me to... become temporarily incapacitated... and by the time I regained the ability to fight again, you and Sorin were already out of reach."

"Why did you not say that when you first arrived? When I asked the first time?" I try to keep the suspicion out of my gaze, but it is hard. The prince slowly walks over to me and sits on the edge of the bed.

"Dove..." He lifts a hand and gently moves some hair away from my face, I flinch involuntarily. He turns away from me, resting his hands in his lap. "It is better that the kings think that we are at odds. The more they see us as conspiring together, the more likely they will keep us apart. If there is any chance that we are getting out of here, it won't be without a little trickery," he casts me a sideways glance. "I wasn't certain of your acting skills. So I thought it would be easier to let you decide on your own what you were willing to believe."

"Why change that now?"

"Because," he sighs, "I'd rather you be in on this particular plan than for you to believe I am capable of my own father's cruelty." He turns towards me again. "Besides, I am still allowing you your own beliefs. Whether you believe my story or not is completely up to you."

I nod. He stands from the bed and walks back over to the door.

"Prince?" I look back over at him.

He hesitates once again in the doorway. "Yes?" He says, tilting his head at me.

"I still do not trust you."

He smirks. "Good." With that, he slides the door open and walks from the room.

CHAPTER THIRTY

Deals

Alaceandra

It was another hour or so before I heard a knock on the door again. Slowly, I lifted myself from the bed and padded over to it. Luckily, physically I was already feeling a lot better. The nausea had calmed down not long after the prince left and the aching of my body had become a dull throb. *Who could be at the door?* I had realized that I was not in the prince and my shared room not long after he left. The room I was in was actually quite plain. It only had a bed and a bathroom through one of the doors. The bed was basic. Made of a strong wood frame and a soft mattress with white sheets and a pale yellow comforter. Otherwise, there were no decorations in this dwelling. The only other furniture was the little side table beside the bed.

"Who is it?" I yell through the door. *If you are going to knock, I am going to ask.*

I get no response. Darting my gaze around warily, I decide to open the door only a crack to see who was behind it. My peek reveals Sydon. His arms are crossed and he looks lost in thought as he waits on the other side of the door. As soon as I spot him, his eyes lock on mine.

"Princess," he greets.

"Hi, um..." I open the door a bit wider, looking behind him. A couple of soldiers are milling around the halls, but no one seems too interested in our interaction. "Why are you here? What time is it?"

"I need to convene with you by order of the king," Sydon says stiffly.

Which king? I wonder nervously. Outwardly, I nod. "Okay."

"Follow me."

I look back at the bed, still rumpled from me laying in it and then down at myself.

"Can I change?"

Sydon sighs. "No, princess. Do not worry over your appearance, we need to move quickly. We cannot keep him waiting for long."

Hesitantly, I leave my temporary quarters, doing my best to smooth down my hair. It refuses to behave, but I continue to try as we weave through the halls. After a couple of minutes, the milling soldiers start to appear less and less until I notice there is a lack of them completely. I look around. *We do not look like we are going to the throne room.*

"Where are we going?" I ask Sydon.

"You will know when we arrive," he responds flatly. As strange as he is acting, I do not get the sense that he is leading me towards any kind of danger. My footsteps echo behind him as we make our way deeper and deeper in to the palace. My tattoo warms along the way, pleasurable tingles increasing with each step we take. Finally, we turn a corner and I recognize my surroundings. *Sneaky bastard.* I stay quiet as he leads me into a nondescript room.

The man laying on the bed in the center of the room makes me smile.

"You took me to see Sorin."

"As I said I would," Sydon responds.

Something within me hums with appreciation.

"Thank you."

"No need. We have a deal. I will keep up my portion, you keep up yours."

His surliness does not dim my smile. I walk over to Sorin and sit at his bedside. I go to lift my fingers and run them down his arm, but Sydon stops me.

"Do not touch him, Alaceandra," he warns.

"Right," I whisper. My fingers tingle with want. I sit by Sorin's side for around an hour in silence, watching his chest rise and fall. Quietly, I demand. "You will take me to see him again tomorrow."

"We have yet to discuss the frequency—"

I do not look at him. "If it is in exchange for my compliance, I will decide it. If I have to masquerade each day like I am following yours and the king's lead, then I will see Sorin at the end of each charade," I say firmly.

"How am I to believe in your compliance? You set the dining hall on fire only a couple of hours ago, princess, that is not compliance."

"That is what the prince said, yes."

"That is what happened."

"Either way. If you had to experience what that king did to me in there, then you would have acted the same to get away from it." I stare at him hard.

"Maybe so, but we cannot have you setting the palace alight each time one pisses you off."

I roll my eyes. "I will not. As long as I feel like my life is not in danger, I will play by your rules," *for now,* "but only if I am able to visit Sorin every night."

He takes a deep breath. "I will not leave you alone with them again."

I nod.

"And you will let me see Sorin," I press.

"I will see what I can do."

"That is not good enough."

"If I am able, I will bring you here, princess, but if there are factors that would not allow it—"

Finally, I turn my head to make eye contact with my prison guard. "Make them allow it. Or that is the day that this truce ends."

He narrows his gaze at me. "Fine."

"Good."

"What is your relationship to this Sorin," he pauses before adding "and that prince?" almost like he was trying to make his question seem more like an afterthought.

"Hmm?" I say. Sydon is once again leaning against a wall studying me.

"There is obviously something with this one," he grumbles, motioning towards Sorin. "Or else we would not be in this room, and you would not fight so hard to see him. So, what is it?."

"We were childhood friends," I say noncommittally. "Then he grew up and decided to become my guard in Tikilium. I owe him many life debts."

"Seems like there is more than a friendship there," Sydon says, more under his breath than to me. I ignore the statement. Louder he asks: "What about that prince? I know you are betrothed to him, but the way you act towards each other is very... familiar."

"Why are you asking?" I now turn fully in his direction.

"Call it general curiosity. I was not expecting the man to show up."

"Trying to sniff out ulterior motive then. To see if he will help me escape whatever plans you have with those kings of yours?"

"Something like that."

"Well, worry not," I say flippantly. "I only met the man in Helomasi. Although, it seems I am meant to be his bride, I would not consider us more than acquaintances at best." *An acquaintance whose cock you have had in your mouth, Lace!* My brain screams at me. I keep my face carefully blank. Turning back around, my palm briefly brushes Sorin's. As if in response to this touch, Sorin's body twitches, causing his hand to close. Excitement fills me. *He moved again!*

"We need to get you back to your rooms." Sydon's voice startles me. I frown. "What, why?"

"I have had you gone for too long. We are leaving now."

I search Sorin's face, but he remains still. My shoulder's slump.

"Now, Alaceandra."

Gritting my teeth, I turn back to Sydon. "Fine."

He motions me closer to the door. He opens it only slightly, allowing me to slip out before he does so himself. Sydon's form radiates tension as we weave through the halls. The tension between the space builds thicker and thicker as we quietly walk back to the room that the prince and I share. Before he can open the door to my quarters, I stop him.

"Why do you seem so on edge?" I ask.

"I am not," Sydon snaps.

"You definitely are," I say back.

He turns to me, and a barrage of emotions are present in his eyes. I recognize confusion, anger, and suspicion. The sight has me stepping back slightly. Noticing my reaction, Sydon looks up towards the ceiling in what I can only assume is an attempt to calm himself. When his eyes once again meet mine, his expression is blank. "It is not for you to know."

"What can I know then?" I ask.

"I do not enjoy the changing of plans."

"What plans have changed?"

He gives me a bittersweet smile. His eyes searching my face. Then he sighs. "I will retrieve you both in the morning." He turns back towards the door and opens it.

"But-"

"Goodnight, princess," he says, gently encouraging me to enter the room. Once he has successfully made me clear the threshold, he shuts the door, and I am left staring at it in confusion. *What the fuck just happened?*

I turn around to see the prince watching me.

"I take it you are feeling better," he comments from his spot on a chair that has appeared at the corner of the room. In his hands, he is holding a small leather bound notebook.

"A little," I reply, walking into the room. My eyes catch on the window as little yellow wings flash against the blackness of the night. *I wonder why the elvisera keep gathering there.*

"What was that about?" he asks, pulling my attention back to him.

"What was what about?"

"With the guard. Sydon, is it?"

"I do not know what you are talking about."

He sighs and sets the little notebook down. Standing, he walks over to me. "What were you both talking about on your way in?"

"He said he would retrieve both of us tomorrow morning."

"Ah. Okay," he continues to search my eyes before nodding. "Am I going to have to fight you about sleeping arrangements again, or are you going to climb in the bed?" He motions behind him.

My eyes dart over to the singular bed in the room. *Oh Ptheryeth, give me a break.*

Although I had just woken up from my unconsensual nap, I still feel exhaustion heavily weighing down on me.

"It is your lucky day, prince," I mumble walking past him to throw myself into the bed.

"Seems it is," I hear him whisper, and then I am asleep.

CHAPTER THIRTY-ONE

Hypocrisy

Alaceandra

"*O*pen *your mouth, little dove... good, that's good." My mouth is around the prince's cock as he watches me with eyes sparkling with lust. My heart is hammering as I do my best to swirl my tongue around his length and suck him gently as he pushes in and pulls out with measured control. His cock glistens beneath the light each time it appears to me, and I do my best not to choke on my moans when he reaches the back of my throat with yet another thrust. My pussy is soaking wet and tingles fill my body. I squeeze my thighs together, trying to find more friction. The tingling intensifies, turning my arousal into a blazing inferno, almost instantly, as I feel the prince's hands tighten in my hair. A whimper escapes me. The prince tilts his head down causing our gazes to collide, but it is not the prince's eyes I find myself gazing into. Fear zips through my body as the man in front of me steps away and transforms into someone else entirely. Someone with eyes reminiscent to the night sky. Someone who is soaked in blood.*

I wake up plastered against the prince's bare chest, breathing heavily. Strange emotions curl in my chest as I try to decipher my thoughts. *Did I really dream about sucking his cock?* A burning sensation fills me as embarrassment and desire war with each other. My nipples are hard, and there is an ache deep inside of me that my body begs for me to scratch. *But what was that ending?* I rack my brain to try to figure out who exactly I was dreaming of when the aching in my body intensifies, causing my thoughts to scatter. I bite my lower lip. *It was just a dream, Alaceandra. You cannot trust him. You said you would keep your hands to yourself.* I try to convince myself to calm the fuck down, but it does not seem to work. Instead, a little noise of frustration escapes me as the last kiss I shared with the prince rips through my memory. I do my best to squeeze my thighs shut.

"Morning, dove," the prince's rough morning voice startles me.

I glance up at him and then try to scramble away. The thick band of his arm, though, holds me in place. "Morning," I echo back, my voice a little shaky. The room is still dark, sunlight not yet peaking through the small window. "What time is it?" I reply quickly, trying to ignore how the sound of his voice has my toes curling.

"Still early." He tilts his head, before bringing one hand up to trace the side of my face. "What woke you up?" A small smirk is present on his lips.

"What woke you up?" I reply quickly, defensively. His soft touches are causing my brain to fog over even more, and I do my best to slow my breathing so I am not panting like a fucking animal in his arms. *What the fuck is going on with me?*

A huffing laughter brings my attention to the headboard. A glowing white Baldar stands there, balancing precariously. *"Feeling a little...warm are you, Alaceandra?"*

Anger mixes with my arousal. *Does Baldar have something to do with this?* I think internally. I glance towards the prince, but notice he does not seem to notice the little creature on the headboard. *Ah, right. He cannot hear him unless they are touching. How convenient.* I think sarcastically.

"Yes. Do you know why?" I grit out in response, doing my best to project my thoughts to the glowing being. I shift against the prince. My nipples brush against his torso and I have to hold back a hiss. Accompanying my embarrassing arousal this morning seems to be bodily hypersensitivity, even the sheets cause tingles to race up and down my skin. *Well, that is just great.* I think to myself sarcastically.

"You, actually," the prince says. "You pulled me to you in your sleep and then started whimpering. I thought, maybe you were having a nightmare, but then I heard you moan."

"I was... what?" My eyes fling back to the prince's. I am sure my face is bright red at the moment.

"I couldn't sleep after that." The prince shifts slightly. "So tell me, little dove, what had you making all those noises?"

"If you are going to explain, Baldar, this is the time to do it," I project to the ferret urgently.

More huffing laughter follows that thought. *"Your body is trying to... recharge. It knows one that you have already connected with is nearby. Do not worry, Alaceandra. You do not have to give into it. You could just go and shower. A good night's sleep will recharge your body enough to survive the day tomorrow. I would leave the room soon though if you are going to resist it."* The huffing laughter continues.

I get the sense that he is correct. As much as climbing on top of the prince is... tempting, the heightened senses of my body are not forcing me to do much of anything. It is only making the sensations around me more pleasurable. *I could just get up go take a shower and—*

"Well, dove, what is it?" He places a finger under my chin gently encouraging eye contact with his touch. I swallow roughly.

"We will begin our lessons tomorrow, Alaceandra." I feel more than see Baldar disappear, leaving me alone with the prince.

163

"Well, fuck you too then," my thoughts grumble after him angrily. Silence is my only response.

My heart starts to race and, as it does, my arousal only seems to grow more intense. My gaze drops to the soft stubble lining the prince's jaw. Images of him between my thighs start to surface. *What would it feel like to have that same stubble scraping me while his tongue plunges into my folds? His hands pulling my ass closer as I moan his name...fuck, I do not even know his name,* I think guiltily. Despite this, the images continue to torment me as I stare at his smirking mouth. I take in a shaky breath.

"Dove?" I glance up and notice that his eyes are now shining with amusement as he stares down at me. I can feel his cock pressing against me. I know he is turned on right now, just as much as he knows I am. The only question now is... what should I do about it?

He confirmed he was never involved in the kings' plans. A part of me whispers. *If he never betrayed you, why should you hold back?*

He is keeping secrets, though. Another part of me argues. *Just because he was not involved in my kidnapping does not mean he is not involved at all. You cannot trust him.*

I could not trust him the first time he was in my mouth. What has truly changed now?

You are quite literally in enemy territory.

I sort of was then too.

The aching starts to overtake my entire body as the prince re-positions his arms until his hands are under my ass and pulls me up to his eye level. Each ridge of his torso brushes against mine as he holds me close to him. I bite back a moan. Our faces are now inches apart.

"Hey, what is going on?" A soft sheen of sweat has broken out on my forehead, he rubs a thumb across the moisture to wipe it away. "Something seems off."

Oh, and now he is choosing this moment to not be an asshole. Great.

I open my mouth, and a whimper escapes me. Concern flashes over his features.

"I- I am okay just-" I stutter out. The prince licks his lips, and it feels like an elvisera carrying a load full of pure sexual yearning slams into me. I choke on my words. "If you double cross me prince, what you saw in that lunch room today will look like child's play in comparison to what I do to you. Do you understand?" The statement jumps from my lips, unprovoked.

"Alaceandra..." he whispers, before a cocky smile takes over his face. "The battle would be an honor, but I am sure it can be avoided."

What the fuck is that supposed to mean? "Could you talk to me plainly just once?" I grumble, because despite his annoying remark, my body still tingles with need. I made my choice with the prince the moment he kissed me when he arrived. Try as I might to deny it, there is only one way I want this to go.

"Likely not."

"You are such an asshole," I say angrily, then I slam my lips against his. His body only stiffens in surprise a moment before he is pulling me closer. His hand warms its way down my spine before he cups my ass and continues to pull me into him. I hook my leg around his waist as his fingers dig into me, my arousal spiking. His tongue coaxes my mouth to open, and I give into its beckoning, then he is consuming me. His kiss is not sweet like Sorin's. No. His kisses are demanding. Controlling. Dominating.

I moan into his mouth. My power is alive under my skin, racing through my body— caged but unable to break free. He pulls his lips off of mine and stares into my eyes, breathing heavily. "We are in dangerous territory here, Dove." I start to push towards him, to capture his lips once more with mine, but he fists the hair at the nape of my neck firmly. "Alaceandra," he growls, his eyes a blazing lavender. "As much as I would like to continue this, we do not want to cause another portal to appear."

"It would have already if it was," I whisper, somewhat confident. My eyes flick down to his lips, and I clench my thighs against another surge of want ripping through me. "I am drained of power right now. I do not know if I could open another portal if I wanted to," I all but moan. I feel semi-rabid, my heart is racing a million beats per minute, but the prince continues holding me away from him.

"Something is different with you right now," his voice remains a low rumble. I can feel his erection flexing against me as he speaks. A small whimper escapes me causing him to groan. He pulls my head closer so our foreheads meet. "What is going on with you?"

"I, um, am in need of a bit of a recharge." I allow my palm to skate down his torso and brush over the bulge pressing into me.

He places a hand on my wrist. "Then why are you not sleeping?"

"Seems I am more in the mood for a different kind of restoration." I squeeze him gently.

He pulls my hand off his erection. "Are you sure? Only yesterday you were telling me that you would never—"

"We can speak of my hypocrisy at the moment or we can," I clear my throat, "not, but it will do you well to remember your own posturing, prince."

He growls in response to my words, before flipping me onto my back and pulling my clothing off. "Oh I remember it, but it is not expected of you, little dove, so let's compromise here." Before I know it he is between my legs, one thigh in each of his hands. A breeze enters the room, rustling my hair and causing me to shiver. "You are going to be a good little dove and let me take my fill of your pussy until I am good and ready to stop, and if you are fine with this interaction tomorrow morning we can discuss going further."

A growl of protest escapes me. "But I want your co-"

"Unfortunately for us, I do not trust that want right now. You are acting strange, and I would rather be safe than sorry. This is what I am willing to give, do you agree to my terms?"

We stare at each other in a silent challenge. Frustration and desire mix within me, swell until I cannot stand the silence any longer. "Fine."

"Perfect." He smirks. "I play a little different than that Sorin of yours. I like a little more... control. If at any point you find yourself not enjoying the experience, just say..." he snorts at his own thought. "Baldar."

I blink at the name. *Why would I need...*

"Do you understand, Alaceandra?" The prince asks, his voice a bit more serious.

"I- I understand," I say shakily.

He gives me a look full of pure seduction. "Show me. What do you say if you want things to stop, dove?"

"Baldar."

"Good girl." The prince's fingers skate over my thighs and, as they do, it feels as if five other hands join his on my body. A cool touch traces over my nipples. "I will go easy on you this time." Another warmer one traces circles on my belly. Another seems to brush through the strands of my hair. The feeling of two other hands join his own on my thighs.

"What is that?" I ask, my voice high pitched and breathy.

The prince traces his finger up and down my slit, teasing my pussy without fully penetrating any part of it. "Oh, those?" The prince says slyly, his voice full of arrogance. "Still me, dove." He allows his finger to finally get past my first set of folds, but only traces around my clit, staying away from any direct pressure. The touch on my nipple switches from warm to cold, causing them to become stiff peaks. My body starts to feel like it is filled with a low hum of electricity. I clench my hands at my sides, willing myself not to move too much. The sensations around me are all encompassing and borderline overwhelming, but I cannot help to be excited for the prince's next move; his next touch. "I think you saw how my powers allow me to create things made of wind, did you not, dove? I have found a way for that to be... let's say *beneficial* in the bedroom." A little swirl of wind makes a tiny tornado on my nipple, causing a pinching sensation that makes me gasp. The prince chuckles.

Slowly, and deliberately, the prince swipes one of his fingers over my clit causing me to clutch at the blankets. "Such a pretty dove." He leans down and with the same aching slowness swipes his tongue up my pussy. A low growl of appreciation rumbles from him. "Get comfortable," he mumbles into me. "I am going to enjoy this." With that statement, his mouth fully encapsulates my clit. I close my eyes against the pure amount of sensation that overwhelms me. I breathe heavily as the wind around me takes on a life of its own. It becomes cold then hot as it tickles the length of my body, amplifying the sensation of the prince's mouth on me. My hands move from the sheets to the prince's long inky braid. I use the leverage to pull him closer to me as my hips wiggle beneath him. He clamps one arm on my lower stomach forcing me to be still. I whimper out in protest. Tiny currents of pleasure pulse their way through my body as I get closer and closer to the edge. As if sensing this, the prince's tongue turns more ferocious, his gentle patterns becoming more of a carving on my flesh. Just when I am about to fall over the cliff though, he stops.

I cry out from the loss. "Prince!"

Ignoring my hand on his head, he lifts up slightly and restarts his tracing along my pussy with his thumb. "Yes, dove."

"I," I jerk as he gently traces over my clit, a soft breeze follows his finger, which only causes my body to coil tighter. A moan overtakes my sentence, "I was about to come," I finally blurt out, frustration present within my voice.

"Oh?" The prince says, his tone telling me he was well aware of my predicament. "This is how we will play this game. Your challenge is to ask me to come right before you topple over the edge. If you ask in time, I may let you. If not, we will work back from this position until you can do so successfully. Do you understand these rules?"

Desire curls my toes at his words. "What if I do not tell you, and I come before you can stop me?"

A husky chuckle escapes him. "Is that a challenge, dove?"

Warning tingles at my scalp. My heart races. I search his eyes. They are a deep lavender and sparkle with mischief. I get the feeling I will lose this battle if I were to throw down the metaphorical gauntlet. I nibble my lower lip before shaking my head.

"I didn't hear you, dove."

"No. It is not a challenge."

He smirks. "Maybe next time," he says. Before once again resuming his position between my legs. "Remember the rules, dove," he whispers before he once again devours me. The breath leaves my lungs as my mind goes blank. The prince's wind flirts with my body, teasing it until I am a mess of sensation whose salvation lies at the will of the prince's tongue. His hands grasp my thighs firmly. His mouth is latched on to my clit creating gentle suction as his tongue swipes across its surface. I cry out, doing my best to keep my voice down, unsure about how far it will carry within the palace. The prince's wind magick swishes past my ears making it hard for me to hear anything other than my own heavy heart beat. My hands join the wind. I play with my breasts as I watch the prince between my thighs and moan as my pleasure intensifies. My skin tingles as my orgasm builds quickly. Almost as if it had never fully went away. I stiffen.

"The rules, dove," the prince warns, nipping at my inner thigh, before continuing his onslaught on my bare flesh.

"C-can I?" My voice is crackly. My words are hard to find. The thoughts haze over as the prince sucks on my clit gently. "Fuck," I whimper.

The prince pauses, and I want to cry in frustration. "Can you what, dove?" His thumb is once again back to circling my clit, but instead of having a light pressure, his thumb circles me firmly, insistent.

"Cum!" I practically yell. "Can I cum?" My legs do their best to pull the prince closer.

"You may," he says before slipping two fingers inside of me and curling them upwards. As he does that, he returns his mouth to my sensitive clit. The orgasm crashes into me faster than I can blink. My pussy convulses around his fingers as I grab a pillow from beside me on the bed and scream into it. I soak in the afterglow of my orgasm. My body has calmed somewhat. The intensity of my arousal is now a soft energy beneath my skin. The prince's face greets me when I finally gain my bearings enough to remove the pillow from my face. He has moved up my body and is now leaning over me. He gives me a soul capturing kiss, and I can taste myself on his lips. I nip him and he chuckles before raking his hands through my hair, tugging on the strands and pulling me into him to deepen the kiss. The stinging of my hair mixes deliciously with the after tremors still rolling through me, making my body once again awaken with desire.

When we part, I marvel at his muscular chest and trace my hands down his torso once again until my hand lands on his shorts. He stops me. "Alaceandra..." he warns. Grabbing my hand, he brings it up to his lips and kisses my palm before once more descending between my thighs.

"What are you...?"

"You didn't think I was done, did you?"

This time he throws each leg over his shoulders ensuring that I am completely open to him. One of his hands grabs my hip and the other grabs my breast. He firmly massages and twirls my nipple between his fingers with one hand while the other holds me close to allow him to rain torment on my pussy with his tongue. After another moment, the hand massaging my breast snakes down towards my pussy and he starts two pump to fingers in and out of me. I squirm beneath him and his grip on my hip becomes more unyielding. The intensity of sensation rolling through me makes me unsure of whether I want to cry out or laugh. His fingers continue to pulse in and out of me in a delightful rhythm, unperturbed by my body's involuntary movements.

"Can I cum?" I gasp out as I feel another orgasm cresting.

The prince replaces his mouth with his thumb and continues to pump in and out of me while his thumb starts to circle my clit firmly.

"Of course, dove."

The waves of the orgasm crash over me and I once again throw the pillow over my face to dull the sound. Just when I think the waves are over, the prince continues slowly lapping at my clit. I shiver, and my eyes shoot open.

"Prince!" I say, admonishing him.

"Shhh... you can give me one more."

"I cannot," I whine.

"You can." He adds another finger inside of me, curving them when he enters so that he hits just the right spot. My breathing is ragged and little speckles of light start to sparkle on the surface of my skin as another orgasm swells from deep inside of me. "Good girl," the prince soothes. "You don't have to ask this time. Give it to me." I do not have time to cover my mouth before my orgasm rips through me with such intensity that I almost pass out. I briefly notice the sparks on my skin rising up before bursting into tiny sparkling confetti around us. I continue to shake as wave after wave of ecstasy courses through me. My eyes flutter open when the waves subside. The prince is still between my legs, a small smile tugging the corners of his mouth as he rubs my thighs. When he notices my gaze on him, his smile grows. Crawling up my body, he captures my lips with his. The taste of my juices coats my tongue as his plunders my mouth, leaving me breathless.

"You did great, dove," he soothes. "I will be right back." Slowly, he rises from the bed and walks into the bathroom. My heart drops briefly at his departure, but he returns quickly with a warm cloth and a small piece of something wrapped in paper. He hands me the object and I open it up to find an unfamiliar piece of candy within. I look at him with wide eyes.

"Eat it," he says gently before placing the warm cloth against my pussy and cleaning me up. I shutter at the stark change in temperature from the cold room, though cannot help but enjoy the warmth. I pop the little piece of candy in my mouth and hum with happiness as its sweet and nutty flavor melts in my mouth. "Good, right?" the prince remarks.

I nod, savoring the candy instead of chewing it.

"Good," he removes the cloth and brings it back to the bathroom. I watch him as he runs it under water and places it in a small bin for washing. He returns back to me and holds out a hand. "Time to shower."

I glance out the window and notice that the sun is just starting to cast its rays into the room, surprisingly though I find myself not as exhausted as skipping a night of rest might otherwise make me. Energy still hums low under my skin and other than a want for more sleep, I realize that

I do not truly need it. I swallow the last bit of the candy and grab the prince's hand. "A shower it is."

CHAPTER THIRTY-TWO

Riddles

Alaceandra

We shower and walk back out into the amber soaked room. I still have a towel wrapped around my body due to the fact that I neglected to think about grabbing another set of clothing before rushing into the shower. The prince, on the other hand, did not have that problem. He is sporting a teal pair of long silken pants and a white shirt. My body is buzzing with a strange, yet comforting, energy under my skin, and I no longer find myself as exhausted or on edge as I once was. Despite this feeling of new energy, a sense of unease also mingles in my chest. Suddenly, a yawn overtakes me and I look back at the bed with longing. *I would never say no to another nap.*

"Do you think we have time to get a little more sleep?" I ask the prince.

He smirks at me and then glances back out the window. "Maybe fifteen minutes."

I sigh. "So then no, not really."

He gives me a subtle shake of his head. I grumble and walk over to the bed anyway, plopping on the edge of it.

"You probably don't want to lay there anyway," he remarks. "You made quite the mess."

Heat rushes to my face, and I glare at him.

He chuckles. "Go get ready for the day. Let me switch the bedding."

Grumbling some more, I peel myself up from the corner of the bed. Standing, I proceed to walk over to one of the little duffles in the corner. Rifling through it, I pick out a burgundy sleeveless top and some athletic shorts. I glance at the prince before making my way back into the warm steamy bathroom and shutting the door behind me.

As soon as the door is closed, Baldar appears in front of me looking smug.

"What?" I whisper at him.

"*Won't be a problem, Baldar, we are not a bunch of horndogs.*" Baldar mocks.

Heat rushes to my cheeks. I roll my eyes and clutch the towel closer to me, trying to deflect from the guilt and embarrassment already creeping up my chest.

"Do you have to be in here for something or...?"

"*Oh, don't get all huffy,*" Baldar says climbing to the counter tops. "*I knew it would happen when you overloaded your power.*"

"You did?" I whisper back.

"*Of course. For all of your bravado, I know that you missed the prince. No matter how annoying he is. You just needed a little push and a lack of magical energy was just that. Now that you have replenished yourself. This is the perfect time to start training your demoni powers.*"

"My what?"

A knock sounds at the door and Baldar skitters behind me.

"You alright in there, dove?" The prince asks.

"Yes!"

"Who are you talking to?" His voice rumbles from the other side of the door.

"Myself. Sorry," I quickly reply.

A pause elongates between us before his reply comes back. "Okay." There is a pause. "I think your assigned guard will be coming soon. He did say he would be the one to retrieve you in the morning, no?"

"Oh yes, he said he would get us both. I will be out shortly."

I hear the prince's footsteps walk back into the bedroom and let out a breath.

"This is why I told you to use your inside voice," Baldar scolds.

"I forgot you could hear it," I respond.

Baldar makes a little noise before climbing back onto the counter.

"Meet me back in here after your combat lesson today, and I will tell you more of what we will do to prepare. Until then, Alaceandra, do be careful with your interactions with others. You are... a little more charged than usual." I watch as Baldar gives me a once over and then disappears.

"Wait," I try to stop him with my words, but he is already gone.

Well fuck. I complain mentally, before quickly getting dressed and leaving the bathroom.

The bed is now decorated in a pale green linen. The prince glances at me when I leave the bathroom, his eyes raking over me hungrily.

"Thanks for making the bed," I say after a moment.

He nods before studying me. "Have you given any more thought to my riddle, dove?"

"Which one?" I put my hands on my hips and study him right back.

He gives me a dazzling smile before walking closer. I watch his approach semi-warily, but remain in place. When he arrives in front of me he places one hand on my chin and with the other he moves a strand of hair behind my ear. "The one about my name," he whispers.

"Oh," I try to think about the riddle. *My name lies in the multitude; it begins at the hands of where crop and life ends.* "Briefly."

He traces a finger down my face, his smile shining bright as he looks at me. "How about I give you another hint?"

Any further insight into the man in front of me would be helpful, but... I narrow my eyes. "Why would you want to do that?" Unfortunately, I cannot help but be suspicious of the prince, despite our intimacy. *The man is such a puzzle. I do not know if I can ever truly find comfort in him until I figure out what he is up to.*

He responds without hesitation as if he was sure I would ask. "You are getting stronger. I can feel it. When my little dove flies, I think it is best she is rewarded," his voice is a gentle vibration in the air, and I have to hold back the tiny elvisera dancing within my stomach as his fingers trace over my collarbone.

"Okay. What is the hint?" I reply softly.

He tilts his head. I can tell from his expression that he is pleased with my answer. "I am an object a reaper holds. When you speak of me, it is to describe a diverse range of intricacies." As his words weave their way into my mind something moves inside of me. My hands tingle with a sense of urgency as my mind tries to unscramble his strange words. More than before, my brain reaches for an answer to his riddles.

I stare at him quizzically. *'Begins at the hands of where crop and life ends'? 'Reaper'? Those two must be related. Maybe something to do with what is used by those who handle crops and death.* I wrack my brain for an intersection, but am coming up blank. *Maybe there is a library they will give me access to? If I had one, I could look into commonalities between those two things. What about this 'lies in the multitude' and 'diverse range' section, though? What could that be trying to point to?* As I am about to ask him for more information, a knock sounds on the other side of the door.

"Ah, there is that guard," he says before leaving me by the bathroom and walking over to the door. The sound of it clicking open jars my thoughts.

I look over to find Sydon standing in the doorway.

"Alaceandra," he greets.

"Sydon."

"Have you checked over your schedule for the day?"

"I have not."

"Please do so now and then take the prince here and follow me. It is time for breakfast." He grabs the door and slams it shut.

The prince stares after him for a moment. "What schedule?" he asks.

"Hmm?" I had already walked over to the place where I had last thrown the stupid schedule and started to unravel it. "Oh, yeah it is this paper." I gesture to it. "That is so odd." I murmur under my breath. I had just finished unraveling the paper.

"What is?"

"This?" I say, turning the paper over to him.

On it was written:

> *Today for the princess~*
> *First: Retrieval*
> *Then: Breakfast*
> *After: Training*
> *Then:* *************
> *Finally:* ************
>
> *Remember:*
> ******************
>
> ********************************

****

Everything after breakfast was smeared and unreadable with only the first two sections of the day having any sense of legibility.

The prince wrinkles his eyebrows and glances back at me.

"There is nothing written on there."

"What?" I turn it back to face me and look at it, but the weirdly half filled schedule is still present. "Yes, there is." I walk over to the prince and present the paper to him once again. "Look, the schedule is right there. You can see the first two steps of the day, but it looks like the rest is not readable for some reason." I point to the words on the paper.

The prince looks at it again before shaking his head. "Dove, it is blank. At least to me. I do not see what you see."

"What?" I stare at the page, but the black lettering does not shift in the slightest.

A knock on the door sounds again and the prince goes over and opens it.

"Good. You have seen the schedule. Come on now, Alaceandra, you cannot be late."

My head whips up to meet Sydon's eyes.

"But-"

"You must follow the schedule, unless of course..." He lets his words trail, but I know his meaning. My other hand turns to a fist.

"I am unsure what the second half of the schedule states," I say through gritted teeth.

"Then follow what you can for now and you can look at the rest when you no longer know what to follow, but I am sure breakfast begins the day as you are being waited upon so please follow me." He turns and walks out the door.

I throw the stupid scroll onto the bed, tension present in my shoulders.

"Lets go, prince," I grit out before walking out the door and following after Sydon's disappearing back.

"Interesting..." I hear the prince mutter before I can feel the heat of him at my back.

My stomach chooses that moment to growl.

"Guess it is a good thing we are getting breakfast." The prince's breath brushes against my ear as he whispers to me, his voice is full of amusement. *I am glad he finds this situation entertaining,* I think to myself grumpily. *Wonder if it would be any different if his loved ones were on the line.* I internally snort. *Does the prince even have anyone he loves?* My brain races over those I know in the prince's life. For the life of me, I cannot think of anyone, that I have seen at least, the prince had not shown a minuscule amount of disdain for.

The thought of that saddens me slightly. My shoulders slump, and I decide it best to answer his original statement. "Guess it is."

CHAPTER THIRTY-THREE

Electric Fire Cannon

Alaceandra

The breakfast hall is silent when we enter. A couple of people mill about the space this time, and I stare after them trying to figure out what group they are from. Unlike at dinner, these soldiers were in more casual dress with no color denoting which kingdom they were here to serve.

"The kings thought it better to limit who actually ate in your presence due to yesterday's... events."

I cringe a little as we make our way up to a newly curtained table in the center of the room. I climb the steps slowly as bits and pieces of memories about black fire come swirling into my mind. I try to focus on one and call back exactly what happened after the voice in my head took over. The more I focus on the images, though, the more the flashes of events become hazy, so instead I bite my bottom lip and attempt to push the thoughts away.

"About that," the prince cuts in. "Will Alaceandra be facing any consequences due to her actions yesterday?" My heart drops in my stomach as dread tries to overtake me. *That is something I had not even considered. Of course there will be recourse for my actions. Whether I remember what occurred yesterday or not, I doubt I will be able to get away with attacking the king of Helomasi.* Glancing at the prince, I notice that he still has his ever present bored mask. My mind flashes back to that same face between my thighs only a couple of hours ago, and I have to bite my lip to keep the memory at bay. That unease from earlier starts to couple with guilt. *How am I so weak as to allow that when I am still unsure of his intentions? Has what happened in Olvaria taught me nothing? No matter where I turn, I must remember that I am surrounded by danger.* I try to force my emotions not to show on my own face and instead eye Sydon awaiting his answer.

Sydon looks at the prince suspiciously before replying. "King Demetrius has not yet decided how to punish the princess."

The prince lets out a puff of air. "So my father has yet to regain consciousness."

The mention of King Demetrius' state pulls me completely from my thoughts of last night. *Regain consciousness? They did not mention that the king was unconscious...* I look back and forth between them to try to see if the prince's words hold any truth, but Sydon only glares at the prince. *I guess that is confirmation enough...he was definitely knocked unconscious, but was it by me? It had to have been. Why else would the prince bring it up in regard to my punishment? Great. Perfect. Amazing. I am definitely not panicking. No, I am not.* Sydon pulls out my chair and gestures for me to sit. I follow his lead and sit, trying my best not to bounce my leg under the table. The prince sits on my right, and Sydon takes his place to the left of me. *I am so fucked. If not dead. Who knows what the king will demand for punishment as soon as he wakes up?* I ignore the two men and stare down at my food. In front of me, looks to be some kind of patterned bread stacked high with yellow fruits and dusted with sugar. Next to the plate, sits a pot filled with a thick, amber liquid and a cup of juice. My stomach grumbles again as the scent of the food wafts up, distracting me from my devolving thoughts. I pick up the little pot of amber liquid and inspect it carefully.

"The liquid is meant to be poured over the food— it is a syrup— it will make it sweeter," Sydon's voice interrupts my inspection.

My eyes dart to him in confusion before returning to my plate. *Okay...this could be your final meal, Alaceandra. Might as well enjoy it.* Carefully, I drizzle the pot containing the viscous liquid over the bread and cut out a little bite, before handing it over to Sydon.

Sydon takes the fork from my hand and eats the food without complaint. I watch him chew and swallow it before I nod in satisfaction. He hands the fork back to me, and I wipe it with a napkin before continuing to cut another bite from the stack in front of me. I try to move slowly in case there is a slower acting poison present. Just because Sydon said there has yet to be a decided punishment does not mean that he is being truthful. *Given past events, I can never be too careful. They drugged me to get me here. What is to stop them from doing it now?* After I watch his face for a couple of minutes I pick up my fork once again. Bringing the food up to my mouth, I take a small bite. A soft moan escapes me as sweet and savory collide together on my taste buds.

"Is that good?" The prince asks, his voice a low rumble.

I glance at him and nod, before returning to my food to slice off another bite. *Ptheryeth, I hope this is not poisoned. It is too good not to eat.* Once I have successfully downed half my plate, I look at both of the men to notice that their eyes are now firmly fixed on me.

"Um..." I say my cheeks heating. "Are you both going to eat?"

Only the prince has a plate in front of him, and he nods, but does not take his eyes off of me.

"I have already eaten," Sydon says before clearing his throat. "We only have about twenty minutes here before we need to get to training. Please hurry with your meal, Alaceandra."

I try not to pout wishing that I could savor the meal more.

"Okay."

I eat in silence, my gaze occasionally flicking to the prince who barely touches his food. *Is that a sign? Or is the prince being cautious like me?* I narrow my gaze as I watch him, chewing more slowly. The prince smiles at me and shoves a bite of food in his mouth, swallowing noticeably. *I am not sure if that makes me feel better or worse.* I take in my surroundings. Only the sound of indistinct chatter and metal on ceramic echo through the space. *Nothing quite so suspicious at least.* I sigh and decide to finish my food quickly. When my plate is empty, I push it away and the prince does the same.

"Are you not going to finish eating?" I ask the prince suspiciously.

He gives me a look. "Would you like more?" He gestures to the plate in offering.

A blush once again overtakes my face. "No," I snap.

He smirks. "Then what is next?" He directs his question over to Sydon. I blink at him in disbelief.

"Training," Sydon responds.

"Lead the way," the prince says, standing from the table. Regaining my bearings, I stand from the table as well, crossing my arms around my middle. *My stomach seems happy at least. No pain or nausea. I wonder why the prince did not finish eating...*

Sydon nods before standing as well and walking out of the dining hall. We follow closely behind him. When we finally arrive at the gym, Sydon turns to the prince.

"Prince, you will find that room to be compliant with your needs." He points to a room at one end of the gym. "Please change into the clothes you find within."

"What is going on in here?" The prince asks, glancing at all the trainees in different colored uniforms.

"Your father requested you be a part of today's training session before yesterday's incident, so you will be training with Alaceandra today. More will be explained after you change, now please," he gestures back over to the room. The prince's eyes momentarily flicker to mine before he nods and walks away.

Sydon turns his focus to me. "I trust you know where you are going."

I nod then walk into my changing chambers and switch clothing quickly before walking out. The trainees stand around me huddled in groups of teal, silver, black, and bronze. I scan the crowd for Lylane and Jaq and find them in the farthest corner of the gym. Fortunately, they are easy to spot. In the sea of soldiers, they are the only two hanging out outside of their colored groupings. They turn to me, and I give them a small wave. They wave back and start to walk in my direction. A warm presence at my back has me spinning around. The prince stands behind me in loose teal pants and a pink sleeveless top.

"Who are they?" he asks in a low tone.

I consider not telling him for a moment, but then decide there is no harm in him knowing. "Jaq and Lylane," I whisper back.

"Hmm... that man seems familiar..." the prince says more to himself than to me.

"How so?" I ask, tilting my head in confusion.

A look akin to realization crosses the prince's face before a cocky smile paints his lips.

"Trainees! In position!" Rafton screams from the front of the room, before blowing three short bursts from his whistle. I turn to look at him and notice that Sydon is standing directly behind him, staring at me. I look away. My eyes then meet a scowling Huermond standing off to the side of the gym, studying the prince and me.

"What about that man?" The prince's breath caresses my ear.

"Trouble."

Luckily, Huermond turns away from me, a look of disgust present on his face, and starts to converse with some of the other bronze uniformed men around him.

"Why is that?" The prince asks.

"Long story," I mutter.

"Come on, Alaceandra!" Lylane yells at me, just now catching up. "You do not want him to ask again." She gently grabs my hand and pulls me to the front of the room. Jaq follows, and the prince whispers something to him, causing Jaq to give him a sharp look. I do not quite catch what they say though as Lylane continues to lead me to a spot to the left of Rafton. The chatter of the people around us grows louder and louder. A long whistle later and there is silence. Lylane, Jaq, the prince, and me all stand in a grouping, and I notice that all around us trainees are similarly paired in groups of four.

"Today we will be working on mixing skill sets. Once you can prove to me that mix has been completed, you will be released. Until then you will remain in this gym. Do you understand me?"

What does he mean mixing skill sets?

"Yes, sir!" The crowd around me responds before I even have a chance to process his words.

"I can't hear you."

"Yes, sir!" They all scream in unison.

"Move it!" The whistle blows again. The crowd disperses around the room until only the four of us remain in the middle. Rafton eyes our group before moving to the back wall with Sydon. They start to speak in low tones.

"Well, this should be interesting." Jaq draws out the words rocking back on his heels.

I nod.

"I think the best way to start this is for us to share what skills we have. We already know you can control fire, Alaceandra, but what about you..." Lylane trails the end of her sentence awkwardly, coaxing the prince to divulge his name.

I look between the two of them.

The prince arches a brow at her.

"Okay..." She widens her eyes. "I will go first. I can create light boxes with these sparks." Suddenly, between the group, tiny sparkles appear. They vibrate for a moment before gelling together, creating an almost invisible box. "I can also shape them into different things." Before our eyes the box transforms into the shape of a human, a tiny elvisera, and a pen. "Once I form this box around a person they can either enhance their abilities or dull them depending on intention." The box starts to flicker, before the sparkles once again separate and disappear. "Unfortunately, I am not very great at this skill yet..." she mumbles. "I cannot hold it for terribly long, but it should work for the exercise." She smiles shyly before shoving Jaq forward. He almost falls on his face with the force of her shove. "Jaq, you are next."

"What the fuck, Lylane?" Jaq growls, righting himself.

She shrugs at him. "Tell us what you got."

Jaq grimaces. His eyes flick to the prince suspiciously before meeting my gaze, then he looks back at Lylane.

She rolls her eyes. "We know her powers. Tell her yours. It is only fair."

He sighs. "Fine." He lifts a hand and blue sparks appear. "Minor electricity. I can move quickly or imbue things with spark. Not super strong, but good for being quick, I guess."

All eyes turn to the prince. A breeze whips through the group. "Wind," he says, but neglects to expound on what exactly he can do with said wind. I also choose not to offer up any more information. Although I have seen him in action, and Jaq and Lylane seem kind, I would be a fool to trust them with too much information. I have quickly come to learn that hidden agendas are a specialty of the people of Ptheryeth. It would be silly to think that their kindness comes without price or expectation.

"And your name?" Lylane presses.

"You can call me the prince."

"Okaaayy."

"So..." I start breaking the tension in the air. "How do we combine them?"

Lylane taps her chin. Jaq scratches the back of his head. The prince stares at us dully.

"Do we have to complete this exercise?" The prince asks.

"If we want to leave," Lylane answers sweetly.

"How are they going to stop us from just walking out?" The prince asks.

"I mean... the room is full of trained and training soldiers. You would not get far," Jaq replies.

The prince rolls his eyes. "Okay, then can we get on with it?"

"Do you have any ideas?" Lylane asks.

The prince remains silent, but turns his gaze to me, tilting his head.

I sigh. "We can probably use my fire as a base," I offer.

"A base?" Jaq asks. "What do you mean?"

"I mean that my fire can probably hold some of yours. Jaq, you said you can imbue things with electricity, yes?"

He nods in confirmation.

"Great, so we can try to have you imbue the fire with electricity then." I look at the prince. "The prince can direct the fireball into a target and...." I look at Lylane. "Maybe if you form a box around the fire once it is in the air you can make it bigger and shape it into something? So it is a more targeted attack?" I check my inner threads to see if I can even sense my fire abilities after what happened yesterday and find that the thick strand that I pulled from earlier is almost bursting with green energy. Mentally, I lay a hand on it and feel magick rush into me. *Perfect.*

Lylane's eyes sparkle. "That is a great idea, Alaceandra!" She bounces on her toes. "Let us practice!"

We spend a couple of hours trying to get Jaq's abilities to play nice with mine. It is quite the challenge because Jaq is mostly familiar with imbuing solid objects with electricity. Since fire is not solid, getting the two to mix seemed quite impossible. The prince has less of an issue pushing Lylane's boxes through the air with ease.

"Okay, okay. Maybe do not imagine the fire as fire," I instruct Jaq. "Maybe instead you imagine it like a solid ball?" I form my fire ball again. "Try to hit the center of it. I think where we are failing is trying to hit the flames which are dancing about instead of targeting the source." I hold out my palm.

"But what if I hit you with it?" Jaq asks, his tone filled with trepidation.

"Then I will hit you with my fire so we are even," I joke back.

He takes a step away from me. "That... is not encouraging."

I sigh. "I am joking. I do not think you will hit me."

"How can you be so sure?"

"Just try it Jaq!" Lylane yells, rolling her eyes.

"Fuck. Fine." Jaq gathers his electricity in his palms before shooting it at my fire. My hands tingle as the sparks make brief contact with my skin, but my eyes widen as the energy quickly redirects and races into the fire causing sparks of blue to now mingle with the red flames. In awe, I study the ball of energy. I now hold in my palm a ball of electric charged fire.

"We did it!" I scream excitedly.

"How interesting," The prince mumbles.

"Definitely cool," Jaq responds, sweat beading on his forehead. "I think we may have only one shot at the whole throwing portion though, not sure if I can do that again for a while."

I nod.

Lylane motions Rafton over. He sees the fireball and nods. "I sense fire and electric. Where are the other two skills?" he asks.

"We will show you," Lylane says confidently. "But we need a target. Preferably something hard to hit."

Rafton nods and walks away. When he returns, he brings with him a piece of parchment in the shape of a tentacled creature.

Lylane nods to me. "Ready?"

"Yes," I confirm.

She turns to the prince. He nods.

"Fire away," she says.

Fast as lightning, I throw the electric fireball forth. It sails through the air towards the target. Lylane forms her little sparkle box around it, forcing it into the shape of the tentacled parchment and the prince pushes the box forward, increasing its speed. Before we can draw our next breath, it hits, and the parchment is decimated. I release the tie to the fire and it simmers into nothingness. I sense when everyone else pulls back their ability as well. We all cheer.

A clap sounds from behind us. I turn to see Sydon nodding approvingly.

"Great work. Your power lies in your allies. Without team work you can only be so strong. Remember that," Rafton says, his hard gaze on both Lylane and Jaq. "You all are dismissed." He turns and walks away.

CHAPTER THIRTY-FOUR

Choices

The Prince

Watching the little dove's interactions with her supposed prison guards has been quite... disconcerting. When Sam and I were speaking, before we finally decided I would be the one to go in and retrieve the dove, we had thought that she would, at the very least, be more resistant to her captors. I didn't think that she would be more open to me due to this resistance, but her docility when it comes to her supposed schedule and eating regime is quite unexpected. If she is happy in this new prison of hers, it will be much harder to ensure her compliance when it is time to escape it. I communicated this to Sam, and he has the thought that they must be holding something else over her. That she would not be so easily swayed by a good meal and training regimen to gain her respect and compliance, but I am not so sure. Maybe her father's presence here is having some effect, but I need to get to the bottom of it before Sam enters the palace. If she has some other agenda that is keeping her here, that needs to be taken into account so that our plans do not fall apart.

Unfortunately, I have also not seen her other guard dog, Sorin, around. Which either means he is still somewhere out in the Dark Lands, hiding out somewhere in this palace, or... worse. *I hate to think what it would do to the little dove if one of her guards has perished in Olvaria's battle, but if he is a factor in this mystery it would only make sense why she would not have much fight in her at the moment.* I watch her as we walk through the corridors and back to the quarters that we have been assigned. She moves fluidly through the halls as if she has gained some sort of familiarity with them in her short stint here. My gaze moves to the man who walks beside her and an emotion, akin to jealousy, worms its way into my heart. Another thing she seems to have an unfortunate familiarity with is this man. She shows no fear in his presence, instead they seem to have a strange friendliness between them. The man even eats her food before she consumes it. *That behavior is quite unlike any prison guard I have come to know, I wonder what his plans are with her. His kindness can't be without some motive.* I grit my teeth, anger starting to course through me at my thoughts. Although I am glad to know that these men have not seemed to harm Alaceandra, the fact that she is comfortable enough here to not have fear and to even make friends does not bode well for my plans to take this place down. *What if she is unwilling to battle those she has grown close with to escape?* The thought of her resistance fills me with annoyance. *I must not think the worst at this point.* I sigh, trying to remain calm. I should be receiving a response from Sam today updating me on his progress in retrieving the necessary items for our mission.

My mind wanders back to last night. A smirk breaks out on my lips, and I do my best to hold it back and remain impassive to those around me. I had been craving to taste my sweet little dove from the moment I laid eyes on her. Watching Sorin devour her in our short time together in Olvaria had only made my want to get between her pretty thighs harder to ignore. The wait was nothing though compared to the reward of having her tremble beneath me as I tasted her. My only regret is that I did so when she seemed so unlike herself. The desperation she had was unnatural and I have to wonder what brought it on. It seems this encounter has also connected us somehow. My desire for her growing almost overnight and I have to warn myself to tread carefully. As much as I would like to think that my dove craves me as much as I do her, the fact remains that she is still quite distrusting of me. It is hard for me to believe that the woman who so passionately told me that we would never kiss let alone touch again is the same woman who begged for more than just my tongue last night. I will have to inquire more about this sudden change. On the bright side, if this is a permanent behavior shift, her welcoming my touch will make our charade in front of the kings much more believable.

There is another benefit to this shift as well, it seems our interactions also invoke her abilities. If we can somehow sharpen her connection to Unduli, that would ensure that my own agenda can come to fruition as much as it would ensure that this prison sentence will soon be over. The kings are not the only ones that need her to be strong enough to open the portal completely, although I'm not so keen on letting the creatures of that world out. It is bad enough that Alaceandra now has the one she calls Baldar hanging around her. Or did. I have not seen the ferret creature since our battle, which is for the best. A creature of Unduli can only bring misfortune. I only hope that she will be able to handle the opening of the portal without letting more creatures like him through, because if not... Unease curls my stomach. I always considered the fact that her powers could be her demise. That this portal could lead her to either falling completely over the edge and let her other nature break through or that it would kill her entirely in the process. If I am honest with myself, I counted on that outcome from the start, but as I am learning more about the princess of Tikilium, I find myself second guessing my original plans. Her ties to the portal should grant me immense power after it is completed. Enough to take down my father and Alaceandra herself if she becomes a threat, but... *do I really wish for that kind of strength if it means I must lose her to achieve it? Can I really allow my father to take rein over Ptheryeth to save one woman from a fate that she is destined to follow?*

I watch as she speaks with the guard— Sydon— and then walks into the room. I follow her. She immediately lays on the bed, exhausted from the day. I can't blame her and the sight ensures that the smirk that was once fighting to show itself on my face, finally breaks through. Turning away from her, I pace the room in front of the window. The elvisera that I have been using to send messages to Sam swirl around on the other side of the pane, excited for their friend to come back with Sam's message as much as they are excited to be given another task. The young elvisera always had zeal when it came to their duties. They had not yet been hardened by how ugly those duties could get. I sigh, my thought returning to Alaceandra. She is much like these creatures, only just now getting started in the world. Only now learning the horrors of what her future holds. I look out the window once more. *If I forsake these creatures and my duties to Helomasi all for this woman, would that really make me any better than my father? Or would I be more of a monster to sacrifice the lives of so many for one? Time is running out, I must figure out what I must do, before it is too late.*

CHAPTER THIRTY-FIVE

Suspicion

Alaceandra

I am laying on the bed. My body is exhausted from training today, but luckily not as bad as it was last night. This was the first time I was able to actually combine my powers with others and the feeling of that was invigorating. I smile to myself and look at my hands. *I wonder if we will continue practicing that skill or if it was more of a one off. I hope we will. It could be useful later on.*

"Are all your lessons like that?" The prince's voice startles me from my thoughts. I glance over at him and notice that he seems tense. His shoulders are drawn up and his face screams turmoil. I watch as his attention flickers back and forth from the window that he is pacing in front of slowly, as if he was expecting something. I do not think I have seen him ever so distraught. I sit up in the bed and watch him carefully.

"Not particularly. Although I have not had many sessions, so it is hard to say whether they are or are not."

Sydon dropped us both off in my chambers before he left, promising he would be back for us in a little while. When we first arrived back in the room I re-checked my schedule to see if any of the hazy words had become more clear. Unfortunately, nothing else appeared for after training, so my captors' plans for the rest of the day remained a mystery to me. *Not necessarily a bad thing though. Might be a good opportunity to scope out the palace. I wonder if the door is still unlocked.* My gaze flits over to the door in question before the prince's approaching footsteps cause me to jerk my eyes back over to him. He places one hand on my hip to move me closer to the edge of the bed and moves a bit of sweaty hair from my forehead. My breath catches in my chest.

"Hmm... seems you have made some friends here?" My brain takes a minute to catch up to his words. *That is a weird change of subject... were we not just talking about training?* I look into the prince's eyes and marvel at how clearly I can see his troubled thoughts. *What is going on with him?*

"W-what do you mean?" My voice comes out a bit shaky.

He smirks. "That Lylane and Jaq. They seemed friendly towards you."

I tilt my head slightly. "Oh. I guess. I only train with the two of them. I think that they were the only people who were not completely disgusted with my arrival so..." I trail off, not really knowing where he is going with his line of questioning.

"So they became your friends."

I clear my voice. "I would not go so far." Because I do not really know where I stand with the two of them. I had only met them on a handful of occasions. It is strange that the prince would be so interested in my relationships.

It must play into his plans in some way, maybe he wants to ensure you are isolated, Alaceandra. That sickly sweet voice whispers in my ear. *That is why he is grilling you for information on them. To see how best to ensure you are apart.*

That would not make any sense. Why would he want to isolate me? I snap back at the voice.

Exactly the reason that Rafton said at training, the more alone you are, the weaker you will be. He saw how powerful all your abilities were when combined together. He wants to make sure that you will be unable to use something like that against him.

I grit my teeth in annoyance. *Go away.* I demand of the voice. I know there could be truth in its statements, but hearing my doubts so clearly only causes more of that same guilt to slam into me. *I should have walked away last night.*

"That is interesting then," the prince says.

"What is interesting?" My attention returns to the conversation at hand.

"If you have not started to make attachments here, then why do you seem so content to stay in these chambers following your captors' rules?"

I pull completely away from him. *What an odd thing to say.*

"I am not content."

"Aren't you? In Helomasi we could not keep you locked in your room, and yet here it seems you are following their schedule and training regimen without complaint. Why is that?"

Defensiveness claws at me. "There is more going on here then when I was dragged to Helomasi. You are speaking on things you have no knowledge of. "

"Do enlighten me." The prince watches me with calculating eyes.

"I am still not fully convinced that you are not working with my captors. Why should I tell you all of my secrets?" I spit back at him.

"Oh, so we are on that again."

"Of course we are on that!"

"Tell me this then, dove. Say I was here to help you, not to trick you. How can I be sure you will not hinder your own escape due to some sense of loyalty to these newfound friends of yours?"

"Why would my relationship with the people here hinder my own escape?"

"Would you be able to slit their throats if it meant that you could escape your fate?"

Shock registers through me, and I stare at the prince in disbelief. My words become stuck on my tongue, and I growl in frustration before pushing the prince away from me and stalking over to the window at the corner of the room. The prince follows me and traps me there, his arms bracketing themselves on either side of my body.

"See? This is what I am talking about. If you have any chance of getting out of here, attachments are your enemy."

"Why are you saying all this? Are you admitting to the fact that you actually are here to aid in my escape?"

"I did not say that."

I turn in his arms. "Maybe not directly but how else am I suppose to take your statement? As a means of helpful advice? Something tells me you are not gracious enough to hand that out unless it is to help yourself."

"Those are some cruel words, dove."

"Cruel does not mean untrue, unless of course you are denying them?"

He stares at me. Silence spans between us for a beat.

"That is what I thought," I mumble before pushing him to take a step back. He complies, but does not move too far away. Instead he watches me silently. Those walls he has carefully built seem to draw back up before my eyes, making his expression once again unreadable.

I turn back to the window. Tension builds in the room around me making me switch from one foot to the other uncomfortably. I try to turn my attention to the outside world to escape it, but my vision is blocked by fluttering wings. Many tiny yellow elvisera are gathering around the glass, their bodies darting excitedly through the air as they circle each other furiously.

With a sigh, I try for a change in subject. "What is with the elvisera lately?" I mumble more to myself than to him.

"What do you mean?" The prince replies nonchalantly. I feel his warmth caress my back as he moves a bit closer to peer out the window with me.

"They seem to be really attracted to our room."

"Hmm... maybe there are some sydryia bushes nearby?"

"Sydryia?"

"It's a plant. They like to snack on it. If someone wants to attract an elvisera outside of their usual flying zones, some of the plant can be used to gain their attention. Would make sense why there are so many around if it is nearby," the prince says this with so much confidence, I give him a sideways look.

"Oh. I have heard of those before, I just never knew the name." Turning back to the window, I place my palm on the glass. "Seems you are an expert in the subject?" One of the elvisera caws and dives for my palm as if to grab something. I squeak and step back before tilting my head. *Odd.*

"You can say they are of special interest to me, yes."

I think on that for a second before responding. "These are so young. Strange that they would know how to grab something from someone like that. Their behavior is... different."

"You are very insightful. Yes, usually the younger of their kind have not yet learned how to fetch and deliver," he says this matter-of-factly and my suspicions continue to grow, but I decide to ask my next question anyway.

"Then why do you think these ones—" A crashing against the glass causes me to jump back.

The prince chuckles. In front of me stands a yellow elvisera with red and orange wings holding a little scroll of parchment in his beak. I would guess this one is closer to adulthood than the fully yellow ones surrounding it, but still quite young in comparison to those around Tikilium.

"Why do these ones seem to know how to deliver letters?" The prince finishes my question, gently moving me from the window. He fishes a hand in his pocket and pulls out a little auburn branch with white and yellow flowers decorating its surface. Gently pulling the window open the couple inches that it allows, the prince places the branch at its entry point. The elvisera flaps excitedly before shoving the letter through the tiny opening and snatching the branch as a reward. Then it flies off, its younger kin following closely behind.

"So you are the reason then," I say dryly.

"It seems so."

Confusion thrums through me. "Who is the letter from?"

The prince smiles. "Ah ah ah. Secret for a secret, dear dove."

I narrow my gaze. "What are you asking me to divulge?"

The prince's smile turns more arrogant. "Let me know one of the things you have endured here."

"Anything?" I ask.

The prince narrows his gaze. "Of substance." The prince amends.

I tilt my head. "When I first encountered my father within these walls, he made an attempt against my life."

The prince stares at me. "And yet you still follow their rules and schedules. Would that not make you want to rebel more in your prison rather than happily waiting to be fetched by your prison guards?"

"I did not say that was a reason why I do so, only a substantial thing that has happened."

"Well then tell me-"

"No. Who has written to you here? I have given you my secret. Reveal yours."

The prince rolls his eyes and hands me the letter. "See for yourself."

I unravel the scroll and stare down at the familiar neat handwriting in utter disbelief.

> ROYAL PAIN IN THE ASS,
>
> THE NECESSARY ITEMS HAVE BEEN RETRIEVED AHEAD OF
>
> SCHEDULE.
>
> PREPARE FOR NEXT STEPS.
>
> -S

"Is this from..." I trail off, shock still taking hold of me.

"Yep," the prince says taking the note from me before scanning its contents and walking back out to the window. One of the tiny elvisera that had stayed behind blows a tiny stream of fire on the paper, turning it to dust.

"You have been speaking to Sam? This whole time?" I ask, my mind reeling from the new information.

"I have."

"You both are working together?"

"Is that so hard to believe?"

My mind drifts back to their endless bickering in Olvaria, and I raise my eyebrows.

The prince huffs.

"What is phase two?" I ask, slowly walking over to the bed and sitting down. *If the prince is actually working with Sam, does that mean he actually is here to help me escape? Or does that mean that Sam has also been working with the kings this whole time? He was pretty on edge those last few days.* I shake my head. *No, Sam is not a traitor. He has been my protector for so long now. Why go through all of that work just to hand me over to someone else?* Guilt fills me at questioning Sam, but I shake it away. *Everything is just so confusing right now.*

"Phase two in our mission to take down the palace," the prince replies dryly. The prince starts to approach me, studying me intently.

"I am so fucking confused."

"Why is that?" The prince asks. He now stands directly in front of me.

"Why did you not just tell me from the beginning that you were here to help me instead of betray me? Why go through all of the riddles just to tell me now?"

The prince gives me an odd look. "I never said I was betraying you, dove. I only confirmed that you should not trust me." He picks up a strand of my hair and twirls it between his fingers. He continues to study me, turmoil present in his gaze.

I shake my head at his words, successfully dislodging my hair from his grip. "That makes no sense. Why should I not trust someone here to save me?"

"It might be better to ask yourself that question, dove." He kneels down til he is at eye level with me.

I pause and then ask the only questions I can think of. "What is your motive?" Silence spans between us and I narrow my eyes. "Once the palace is destroyed, are you planning to take me with you? And if so, where to?" *There are only so many places left in Ptheryeth without these kings' influence.* My mind flits briefly to my friend, and Areletos' princess, Philos. *Maybe safe haven could be found with her?*

"Ah, those are better questions." He stands and circles the bed until he is behind me.

"Prince..." I say in warning, doing my best to keep my eyes on him. That stinging feeling of betrayal has started to creep its way back in, and I swallow against the emotion I feel building up in my heart. Although the prince has not admitted outright that he worked with Sam to get here, that is the feeling I am getting. I am also getting the feeling that he has not yet decided to take me with him when he leaves. I can only hope that Sam is not privy to that information, but with my luck that is unlikely. Dread continues to fill me as I feel the prince's body heat radiate at my back. The bed sinks as he leans forward towards me, his breath ghosting across my ear.

"Have you really not given any more thought to my name?"

I move away from him. "What?" *Is he trying to change the subject?*

"You continue to call me prince even though I have given you two hints as to my name. I thought you would have cracked it by now."

I furrow my brows. "I am not sure what this has to do with the conversation and I am getting sick of your toying with me. You are either on my side or you are not. Make a decision. Maybe then I will play into your stupid games." I stare at him angrily, my fists clenched at my sides. He only smirks in return.

"I would reconsider, dove. As I told you before, names have power. Figure out mine and you might finally find the answers you seek."

CHAPTER THIRTY-SIX

Regret

Alaceandra

"*I think this is my cue.*" A small voice causes me to jump. The prince moves quickly, appearing on the other side of the bed in a flash of wind. I shiver at the sudden temperature change. I stare at his back for a moment confused on why he moved in front of me when he so obviously has such little care for me outside of his plans, but give up on trying to figure him out. Despite my energy boost this morning, I am finding as the day goes on that I only feel more and more exhausted. I peak over the prince's shoulder to see the creature I know is standing at the edge of the bed.

Baldar smiles up at me from the other side of the prince. His form is less ghostly and more solid than it had been over the last couple of days. I give him a curious look and he only tilts his little head at me in response.

"Baldar." The prince growls from behind me.

"Oh, so you can see him too," I mumble. *Of course he can, what else would he be blocking you with his body from at the moment?*

"Of course I can, why would I not be able to see him?" The prince echoes my thoughts.

I shake my head. "No reason." *Probably best not to give away that I have been seeing him over the past couple of days right now.*

"Anyway," Baldar interrupts. *"I think it is time for you to start training your other powers."*

"What are you squeaking about now?" the prince asks exasperatedly.

Right. He cannot understand him.

"He wants me to begin training my other powers."

"Which ones?" The prince asks with interest.

"The ones that created me," Baldar replies simply.

I repeat his statement.

"Interesting," the prince says in a low voice.

"Why now?" I ask Baldar internally.

"I have a feeling they might be useful to you in the coming days. Call it a hunch."

I ponder his answer, but decide not to question it further. As weird as this little ferret creature is, his teaching me about my fire did prove useful in Olvaria. Not at saving me from capture, unfortunately, but at least ensuring that not all of my men were injured during the fight. There has to be something to that. *"How do we start?"*

"The same way we started with Sorin."

Miniature elvisera take over my stomach at the thought. I do not know whether the thought makes me nauseated or some other emotion I do not feel the need to acknowledge at the moment. The prince continues to prove that he is not worthy of my affection. I would have thought that at the very least our closeness yesterday would make him open up a bit more, but it seems all it succeeded in doing was making him more cryptic and me more hurt. I was stupid to go against my instincts and allow what happened last night. I am sure of that now. I nibble on my bottom lip.

I glance back at the prince and weigh my options. As good as it sounds to do this completely without him, the issue is training my powers could prove to be a powerful tool in my escape. Especially if I cannot count on outside help to aid me without some motive of their own. If I can have more creatures like Baldar at my side then maybe, just maybe, I will have a chance to get cut of here alive. I sit up straighter as I come to a decision. I will try to train my demoni powers as long as it is safe to do so. The moment the prince fucks up and reveals that he is truly against me, our training will end, consequences be damned. *There might even be a way that we do not have to... be so intimate to gain my powers. I never even asked for another option with Sorin.* If I am going to embark on this kind of training with the prince, I have to ensure that we keep our distance while doing so. *It is the safest option. The prince himself cannot even reassure me as to where his loyalty lies. If I do not take his words as a warning, who knows where I will end up?*

"Be honest with me Baldar. You cannot expect me to kiss the prince. Is there some other way we can start training?" I try, giving Baldar a look of desperation.

I can see the sass enter Baldar's small form. *"Like you were not doing more than kissing last night."*

My face heats at the reminder, and I glare at the little ferret, resentment filling me. *"That was different. You did not have to leave me alone with him when I was in that... state."*

"Was it different, Alaceandra? I distinctly remember informing you that you could have left at any point and taken a shower. It is not my fault that you did not heed my advice. Are you really going to sit there and tell me you did not want yesterday's events to occur?"

I let out a frustrated growl. *"Maybe I did, but that was a stupid decision. Getting in bed with a likely enemy is not exactly something that I am proud of. There has to be another option."*

Baldar huffs at me in response.

"What is he saying?" The prince asks. I turn to him and see his gaze switching from Baldar to me with interest.

"Nothing."

The prince tilts his head. "Somehow I do not quite believe you, dove." A smirk is playing on his lips.

I sigh, rubbing my face. "Baldar was just informing me on how to... compel my powers to appear for training."

"Ah." A twinkle has entered the prince's eye. I can tell he also remembers how this training started last time.

That is just great. If the ground would like to swallow me now, it would not be unwelcome.

"Are we sure this is safe? Especially after what happened the other day?" The prince studies my face.

"I do not know exactly," I slump a little. "Baldar seems to think it is necessary and he was not wrong about training my fire, so..."

"So you are willing to touch me after all."

Already regretting my decision, I scrunch my nose in disgust. "I never said that," I snap. "And if I was... it would be to enhance my abilities only. Do not think otherwise."

"And our interactions last night were for the same reason then, I guess."

I look away from him. "It was for a similar means," I reply curtly.

"I see. So you're afraid then."

"What would I be afraid of?"

"Afraid of touching me. Scared of a repeat performance of last night. Think that you will like it a little too much, dove?"

Anger and embarrassment flood through me. I turn towards the prince. "Condolences to your ego, prince, but that will not happen. Last night was a mistake. Whether we train or not, there will not be a repeat performance."

"Oh, won't there be?"

"No. There will not."

"So you are telling me you haven't thought about my tongue bringing you to orgasm over and over again last night at all today?"

My cheeks burn. "Has not even crossed my mind once."

"Great. Then you will have no issues with these lessons. We should start soon."

"I never said we would start the lessons," I bite back.

"No?" He runs a finger down my arm causing me to shiver. I bat at his hand.

"No. I do not think that it is a good idea."

"So you would rather not have a small army of those guys running about to help you out of here if it means kissing me?" he motions towards Baldar with his statement.

"Oh, I am sorry, are your feelings hurt?"

"Not at all. I just wanted to clarify."

Baldar climbs between us and places a paw on the each of our hands . *"Quit your bickering!"* he squeaks.

We both stop glaring at each other and turn to him.

"I could hear him that time," the prince mumbles.

Baldar looks up to the sky before saying anything else. *"Look. My job is to train Alaceandra. As I was saying before, I have a hunch that she will need these lessons quite soon. Either she can learn from us or she can be forced to train incorrectly by those who wish her harm. Alaceandra, show your palm.*

I grit my teeth and present it. The red swirl shows itself starkly on my skin.

The prince stares at it. "What is that?"

"A warning," Baldar says. *"Too many of those would mean bad news for Alaceandra and the world at large. The creatures of Unduli are already trying to get out by any means necessary. If we are not able to control Alaceandra's power, then when they succeed it will not be pretty. So can you both put aside your stupid fighting at least during training so that we can figure this out?"*

"I do not trust him," I say under my breath.

"What is new? Between the two of us I do not either. I sense that there is more to him than meets the eye, but at the end of the day, he is what you got. You already started to bond with him, more so after last night. There is no backing out of it. Your powers will continue to develop with or without him. Whether you are able to control it or not is totally up to your ability to work with him. Unfortunately, Alaceandra, the heightened state your body is in when you are connected to your bonded is what invokes your powers. There is no other known way to jump start them, and I have a feeling we do not have the time to find one. Now, what will it be?" Baldar turns his tiny face towards me and gives me a hard look.

I look at the prince who only raises a brow at me. Taking a deep breath, I square my shoulders. "Fine. How do we start?"

CHAPTER THIRTY-SEVEN

Tiny Claws

Alaceandra

"We do not have much room in here." I point out. Our quarters are not cramped, but the thought of opening a portal to Unduli does not fill me with confidence.

"It is for the best. We will be able to see where the cracks start easier in here."

"What if Sydon shows up in the middle of this?" I ask, wringing my hands together. Nervousness makes me shift from foot to foot.

"He won't."

"How can you be so sure?"

"Stop stalling. Get to the middle of the room."

I lick my lips. "Fine."

I walk to the most clear area of the space and the prince stands in front of me.

"Okay, start," Baldar commands.

I stare at the prince. He stares at me.

"Are you going to...?" I start.

"I would much rather you did, all things considered," his tone is seductive and teasing.

Somewhere behind me, Baldar sighs.

"Whatever," I mumble, before taking a step forward and grabbing the prince's shoulder. I push up on my tippy toes to reach him, and he complies with my pull by leaning down. I pause before our lips meet. "Do not think this changes anything," I whisper against his mouth.

"Wouldn't dream of it."

With a growl, I capture his lips with mine. Quickly, the prince grasps me around the waist, his lips taking over mine in a primal tangle of tongues. I gasp beneath his lips as tingles of pleasure start to swarm my body. The prince holds me closer picking me up so that I can wrap my legs around his waist. I do so, and the tingles intensify as one of his hands wanders my body. A small moan escapes me, and just as it does, I hear Baldar clear his throat.

"Ahem, horn dogs!"

With a small noise, I push the prince away and look around. He lets me down reluctantly. Around us, glowing orbs fill the air. Once I notice them, they surge into the ground. A crack forms.

I start to step away from the prince, but Baldar's voice stops me. *"Keep your connection with the prince, Alaceandra."*

"Why?" I snap back.

"Releasing him will weaken the magick."

"That did not seem to be a problem when I was summoning you."

"Lucky for you, I am unlike any other demoni. Otherwise you would have started out with a swirl a lot sooner in your journey. Now stop complaining and stay connected to the prince, please."

"Fine." I force myself to lean into the prince's touch. The prince wraps his arms around me protectively as the crack grows.

Baldar skitters over to us moving his body so that he is able to make contact with both the prince and me.

"*Okay now, Alaceandra. I need you to focus on that crack there. What does it feel like in your body?*"

"Feel like?" I echo aloud.

"*Yes. You are connected to it somehow. What does that look like?*"

I delve into my mind trying to imagine the connection point just like I did my fire. The green thread remains steady in my head but it is not that that is connected to the quickly growing crack in the floor. No, instead another thinner thread now sits beside it. It is almost transparent and looks much weaker than the green one.

"A thread," I say aloud. "It sits next to another, stronger green thread, but I do not think the other one is connected to anything in this room."

"*That is a good visual,*" Baldar says encouragingly. "*What color is the other thread?*"

"Purple, maybe?," I reply examining it.

"*Can you touch it?*"

I hear a grunt and my eyes fly open.

Tiny clawed hands are reaching from the floor, trying to find purchase around it. Baldar has left our feet and is now doing his best to keep them at bay, scratching and biting the little hands as they appear. He spots me almost immediately and hisses at me.

"*Keep your eyes closed, Alaceandra!*"

I slam my eyes shut quickly.

"*What is going on out there?*" I ask, internally this time.

"*Do not worry about that. The prince will keep you safe while we go through the exercise. Now, tell me again what color that thread is, Alaceandra.*"

I try to retreat back into my mind and visualize the thread. The image comes back to me but hazier than before. I walk over the lines that are floating through the air in my mind and inspect the smaller one. I get as close as possible, until my vision on the thread starts to sharpen and a pale purple color reveals itself to me once again.

"*Purple. It is purple,*" I respond to Baldar.

"*Good job. Now, can you touch the thread?*"

I extend my hand out towards the thread and try to grasp it in my hand. I feel the sharp tingles of magick more through my system, but just as I try to capture them they slip through my fingers and fall away. I try again to grab at the small thread, but again, instead of having a more corporal form, I feel the magick of the little strand move through my hand before I see it appear again on the other side.

"*No,*" I say after a minute of trying. Growling and the sound of frantic movement start to reach my ears, but I remind myself to keep my eyes closed. My body shifts slightly to the right and then to the left as it feels like the prince is swaying me in his arms. *What is going on out there?*

"*No?*" Baldar repeats.

"*No,*" I confirm.

"*Well, isn't that inconvenient...*" I hear Baldar mumble.

Concern curls my stomach. "*Why is that?*"

"*Do not worry yourself with that. Walk down your line of thread. Do you notice anything different about it? Is it torn? Stronger in areas? Let me know what you see.*"

Obediently, I follow his advice and mentally walk down the line of thread, inspecting every piece to see if I can find any piece of the thread that looks different than the rest. A couple of steps later, I find it. There are two pieces of thread that are thicker than the rest. Connecting them is a thinner thread. It is as if these two pieces of thread were once connected, but have recently frayed apart leaving both ends in excess of magical energy and the middle lacking. I continue looking down the thread and notice two other pieces that are similarly frayed. I relay my findings to Baldar.

"That is not great, Alaceandra, but we can work with it. Try to see if you can grab both of those thicker ends."

A horrendous scream meets my ears, and it takes everything in me to keep my eyes shut and focus on the task at hand. I try to grab at the two ends of fraying thread. Surprisingly, I am able to successfully grab them.

"Got them!" I say excitedly.

"Perfect. See if you can pull the two in front of you together. The thread should heal itself pretty quickly if you can get those strands to meet. That is what we want to happen."

I nod, but I know that he cannot see me. I tug at the little thread, doing my best to bunch the two sides together. The magick fights me. Little ripples of energy make their way up on either side and bite at my hands making me release the thread.

"Alaceandra, I need you to focus!" I hear Baldar yell before more grunts follow.

"Sorry!" I yell back. Placing my hand back on the thread, I tug again. The magick energy again fights back, and I wince against the small bites that attack my hands. Using all of my strength, I finally am able to pull the thread together. I smile in victory as it starts to weave around itself, healing the fraying edges.

"Good job, Alaceandra!" Baldar praises me before I can even tell him the good news. *"Fuck! Watch out!"* Just as the threads are about to fully knit themselves back together, a searing sensation travels up my arm. I scream, and my eyes fly open. My bracelet is burning an angry scarlet, searing itself into my wrist and if that were not enough a tiny rat like creature has attached himself to my arm and has bitten down hard. The

prince bats the creature away, but I notice that the entire room is being almost overrun with the little beasts.

"What is happening?" I whisper, both terrified and amazed by the creatures around me. I hold my arm in my hand as blood starts to leak from the wound that the little rat-like creature created. I am in the prince's arms. He holds me tightly as he sends bursts of wind magick at the small creatures in an attempt to keep them at bay in their portal. Baldar does his part ripping into the ones attempting to climb from the portal. The one that bit me must have snuck through their defenses.

"Alaceandra, no!" Suddenly, the smaller crack in the room expands and more creatures start to escape flooding into the room. *"Shit! Abort. Alaceandra, say the closing spell."*

"The closing spell?"

"The phrase I taught you the last time this happened."

Beams of light start shooting from Baldar's body and into the creatures forcing them back into the crack in the ground.

Ignoring both the pain in my wrist as well as the actively bleeding wound in my arm, I wrack my brain for what he is talking about when the words come to me. "Back into the portals of where you once were. Your time in this battle has yet to occur."

The little creatures hiss at me and scramble back into the floor. Baldar backs away quickly as a blackened light shines through the room and the crack slowly starts to become smaller and smaller until it vanishes all together. We all stare at one another for a minute, before I sweep my gaze around the room trying to see if there are any more of those creatures remaining, but do not spot any. Luckily, I am not quite as tired as when I created that crack with the prince the first two times so instead of passing out, I just slump in the prince's arms.

"What the fuck just happened?" A familiar searing sensation burns its way through my palm and I glance at it. Another swirl has made an appearance at the base of my ring finger. "Another failed portal then?"

"Unfortunately," Baldar mutters making his way over to the bed and slumping on its surface.

The prince walks us over to the bed as well and sets me on the mattress before sitting beside me. Baldar stands up one more time, but only to situate himself between us so that his body is making contact with the both of us.

"We only have so many attempts, Alaceandra. You have to stay focused," Baldar chides, tiredly.

"I was bitten," I defend aloud.

"Which is something that might happen. Since we do not have all your men here, it will be more difficult to keep those creatures away while we are preparing them to listen to you. They are angry assholes."

"Why is that?" I ask.

"Unduli's ruler is missing for one, but also that frayed thread could also be a cause. They only really listen to those they are connected to. If your connection to them is damaged, it will be harder for them to discern if you are friend or foe."

"And this is a needed lesson right now?" I clarify once again.

"I am afraid so."

"My apologies that one got to you, dove." The prince sounds distraught. I look at him. "I do not know how they passed my defenses."

"Oh don't beat yourself up," Baldar snickers. *"They were overwhelming us. I knew some would be waiting at the portal's edge but was not aware of the sheer magnitude. They must be really feeling antsy down there. It was quite impressive how much we were able to accomplish today. I felt it when*

Alaceandra connected her thread. The next time they should be a bit less aggressive."

I groan. "Next time?"

"Yes. You need to be able have some mastery on this skill soon. At least enough to be able to get some of the demoni to follow you. I promise it will make your life a little easier and prepare you for the next stage."

"Next stage?"

"Nothing to worry about now." Baldar almost imperceptibly removes his little leg from the prince's form so that his next words are only heard by me. *"I will let you both get some rest. As a note, Alaceandra, your powers should be a bit more stable for the rest of the night so do not worry about any... mishaps due to your horn doggedness,"* he teases. *"I will see you tomorrow."* Baldar's little form vanishes into thin air. *Ugh, great.*

CHAPTER THIRTY-EIGHT

Exploration

Alaceandra

I need space. I stare down at the prince sleeping beside me on the bed. Slowly, I maneuver away from him doing my best to not shake the bed too much as I extract myself. Luckily, the prince does not seem to wake up, too exhausted from our training session with Baldar. The cut in my arm has thankfully scabbed over since that little rat bit me, and I thank Ptheryeth that the wound shows no sign of being infected. My wrist is starting to look better as well, the skin around my bracelet more of a dull red now instead of glowing and irritated. Keeping my eyes on the prince, I back away from the bed on light feet and cross to the door. Once I have successfully made it over, I try the handle. *Unlocked again. How strange.* Peeling the door open with the utmost care, I cringe as it creaks on its hinges. My eyes shoot to the prince's form still unmoving on the bed, and I breathe a sigh of relief before sliding my body out of the room and carefully shutting the door behind me. No movement meets my ears from the other side of the door, and when I look around me, there are not any guards immediately present. *Well, that is a plus at least.* With the prince now being a suspect on my radar and Sam seemingly working with him, it has made it even more clear to me that I am on my own in finding my way outside of these walls. In order to do that though, I need to learn more about my environment. I have stayed in the dark too long. It is finally time I search for answers on my own.

I dart through the halls of the palace, in search of sanctuary. I would go to Sorin, but I know that I will be quickly found out if I do. *No, there must be other secrets in this palace that I can find. I just have to keep searching.* The dark halls almost seem to close in on me as I run. Unlike the halls around my room, soldier's are patrolling these corridors. As much as I want to avoid them, the sheer amount present make it hard for me to stay undetected. I see them spot me as I weave through, but not one stops me from proceeding forward. *I am not sure whether to be thankful of that fact or suspicious,* I think to myself bitterly. I do see some of the guards start to run towards something upon sight of me, so it is more than likely they were asked to report my movements to someone rather than stop me from leaving my room. As if on cue, a voice startles me from my thoughts as I round a corner.

"I think she went this way, sir."

"Thank you." Sydon's familiar voice echoes through the halls. I hear his footsteps echo closer and panic seizes in my chest. A door slightly ajar in the hall catches my attention, and I quickly throw myself through it. A long, dark hall greets me on the other side, and I carefully make my way down it. My bare feet cold against the stony floor. At the end of the hall lies a spiral staircase that disappears downwards into darkness. It looks like no one has been down this pathway in years. Little bugs scuttle across the wall, and there are multiple webs hanging dangerously low from the ceiling. I shiver and glance behind me for a moment, considering going back. *You said you wanted space, Alaceandra. What better space is there than down an abandoned staircase?* Licking my lips, I trace a finger over where my pin lays tucked into the clothing at my side, and carefully descend.

Sydon

When the guards told me that Alaceandra was walking about the castle, I was impressed by the princess' growing boldness. I instructed the guards to keep her quarters unlocked. Until today, the princess had not even attempted escape since her last foray through the castle looking for Sorin. Obviously, I was curious as to where she would end up, so I instructed them to keep a close eye on her, but not to stop her until her final location is known. I also told them to let me know where she stopped along the way. Unfortunately, one of my guards got a little bit nervous about her wandering near places that she should not be and hurried me to find her, by the time we arrived though, she had disappeared.

"Has anyone seen where the princess went?" I ask the remaining guards in the hall.

"No, sir. Sorry, sir. She was just here," one of them answers.

"Fan out and find her then. Her last location was near a restricted area of the palace. If I find out that she went down there, your asses will be on the line," I growl.

The guards run in each direction searching for the missing princess of Tikilium. Unluckily for them, I am sure that Alaceandra did, in fact, venture into the library. I have to hold back a smirk. *These guards need better training.* I think to myself, amused. *I am sure Rafton will give them hell in their lessons, though. A couple of extra exercises should be enough to teach them something.*

I stare at the door to the library staircase. The palace was built around this very library in the foothills of the Dark Lands. It holds an ancient magick that can be helpful in ensuring wanderers find what they seek when on the hunt for answers. Although I assumed that Alaceandra would find herself down there at some point in her stay, I had not guessed it would be so soon. Once a wanderer finds itself in its depths an archaic spell is cast over the space, keeping them safe from outside elements to research for two hours. *Which means I will not be able to retrieve her until those two hours have passed.* I sigh. *I hope she does not find anything that will get her in too much trouble.*

That library has also been, regrettably, where I had been doing much of my research on Alaceandra's prophecy. The text that remains in the Dark Lands is unfinished and manipulated from the original. I have been trying to figure out why that is. If she finds that research in the stacks of books it would be... unfortunate. I will just have to hope that something else occupies her time down there. I sigh and return to my own room. It is one of the largest rooms in the palace, decorated in deep shades of blacks and blues. The ceiling of the room twinkles with yellow gems mimicking stars in the night sky. I walk over to my desk in the corner and find one of the blue gems within. The rock will turn red the moment the spell is released. Until then, the best thing to do now is wait.

CHAPTER THIRTY-NINE

New Knowledge

Alaceandra

When I reach the bottom of the staircase, the smell of old paper and mildew greets me. My hand knocks a small button on the wall, and slowly, firelight starts to twinkle around the room. My mouth drops open in surprise. In front of me lies an old library. Huge wooden shelves line the room filled with leather and velvet covered books. A warm magick settles over my skin, but the feeling of it does not startle me. Instead, it encourages me to explore the room further. Slowly, I walk deeper into the room and see that there is one book laid open on one of the tables, as if someone had not finished reading and had left it to take a short break elsewhere in the palace.

What do you say? I let my fingers brush the edge of the pages, trying decipher the unfamiliar words. As I do, a soft glow shines from the page, and the words reconfigure themselves to a language I can understand. I jump back in surprise, but the text remains the same. Slowly, I approach the magical text again and, picking a random line in the book, I squint down and read the words:

Diaries, Dictionaries, and Drawings .... 423.1 TEL

I search through the other lines of the book only to find more titles paired with number and letter characters. *Is this some kind of directory?* I do my best to try to decode what the little number and letter pairings mean but become stuck quickly. *I think the best thing to do is to walk the place to get my bearings. Maybe the numbers will make sense after.* I start to explore the little library, its silence bringing peace to my racing thoughts as I search each title on the shelf carefully. Finally, I stumble upon the book that I saw in the little directory. My fingers trace over the gold lettering on the side of the leather bound behemoth of a book and I pull it away from the shelves. Carrying it away, I walk towards the back of the room where I find some leather chairs and sit in one of them.

Other than the cobwebs, the room itself had very little presence of the bugs that made them. I cross my fingers and toes hoping that remains true. *If I encounter a spider down here, the entire palace will know where I am hiding,* I think to myself wryly. The walls down here are smooth. Smoother than those in the gym or halls, making me think that this library was once lively and packed with people. Why else would they have taken such good care of it? I snuggle down into the chair and flinch as my arm grazes its leather. *Ow!* I shift slightly, inspecting my wound. It looks to have scabbed over, but the skin around it is now inflamed. I grit my teeth and carefully lower my arm and crack open the book.

Words and their definitions meet my eyes. Some are printed within the book by some sort of stamping tool and others look to be handwritten. I flip through the book; as I do, I notice that some of the words are paired with anecdotes on where what they describe can be found and some are paired with drawings. *How interesting.*

I start scanning the pages marveling at the beauty of the drawings within the book when the picture of a creepy feline creature catches my eye. The creature is colored black and the eyes of the picture are left blank as if the eyes are devoid of pupils. I shiver. *What is this?* This creature's definition was written by hand.

Grantador: Need portal to summon.
Origin: Unduli.
Can grant wishes, but **beware** volatile creature. Services come with a price.

Next to the description, a star is written in a different colored ink. The words *this one!* are written beside the star in strangely familiar handwriting. I run my finger over it, trying to remember where I had seen the handwriting before. A strange sort of magickal energy races through me, and I pull my hand away. Glancing at the picture again, I cringe and turn the page ready to have its haunting eyes off of me. *Okay, no more of that... I wonder what else this book has in it.*

I continue flipping through the book until something else catches my eye. Taking up an entire cross section of the book is a long handled sword with a crescent shaped blade. The blade looks like it has some sort of pattern drawn on it that echoes down the handle. Not learning my lesson from the last time I placed my hand on this book's pages, I trace the pattern. Luckily, no more weird energy runs up my arm. Along with the dark inked etchings in the blade and handle, it looks like someone has added some leaves and skulls around the drawing. My fingers drift over those too, and I smile down at the page. *Pretty.*

My eyes flit to see if I can figure out what this blade is called. In small lettering on the corner of the page, I find it.

> **Scythe:** *Used for reaping plants, grains, and souls.*
> **Synonyms can include:** *Sickle, pruner, blade*

I blink at the description. *Plants, grains,... and souls? What an odd combination.* The memory of the prince's riddles echo through my brain:

My name lies in the multitude; it begins at the hands of where crop and life ends.

I am an object a reaper holds. When you speak of me, it is to describe a diverse range of intricacies.

Then his other statement about thinking that I would know the answer by now rings through my head making me scowl. *Pompous asshole. Watch me solve it.* I stare back at the word and picture in front of me. This word seems like it can apply to the reaper portion of the riddle, but which iteration of the word could it be? I flip through the book and look for sickle, pruner and blade. The only other word related to a Scythe that could maybe fit is the word sickle. A smaller blade is pictured next to the weapon, but this tool has no drawn engravings on it.

> **Sickle:** *the cutting device (as of a reaper) consisting of a bar with a series of cutting elements.*
> **Synonyms can include:** *bayonet, scythe, shiv*

That definition also contains the word reaper, but nothing about souls. *Hmm... It is more likely the first half of his name has something to do with the word Scythe, but what about the second...* I flip through the book looking for the word multitude. Finding it, I read through the definition.

> **Multitude:** *describing something that is numerous.*
> **Synonyms can include:** *horde, abundance, heaps*

I wrinkle my nose at the definition. None of the words seem to sound like exactly what the riddle was describing. *Lies in the multitude....* My brain fixates on the wording for another moment. Throwing a shot in the dark I look up the word numerous. *Technically the word lies in the definition...*

> **Numerous:** *Great in number; many.*
> **Synonyms can include:** *copious, countless, various*

Okay... not super helpful. I sigh, rubbing a hand across my face. *Do any of these synonyms describe something that is a diverse range maybe?* It feels as if I have spent an hour digging through this book. I doubt Sydon has stopped looking for me, but luckily it seems nobody saw me disappear into this room. I look around. The library is still quiet, nothing moving, nothing out of place. I would stop my digging, but I feel as if I am so close to solving the prince's stupid riddles. I nibble on my bottom lip and flip to the front of the book searching through the "c"'s. *Okay so not copious...* I think to myself looking at the definition. I search the words looking for the next word. *Nor is it countless. Ugh.* Finally, I flip to the back of the book and stare at the description for various.

> **Various:** *To describe a diverse range of several different kinds of people, things, places, etc.*
> **Synonyms can include:** *Diverse, varied, numerous*

Well, that is too easy.... I look at the page in disbelief. *So it has something to do with a scythe and the word various..., but what?* Footsteps cause me to shut the book quickly and stand up from my chair. Racing back over to where I found the book I slip it back in its place and hunker down in the aisle. *No, no, no! I was so close.*

"Princess, I know you are down here." Sydon's voice echoes through the room. "I will ignore that fact if you come with me now." Sydon's voice gets closer and closer. His voice is a mix between annoyance and amusement. I stay hidden in my little corner of the library, unwilling to reveal myself. "I am going to find you soon enough. Do not waste my time." He sighs. Slowly, I creep through the stacks of books, using his footsteps to track him through the library, I carefully move around him. *I just need a little more time to myself...*

His footsteps stop suddenly causing me to freeze. "I can hear you," he whispers. My heart jackhammers in my throat and suddenly I am up and speeding towards the spiral staircase. His footsteps pound into the floor behind me, and I am just about to reach the first step when his arm wraps around my waist causing me to fall into him. I squeal and kick out, nailing him in the knee. He grunts but does not release his grip.

"Stop struggling!" He growls.

I ignore him twisting and turning in his arms trying to break free. The ferocity of my struggles causes my wound to once again break open. I hiss in pain. "What. Do. You. Want?" I puff out, clawing at his arms. My blood starts to trickle down my arm.

"Alaceandra! Stop!" My body freezes.

He releases me, before turning my body around. Grabbing my arm gently he picks it up and inspects my wound. "You are injured," he says matter-of-factly. I do not respond. I cannot, my lips frozen by some kind of magick that this man holds. The only part of my body that still seems to be functioning properly are my eyes. I narrow them at Sydon dangerously. My heart races as I try to force myself not to panic. *Stupid powerful man.* Placing his hand over my wound, a warmth fills my arm. I watch warily as the skin knits itself back together, until the only trace of the wound left are the flecks of blood covering my skin. The redness around my bracelet also fades away until not even a hint of its existence remains. "I am going to release you from my magick, but if you try to run I will cast it again. Do not test me. Blink twice if you understand."

I comply. The magick falls off of me quickly, and I cross my arms. "I do not like it when you do that," I mutter.

"Then stop disobeying me."

"What do you want?"

"You need to go back to your rooms."

I tilt my head. "Why?"

"You should not have left to begin with."

I let out a puff of air. "If you meant to keep me within my quarters, why not lock the door?"

Sydon rolls his eyes. "Come." He starts to ascend the staircase.

Begrudgingly, I follow.

CHAPTER FORTY

Passages

The Prince

I knew the dove was leaving the moment she left the bed. Feigning sleep, I wait until she slides through the door before getting up to follow her. *What is she up to?* I was surprised to see that the door to our quarters was unlocked. I would have assumed that they would have kept us secure in here, but it does not look like that is the case. *How idiotic.* I observe the dove as she flits through the halls. She races through completely unaware of me behind her, which is unsurprising. The wind makes my footsteps lighter and harder to detect. Couple that with the fact that the dove looks completely preoccupied with something on her mind and she makes for an easy victim. *We will have to fix that.* I follow her until I spot the first guard. A bronze guard that studies her curiously as she passes by. Seeing that she has his attention, and he does not seem like he has much intention to stop her wandering, I take a left instead of continuing on my pursuit. *Let the dove find her own path. I have some scouting to do before Sam arrives.*

The walls down this part of the palace are less worn than those near the dining hall and the gym. These halls have jagged edges. The flooring uneven in its rockiness. I stick to the walls and glide through them quickly, searching to see if I can find anything more nondescript to explore. *This place must hide some more secrets. It would not be so large if it was not trying to keep things cloaked deep within its walls.* Finding another hall that looks even more jagged, I turn down it, keeping an eye out to see if I can spot any soldiers patrolling the area. Turning another corner I spot three teal guards. Two pace the intersection in front of another hall. The other stands at its entrance.

"Patrol duty sucks." I hear one of them say.

"It's necessary," the one standing at the hall's entrance says. "With the king out of commission, we cannot have anyone wandering down here and finding our only hold on the princess."

"I feel like we have much more leverage than just this one man," the other pacing guard mumbles. "He is passed out anyway, it's not like the princess is going to carry him away without being spotted."

"Stop questioning our orders," the middle one hisses. "King Demetrius says this is important so it is important."

"I guess," the first one mumbles. "But I heard rumors that Sydon is taking her down here to see the man anyway. If he was so important to keep her away from, why would she even get visitation privileges?"

"Idiot, it is so she knows he is here. If she thinks he is dead then we will have much more trouble controlling her. By the sounds of it, they are lovers." The other pacing guard reports.

A look of disgust crosses over the other guard's face. "Ew. The princess is fucking her guard? Does the prince know?"

The other pacing shoulder shrugs. "Not sure. Not that it matters. His duties don't change either way."

"I guess..."

"If you both do not shut the fuck up, I will make you."

The other two guards' mouths close with a snap.

"Thank you," the middle guard says peering around the room. Looking for any movement likely.

Interesting information... I think to myself. *My father would not be pleased with them talking so freely about what they are guarding, but I am quite grateful for their inadequacy. It seems Sorin is here after all. That does explain the dove's compliance with the kings. I know how much she cares for her guard. Seen it first hand.* I chuckle to myself. *Now that I know where he is, he will need to be extracted before I can convince the dove to go with our plans. Which means I need to inform Sam.*

Carefully, I dig in my pocket and grab a small tracking device and place it on the wall. The device is small enough that it should not be detected by any of the guards patrolling the premises. Sam and I agreed that this would be the best way for him to make quick work at retrieving Sorin if he was indeed in the palace walls before he came and aid in our escape. Turning around, I carefully make my way back to our chambers and sit on the bed, pondering my training with Alaceandra earlier. It was strange to see her change so suddenly in her mood towards me. Although I know that my dishonesty and secrets annoy her, I had not suspected that it would cause this much agitation which might be foolish of me. After all, this is a high stress environment and I do tend to bring out a sense of rebelliousness in her. I smile. I would be lying if I said I did not like to see her so passionate. It has been quite a joy to watch her evolve. That shy little princess that arrived in Helomasi is not the same as the fierce warrior that I saw today in this palace's so-called training course. I wonder how her upcoming trials will shape her. *If she can survive them.* Sighing, I lay back onto the bed. I know her inner turmoil about me can only last so long. Even our brief kiss today has our souls calling louder for each other. It seems the stronger we make each other the more our bodies crave the other. I know she must feel it too.

A sting of regret hits my chest and I grit my teeth against it. *Maybe there is a way to save Helomasi and keep the little dove?* That ferret hinted that it might be possible for her to conquer her portal powers without it being the death of her. Watching her glow with magick as she cracked open the realms was a bit inspiring. I have a feeling she might have been able to get control of those creatures if it were not for that demoni-rat getting through my defenses and biting her, breaking her focus.

Suddenly a zap of magick zings through my body, causing me to smile. *Ah, she has figured out my name.* Pure satisfaction sings within me with the knowledge of what exactly my little dove was up to on her trip outside of her quarters. *Yes, she is a lot stronger than when I first met her. Let's hope that is enough.*

CHAPTER FORTY-ONE

Answers

Alaceandra

Sydon leads me down the halls, keeping a close eye on me as we make our way back to my room. Nevertheless, my mind is hyper fixated on the prince's riddles. I know I am on the verge of figuring out his name, I just need to figure out how to get the pieces together. *Does the prince mean that his name is literally the words Scythe and Various? Like a first name last name situation? Or some amalgamation of the two words? Maybe he means that the name is something related to them? No. If that was the case the riddles would not have directed me to them so obviously. I test out different iterations in my mind. Various scythe man. Varscythious. Scyvarious? Or maybe Syverious? That would be a much more common spelling...* I let out a sound of frustration causing Sydon to look at me briefly.

"What is on your mind?" he asks before turning his attention once again forward. "Your thoughts are so loud I can almost hear them," he grumbles.

"If you could hear them then you would know what it is I am thinking about," I snap back.

"Fair," Sydon acknowledges. "But as I said I can *almost* hear them. What your mind is actually turning over is unknown to me."

"Likely due to the fact that it is none of your concern."

Sydon snorts. "When it comes to you, everything is my concern."

"I am sure that has to do with me becoming a precious investment, yes? To you and your corrupt kings?"

"Something like that." He laughs causing me to stare at him. "So what is it? Does it have something to do with why you were wandering around the library?"

I do not answer him. Instead, I glare at his back.

"I will take that as a yes then," he mumbles.

"I will not be providing you with more information to use against me."

Sydon chuckles. "That was not my intention."

"As if I am to believe that." Silence spans between us for a bit of time. I follow closely behind Sydon as we weave our way back through the halls. The pathway feels longer somehow. Likely due to the fact that we seem to be in no rush ever since we made it back up those spiral stairs. "You seem to be in a good mood today," I comment.

"I am most certainly not in a bad one."

"And that is because..." I lead.

"I will not be providing you with more information to use against me," he echoes.

I roll my eyes. "Right." Another few moments of silence. "Thank you for healing my arm," I mumble, spotting the door to my chambers up ahead.

"Do not mention it," Sydon replies, humor apparent in his tone. "I would not guess you would be willing to share with me how you got it.

I am not aware of any animals that would cause that extensive of a bite mark on the premises."

"It is unsurprising you would not be aware. The palace is so vast, why trouble yourself with a rodent problem?" What I am surprised about though, is that he makes no mention of the reddened wrist he healed. He has to know that I was using magick. The band around my wrist is his best indication as to that fact, yet, although he has every opportunity to comment on it, he does not. *What is your game plan?*

We arrive at the door and Sydon eyes me suspiciously. "Why indeed," he says more to himself than to me. Moving around me, he opens the door to my chambers. "Your dinner will be served in your rooms today. If you run into any more... problems. Please do tell a guard. I will have one posted outside to satisfy your requests."

I am sure that is their exact purpose... not. I give Sydon a sardonic smile. "How very kind of you."

"I do take pride in being a kind captor, Alaceandra."

"Hmm... if you keep working on it, maybe one day it will be believable."

He smiles at me. "See you in the morning."

I give him a tight-lipped smile in return and walk into my room without replying to him. Slamming the door in his face, I let out a frustrated sigh as I hear him chuckle once again on the other side. *Bastard.*

"I trust you enjoyed your outing then," the prince says from the bed. I jump in surprise.

"I thought you would still be sleeping."

"Did you?"

"Yes," I reply feeling all kinds of flustered.

"So you decided to... what? Go out and flirt with your captors?"

His statement catches me off guard causing me to give him a sharp look.

"I was not flirting," I snap.

"Oh, dove, I have watched you for months now. That was definitely flirting."

I glare at him. "You know what? I am not surprised that you would mistake hateful barbs for playful banter. It is your specialty."

"More like yours," the prince says, sitting up. I notice that the prince looks tense instead of his usual carefree self and a small smile takes over my face as I come to a realization.

"Sounds like someone is jealous."

The room seems to grow ten degrees colder as a chill sweeps through it. A shiver rolls over me and I look back to where the prince once was to find that he is now closer than before. He stands about a foot away from me. Oh so slowly he starts to circle me, his expression dangerous.

"And if I am, little dove?" His voice is icy.

"I-" I stutter a little on my words, his body language taking a turn from what I expected of him. "I did not take you for the jealous type."

"Why is that?" The prince is now behind me, his fingers twirling a strand of my hair. I turn quickly. *He is so close.*

"You did not have a problem with—"

"Your guard dogs, dove? No. I didn't, but they are not the same as you placing your affections with that guard now, are they?"

"I am not placing my affections in him," I defend.

"If you say so. Just remember what we talked about in Olvaria."

"And what is that?" I ask, my fingers are clenched into fists as I do my best to keep him in my line of sight. He has started to circle me once more. Once he has me where he wants me, he starts to advance. I back up in time with his steps forward, doing my best to maintain my distance.

"You. Are. Mine." He growls. His statement makes it hard for me to breathe. My heart races in my chest as my brain tries to deny his words. My back is now placed firmly against the wall of the room. The rocks dig into me as I shrink against it, their roughness a welcome distraction.

I place my hands against his chest attempting to push him back, but he does not budge.

"I am not yours," I growl back at him. "I am no one's property and even if I was, I would not give myself over to someone who loves to try to play both sides."

"Playing both sides is what wins this war, little dove."

"That is not true—"

"It is."

"It is not. It is what ensures that you will never know stability in your relationships, though. How can you expect anyone to desire someone who plays such dirty games?"

"You love my dirty games, dove. That is why, although I know you are pissed off at me right now, if I were to stick my fingers in your little cunt they would be soaked with your juices. You live for my games, dove. Whether you like them or not."

"That is not true."

"Is it not? Would you like to wager that?"

I clench my thighs, pissed off at my own body's reaction to his nearness.

"Just as I thought."

"You know nothing. It is a biological reaction. Nothing more."

"No? Then let me prove I have your mind as well." He places a hand on my face before raking his fingers into my hair. "What did you get up to when you left our quarters earlier?"

I scrunch my nose in confusion. *He cannot know what I was doing.*
I would have seen him if he was watching me in the library. I open my
mouth to deny I was doing anything, but he speaks again before I get the
opportunity.

"You were solving my riddles, weren't you?"

I start to shake my head, but the prince only tightens his grip on my
hair. Not to the point of pain, but just enough to stop the movement.

"Do not try to deny it, Alaceandra. My magick can sense when this
particular riddle's answer is found. Now tell me, what did you come up
with?"

My mind races through all the iterations that I thought up until it
lands on the one that would make the most sense. "Syverious?" I whisper.

He hums in satisfaction. "You got it. Remember that name. I intend
to make you scream it before the night is over." Then he kisses me.

CHAPTER FORTY-TWO

Threads that Bind Us

Alaceandra

I do not push the prince away. Instead, my body melts into his as our lips collide. The prince makes quick work of scooping me up from the wall, depositing me onto the bed, and ripping off my shirt, allowing my breasts to be fully exposed. My hands rake through his hair and I tug on the strands as he hovers over me on the bed. I am rewarded for my efforts by a quick nip on the lips. I yelp, pulling a chuckle from the prince.

Quickly, my pants are being ripped down my legs, exposing my pussy to the cold air. I shiver at the sudden temperature change. The cold of the air is replaced by the prince's warm fingers as the part my folds, testing my aching pussy for wetness I know he will find. A growl of appreciation fills the room as the prince's fingers make contact. He pulls said fingers up to show me how soaked they truly are.

"Open your mouth, dove," his gravelly voice commands me. "Taste what I do to you."

My heart stops and then restarts at his words, but I comply with his demand, letting my lips fall open to his invading fingers. He rubs them up and down my tongue, his movements in and of themselves erotic. I cannot help the moan that escapes as my own wetness coats my tongue.

"Fuck, dove," the prince says, his eyes a blazing lavender. He pulls his fingers from my lips slowly tracing his thumb over them before he completely pulls away. "My turn." His smile is predatory as he sinks in between my thighs. "Do you remember my rules?"

"Yes," I say softly, embarrassment coloring my cheeks.

"I didn't hear you."

"Yes," I repeat more firmly.

"Good girl."

I gasp as I feel his warm breath dance across my pussy before his mouth closes in. As his tongue circles my clit, the breeze also joins in on tormenting me. Warm and cold wind skates across my nipples teasing them into stiff peaks. The prince's hands dig into my hips as he laps at my clit like it is his favorite meal. My orgasm crests quickly almost taking me by surprise. I rush out the words the prince wants to hear quickly.

"May I come?"

He pauses in his assault. "Depends. Do you remember my name, little dove?"

I nod.

"Then tell me, what is it?"

"Sy—" He plunges two fingers into me, curling them until they hit just the right spot all while resuming his assault. "VERIOUS!" I finish his name on a scream.

He laughs, his face still buried in my pussy. His movements slow, before he pulls his fingers out of me and sits up. I whimper at the loss, aftershocks still racing through me.

"I am going to fuck you now." Syverious states. "If you are opposed to that, I would recommend letting me know." He stays still in his position between my legs, his eyes devouring me as much as his mouth did only moments ago.

Do I really want this? I ask myself. *Am I really going to let this temporary insanity go that far?* I stare into the prince's eyes and the answer hits me with so much certainty it almost takes my breath away. *Yes. I do. As much as I do not trust this man, it is very likely that I may only have so many pleasurable experiences left in this world. Once the king wakes up and decides on my punishment, it is very likely that the result of that will not end well for me. If the prince decides to fuck me over after all of this so be it. At least I can say when I had the chance I lived without regret, because the prince is right. As much as I would like to deny my attraction to him, the man catches both my body's and my brain's attention with just a simple glance. It would be a shame to not know if that outward arrogance translates to performance in the bedroom.*

"I.. I want you to fuck me." My words are breathier then I intend them to be.

"What was that?" The prince asks. The smile on his face letting me know that he heard those words, he just wants me to repeat them.

I nibble my bottom lip before repeating my words. "I want you to fuck me," I say. This time my voice come out stronger, more steady.

He leans forward and captures my lips with his, dominating me with his mouth. My fingers claw at his shoulder blades as my body wills me to get closer to him. Finally, he releases my lips and strips out of his own clothing. My breath catches in my throat as I take him in. He turns to toss his clothing behind him and my eyes race over the gorgeous elvisera tattoo on his back. He turns back to me and my eyes drink in each ridge of his chest, his abs, his... My eyes widen. I had almost forgotten how impressive the prince's cock is. I swallow as the memory of having it between my lips flashes in my mind's eye.

I wonder how he will feel inside of me. The prince notices my eyes and smirks at me before walking back over to the bed. Grasping both my thighs firmly, he pulls me until my hips are balanced right at the edge of the bed. Then he snakes a hand down my body testing my entrance with his finger before tracing tight, slow circles around my clit.

I jerk against him and moan. I hear his growl of appreciation in response and then... then I feel his cock nudging at my entrance. My eyes fly open. I had not even realized they were closed. They connect with his lavender ones as he, oh so slowly, pushes into me. I feel every inch of him as he seats himself inside of me. Once every inch of him has entered my body, he hangs his head.

"Fuck, Alaceandra, you are so fucking tight," he groans. "Hold on, dove, I am afraid I will not be as gentle as you are used to."

I lick my lips and nod. He continues to work tiny circles around my clit as we sit in stillness for another moment. I wriggle against his grip on my legs, but he holds me steadfast.

"You can come as much as you like," he says. "As long as it is my name on your lips when you do. Understood?"

I nod again.

"I want to hear it."

"I understand," I say on a moan.

"Good."

He starts to move. Slowly at first, but then his pace picks up until he is slamming in and out of me. His finger continuously circles my clit in time with the movement of his hips forcing my pleasure higher and higher. I moan as waves of pleasure rip through me. My body jerking back and forth on the bed with the force of his thrusts. The angle of his cock hitting that perfect place inside of me. My moans quickly become louder and louder as my orgasm builds until suddenly warmth covers me as my orgasm hits me abruptly, his name a plea on my lips. He pulls my legs higher, deepening the angle of of his thrusts and prolonging the delicious shocks racing through my body. He pauses for a moment as my body spasms around him, his panting breaths a beautiful symphony to my ears.

Before I can catch my breath, the prince is moving once again, his thrusts now more measured than before. Sparks start to light on my skin before they are sucked away almost instantly, causing twinkling lights to dazzle throughout the room. The wind continues to tease at every inch of my skin not covered by the prince's body causing me to pant as tiny tingles of pleasure zip their way across my skin. Syverious leans over my body to smooth away the hair from my sweaty face, never once losing his rhythm. I clench around him and he hums beneath his breath.

"I wish I had a mirror to show you how gorgeous your face looks right now. You look so fucking pretty when you come all over my cock."

Holy shit. A whimper falls from lips at his words. His thrusts start to become more uneven. I scratch at his back as I rock against the bed, doing my best to pull him closer as my mind becomes more and more hazy. His hand travels between us, his fingers once again causing my brain to go haywire as he traces tiny circles around my clit. I feel stuck in a perpetual state of pleasure, my first orgasm never quite ending as another one picks up where the other left off.

With a scream, my second orgasm hits me. Darkness takes over my vision as the feeling of something snapping into place overwhelms me causing tears to spring to my eyes. I feel Syverious jerk as his own orgasm takes over and he fills me with his cum. We fall together in a heap onto the bed, our bodies humming with satisfaction. The prince lifts up slightly and allows his hand to trace the side of my face. A small smile present on his lips. I smile back at him slowly. After another moment, the prince stands, the lack of his body weight leaving me cold.

"That position can't be comfortable for you," he says more to himself than to me. He pulls me from the bed and lays us both down so that we are no longer hanging off the edge.

We sit in silence for a couple of minutes. My body now laying comfortably on top of the prince's as he runs his fingers soothingly over my hair. My heart is still racing from my orgasms and I can tell from the prince's racing heart that he is feeling much the same. The thought is strangely comforting. A knock sounds on the door breaking us from our moment of peace.

"Dinner!"

CHAPTER FORTY-THREE

Tattoos

Alaceandra

The prince— Syverious— and I sit across from each other on the floor, our two plates of food at our feet. The contents of our dinner today look to be some kind of noodle dish with a white sauce and a sprinkle of some kind of green herb over top. Syverious is shirtless, the expanse of his muscular chest on full display as he brings each twirl of noodles to his mouth and sucks them down. I, on the other hand am dressed in Syverious' missing shirt. I blush slightly as I eat my first bite of food. I watched as Syverious ate the first few bites of both food to make sure that the meal was safe and I cannot help but be a bit touched by the fact that he noticed the tradition between Sydon and me. Even though I have yet to be poisoned here, the anxiety that I have around food is still quite severe. It is strangely comforting to know that Syverious would be willing to be poisoned in my stead.

A tangle of emotion fills my heart at the thought. That frustrating sense of guilt and regret accompanying the warm fuzziness of the evening. *I have once again found myself in bed with the prince and I cannot even say that I would not do it over again given the chance. I am such a hypocrite.* I groan a bit internally. Despite the danger that Syverious holds, part of me cannot help but fall into his trap every single time an opportunity presents itself. It is frustrating that I have such little control over my emotions or my bodily reaction to the man, but unfortunately that is the truth of the situation.

My brain mulls over this night's hypocrisy and my belly cannot help but flutter at the memory. *At least the man is good in bed.* A blush takes over my cheeks at the thought. A hot tingly sensation overtakes my thigh in that moment causing me to set my food down and take a look. Next to the vine now sits a band of wispy clouds, reminiscent of a breeze encircling my thigh. Instead of being gold in color this band is stark white. *Oh shit.* Quickly, I pull down my shirt again, trying to hide the band from the prince's view.

Syverious gives me a curious look. "What are you looking at?"

"I thought I dropped a noodle," I say quickly.

"You have barely touched them."

"They are slippery," I defend.

He sets down his plate. "Fine. Have your secrets." Then he smiles. "But I will reveal one of mine."

That catches my interest. "I am listening."

"You were not the only one wandering the palace halls this afternoon," the prince says conspiratorially.

"What do you mean?" I lean forward.

"I may have done some exploring on my own."

His eyes flash lavender in satisfaction at my surprised expression. "You really were not sleeping were you," I say dryly.

He only smiles in response. "Would you like to know what I found out?"

"Obviously. What did you see?"

The prince pauses and his eyes watch my face carefully. "Sorin is being kept in the palace."

Silence rings between us. I force my expression to remain blank.

The prince leans back with self assurance, picking up his food to continue eating. "But you knew that, didn't you?"

Still I remain silent. I could not say anything if I wanted to, the hold on my tongue still in place from my and Sydon's agreement.

"Ah, so what the guards were saying is true then." Syverious confirms. "That *is* what they have against you to keep you in line." He takes another bite of food watching me carefully as he chews and swallows it. "You know it would have been good to know that before now. Good information to communicate to Sam," he says nonchalantly.

I lick my lips.

"But..." the prince continues. "From your silence I am also gathering that they spelled you against speaking about it, am I right?"

Finally the shock of his knowledge registers on my face.

"Right," he confirms more to himself than to me. Finishing his meal he places the plate on the desk in the corner before walking over to me. Leaning down he places a gentle kiss on the top of my head. "Unfortunately for them, there are very few secrets that I cannot find out." The statement feels more like a warning than a comfort and I lick my lips nervously in response.

Just then a knock sounds on the door.

"Your presence is requested princess," Sydon's voice echoes faintly through the room.

"Enjoy your time with your guards tonight, dove. I will see you in the morning." Syverious bends down to drop another kiss on my head again before walking over to the bed and plopping down on its surface.

On slightly shaky legs, I stand up and pull on a pair of loose pants and a cloak to cover the prince's shirt on my body. Pulling open the door, I come face to face with Sydon.

"Are you ready to go?" he asks.

"Yes, I am ready."

CHAPTER FORTY-FOUR

Movement

Alaceandra

S ydon leads me back down the corridor and down the familiar path to Sorin's room. I rub Sorin's tingling spot on my thigh in appreciation- the sensation now a familiar comfort- before pushing the door open. Sydon leads me inside. I yawn, a bit exhausted from the day, but smile when I see Sorin's familiar body wrapped in vines on the bed. He has more color in his cheeks today. Even his vines are more green than they were previously. All in all he looks more *alive*. My hands twitch craving to run my fingers over his body.

"How is he doing?" I ask Sydon, wanting confirmation of my thought.

"Better today," Sydon replies softly.

"Do you know why?" I ask.

"No, not really. He randomly started improving sometime this afternoon."

"Hmm.." I hum to myself thoughtfully. "I wonder why."

"I do as well."

Sydon moves closer to my spot by Sorin's bedside. "Speaking of people who are doing better, I think that the king is going to wake up soon."

My gaze whips to Sydon's, my heart now in my throat. "Why do you say that?"

"I was informed this evening that his vitals started to improve sometime this morning. It is only a matter of time."

"What does that mean?"

Sydon sighs. "He is going to want some kind of retribution for what you did to him, princess." Sydon looks almost regretful of his words. "I can try to ensure that it is not severe, but... you know King Demetrius, just... keep a low profile over the next couple of days, okay? The soldiers are likely to be more agitated."

I give him a quizzical look. "Why are you telling me this?"

Sydon paces the floor of the small room. "Look. You seem like you are close to where we need you to be in training. I am not sure if you know this or not but when our skills are pushed too soon... it can lead to sometimes dire consequences. I do not want that to happen to you so... just be careful."

"I did not realize you were this invested in my well-being."

"Caring captor remember?"

"Right," I say narrowing my eyes in suspicion.

He sighs. "Just trust me on this okay."

I shrug. "It should not be a problem."

"Good."

As if to illustrate his earlier point, something or someone crashes into the door causing us both to startle. Muffled screams start to filter in shortly thereafter. A look of annoyance and indecision crosses over Sydon's face and he looks towards the door before looking back at me. More muffled yelling filters in from the hall before the room shakes. *What is going on out there?* Whatever it is it does not sound like it is stopping anytime soon. I bite my bottom lip nervously as we stare at each other in silence, waiting for the commotion to calm, only it does not.

Sydon sighs, clenching his hands into fists. "Stay here," he commands before turning and swiftly exiting the room.

I watch the door close behind him and my eyes widen. *This could be my chance.* Quickly, I turn my attention back to Sorin on the little bed. *This might be my only moment alone with him. Maybe there is something I can do to help him wake up?* Every time I have made contact with Sorin's body so far it has led to more movement from him. His condition only seems to have been improving as the days go on as well despite me brushing against him on these visits.

My ears prick as the noise outside gets louder and I try to strain them to listen for any signs that Sydon might be returning. I reach one of my hands out to Sorin. His hair is a bit longer than I remember it. His beard a bit more scraggly. But he is Sorin all the same. Yearning fills my heart at the thought of seeing his eyes open again. *Let me just try...* I run my fingers over the closest vine. They jerk at my contact before slowly unraveling itself from Sorin's body and sinking back into his skin. Delight fills me at this new revelation. *So my touch actually causes the vines to go away! Is that a good thing?* Sydon's warning echoes in my head, but something in my body urges me to ignore it.

Trusting the words of your captor will only keep you here longer, Alaceandra. We could kill him and take Sorin now. That overly sweet voice tries to make an appearance in my head, but I push her away quickly.

*She does have a point though. Trusting my captor **will** only lead to a longer sentence.*

Kneeling at Sorin's bedside, I do the one thing I have been craving to do since I stepped foot in this Ptheryeth-forsaken room all those days ago. I kiss him. I pour every ounce of love, fear, and want into my kiss, hoping that it will reach him in whatever in-between state he is currently battling. Nothing happens at first, but slowly, I feel his lips start to twitch in response to mine. My tattoo warms exponentially and the feeling of something soft wraps around my thigh. Startled, I glance down only to see one of his vines has wrapped itself around me. My eyes dart back to his face and I catch one of his eyelids twitch. *It is working!*

Quickly, I press my lips against his again. His vine tightens against my thigh and my mark burns as if it is on fire. I could almost burst with the relief that feeling brings me. More vines join the first and before I know it I am being lifted on top of him. The vines do their best to press every part of us together and form us into a cocoon of warmth. I smile as my fire prickles along my skin, straining to break free. The inner thread tying me to Sorin swells excitedly. *You are alive.*

Tears well in my eyes and I end our kiss. As I pull away from Sorin's lips, a gasp escapes me as a small, golden firefly tattoo appears on his collarbone and his vines release me. I stare at his face, but although his lips were responsive to my own, his eyes refuse to open. I stay on top of him for a couple more moments, tracing the new tattoo. It seems to buzz under my touch.

"Please, Sorin, come back to me. I need you," I whisper, before allowing my hand to fall away from his body.

Crawling off of him, I allow my feet to touch ground again. The noise outside the room has started to quiet and I know I do not have much time left with my gentle guardian. I plant one last kiss on his forehead and watch as his hands clench in response. "Please," I whisper again, my voice breaking with emotion.

The door opens behind me and I step away from Sorin, quickly wiping at my eyes. I turn towards Sydon who is staring at me, his eyes narrowed.

"We need to get back," he says. "Training will start earlier tomorrow. You need your rest."

Ensuring that my body blocks Sorin's vine-less upper half, I start toward him. "Yeah, okay," I reply, pushing past him and out the door. *Focus on me please, prison guard. Not the man on the bed.* "Let us get going then." My voice is pitchier than normal, but he does not seem to notice. His gaze, thankfully, does follow me, a look akin to incredulity on his face. He seems unmarred from whatever disturbance was happening outside the room.

"Are you not going to fight me more on that?"

I shake my head, continuing down the hall. I look around. Blood stains the walls, but other than that there is no indication of the earlier noise. I blink at it, before continuing down the hall. Sydon follows closely behind me shutting the door quickly. "No. You are right. I need to keep a low profile if the king is waking up. Showing up tired to my lesson will do me no favors. What happened back there?"

"A mere squabble. I have it sorted, but do remember my earlier warning. At the moment it appears things are... unbalanced. Do not make yourself a casualty of that."

Yay more riddles. I think sarcastically, but instead I reply. "Understood."

We walk in silence for a while until we arrive back at my quarters. Finally, Sydon replies.

"Glad to see you are cooperating," he says slowly.

I turn to him and roll my eyes. "Look, I am not saying I like it only that I am not trying to make things any worse for myself. If I need to be more vigilant because the king I apparently injured is out for blood, then fine. If going to bed a little early can save me from the other kings' ire, then fine. I know the fury of the kings. I have seen my father's on more occasions than I care to recall. Frankly, I would rather make it out of here alive, so call it cooperation if you must, but truly it is survival."

"I see," is Sydon's only response.

If today was any indication, sometime soon Sorin will wake up. I promise myself that no matter what King Demetrius' plans are, I will survive long enough to be there when he does. *I need to.* From this point forward, their threats are just a part of my waiting game.

"Goodnight, Sydon," I say after Sydon opens the door to my room.

"Goodnight, Alaceandra."

Shutting the door behind me, I only shake my head at the prince's raised eyebrow. In response he lifts the blanket. Quickly, I strip my clothes until I am once again just in his t-shirt and a pair of panties. Yawning, I make my way over to his open arms and lay beside him.

"How was that?" The prince asks softly, his thumb making circles on the side of my body.

"Enlightening."

I feel the prince nod behind me. "You should get some rest."

It is my turn to nod. With one last kiss on the back of my head, the prince settles in behind me. My mind races over the events of the day. Another yawn overtakes me as exhaustion starts to eat at me. *I will see you soon, Sorin. I just know it.* The prince's measured breathing starts to echo behind me. I smile and snuggle into him before allowing my eyelids to fall shut.

CHAPTER FORTY-FIVE

Ominous

Alaceandra

I stand in a grassy field unfamiliar to me. My hair is in long braids down my back and I am wearing a black, flowy dress that lands about mid thigh on my frame. My feet are bare, as they are most times in these dreams. It is sunny and just the right amount of warm outside. I turn my head up to the sun and take a deep breath. Before long I feel a presence at my back.

"So we meet again," I mumble, doing my best to remain unmoved by his presence.

A low laugh echos behind me. "We do."

"What do you want this time?" I do not try to turn towards him. I know my body will not let me so there is no point. Instead I stare at the sky as I feel him walk closer. His heat radiating on my back.

"I see you have ignored my warnings."

"What about? You have given me so many."

He hums. "The man you lay beside even now."

"How do you know who I lay beside?"

"I know everything when it comes to you."

That statement is bizarrely familiar, but I cannot quite place why that is. I sigh. "Do you have any truths today or have you just come here to scold me?"

The mysterious figure behind me snorts. "Just one."

"And that is?"

"Change is coming to you quickly, but it is not exactly that which you hope for."

I narrow my eyes. "How ominous."

"It does not have to be."

A gentle breeze toys with my hair causing my braids to swing to the right. "What am I supposed to do with that?"

"Whatever you wish. I recommend that it may be time to prepare yourself."

"Thanks for the help," I whisper, my tone sarcastic.

"It is a pleasure of mine," the figure answers seriously. "It is time for you to wake up now. Do not forget that you have these to guide you."

The small stars on my back heat with the his words. "If you need me, call upon the stars."

I wake up with a start, my eyes opening quickly before being blinded by the light of a new day.

"Hey, are you okay?" The prince whispers, already awake next to me.

I glance at him and see that his eyes are filled with concern.

"Yes," I whisper, trying to shake off the remnants of my dream last night.

The prince stares at me for a moment his hand once again making circles along my skin. "I think your guard will come soon to retrieve us, you should ready yourself for the day."

I nod against him. Pulling myself from the bed I make my way over to the bathroom and shut the door behind me before leaning against it. As expected, as soon as the door shuts Baldar appears.

"*Good morning, sleepy head.*"

"*Morning, Baldar.*" I grumble at him, starting the shower.

"*Slept well, I trust?*"

"*Sure.*" I close the curtain to allow the shower to warm up before turning to look at myself in the mirror.

Baldar skitters in front of my view, forcing me to meet his gaze. He looks smug. "*There was quite the power surge yesterday evening.*"

"*What?*"

He continues his statement, as if I had not even spoken. "*Makes me think a certain two somebodies might have completed a bond?*" I get the sense that if Baldar had any eyebrows he would be waggling them at the moment.

I roll my eyes in response. "*It is not a big deal,*" I mentally mumble.

"*Oh but it is!*" Baldar retorts. "*With this increase in power you should be able to finish stitching the power connected to your demoni abilities together. Which means!!!*" The excitement present on the ferret's face is almost ridiculous. "*You might be able to successfully create a portal!*"

"*Why do you seem so excited about this?*"

Baldar rolls his beady eyes. "*It is my job to train you, Alaceandra. The closer you get to your powers, the easier my job is. My assignment does not stop just because you want to reject your bonds. Think of it this way, you have just made my life incredibly easier.*"

I give the ferret a hard look. *"Who assigned you with this job?"* I ask suspiciously.

"Oh do not give me that look! Just because the other people you place your trust in are assholes does not mean that that same suspicion should be cast on me. It is offensive!"

"You are not answering my question."

"You would be unaware of the meaning of my answer even if I did, grumpy pants. Go take your shower. I will see you again later." He disappears.

I let out a frustrated sigh and strip down. Glancing at myself in the mirror I admire the new tattoo on my thigh. The design is quite pretty, even if its complete absence of color is a bit unsettling. I run a finger over it softly. I do not know how the prince would react if he realized that he too marked me the same way Sorin did. *He would probably be quite smug about it.* My mind offers. I smile to myself. In all honesty, it did not feel right to show him the mark last night. Although I feel as though I have come to a gentle truce when it comes to my feelings about him, giving him the satisfaction of knowing that he is now permanently embedded on my skin after his whole "I own your body and mind" speech felt too much like I would be letting him win that argument. He can learn of the true consequences of our union once I figure out his final game plan. For now, I will keep the mark to myself.

Turning around, I also reinspect the marks on my back. The five tiny gold stars are unfortunately still present. If the prince saw them at all yesterday he neglected to mention it. *I should be grateful either way, I would have no way to explain the strange markings even if he did ask.* Sighing once again, I move away from the mirror and step under the warm spray of the shower. *There will be plenty of time to worry about that later. For now, I will take this moment to relax.*

CHAPTER FORTY-SIX

Elimination Style

Alaceandra

A couple of hours later, I am being led to the gym by Sydon. Syverious decided to stay behind in the room, despite his father's request for him to train. Surprisingly, Sydon did not fight him too much on his request. As we were leaving, I saw Syverious chatting with one of the soldiers that are now posted outside our door.

What is he up to? I ponder that question as Sydon leads me away. The walk this time is silent, neither of us willing to speak first and break the peace of the morning. My muscles are more relaxed than they have been since I arrived. The routine of this place now becoming more of a comfort than an annoyance to my system. *That could be dangerous.* A small voice inside me warns. I lick my lips and keep my eyes forward, wondering what we will be training on today.

As we enter the gym, Huermond catches my eye. I watch as he takes in the fact the prince is not present in the gym with me today. The information causing his face to twist into a sneer. Doing my best to ignore him, I search the room for Lylane and Jaq again. Finding them quickly, I give them both a wave which they return.

"Go get changed," Sydon commands, making him the first to break our silent truce.

"Okay." Walking confidently over to the small room that holds my athletic gear, I change quickly. The little pin I have kept on my body since the first day I arrived in this place hits the ground as I whip my shirt over my head. I scramble for it, quickly snagging it just before it falls down one of the vents on the floor.

That was close. Holding it tightly in my hand, I wrap my binding around my chest and tuck it neatly into the fabric. Although this little pin has yet to prove useful to me, it has become a kind of emotional support. As long as I have it on my person, I feel as if I have at least a sharp tool that I can stab someone with if worse comes to worst.

Truthfully though, I had grown so accustomed to having the dagger that Sam gifted me with when we were out in the Dark Lands on our own, the thought of being without anything now except my powers as a form of defense goes against everything that Sam had taught me. Both back in Tikilium and in our short lessons at Sylvie's house. Strange as he was being in Olvaria, Sam has always stayed true to one thing in his interactions with me. He has always done his best to keep me safe. It would be silly to not keep his lessons in mind, even when he is not here to continue to teach them.

A sense of anticipation fills me at the thought I might see him soon. If his note to the prince had any truth to it, it would mean that he is close to infiltrating this palace. *The only question now is how soon is soon?* A knock sounds on the door to my little changing room jerking me from my thoughts. *I better get out there.* Quickly folding my clothes on the bench seat, I exit the room.

Sydon narrows his eyes at me suspiciously. "What took you so long in there?"

"I got tangled in my shirt," I reply quickly. He gives me a dubious look which I return with an eye roll. "Do not act like it has never happened to you. Now come on."

I walk further into the gym and over to Lylane and Jaq. Sydon watches me but makes his way over the front of the room, taking his usual place near Rafton.

"We will return to a regular cadence with our lesson today," Rafton announces. "Good old hand-to-hand combat. Trainees find your group of three and a mat. I will pair each of you against another group. The challenge will occur elimination style and solo. Each member of your team will face a member of the other simultaneously. The groups that win the most matches, win the lesson for today. Do you understand your assignment?"

"Yes, sir!" The group yells.

"Then take your places."

Lylane grabs my hand and races over to one of the mats on the left side of the gym.

"Woah! Why are we racing?"

She laughs. "Those who do not find a mat in time will be assigned one. I would rather have a home base then to have to impede on another's."

"I guess that makes sense."

"It does," Jaq says. "These tournaments can get crazy. Best to be in a spot you are comfortable in than to be assigned one across from say, the bathrooms." He hooks a thumb at the doors in question that apparently lead to said bathroom.

"Yeah..." Lylane says, widening her eyes and shaking her head no at me.

I laugh. "Okay, so what happens next."

"We fight," Lylane says solemnly.

"I will begin the pairing process," Rafton announces. I glance over at him to see that all of the groups that did not find a mat in time now stand against the back wall preparing to be matched with those on the mats. My eyes once again meet Huermond's and a sinking feeling hits my stomach.

"Are there any limitations on who we get paired with?" I ask Lylane and Jaq.

"No, not really," Jaq says distractedly. He has started stretching. I mimic his movements.

"That does not seem fair, we are not all at the same skill levels are we?"

"Maybe not in hand-to-hand," Lylane says. "But usually what you lack in melee you make up for with your abilities."

"Are we allowed to use those?" I watch as Rafton gets closer, pointing to groups and directing them to mats. Our mat looks like it is one of the last ones that will get a pairing. I glance over to the back wall to see Huermond still standing among the unpaired trainees. I glance towards where Sydon was standing and notice that he has disappeared. Looking around, he is nowhere to be seen.

"We are, but only in the second round," Lylane replies.

"How many rounds are there?"

"At most, three," Jaq answers this time. "First one is hand-to-hand only, second is melee and magick and the third is the tie breaker." He starts to jog in place. Again, I mimic his actions.

"This group. Here." Rafton's voice startles me. He is pointing at our mat. My eyes flick to the group he beckoned. Just as I had feared, Huermond and two teal soldiers step forward.

Lylane glares at the group, looking just as happy with the pairing as I am. Rafton walks away quickly, returning to his spot at the front of the room. Sydon remains nowhere to be seen.

"Hello, Alaceandra," Huermond says, his voice full of malice.

I do not reply, instead I finish walking through my stretches with Jaq. Huermond's eyes narrow on me.

"Alright, trainees!" Rafton's voice echoes through the room. "Pick your opponents."

"I will be facing the princess," Huermond says quickly.

"No, you will not be," Lylane snaps back. "She can face one of your teammates."

"We refuse to face her," The teal trainees say in near unison.

"And why is that?" Lylane asks, her eyes narrowing.

"It is against our code to harm a future monarch. As she is set to marry our prince, we cannot fight her," one of the men explains.

"I have never heard of such a code," Jaq says.

The other teal man shrugs. "Whether you heard of it or not makes no difference. We will not face her."

Huermond smirks victoriously.

You can take the fucker. The voice in my head is back. *He is a weakling. Let him test our power. He will soon regret it.*

"Rafton!" Lylane calls. Rafton walks over to us, his eyes flicking over our forms.

"Yes, what seems to be the problem?"

"These trainees are refusing to fight Alaceandra."

"Not all of us," Huermond cuts in. "I have no problem facing her. It is she who is refusing to fight me."

"Why the refusal?" Rafton questions.

"It is against our code." The teal trainees supply without hesitation. "We cannot harm a future monarch."

Rafton rolls his eyes before he looks at me. "And you? What is your reason to refuse the fight?"

"He has threatened me on multiple occasions," I say softly.

Rafton shrugs. "Looks like there might be a grudge then. It is the perfect situation to work those out. The round ends once one of you are put in a "kill" position, but no true harm will come to you here. If he wants to fight you, I see no problem in letting him. Work it out among yourselves." He turns and walks back towards the front of the room.

Huermond eyes me expectantly.

"On the mat," I command Huermond through gritted teeth.

"Gladly."

CHAPTER FORTY-SEVEN

Allies and Family Ties

The Prince

I decided against following Alaceandra to training this morning. *It is time to visit my father.* I follow the teal guard that was stationed outside of our quarters down a few hallways to the opposite side of the palace. As we walk down the extensive hallways, my mind drifts back to last night. Being with my dove was... extraordinary. Her body undulating beneath me is a picture I will not forget for decades to come. *I hope to experience it again.* Not only that, but the noises of the castle fell to utter silence with her in my arms. The near constant chatter submitting to the indomitable aura that she presents. A part of me seemed to align when we fell together, leaving my brain more clear than it has in all my years of life. Her effect on me continues to leave me pleasantly stunned.

Too bad you must ruin it. My brain snaps at me.

But must I? I argue back. *The ferret did say there is another way. A way that what needs to happen is done, but I do not lose her in the process. Can I allow my plans to be swayed by her strange familiar?* I find that, despite everything, I would like to.

We arrive at a thick metal door that flashes silver in the candle light. The guard opens the door and is prepared to walk in with me when I stop him with a hand.

"I would like to see my father alone."

"That is not advisable, my prince," the guard looks nervously from side to side.

"Think not of me as a prince, but as a son who wishes to see his father. I do not need long. I only would like to have a vulnerable moment that is not observed. I think that the king would appreciate fewer soldiers seeing him in his current state as well. I promise the visit will be short."

"We were instructed to not leave anyone alone with the king," he says, shifting from one foot to another.

I place my palm on the guard's arm. "An admirable task indeed, but again, I am his son. I have been apart from my father for too long and now he has been injured. Is that not something deserving of even the slightest bit of privacy?"

The guard seems slightly placated by my words. "Okay. I- I can give you ten minutes, but that is all. I do not want anyone patrolling to know that I did this, prince, so please be quick."

"I will be. Your empathy will be notated favorably. Thank you."

"You're welcome, my prince," the guard bows and opens the door. I smile as I enter the room, the door closing with a bang behind me.

In front of me is a simple room. The walls are stark white in appearance, something that I am sure is hard to do given the blackened rock used to make this place. Tiny monitors fill the space, beeping in time to a heartbeat and little jars are scattered about the room holding various medical equipment. Fortunately, the room seems empty of all other bodies besides my own and the one attached to the medical equipment itself. That person being my father. I walk further into the room and observe the man who contributed to my birth laying on the medical bed in front of me. He looks... peaceful. Much more so than I have ever seen him. Anger fills me at the image of him resting so serenely. *He is undeserving of such a rest. Not after all that he has put his kingdom through. Has put me through.*

I breathe deeply trying to calm my racing heart and walk up to his bedside. With a gentle hand, I search his body to see if I can find the totem that has held me captive for many years on his person. *Luckily Alaceandra was able to get rid of hers. If I can find mine it would put me at an advantage in the days to come.* After a thorough search of his body I come to the frustrating realization that the totem is not on his person. *But where is he keeping it?* I stare down at my aging father in disgust. My mind reeling on where in the castle he could have placed it. *Maybe in his quarters? Where would that be? But no, he would have had it on him when he went to confront Alaceandra. Maybe someone else took it when they saw him passed out? And if that is the case who?*

My hands grip the side of his bed and I have to actively work to keep myself calm. I would be lying if I said seeing my father like this does not have thoughts of killing him racing to the forefront of my mind. As tempting as that may be, the guard poses too much of a barrier. I know that he reported to his command where he was taking me. If my father somehow ended up dead after my meeting with him, no matter if I killed the guard in the process or not, it would cause too much suspicion.

As if to prove a point, a knock sounds on the door ending my inner monologue.

"It has been ten minutes, prince," the guard says, his eyes cast away from me. "I need to take you back to your room."

I nod at him. "Alright." With one last glance at my father, I exit the infirmary and walk back to the dove's and my shared quarters. We move through the halls at a quicker pace than before and I have to wonder what the guard's rush is, but decide not to question him. He has already been plenty helpful to me, no need to cause him any more nervousness with extra questioning. *I will have to worry about the totem later.*

We make it to the room relatively quickly and I bid the guard farewell before entering. Closing the door, I dig into the desk drawer and grab the paper and pen that I have been storing within it. Doing my best to be swift, I jot down a little letter to Sam.

```
                    S,
Your insistence on calling me names will
someday get old. I have an update. I have
located your fellow dog on the premises.
Enact retrieval system four. He is located
on the west wing. I have left the agreed
upon marker on the wall across from his
                   room.
              Before Long,
                    P
```

Rolling the piece of paper, I grab some sydryia and stick it in the middle of the scroll. Walking over to the window, I smile as the little yellow elvisera dart past it, excitedly looking for their next treat. I pull the window open the inch it allows and lay the little letter in the opening. The orange tipped elvisera darts in before its siblings can beat it and snatches the letter with its beak before soaring off in the distance. The smaller elvisera follow hoping for a piece of the branch for themselves. A small chuckle escapes me at their antics.

Suddenly, the orange elvisera darts straight down. Nosediving into some trees near the palace. *Ah, so he is close.* I wait a couple minutes watching the patch of trees. I do not have to wait long before the little guy soars back into the sky and makes his way to me, his yellow companions flying close behind. He drops a new letter at the edge of the sill before using his beak to push it through.

ROYAL HYPOCRITE,

I WOULDN'T COUNT ON IT IF I WERE YOU. THE WINEMAKER'S
PRESENCE HAS ALREADY BEEN ACCOUNTED FOR.
SEE YOU IN TWENTY FOUR.
S

Winemaker's? I did not realize that either of them knew the craft. *What an odd nickname.* At least now I know that Sam's presence is imminent. *Only twenty four hours until this place gets blown away.* My brows furrow thinking about how the dove still has yet to complete a stable portal. The question I have been stuck on since I arrived in this place echoes through my brain. *If we cannot figure something out tonight then I really will have to choose between Alaceandra and revenge.* I sigh as dread fills my stomach. *Let's hope I choose wisely.*

CHAPTER FORTY-EIGHT

Kill or Be Killed

Alaceandra

H uermond and I circle each other. Rafton has already given out his long whistle calling the first round of our little exercise. Lylane and Jaq stand on the sidelines of the mat. Lylane looks more anxious than I currently feel. Sydon has still not returned to the gym. Huermond stares at me with the eyes of a predator, a sick smile plastered to his face.

"Are you going to attack me?" He jeers, continuing to move around the mat.

"I can ask the same of you," I reply. Realistically, I know that Huermond has much more experience in hand-to-hand combat. The only true skills I have learned are how to get out of holds and evade. My punches are relatively weak, and other than the pin woven snugly into my binding, I have no weapons. Huermond, on the other hand, has been working at this for likely his entire life. His movements in class have been precise and near deadly and he does not seem to be someone who would hold back just because of my royal status. The likelihood of him winning at least this round is quite high, but I cannot help but scowl at the fucker.

In all fairness, it seems as if this fight is rigged, and not in my favor. If this was just some sort of small squabble like Rafton had suggested,

I would be less afraid in this fight, but it is not. I can tell from the look in Huermond's eye that he has been out for my blood since day one. He blames me for Fadres and Credour's disappearance and is seeking retribution. I would say that the fact the kings need me for whatever plans they may have would stop him from causing too much damage, but somehow I fear that is not the case. Huermond does not look like someone afraid of consequences. He looks like someone with one narrow focus and that focus is unfortunately on punishing me.

Huermond darts into the circle attempting to grab at my waist. I move back, just barely missing his hands. I move in, using his bent over frame to my advantage and knee him in the face. He backs up, rubbing his nose. His eyes look like they have gotten a silver tint to them and my heart beats into my ribs. Adrenaline and fear are heavy in my body. He darts in once again and I evade, kicking his stomach. Instead of backing away, he grabs my foot. With a grunt, he pulls me forward and kicks at my remaining leg, his foot crashing into my knee. I fall onto the mat with a heavy thud. Moving over top of me, Huermond reels his fist up and punches me in the face. My face whips to the right with the impact. The hit so hard it causes me to black out momentarily. Anger surges through me as my head pounds.

"You are dead," Huermond growls in my ear.

"Point Huermond." Rafton's voice rings through the air.

Huermond backs away from me. I get to my feet quickly, but the room seems to spin with my movements.

Give in to me, Alaceandra. I can prove to him who truly is more powerful here. That saccharine voice purrs.

No. I got it. I snap back.

"Round two, begin!"

Instead of allowing Huermond to invoke the attack, this time I dart in, landing a kick straight to Huermond's balls. He yelps out in pain and I smirk, bouncing on my toes after evading his attempt to grab me.

A grumble escapes him as that silver in his eyes darkens. The floor beneath me quakes ferociously.

"Powers! You can use your abilities this round!" Lylane yells out. I glance at her to see that she has already trapped her opponent in one of her boxes.

I pay for the momentary distraction. Huermond crashes into me taking me down to the mat. Quickly, I visualize my threads. The one connected to my fire is still as lively as ever. The other purple, frayed thread remains as well, but instead of it being translucent this time it has grown in thickness. It glows happily beside the green. *Odd. What changed?* Ignoring the development, I grasp at the green thread and it sends magick into me. Re-opening my eyes, I blast fire at Huermond. He falls off of me and rolls onto the mat, doing his best to extinguish the flames.

"You bitch." Huermond whips out a hand, grabs my ankle and attempts to pull me to him. I kick, trying to dislodge his hand. "I am going to enjoy watching you die." One of my kicks manages to nail him in the face. He releases me and I scramble to my feet.

The ground beneath me quakes again and I realize that Huermond is the cause. *So he can cause concentrated vibrations beneath his opponents in order to distract them. Not the best ability, but certainly not the worst.*

A flash of something snags my attention as Huermond's fist comes barreling towards my face. *Is that a dagger?* I dodge him just in time. The object in his hands becomes more visible. *It is!* Shock registers through me as I realize that his grumblings about my death might not just be empty threats. Huermond notices my eyes and smirks, fitting the dagger back into a sheath on his sleeve before running at me. Right before his fist connects, he extracts the dagger from his sleeve again, I move quickly once again dodging him.

He is going to kill you if you do not let me take over. That voice in me coos.

"What the fuck are you doing?" I yell at Huermond.

"What I should have done the second I saw your disgusting face. I got news that they found Fadres and Credour's bodies near their favorite tavern, Alaceandra. Did you really think you would get away with killing them?" He sneers before darting at me once again.

"I did not kill them," I say, dodging his blow and shooting another beam of fire at his abdomen. He dodges it.

"Liar!" He growls. The floor shakes more violently beneath me causing me to lose my balance. He takes his advantage and tackles me again. We roll on the mat, each of us fighting for an upper hand.

Alaceandra! The voice urges. *We need to act now.*

He gains control, forcing my back to dig into the mat. He raises his hands the flash of the blade present in his grip.

Now, Alaceandra! The voice has lost its syrupy sweetness, its alarm overtaking its regular intonation.

Fuck! Fine! I scream at the voice as the dagger soars towards my throat.

Black fire bursts out of me, smashing into Huermond. As the flames connect, a loud cracking noise echoes. I glance down to see the red band on my wrist has fractured again, before turning my attention back to my attacker. He has fallen backwards off of me with the force of the attack, his skin sizzling as the hot flames eat through his clothing and flesh. An agonized scream falls from his lips as he does his best to extinguish the fire now burning brightly on his skin. My body moves on its own accord. A smile creeping on my face as the sound of his pain meets my ears.

"You know it is not polite to fuck with a princess," I hear my voice say, that sweet tone that is usually only present in the recesses of my brain now falling from my lips. "Did you really think that you would get away with killing me?" I echo his own words, another ball of fire building in my palms as I approach his body on the mat.

"Alaceandra?" A stunned voice calls my name. I turn my gaze to it and see a woman in silver looking at me with a tilted head, a smile just barely registering on her lips. "Ah I see, it is you." The woman bows her head.

Satisfaction rings through me at the sight. Suddenly a searing pain rips through my arm. I turn back to see that the man attacking me has successfully embedded his blade into my arm. *Stupid man.* Flicking my hand, I send another fireball at him. He tries to move out of the way, but the flames nick his arms, pulling another scream from his lips.

"That is enough!" A man screams. "Alaceandra, get control of yourself."

I ignore him, advancing once again on my opponent, creating another sphere of fire.

"I said that is enough!" A palm lands on my arm and I whip my attention to the intruder. A bald, muscular man is grabbing me firmly. I toss the fireball at him. He moves out the way. His eyes connecting with my own. "Fuck," he says aloud, before backing away from me and running from the room. *As he should.*

Pain continuously radiates from my arm and I realize I have yet to remove the dagger from my skin. With a sigh, I pull it free before dropping it to the floor. Blood runs in ruby red rivulets down my arm. Voices around me gasp. Turning back to my original attacker, my brows scrunch as I realize that he is not in the place I left him. I scan the room and spot him dragging his body to one of the locker room doors. Slowly, I advance on him.

"I told you not to pair her with him," a familiar voice snaps behind me.

"I thought it would be good for them! They had to work out whatever rivalry was between them somehow." The voice of the man who grabbed me meets my ears.

"Well, you see where that gets you. Do not defy an order from me again or you will pay with your life."

"Yes, sir."

Tuning the men out, I allow my black flames to build once again in my palms. The people around me scatter as I near them and I smile at their retreating forms. Once the fire has successfully reached its peak, I throw it at the running man. It hits his leg. His agonized scream meets my ears once again and my smile grows. Suddenly, his screams are cut off as he collapses to the ground. Rapid footsteps approach.

"Fuck," I hear someone whisper.

A body grabs me from behind. Warmth overtakes my senses as a man's breath ghosts over my ear.

"*Sleep.*" My body tingles as it registers the command.

Before I can push the invading presence away, the world goes dark.

CHAPTER FORTY-NINE

A Misstep

The Prince

I stare at the window outside, lounging on the bed. The positioning of the sun tells me that Alaceandra should be back by now. I jiggle my foot, worry creeping in. *Why is today's lesson taking her so long?*

The door to the room opens abruptly causing me to glance away from the window. The guard that I had met upon my entrance into the palace stands at the door. She narrows her gaze at me.

"Your presence is requested in the throne room." she says, her voice full of annoyance.

Peeling myself from the bed, I walk over to her. She watches me leave the room and slams the door shut behind me before stomping ahead of me, leading me down the hall.

I stare at her for a moment. "What is your name anyway?"

"Mylindia," she snaps back at me.

"That is a pretty name," I try.

"Do not insult me with your flattery, prince," she snaps.

Okaayyy... I watch her as she moves through the halls at a rapid pace as if she is ready to be done with her duty of retrieving me. *What do the kings need this time?* Finally we make it to the grand doors of the throne room. Mylindia leads me inside before exiting quickly and shutting the door behind herself.

I stand alone in the room after her departure. *Why would she lead me to an empty room?* A door opens on the dais, causing me to whip my head in its direction. What I see there makes my blood run cold. My father enters the room, a glower on his face. I try to keep my expression carefully blank as he hobbles his way to his chair and takes a seat. *But he was just in the infirmary.* My mind tries to grapple with what I see in front of me. *I was told he was not awake yet.*

"Hello, son." His voice rings through the room, his displeasure apparent.

"Father," I say in return.

He leans back, disapproval radiating off him in waves. "I see you tried to pay me a visit."

"I was summoned," I reply quickly.

"We both know that is not what I am referring to."

Pain stabs me in the gut causing me to crumple to my knees.

"Looking for this were you?" My father holds up my totem in his hand, teasingly.

"I have no idea what you are talking about," I reply, my voice coming out raspy.

"Oh you don't, do you?" Another shot of pain shoots through me. Suddenly dust flies from the floor beneath me and images made from the moving particles blink to life the in front of my eyes. "Just as you have had no idea of the princess' capabilities. Just as you have been working for your kingdom this whole time?"

Images of me sneaking through the halls of the palace, light flashes coming from Alaceandra and my shared quarters, scratch marks embedded in the flooring of the room, and elvisera gathered around our window all form from the dust. Then, a video of me searching my father's body plays in silence. I stare at the animated dust, my jaw ticking in frustration, but I say nothing. Any words I deign to speak against him will only be seen as further proof of my guilt at this point. I had considered the fact that there might be other spyware present within the palace, but I had not realized the extent. *I had gotten too cocky.*

"I told you if you made a fool of me again there would be consequences," my father spits. "If your plans were to betray me, you should have killed me while you had the chance. Guards!" Without warning the room fills with teal soldiers. "Take my son to the dungeons and, while you're at it, please show him how a traitor to the Helomasian kingdom is treated." The guards descend on me. Pure agony fills me as both the power of my father's totem and the impact of the guards fists and boots rain down on me. I try to breathe through the pain, but the torment quickly becomes too much for me to bear. Before my body shuts down completely, I surrender to unconsciousness.

CHAPTER FIFTY

Who Are You?

Alaceandra

When I wake up, I am strapped to a chair in the throne room. I blink my eyes hard as the faces of the kings blur into focus. Surprisingly, King Demetrius also sits among them. His body looks weakened, but he still sits firmly on his dais, his finger grasping something roughly in his palm. Dread fills me as he meets my eyes and smirks.

"What- what am I doing here?" I ask, my voice shaky. My brain scrambles to remember what happened before I passed out.

"You caused quite the stir in your training today," King Telvonius says, his tone full of amusement.

Dust particles animate themselves in front of me. I stare at the moving pictures they display and watch as I throw fireball after fireball at Huermond. Black flames lick his skin causing it to peel away from him, I turn away from the dust, nausea pooling in my gut.

"I-I do not remember that," I say softly.

"No? Because that display is strangely reminiscent of what you did to me," King Demetrius pipes up. The image being played out by the dust shifts to footage of the dining hall coated in the same black flames. King Demetrius does his best to get away from me as I hurl a ball of fire at him. I watch as Sydon and the prince run into the dining hall looking panicked. I did not realize that *that* is what I became when I surrendered myself over to that sickly voice inside of me. The knowledge of what exactly I was letting myself do to others causes shame and disgust to roll through me as the image of Huermond's skin peeling plays over and over in my mind.

"No response to that, I see," King Demetrius says.

I just stare at him.

"We think that you have now been trained enough to start fulfilling your duties," my father states. "There is no point in waiting on a useless solstice if you have the abilities to do that, you have the ability to make a fucking portal and release the grantador," my father says more to the other kings than to me.

"Grantador?" I repeat, the name sounding oddly familiar.

"Yes the Grantador, daughter," my father rolls his eyes. His hair is sticking up in a bunch of different directions. He still looks as deranged as he did during our last meeting. "The beast of Unduli. He will ensure that we can take over the land and—"

"Now you are willing to tell your daughter about her purpose?" King Mirksyl cuts in with annoyance. A picture of a giant unseeing feline flashes through my mind and an uneasy shiver runs through me. *That is what they are wanting to summon?*

"It does not matter now," my father bites back. "She will do as she is told. King Demetrius and I have decided she is too much of a loose cannon. We cannot allow her to get stronger. The prince has shown us that her power is dangerous."

The prince? Has he been communicating with the kings about my progress. Although I had considered that he was still working against me, the thought of him convening with these kings after our... sessions... causes hurt to knife through me.

King Demetrius notices the look of surprise on my face. "What? Are you surprised that my son convenes with us, as is his duty? You probably thought you were wrapping him around your little finger again, didn't you?" Disgust registers in his expression. "Well unfortunately for you my son knows that his loyalty is best to be held with his family, not some brat."

"Demetrius..." King Telvonius warns. "Watch your tongue." I am surprised by his defense of me. He looks a bit nervous. "Should we not be awaiting Sydon's return before making any rash decisions?"

I watch the kings silently, my arms starting to ache due to the tight rope binding me to the chair.

"No, of course not! It is time we take back control," King Demetrius states. "Let the replacement deal with the issues at the border, by the time he returns we will already have what we were promised."

"The replacement?" I ask, softly.

The kings turn back to me and King Demetrius rolls his eyes. "Yes, the replacement." King Demetrius says with annoyance. "Seeing as we did not know that my son was still suitable for marriage, Sydon was meant to replace him as your suitor. Why else did you think we had him following you around?" I notice King Telvonius looks slightly bewildered at this statement, but he remains silent.

If the prince had not arrived, I was meant to marry Sydon? The thought causes unease to slice through me. I guess it would make sense, seeing as he did seem quite attached to me since I arrived at the palace, but it is strange that they would want me to marry someone who was not of a noble background. *Unless...?* But that would not make sense. He would be sitting with the kings if he was and he had been acting as if he was more of a servant to them than a peer. *You did notice that they paid deference to him. That could be why.* My brain reels over the new information trying to make sense of it.

"Unfortunately I cannot allow this plan to go forward," King Telvonius says solemnly. "We will need to inform Sydon if we are to continue."

"I am siding with Telvonius with this one," King Mirksyl says dryly.

King Demetrius' face scrunches up into a scowl. I am once again reminded about the fact that there is no clear leader among these men. I get the feeling that they have been squabbling more than they have been making any decisions since they have been here. *If only their arguments did not have to happen while I was tied to a chair.*

My father cuts in before King Demetrius can respond. "You two are correct," he says calmly. King Demetrius gives him a hard look, betrayal flashing over his face briefly. "Please, if the both of you will go retrieve Sydon, we will wait here until your return. It is not like my daughter can go anywhere while he is being fetched," his amused eyes glance down at me.

I glare back at him.

King Mirksyl narrows his eyes. "Would it not be better to call upon a guard for such a duty?" he asks.

"Normally, yes," my father says. "Although, all those we trust are called away on another duty at the moment. We will need his presence quickly and you know the old saying, if you need something done correctly it is best to do it yourself."

"And how are we to be sure that you will not continue with your plans the second we leave this room?"

"You can't be," my father says simply. "So it is best you retrieve him quickly."

283

They all stare at each other and tension continues to build. I look from each man warily, knowing that no matter how this argument resolves, the result of it will not be good for me.

"Telvonius, let's go," King Mirksyl says softly.

"But-"

They stare at each other almost seeming to have a silent conversation before they both race from the room. As soon as they do, I watch as my father walk over to a wall and click a small button. Metal bars descend over the walls and doors. My stomach knots as I realize I am now trapped in a room with two deranged men. One of which happens to be my father that would sooner see me used in some asinine scheme to make a fantasy creature appear than to have any concern over my well-being.

The two remaining kings look at each other before they fix their gazes on me.

"Shall we get started?" King Demetrius asks my father.

"We shall."

CHAPTER FIFTY-ONE

Not So Gilded Cage

The Prince

"I did not expect to find you here." A voice causes my eyes to blink open. My body aches, pain searing through me as I try to regain my bearings. I am laying on a slightly damp, cold stone floor. As my eyes focus I realize that a familiar form stands at my prison door. *I must really be in the dungeons then. Fuck, I hope the dove is okay. How long have I been out?* Blinking again, I stare into Sam's smirking face.

"Has it already been twenty-four hours?" I ask warily.

He scrunches his brows. "Uh, no. Why would you ask that?"

I stare at him blankly. "You said 'see you in twenty-four.'"

Realization flits through his expression. "Oh. Minutes, prince, not hours. Guess I could have been more clear." He scratches the back of his head.

"Twenty-four *minutes*? Who gives time estimates like that?" I ask dubiously.

Sam rolls his eyes. "Did you not see how close I was when you sent your elvisera? Why would it have taken me— never mind— whatever. That is not important. What is important is how you ended up in the dungeons of all places in a singular hour? And where is Lace? Is she here with you?" His eyes search the darkness around me.

I try to sit up, but groan as my body fight against the movement. "No. Last I checked, she was at training. She was taking a while, though, so I do not know if she is back in the rooms or elsewhere."

Sam narrows his eyes at me. "You were supposed to be keeping an eye on her," he growls, his gaze darkening.

"I was. I just needed to handle other business this morning."

"And look where you ended up."

"Yeah. Are you going to help me out of here or...?"

Sam places a palm near the cage, testing its magick. Then he cringes. "Yes, but I will need to retrieve Sorin first." He sighs. "The magick around you will alert the person who trapped you in here of your escape. I would unravel the magick, but I will need as much energy as possible to get us out of here. You are not far from my exit point as it is. It would be better to do this with a bit of backup."

"I do not know what state your friend is in," I say after a moment.

"You don't have to," Sam says. "As long as he isn't dead, he will be an asset," Sam says wryly. "I should get going. I don't want to get caught too soon." Sam's form tenses as though he feels something unpleasant to him. "There is someone here who it would be best if I did not see."

A rustle causes me to turn to look to the left. When I turn back to ask Sam who exactly he might be referring to he had already disappeared. *Just my luck.* I think to myself sarcastically. Another rustle sounds to the left and then footsteps approach my cell. Mylindia now stands in the place that Sam vacated. The first smile I have ever seen on her plastered to her face. Her clothing draws my curiosity. She is now wearing a silky pink dress. The garb is much different than the teal uniform I have seen her in before.

286

"Hello, prince."

I give her a blank look. "Hi."

"Our king is about the start the second stage of his plan. It is a shame you are not there to witness it." Sarcasm is heavy in her tone.

"That is swell," I reply dryly, gingerly crossing my arms in front of me.

"It is, isn't it," she says wistfully. Something gold flashes briefly in her hand and I look at it curiously. "Luckily," she continues. "There is something you can still do to join in on the fun. It is your duty to help your kingdom. Even if you are so good at betraying it. Let's see if there is any more loyalty left in you, shall we? Guards!"

Four men appear behind her.

"It is so fun to say that when it is not referring to myself," she giggles. She turns her attention to the men around her. "If you would please hold the prince while I adorn him. I would hate for him to cause any problems and injure me."

"Yes ma'am," they say.

She unlocks the prison door and as a unit they rush in and restrain me. She walks up to me after she has confirmed that their hold on me is secure. I try to struggle against their grip, but with my body already as injured as it is, the task is difficult.

"Please present me with the prince's arm."

One of the men forces my arm forward and she clicks a thick golden bracelet into place. The inside of the bracelet has sharp teeth that dig into my skin and I cringe in pain as they cause blood to seep onto the floor. Seeing my pain, Mylindia smiles in delight. She places a hand over the cuff and applies pressure, causing me even more agony.

"Once we have used your power to suck the life out of that little whore of yours, your father promised to make me queen. I just need you to know who will be ruling the kingdom once you finally die." She releases my wrist and turns away from me.

"What is your issue with me?" I ask, confused by the anger I hear in her voice.

She pauses before glancing back at me. "I have been loyal to our kingdom since the moment I was born. I gained your father's favor the moment I reached my age of majority. I thought that maybe, just maybe, being in his bed would ensure that I can rule by his side once your mother died, but no. After the bitch was dead, he immediately started to groom you towards taking over the kingdom. Since that day, I have been plotting. Waiting for you to screw up so that I can come into power. It seems you finally did." She turns to me. "So really, prince, it is nothing personal. Just politics." She turns away from me and leaves the cell. "Knock him out before you release him. You can't be sure he won't attack you otherwise." She stands outside the prison door smirking at me.

My brain reels with the information. Confusion, anger—hurt— they all crash into me as I process her words. *Guess my mother might have died by poison after all.* I stare at Mylindia's face. The sad part is that even with her revelation I still have very little memories of her outside of this palace. I have seen many women travel in and out of my father's bedroom, but never once her. *He must have been keeping her somewhere secret for their rendezvous.* With that said, I don't truly believe that he plans to make her queen. Her affection for him has only made her the perfect pawn in my father's game. One that, unfortunately, takes sick pleasure in my downfall. The irony is not lost on me. I consider my interactions with my own future queen and a bit of shame filters through me.

Was I not doing the same with the dove? Using her affection for me to ensure my plans were accomplished? It is time I made a choice. The one

I should have made once I realized that my little dove was a lot more brilliant than I was led to believe. One that should have happened the moment I had her in my arms and realized that without her, the world would lose its beauty. Its peace. If I get out of here. If we can safely escape this place. I swear I will find some other way to get revenge on my father. A way that does not have to end in the dove's blood coating my hands.

The guard approach me, malice clear in their expressions. "Yes, ma'am," the prison guards say. That is the last thing I hear before everything goes dark.

CHAPTER FIFTY-TWO

Loose Cannon

Alaceandra

A small door opens in the flooring near the kings' daises and a woman dressed in a pink silken dress emerges. *Who is this lady?*

"The cuff has been placed," she says simply.

King Demetrius smiles at her warmly. "Perfect, Mylindia."

Okay so her name is Mylindia, but why is she here? I study her and she sneers at me in response. She seems to glide over to King Demetrius' side. He rewards her approach by wrapping her with his arm, patting her butt affectionately, and giving her a kiss on the forehead. She gives him the biggest smile in return. Nausea fills my stomach at the sight and I look away.

"Why don't you go sit over in my chair," King Demetrius says softly. "The show is about to begin."

My father's shoes invade my vision. "Look at me, daughter."

I cast my gaze upwards and stare my father in the eye.

"We have connected your bracelet to another power source. This should boost you enough to create the portal. Cast any magick in our direction and there will be consequences."

"Remember this?" King Demetrius cuts in.

I look over at him and see yet another figurine in his hand. He squeezes it and pain shoots my abdomen. I let out a gasp of pain and double over as much as I can in my restrained state. The pain lessens some after a moment. Unfortunately, even after I catch my breath, a dull throbbing still remains.

"I will keep pressure on this totem until the portal has opened. Complete the task quickly and you should be able to save yourself from too much agony."

"You heard him," my father says. "Do as your told for once in your miserable life and maybe I might finally be proud that I was stuck with you."

Gee, how encouraging.

"And if I refuse?" I ask, glaring at my father. *I do not know how they plan to force the issue other than by causing me pain. Pain I can endure. I have no idea what this grantador is going to do to our world. There is no way I will willingly release it.*

My father scowls at me. "The magick source you are attached to should encourage your cooperation and if it doesn't then I urge you to think of this. We have kept that friend of yours captive here ever since we brought you in. Sorin, is it?" He holds up a small button and clicks it, the dust in front of me flickers to a dual images. One shows a still picture of Sorin laying in a familiar barren room and the other a video feed of guards outside his door. I glance back at the picture of Sorin. He is no longer covered in vines and his skin now has a faint glow to it. *Could that mean?* "Those guards have orders to murder him within the next hour unless I tell them otherwise. So refuse if you like, dear daughter, but know that it will only lead to his demise." The dust returns to the floor. "Now, let us commence." Holding up another button, he pushes it, smirking at me.

Familiar magick slams into me stealing my breath. My own magick reacts, reaching towards the energy like a familiar friend. I watch in horror as tiny balls of light start to sprinkle themselves throughout the room. *No, no, no!*

My father stares at the balls of light, his eyes wide in amazement. I look around to notice everyone is staring at them much the same way,

"I can't believe this is working," my father says under his breath.

"That is your fault for doubting me," Mylindia says teasingly. "Those cuffs were the best investment I ever made."

I ignore their chatter, doing my best to call back my own energy. Closing my eyes, I try to visualize my threads and am surprised by what I see. Instead of my green thread being sprinkled with green magickal energy, it seems like the strand has now fully absorbed it, causing the thread to become fully green in color and twice as big. My heart thuds in my chest, hopefully knowing that that thread represents my connection to Sorin. *He is doing better.* Running over to the green strand I grasp it, sending some of the power thrumming through me through his thread. It seems to hum with life. *Wake up, Sorin. I need you to wake up!* I scream at it. The tattoo on my thigh starts to burn.

"Alaceandra?" Sorin's groggy voice enters my head and I sigh in relief.

"I need you to get out of there. Now, Sorin," I plead.

The thread hums, but I hear no response. *Hopefully it is enough.*

Turning my attention back to the purple strand, I release the green. It too pulses with power, but this power looks unstable. The remaining two fraying pieces pull taut as magickal purple energy slams into the thread, causing the strand to shake violently at the impact. *What is happening?*

I open my eyes to see that the floating orbs have stilled in the air. *The portal is about to open.* Pure panic runs through me. *I do not have much more time.* Slamming my eyes closed, I refocus on my purple thread. Mentally, I try to soothe the little balls of energy into calming down. The middle frayed string starts to unravel further and my stomach drops. *I do not think that it would be good if those fell apart.* My brain resorts to Baldar's last few instructions. In my mind's eye, I run over to the quickly dissolving fray and pull both ends of the thread, trying to force them to come back together. Slowly, both ends of each fray start to reach for the other winding around themselves. The energy in the first half of the thread starts to calm. *Okay... I did not know that would happen, but that is good, right?* I direct my attention to the last fray.

I hear the balls of energy crash into the floor, the ground prying open with a sickening cracking noise. Unlike when the prince and I had attempted this maneuver in our quarters, the energy forming those balls is more uncontrolled. I open my eyes momentarily only to realize that, instead of just one crack opening up in the ground, there are six. Sheer panic fills me. I close my eyes again and mentally run towards the last fray, but as I get closer, the fray only seems to move farther away. *No, no, no.*

I throw my body towards the farthest end of the fray. My hand just barely grasps it before it can move farther away. The magickal energy starts to pound into my body causing me to wince in pain as sharp pain starts to lash through me. My other hand grabs the other end of the thread.

"She is doing something," the woman's voice meets my ear.

"Doing something? What do you mean doing something?" King Demetrius snaps.

"I don't know!" She yells. "The energy is calming down. The cracks look like they are slowing. We need to get her to stop." Suddenly she screams. "What the fuck are those things?!"

I feel tiny feet run across my own. *The small demoni must have started to escape.*

With all my might, I shove the two ends of the thread together and whisper the words that Baldar had taught me. "Back into the portals of where you once were. Your time in this battle has yet to occur."

I open my eyes to watch as each of the portals snap shut. A searing pain fills me and I know why. *Six more failed portals.* I breathe deeply. *I cannot afford another.*

"You!" A shrill voice jerks my attention back to the woman. She has deep gouges covering her face. *A demoni must have gotten her.* I do my best to hide my amusement. "You did this!"

I stare at her blankly before flicking my eyes over at the other two kings. They too are covered in scratches. *At least my magick knew who to attack this time.*

"Grab the girl," Demetrius growls. "It is time for plan b."

CHAPTER FIFTY-THREE

Captured (Again)

Alaceandra

I gasp as I am thrown into a barred cell in the deepest part of the palace. Mylindia stands at the cell door her hands grasping a sword already drawn. The metal of the blade stands out starkly against her pale dress. I cannot help but admire how cool she looks. *Wow, is that how bad ass I look with a dress and a dagger? I should wield one more often.* Mylindia's eyes are steel as she stares at me in disgust. A spark of pain shoots through me, originating at my wrist and I clutch at the glowing red band. Another crack seems to have appeared on its surface. I tug it, but even in its weakened state it refuses to come off of my wrist.

"Stay there!" My father says through gritted teeth. "I knew I shouldn't have trusted you to do your duty. Now it is time you suffer the consequences of your insolence." Fear curls through me as I think about what my rebellion could mean for Sorin, but I choose to push it away. *He woke up. He will be okay.* I try to calm myself. My father continues. "That bracelet you wear? It has been tracking how you manifest your abilities since the moment you awoke in the palace. I bargained with Demetrius for the ancient relic to ensure your obedience. I was obviously wise to do so as it will now serve yet another purpose." He says smugly. "Since you will not cooperate willingly in opening the portal, you will now be forced. That bracelet will drain you of your powers until there is nothing left in you."

I glare at my father. I thought that the band's abilities in the throne room were bad enough, but the thought that it can enable them to use my powers without me present? It makes my skin feel itchy and I have to suppress the urge to yank at it again. My father takes my glare for challenge and strides up to me slapping me viciously across the face. My vision doubles and blurs, but I remain conscious. I spit blood at my father's feet and he yanks me to eye level by the front of my gown.

"We will get this portal open. You will not make more of a disappointment of yourself. All you were ever good for was your power. That is why I have kept you alive as long as I have. I will not allow you to make me into a fool any longer, Alaceandra." He throws me back onto the ground and turns away. My knees scrape against the stone of the floor and I do my best not to react, but the pain is lashing through me with such intensity that it causes my legs to weaken and I crumble to the ground. My father snorts, amused by my weakness. "You better hope the siphoning kills you." My father spits out already walking away from me. "Because if it doesn't I will do it myself and trust me, dear daughter, I will not be as gentle." His statement is accented by another burning wave of agony hitting me.

My father walks towards the barred doors. He has almost left the room when I hear him say, "There is nothing you can do to stop us. We will meet the grantador and restore the lands under our control. There is no one left to save you now, dear daughter." He laughs. "If you don't believe me, feel free to look around." The clang of metal sealing me into what is meant to be my tomb marks his departure. I glance up to watch as my father and Mylindia disappear from the hall.

Look around? Fighting through the pain, I slowly turn my body around to see, who I now know to be, Syverious laying unmoving behind me. *Why is he down here?* His clothing is torn and tattered. Bruises and burns mar his skin. *Why is he injured? Why would they injure him? Did they not just confirm that he was working with them? Telling them of the progression of my powers?* His face looks paler than normal and his body sickly in the low light.

He looks— No. As angry as I was at him, I did not want him dead. *He cannot be dead.* I crawl over to him and shake him, but he does not so much as flinch at my touch. *What did they do to you?* Panic starts to claw its way up my throat and I put a hand under his nose to see if I can feel for any kind of breath. A gentle breeze greets my fingers and a notch of tension releases from my body. *So he is alive. That is good at least, but why will he not wake up?* I glance at the door that my father and the guard left from to notice that the coast is still clear.

Another wave of pain rolls through my body from what I now know is the bracelet siphoning power and I grit my teeth in anger. *Those greedy fucking kings. Taking and taking without a care of the consequences.* I stare at the tiny swirls present on the bases of each finger. *All except one. If they are able to start the progression of yet another portal.* I do not stop the tears from falling from my eyes. *What will that mean for me?* I weigh my options, trying my best to come up with some way I can gain control of the portal and the creatures coming out of it without giving the kings exactly what they want.

I can help you achieve what you seek. I can release you, dear Alaceandra. You know what you must do. That sickly sweet voice echoes in my head. I do not doubt her words. Whatever part of me she is, she is... disgustingly effective. She has ensured I have survived two encounters I probably should not have. I might have more of a mind to actually give into her once again, except... except when I do. I lose all sense of myself. The images I saw in that dust were not me. Who is to say what kind of damage she will do if I let her loose once again.

You are not to be trusted. All you crave is violence, I snap back. *You mean to take over entirely, do you not? I would not maintain control if I give into you.*

You may have no other choice. That voice growls at me. Its sweet act dropping for just the barest bit of time. In a more soothing tone, it continues. *Do you not want to show those kings who you truly can be? Do you not want to make them fear your wrath?* Unease rolls in my stomach.

Not in the way you wish me to. You are... demented.

I. Am. You.

Pushing the voice away, I try to breathe through the pain of the siphoning. I shake at Syverious again, watching carefully for any more signs of life. He remains still. I feel his neck for a pulse. A faint beat greets my fingertips. *Good. It is not too late.*

Noise at the door calls my attention away from Syverious for a second. My eyes dart around the hall but I see no one. A squeak brings my gaze downwards. I am delighted to see Baldar shoving his little body through the cell bars.

"Alaceandra!" He says in a rush. *"I have finally found you. Sorin and Sam are making their way over here."*

"So you have." I say. Another wave of pain rolls through me and I clutch at Syverious' shirt, but it does nothing to dampen my joy at his statement. *"How are they? Sorin? Sam?"*

"They are doing well," Baldar says with a knowing smile. Relief fills me with the knowledge that Sorin is still okay. *"As I said, they are making their way here. They had me scout ahead but when I saw you weren't in*

your room, I went looking to find you. I never thought you would be here in the dungeons. What happened?"

"Too much to explain right now. I am trapped here and as it seems so is Syverious. I need you to get us out of here."

"Syverious?" The little ferret tilts his head in confusion.

"The prince, sorry. That is his name."

"He revealed his name to you then?" I can tell Baldar's beady eyes are studying me *"Curious..."*

"More like I figured it out." I sigh, clenching my fist as I ride another wave of agony. *"Look, we can go over the specifics later. It is not important right now. We do not have much time until the kings open their portal. They have been trying to force me to do it all afternoon and since I did not well..."* I show Baldar my palms.

"Fuck." Baldar says. *"How are they making a portal without you?"*

"The bracelet. Somehow it is channeling my powers to them. I do not really know how it works only that it is working."

"This is not good."

"No it is not."

Baldar stares at the bracelet for a moment. *"It has cracks in it."*

"Yes it happens every time uh.... a voice in my head takes over."

Surprisingly, Baldar seems unmoved by the information. *"Ah, you should have informed me you were hearing her sooner. No matter. It seems that the bracelet cannot handle power surges. Once we get all of your men together, we can channel your energy into it and that should break it."*

I stare at him. *"Okay.... what about the portal?"*

Baldar looks sad. *"We will have to ensure it completes. We cannot have you hitting that many failures this soon."*

"Would that not give them exactly what they want?"

299

"We can handle the grantador when the time comes for it. We just need to make sure you survive this."

"How do you know about the grantador?"

Baldar rolls his eyes. *"Your men are close. I will inform them of where you are. As you said, we do not have much time."*

I am unsatisfied with his answer, but I let it slide. Baldar starts to shimmer out of focus. *"Baldar!"*

His form solidifies for a moment. *"Yes, Alaceandra?"*

"Be careful."

"I will." Baldar sits on his back legs, pausing, before walking cautiously over to Syverious. I eye Baldar warily as he places his paw on Syverious' chest. *"Now that you know his true name... Do you wish for him to awaken?"* Before I can speak Baldar cuts me off. *"Answer honestly, Alaceandra. Although he is alive at the moment, he is on the brink of death. He has been beaten and drained of power. If you want him to live, you must make that choice now and mean it. He does not have much time left."* He cautions.

I stare at Baldar. That evil side of me slips into consciousness once more. *It would serve him right to die, Alaceandra. You do not need him. You do not need any of them. All those you trust are only going to betray you. He already has. Do you want him to do it again? It is better to be rid of him before he can attempt it. Give into me and we will finish this without them.*

He had caused me such pain, and yet...

And yet nothing! He has lied to you. Manipulated you. Give into me, Alaceandra. Only I can get you out of here alive.

Her statement lets doubt creep into my brain. *What is his true endgame?* He always seemed to have one. Every piece of him I had unraveled was complicated, tragic— beautiful. Could I really see him dead before the game was over?

No. I cannot. I think to myself.

I turn to Baldar. *"Yes. I want him to live."*

"Okay." Baldar continues to study the both of us. *"Kiss him then."*

"What?"

"Oh, don't be a prude now, Alaceandra." Baldar chitters exasperatedly. *"No matter what spell they put on him, as long as it has not advanced to the point of death for him yet, that should at least buy him some time. If you have not figured it out already, your magick is directly linked to your sexcapades with these men. Your horndoggedness will quite literally save his life by renewing his energy."*

My eyes flick between the albino ferret and the prince, stunned by his words. *"You are fucking with me, right?"*

"Not at all." Baldar stares at me with a straight face. *"It is why you were so late to achieve your powers. With the amount of magickal energy you are meant to hold, there needed to be something to bind you back to this world. To ensure the tie is strong enough, sacrifices must be made. The ties are a result of that. You fuel each other."*

"O-okay." My brain is scrambling to make sense of his words but before I can Baldar starts to disappear once again.

"Great. I will be back." He vanishes.

I stare down at Syverious and sigh. "Here goes nothing."

CHAPTER FIFTY-FOUR

Fancy Meeting You Here

Alaceandra

Slowly, I lean down and press my lips to Syverious'. Flashes of the past few days glimmer in my mind's eye. Our kisses, our verbal sparring matches, our bodies tangled together in a fit of passion, our fights. The emotions of these events swell in my heart and I allow the feelings of all those moments to find refuge in this singular meeting of our lips. As I do, I use my thoughts to speak to him. *You once promised that you would never let your father win. That you would see Ptheryeth's inevitable rise or demise with your own eyes, without his savagery at its helm. Do not forsake your promise, Syverious. Do not let him win. There is far too much at stake.* With those thoughts projected, I end the kiss.

Slowly, signs of life start to return to the prince's body. His coloring starts to improve first, the ashen pallor of his cheeks turning more pink. Then his fingers start to twitch. That tremor works its way through his body until finally it makes its way to his face. His eyelids twitch as a dull lavender glow takes over his body. Finally as the glow fades, his eyes fly open and he inhales deeply. When they meet mine they are a vibrant lavender. The world stills. The air falls stagnant, unmoving as he studies my face. After a couple of moments, he speaks in a low voice.

"Little dove." His gaze holds intensity that I cannot look away from. He lifts a shaky hand and traces his fingers over my jaw, then up my cheek, until his palm is gently caressing me. He looks around. "Are you okay? Why are you here?"

I sigh. Internally, my thoughts rage. If the king's words about him funneling them information holds even an ounce of truth he should know why I am in these dungeons. I search his eyes for the truth and only find concern present within them. His face is battered and bruised. His hands have open wounds that are trickling tiny rivulets of blood down his arms. And his wrist. My gaze pauses on it. *Is that... a cuff?*

My fingers trace its surface, a tiny tremor going through me. "What did they do to you?"

"That is not important. What is important is that they have not succeeded in their plans yet. If they had we would not be having this conversation." The shakiness of his hand has disappeared. "We must leave here as soon as possible." His eyes close, his expression one of pain. He takes a slow breath, before he looks back at me, his eyes now a blazing lavender. He pulls me close and I let him. Pressing a soft kiss to my forehead, he nods.

"Okay." He pauses, releasing me. I back away from him, gently, and stand. He nods again and stands himself. "Let's go. We have to meet up with—"

"Sam, right?" I say, turning back towards the cell door to hide the pain lining my face. The shock waves traveling through me have intensified and I fight every urge I have to fall to the ground. I clear my throat as it passes.

"Yes. Have you seen him?" Syverious asks.

I shake my head. "No. Baldar came by. He said that they were headed this way." A little noise escapes me as another particularly brutal wave pierces me.

I shiver as Syverious allows a breeze to skate across my shoulder, pushing my hair away from my face.

"Dove? What is going on? Did they hurt you?"

"Siphoning," I manage to say. "They are siphoning my powers through the bracelet. Not sure how, but it hurts." I double over. "Shit."

"Shit." Syverious echoes. He grabs my arm to inspect my wrist. The skin around the band has turned an angry red. The veins surrounding are raised and swollen. The entirety of my arm now hot to the touch. Even with its temperature, the prince continues to hold my arm delicately. "This is not good." He gently tries to tug at the bracelet, but the swelling of my wrist has made it now impossible to move. He traces a finger over the fissures in the bands service, pushing his nail in to see if he can pry the cracks open further. "The bracelet is cracked... it should be weaker. Have you tried to snap it?"

"It will not come off with physical force. The cracks were made by magical energy. I have tried to pry at it and pull it off but the bracelet will not budge."

Another gentle breeze flows over my wrist. The prince growls. "My power is weakened. They must have attempted to drain me as well." He motions to his own bracelet. "Unluckily for them, I saw how they attached it." With a couple of movements, the bracelet falls to the ground. The prince hisses as his wrist starts to bleed profusely. "This one was never meant to be permanent," he explains through gritted teeth.

"Wish the same could be said for mine," I grit out through another wave of agony. "I am hoping with Sorin and Sam's power combined-"

He places the hand not bloodied by his wrist on my shoulder. "Understood."

"Have you seen these bracelets before?"I question, his knowledge of them raises flags in my head.

"No. I only watched how my father's guard adhered it and felt its effects. The rest is surmisable."

Sure. That voice reveals itself again. I ignore it.

"We need to get out of here," I say instead.

"We do, but I am afraid that will prove difficult. Sam said that there is magick over the cell that will alert them if we escape."

"Okay... so then what do you propose we do?"

"Leave anyway. If we can get out of here quickly enough it shouldn't matter, better to be found running than to be sitting bait."

I nod. "That is a good point, but how? We do not have a key." I grit the words out, another particularly vicious swell of pain assaulting me.

Concern takes over the prince's gaze. He wipes at the sweat gathering on my brow before he answers. "You are right we don't have the key, but you do have that pin you refuse to leave behind, right?" He gives me a knowing look.

My eyes widen. I search the banding around my breasts and pull out my golden pin. *Looks like you will prove yourself useful after all.* "How did you know about—"

"The pin? I have undressed you, dove. The thing stabbed me."

I hold back a laugh and the prince winks at me.

"I also know about those stars on your back and that mark of mine decorating your pretty thigh."

That causes my mouth to open in surprise.

He smirks. "As I said before, dove. I am a master at finding out secrets, but we can discuss those once we are out of here."

Syverious slowly guides me to the cell doors. He fits the pin inside the lock, maneuvering it delicately until the pins of the lock fall into place. After a couple of minutes, the door releases and swings open. I take the pin from the prince and stick it back in my clothing. Syverious and I guide the door open slowly, doing our best to guard against any creaking. A yawn overtakes me and my limbs start to become harder and harder to lift. Alarm registers through me as I realize my body is nearing exhaustion in its fight against the siphoning. Syverious tenses behind me as the edge of my vision starts to darken. Suddenly, I am in the air.

"What are you doing?" I say weakly.

"Getting us out of here." There is a terrifying intensity in his tone. Syverious sprints and weaves down the halls. Darting behind walls whenever we hear any voices approaching us. I stay silent and hold onto him tightly. My eyes close and then I feel lips against mine. My eyes fly open.

"What are you doing?" I whisper.

"Shh," Syverious responds. "I am trying to channel more power into you. You are passing out."

"You have already been drained of your own power, Syverious. You cannot be channeling any more into me." I try to protest as we race down the halls.

"I will not let you die," his tone is harsh.

"But—" I start to argue, but realize it is no use. I could not stop him if I wanted to.

You may not, but I still can. Give into me, Alaceandra. We will escape here and burn this place to the ground.

"Shh," he repeats, unintentionally quieting the voice inside of me. His lips meet mine again and I submit to the feeling, sighing gently as I sense his thread thrum within me. He releases my lips too soon.

"Thank you," I whisper, feeling a bit more stable.

"Don't mention it." Syverious says, a smirk clear on his face.

We finally make it to a large lobby area of the palace and Syverious pauses before walking through it. "This room does not have much cover." He looks around the space, muttering to himself. Abruptly, he stiffens. "Footsteps approaching. Stay on guard," he whispers, pulling us back into the tunnel we just exited from. He sets me gently on my feet and I hold onto the wall as I peer back into the large room in front of us. His hands go to his hip as if he was grabbing for a weapon no longer present. His hands clench when they meet nothing. I watch his back straighten, before he takes a breath, preparing himself for whatever may be approaching us.

Multiple sets of footsteps reach my ears from the other end of the room. There is a pause and then the sound seems to disappear completely. *Where did they go?* I squint into the darkness, my heart racing in my ears. I glance back at Syverious and notice that his gaze is firmly fixed on the tunnel across from us. I turn my attention back as three forms slowly and silently come into view. I squint... *is that?* A new fourth form emerges from the trio. A tiny furry creature skittering out in front of them like it is on a mission. *It is.*

"*Baldar?*" I ask.

The tiny creature stops, his eyes zeroing in on us.

"*It is. I see you have escaped your cage and awoken the prince. Good. I have brought the rest of your men.*"

One of the men's mouth starts to move, but no sound travels from it. When the form moves slightly to the left, a flash of red hair catches my attention. *Sorin.* The thought is confirmed by the warming of his mark.

The forms suddenly vanish and my heart stops. *Where did they go?* As quickly as the thought passes is as quickly as the forms reappear, but instead of them being across the room, they are standing directly in front of me. A palm is over my mouth before a scream can escape.

My eyes search the darkness for the palm's owner. A smiling Sam meets my gaze.

"Don't scream," he whispers.

Taking a deep breath, I nod. Slowly, he releases my mouth and instead folds me into a big hug. Tears rush to my eyes and as I hold him tightly. "We thought we lost you, parum bellator," comes Sam's voice whispered into my hair. "You made me work with that fucking prince to get you back." His breaths are uneven, I can tell he is barely keeping it together. "And the fucked up part is I would do it again, just to make sure you are safe. Fuck, I am so glad you are safe." I feel his lips on the top of my head and the sensation causes my heart to jolt in my chest.

Another set of arms pulls me from Sam's and Sorin's familiar scent invades my nostrils. My tattoo hums happily the moment our skin touches. The tears gathering in my eyes now truly fall as I latch onto Sorin with a desperation I did not know was in me.

"I visited you every night," I whisper to him feverishly. "I never would have left without you."

"I know, firefly, I know." His lips capture mine and the warm comfort his presence encourages within me springs to life. Our kiss is desperate. Our hands searching the other's body, doing their best to commit every curve and ridge to memory should we ever have to part again. My skin warms as I feel my fire prickle within me, ready to be unleashed.

A throat clears. We part quickly. My head whips to the third form that was apparently accompanying Sorin and Sam, cheeks burning. Then I blink. *No, it cannot be.* But it is. A man with long white hair steps forward.

"As sweet as this reunion is, there will be time for it later. If what Telvonius and Mirksyl say is true, we only have so much time until the portal reopens," Sydon drawls.

"Shut it," Sam snaps.

"You are lucky I am not dragging your ass back home for showing up here. The princess is under my—"

"I said. Shut. It."

Sydon sneers at Sam and Sam returns his glare.

"Do... do they know each other?" I ask Baldar studying the men.

"You can say that," Baldar's voice is filled with amusement. *"Do not worry about his presence here, due to the Helomazi and Tikilium kings deciding to go against his ruling, he will not pose much of a threat."*

I glance over to the prince who is watching their interaction with interest.

"Against his ruling?" I ask, but as I do yet another wave of pain crashes through me causing me to crumple to my knees. Every bit of relief Syverious' and Sorin's kisses brought me vanishes instantly. I gasp, doing my best to fight through the pain.

"Shit." All the men say in unison.

"We need to get the cuff off of her," the prince says, his voice panicked. "They are using it to siphon her powers."

"What?" The men say in unison once again.

My skin feels feverish and my vision starts to blacken at the edges. Tiny tremors take over my body as the room goes from hot to cold to hot again.

"Did you not know?" The prince asks.

"No," a voice that sounds a lot like Sydon's reaches my ears. "The bracelet was only meant to keep her powers in check should they spike during training. I should have known the kings were up to something when I saw her reddened wrist the first time." Anger laces his words.

"You should have known better working with those kings. The bastards care nothing for the future of this world. The only people they actually care about is themselves," Sam snaps.

"I thought I had them under control," Sydon snaps back.

"And look where that got you."

"What else was I supposed to do. You left to follow her. You—"

"I said to shut it about that stuff. We can talk about it later."

"Both of you shut it!" Baldar's voice cuts through their bickering. *"All of you need to combine your energy now and channel it into Alaceandra if you want her to keep breathing. The kings have already completed the second stage of the portal. The demoni have been freed. She needs to be awake to complete the portal so that she does not have to endure her final consequence."*

My consciousness starts to dim. As if she is summoned, my inner voice returns.

You have to let me out. Let me gain control. You only have so much time left. These men will not be able to save you. Only I will.

I refuse. I fight the voice. *I have seen what you can do. Who are you going to direct your energy to should I let you out? The only ones around me are my allies.*

You have no allies. Only those who will bow to you and those who will burn.

I close my eyes. *That is not true. I cannot believe that. I will die before I believe that.*

Then die. I will overcome you soon enough.

My body jerks as another wave of agony pushes through it. I whimper unable to fight against it any longer.

"Fuck."

CHAPTER FIFTY-FIVE

Nightmare or A Dream

Alaceandra

I am sitting in the grass at the top of a cliff. My feet dangle precariously over the edge and I swing them back and forth enjoying the feeling of the cool breeze against them. Instead of a dress, the clothing on my body takes the form of a loose pair of pants and a sleeveless top. My hair is loose as well blowing behind me. I sit there for what feels like an eternity, balancing precariously on the edge of the cliff waiting for something, but nothing comes. Slowly, I feel my heart shatter as disappointment fills me.

Where is he? *I think to myself.* He should be here by now. *My disappointment grows and grows, but who I am waiting for is actually unknown to me. The only thing I know is that I am waiting for someone, and he is not here. I chew on my bottom lip, swinging my feet more deliberately over the edge of the cliff.*

"*Alaceandra!" A feminine voice yells at me.*

I glance around, confused, but as I search the grassy field behind me, no one appears.

"*Not over there, silly girl." The voice teases. "Here. Down here."*

Hesitantly, I glance below me. The landscape between my feet is a dark abyss. Only the glimmering light of blackened fire can be seen flickering through the space. I search the darkness, desperately trying to find the origin of the voice. Before my eyes a figure cloaked in white appears.

"Hello?" I yell into the darkness.

I see the figure turn to me and smile.

"Hello!" The figure echoes back.

I blink at the person. "What are you doing down there?"

Sweet laughter echoes up from beneath me. "Living, sweet Alaceandra. But, tell me, what are you still doing up there?"

"I- I am supposed to be up here," my voice wobbles uncertainly as I answer her.

"Really? Says who?" The voice asks me playfully. "Seems like you are all alone up there. Would it not be better to come down here and hang out with me?"

"I am waiting for someone," I reply.

The figure tilts its head at me. "I don't see anyone."

"I know," I reply. "They are not here yet."

"Oh," the figure walks closer to the cliff separating us. "Well then I don't think they would mind if you came down here for just a little while. I promise you can climb back up as soon as they arrive." The figure smiles sweetly. "Someone like you should not be kept waiting for so long."

She has a point. *I think to myself. Squinting into the darkness, I chew my bottom lip.* "But it is so dark down there," *I say hesitantly.*

The figure glances around. "I have come to like the dark," she replies. "I am sure if you came down here you would like it to. Besides, I am here. I will keep you company while you wait."

I stare down into the darkness, considering. With a sigh, I stand. I have grown bored waiting all alone. *As I approach the edge of the cliff, a shooting star catches my eye. A voice echoes in my brain as I watch it soar across the sky.* If you need me, call upon the stars.

"The stars," I whisper out loud.

"What was that?" The figure says. "You disappeared. Are you on your way down?"

Something jerks within my chest as I watch the star disappear.

"Stars," I repeat.

"Alaceandra?"

Suddenly, a burning sensation fills my back and I scream. A presence grabs me from behind and I fight against it.

"Shhhhh, princess, I have you," A masculine voice coos into my ear.

The feminine voice that was just moments ago calling me from the bottom of the cliff now whispers to me. Her voice louder than it was before.

"They can only help you escape for so long. Soon, we will be joined again."

I gasp. My eyes spring open. Hands are pressed against my body. On my arms, my legs, and torso. I am leaning against a warm body as hands stroke my hair.

"Shhhh..."

Warmth radiates as what I now recognize is the men's power courses through me. I blink and lift up slightly. The hands retreat. I stare into Syverious, Sydon, Sam, and Sorin's eyes, mine widening as I take in my surroundings.

"Wh-what happened?" I gasp.

The prince smiles at me. Gently, he grabs my hand and brings it up to my wrist. The red bracelet that was once there has fallen completely away. I look down and notice that pieces of it are scattered throughout the floor.

"H-how?" I ask.

"Power surge." Baldar climbs onto my legs. *"I had all the men channel their power into you. It was enough to complete the cracking of the band."*

I look around again, pausing as I realize that the person I was leaning on was none other than Sydon. *"All the men?"* I ask Baldar.

"All of them," he confirms.

"Are we sure we can trust him?" I eye Sydon warily.

"For now," Baldar says coyly.

"What about Syverious?" My gaze travels to the prince.

"We shall see."

The palace shakes. Rocks fall from above us and the men do their best to stop it from hitting me.

"What was that?" I ask aloud.

"Portal," Baldar answers solemnly.

"I thought that removing the band would close it," I whisper.

Baldar shakes his head. *"As I said, we need to complete it. That is the only way you are going to be able to get out of here without consequences."* I glance down at my hand at the offending swirls.

"Then what are we waiting for? It is time to complete the portal."

CHAPTER FIFTY-SIX

Unlikely Allies

Alaceandra

"I will assume from your one-sided conversation that this is not over yet," the prince says dryly, leaning against the wall of the hall. He looks tired, but I can tell he is trying to mask it.

"I have to complete the portal," I answer him sadly. "Otherwise there will be consequences."

"Consequences?" Sorin asks.

I look over at him and smile seeing him so alert. I had grown accustom to watching him on that table wrapped in his own vines. I do not think I have fully processed the fact that those days are now over. He has lost a bit of weight since he was standing last. Although it had only been a few days, I can only assume only having magick to feed you while you are out is not exactly the most nourishing diet. Even still, the man before me is the same old Sorin. My rock in rushing waters. He looks not the least bit fazed as he takes in the scene around him, his only focus trying to find the best solution to the situation. All in the name of keeping me safe.

"What kind of consequences?" Sorin meets my eyes and returns my smile. He looks tired, but life fiercely sparkles in his golden eyes. My gaze pauses on his face as the thought registers. *Sorin's eyes are gold.* Not the flashing dark gold that he gets when his powers surge, but a shimmering gold reminiscent to a blazing fire. The same shade of gold as the little firefly mark that now adorns his collarbone. *But when did his eyes change colors?* I must have been staring for too long because Sorin's eyes dart away from mine, his eyes returning to the group. *I will have to ask him about that later.*

Surprisingly, it is the prince that answers him. "She can die," he starts. "Or fall into a more uncontrolled state. One that will make her wish she died." He says the last part softly.

All eyes in the room turn to him.

"How do you know that?" Sam asks suspiciously.

The prince sighs. He looks at me before observing the rest of the group. Some of his usual arrogance falls away as he seems to come to a decision within himself. "Look we all know that I might have come into this relationship with a couple of... ulterior motives."

Silence is thick within the group.

The prince sighs again. "I might have been told that once Alaceandra gets her portal abilities that those... consequences as you called them would happen, but that I would also get a surge of power of my own. I was going to use that surge to kill my father... and her if she got too out of control."

Shock fills me at his confession and I have to bite my cheek to stop a sob from breaking through. *I knew I could not trust him. Stupid. You are so fucking stupid.* I silently berate myself. More silence spans between us, but Sorin's voice breaks it. "There better be a but coming here or you will be the next on our list to die."

"Of course there is," the prince says his shoulders slouching. "It might come as a surprise to some, but I have actually come to... love... Alaceandra." That revelation shocks me more than the first. Some part of me always suspects the prince's trickery, but his love? The man has only spoken of possessing me, never of loving me. I had started to think he was not capable of such an emotion. He looks nervous as he proceeds. "Enough it seems to even forsake my kingdom and my vow if it came to it. Although I still wanted Alaceandra to grow in her portal abilities when we were working with Baldar, I only really felt okay with it knowing that her refining the abilities would lead her to not meeting the fate that I thought was certain for her." His eyes meet mine and I can see the honesty shining within them. I look away still hurt from his confession. "My dove told me that despite our upbringing, the best we can do for ourselves and our kingdoms is not become the men our fathers are. I believe that there is truth in that. I am sorry for my deception, dove."

"I do not forgive you," I whisper. "But that does not mean I do not think that you should not get your revenge. I have my own to deal out." I stand up. "We can discuss the ramifications of your actions another time. For now, we need to get this portal handled."

The prince meets my eyes and nods. "Understood."

"Good." I step forward and everyone follows. I pause for a moment eyeing Sydon suspiciously. "And where are you going?"

"To help," he says, as if it were obvious.

"To help... us escape?" I say, my voice incredulous.

He rolls his eyes. "Yes, princess."

"But are you not the whole reason I am here to begin with?"

"I am."

"Then why in all of Ptheryeth would you be helping me escape this place?"

"It seems I have aligned myself with the wrong people in a foolish attempt to get back at my older brother. I am now acting to rectify that error."

"Older brother?" I question. I glance between Sydon and Sam, my stomach sinking at the guilty expression on Sam's face. "Sam?" The pitch of my voice is dangerously high.

Sam wipes a hand down his face. "Yes, yes. He is my younger brother. Can we move on now? Don't we have a portal to deal with and all that ready up type speech you were telling us earlier?"

My mouth drops open in shock. "Y-you," I stutter.

"Firefly," Sorin cuts in. "We really should get going?"

I glare at Sam. "You will be explaining yourself later," I growl.

Sam chuckles. "Yes, parum bellator, you have my word."

"You call her little warrior?" Sydon says. "Really?"

"I am so serious right now if you do not shut the fuck up I am going to make you," Sam snaps.

"Onward!" Baldar squeaks, barreling forward. We, of course, follow.

CHAPTER FIFTY-SEVEN

Too Late

Alaceandra

The palace halls become nothing but a blur as we move through them. We stick to the shadows, doing our best to move quickly and yet quietly as to not call too much attention to ourselves. Now that I have been released from the red band my body no longer spikes with pain as we move, the kings unable to siphon from me now that their tether is removed. My body also seems to be healed from my prior injuries. I suspect Sydon might have a part in that, seeing as he was also feeding energy into me when I passed out. I eye the prince who also seems to have made a miraculous recovery in the short amount of time since I have been passed out. As great as it is that the kings can no longer use any more of my magickal energy, the damage has already been done. Which means that we are, unfortunately, headed back to the throne room.

"You will need to be able to be near the source of the portal to complete it." Baldar told me, his feet skittering quickly through the halls. *"You are not advanced enough to achieve this remotely."*

The halls are strangely empty as we make our approach. Come to think of it, I have yet to encounter anyone but my men since the prince and I escaped the dungeons. Unease flits through me as I scan our surroundings. Although not all areas of the palace were heavily guarded, the fact that we could travel so far without the mere sight of anyone is disconcerting. *Where is everyone?*

As if in answer to my question, we round the corner to the guard room and men and women in teal, silver, black, and bronze armor are crowding the open space. Sam has us cloaked in his magick so they do not immediately notice our presence, but the compacted nature of their bodies against each other in front of the room make it impossible to get through and into the throne room undetected. The soldiers are staring straight ahead, their bodies taut as if prepared for some upcoming battle. I scan the crowd of soldiers looking for anyone I might immediately recognize. Three rows in stands Jaq and Lylane. Their eyes dart around nervously, unlike those around them, as if they are unsure about their place in the group.

Seeing the crowd of soldiers we stop in our tracks, trying to assess what to do next. Although, Sam's magick is great at providing stealth. We decide it best not to speak to each other to communicate in order to expend the least amount of Sam's magickal energy. We have no idea what the inside of that throne room looks like and although I feel mostly recharged from the men gifting me with a bit of their reserves, the prince is still quite drained. We will need to be smart if we want to complete the portal and make it out of here alive. *But how to get past these guards?* I do not think that they would be excited to let the prince or I through. Seeing as Sorin is likely still thought to be in a coma, the chance of him getting through is unlikely. Sam is a stranger. That leaves... as if the thought hit all of us at the same time all eyes turn to Sydon. He nods, understanding our meaning. Stepping forward Sam releases him from his cloak of magick.

"What is going on here?" Sydon's voice echoes through the small space. I see some soldiers twitch at his voice.

"Sydon!" A man in silver looks surprised to see him. "A-are you not aware of the decree?"

"Do inform me," Sydon says, his arms crossed angrily. His form screams of someone who has lost all patience with the man in front of him. The other soldiers feel his ire too. We watch as many of them exchange glances, losing the bravado they had when we had first arrived.

"We are not to let anyone through this door... um... including you," he cringes at Sydon's glare, but continues his explanation quickly. "The kings are conducting business in the throne room that is not to be interrupted."

A teal guard pipes up. "The Tikilium princess and the Helomasian prince have been been caught committing treason once again. And they have insiders this time. Anyone caught trying to infiltrate this room is to be considered treasonous as well and to be killed on sight."

Sam, Sorin, the prince, and I all exchange glances.

"Which kings gave you these orders? I was convening with Telvonius and Mirksyl only hours ago and they made no mention of such an order."

"King Demetrius and King Nikoli," A soldier in black now chimes in.

"Ah," Sydon smirks. His eyes seem to meet those of each soldier as he surveys the room. He takes a step forward and all the soldiers gasp simultaneously, their hands falling to the swords at their side as if by instinct. The guards form a loose crescent around Sydon blocking him from going any further. The tension in the space builds as it seems that Sydon and the soldiers around him are at an impasse. "And if I, myself, were to defy the order?"

The sound of a sword drawing catches our attention. A soldier in bronze points his weapon at Sydon, causing Sydon's mouth to form a full on smile.

"That means you would have deemed it your time to die."

Sydon nods, his body tensing as if preparing for an inevitable attack. "So be it then."

CHAPTER FIFTY-EIGHT

Final Push

Alaceandra

As if his words gave the other guards what they needed to react, more guards draw their weapons just as the bronze soldier goes to strike. Sydon is not carrying any weapons. He stares at the sword as it comes hurting towards his face.

"No!" I yell, running forward. Sorin's vines whip out, wrapping along my torso to pull me back, but they do not stop me from summoning my fire. I blast it at the bronze soldier. The fire makes impact with his chest, the flames licking at his armor. He screams and drops his sword, backing away from Sydon.

"Fuck, Lace," Sorin whispers as the soldier turn in the direction that we are hiding. "You can't do that. He was going to be fine."

"But he does not have a weapon," I whisper harshly. "They were just going to slice right into him."

"That is not exactly the case," Sam mumbles.

"Fan out!" The bronze soldier yells. "The traitors have escaped." The soldiers start running in different directions. Searching for us, leaving the hall in front of the door relatively more clear than it was before. Lylane and Jaq continue standing at the door, their posture more relaxed than it was when I first saw them. More soldiers crowd Sydon.

"So that is why you are here? To help the traitors. I never thought you would be one for treason," the same bronze soldier spits at him. "But it looks like you have chosen your path." The man is now reequipped with his sword. He once again attempts to swing it at Sydon.

"Wait for it," Sam says softly.

Right before the blade makes contact, Sydon's eyes flash red and the soldier falls, his sword clanging to the ground. I watch as Sydon smirks at the soldier's body splayed out, unconscious. *What the fuck just happened?*

"What did you do?" Someone else echoes and then suddenly Sydon is surrounded by teal and bronze as they do their best to attack him.

"Now is our chance," Syverious pushes me forward and others follow as we carefully avoid swords and body parts and make our way towards the door. Baldar climbs up my arm and lands on my shoulder.

"I will coach you on what to do when we get inside."

I nod at the ferret.

"I will drop the disguise once we get the door open," Sam says. "It is unlikely that they will believe the door just opened on its own and I would like to reserve some more energy for when we get inside. Who knows what they have unleashed from the portal by now? Seeing as it is likely quite unstable, we will need to be prepared to not only battle the kings and whatever other form of protection they may have but also the demoni."

I nod.

"So how do we get this open?" Sorin asks inspecting the locking mechanism on the door.

The prince and I exchange a look. "I have seen it opened a couple times. Dove, if you would assist me I am sure we can get it open," Syverious says, his usual arrogance now back in full effect. I roll my eyes at him, but nod.

"We got this." Carefully, the prince and I work together to undo the lock on the door. Once we get the final pin in place, the door hisses open and Sam drops the cloak. All eyes turn in our direction.

"Someone is getting in!" A soldier screams.

Bars block the door's entrance and I can kick myself for not remembering to inform the men of this little roadblock. Being so close to my portal my skin starts to sparkle with magickal energy, my stolen magick happy to be reunited with its power source. I breathe deeply as the sensation of magick rushing through me makes me dizzy. I almost do not catch a sword swinging into my face. I flinch, unable to dodge the blade.

Suddenly, the sword clashes with another and I look up to see its owner. Lylane stands smiling at me.

"Hi, Alaceandra! You have gotten into some trouble here, I see."

The bronze soldier that was ready to slice my head off sneers at her. "What are you doing, soldier? You are supposed to be neutralizing the threat, not helping it."

Lylane shrugs. "Where is the fun in that?" With a nod of deference to me, she proceeds to battle the man who had just attempted to kill me. "Go get them, princess!" She is quickly overrun with soldiers now attempting to battle her as well as those in my group. Fear clutches at me as a man sneaks up behind her. My hairs stand on end as the room is filled with a surge of electricity and the sword in the man's hand is quickly dropped as if it shocked him before he is roundhouse kicked to the face. *Jaq?* Jaq catches my eye and gives me a little wave.

The prince grabs my hand and pulls me back towards the bars in the door. Tiny creatures are now roaming the throne room, their hackles raised as they regard the kings and Mylindia. I see their mouths moving as they try to communicate to the demoni, but cannot hear the words.

"Dove, we have to keep moving."

"How are we going to get through the bars?"

"I can help with that," Sam says.

"How is that?" The prince asks, turning to him.

"He can teleport you to another shadow in the room. It'll just expend a lot of his energy," Sydon says.

"I will have to rest for a bit after. It'll mostly be up to you to get the portal secured, parum bellator. The other men will keep the creatures away."

"Why could we not have done that instead of opening the door and getting everyone's attention?" The prince asks.

Sam glares at him. "I have to see the shadow to teleport to it, asshole."

I nod, but do a double take when I realize that Sydon is no longer fighting the guards. "Wait. Were you not surrounded?"

His red eyes sparkle at me. "Was. Take a look around."

I spin around and notice that on the ground lay teal, bronze and black uniformed soldiers. Standing over them, at the ready, are soldiers in silver and a few in black, including Lylane and Jaq. They nod at us when we look at them.

"Are they not going to stop us?" The prince asks.

Sydon shakes his head no.

A roar brings our attention back to the bars blocking our entry into the throne room. A large clawed hand reaches up from the depths of the portal in the ground. Its movements cause the ground to shake beneath our feet.

"We need to move quickly," Baldar warns, his nails digging into my shoulder.

I nod. "Okay, let us get going then."

CHAPTER FIFTY-NINE

Hello, Father

Alaceandra

I n a flash, we appear in a darkened corner on the other side of the metal bars. Sam looks pale as he stumbles away from us and sits at the very edge of the room.

"I should recover relatively quickly. I just need a moment."

"You need to go home," I think I hear Sydon mutter.

Sam ignores him. "Go ahead without me. You got this, parum bellator."

We turn away from him. In front of us is chaos. In the center of it all, the claw tipped paw of a giant animal protrudes from the middle of the crack in the floor, its arm just barely able to fit through the portal. It has gray fur that is patchy and scabbed over in multiple areas. Its claws are pitch black and stained with some kind of red substance that drips onto the floor of the palace. It roars again as it tries to make its way through the crack, but realizes it cannot, its body far to big to breach through the crevice. Sparked on by its roar, ferrets, meresyvils, rats, bradonises, raccoons, and creatures I have never seen before all claw to escape the hole around the giant animal, quickly filling the large room with more and more creatures.

My father and King Demetrius witness this from their dais. My father holds a ruby gem in his palm. I fixate on it, feeling a pull towards the small gem. Purple sparkles jump from the gem and channel themselves into the ground, feeding the portal, allowing it to widen further. Whatever creature is trying to enter, stretches their paw out further, now able to feed more of their arm into this realm. Another roar echoes through the room.

"*Do you see that?*" I ask Baldar.

"*I do.*"

"*Wh- what is trying to get through?*"

"*The Grantador.*" Baldar seems unimpressed as he stares at the giant beast with cold eyes.

"*So they were able to call upon it?*"

"*Seems so.*"

"*What about that gem?*"

"*Looks like that is where they are storing your power, but the gem is a weak tether. Your father will have to maintain focus if he wants to succeed.*"

"*And if he does not?*"

"*If he does not and you cannot gain control of your power in time that will be the final mark, but seeing as this power is not clearly connected to you at the moment I am not sure if we will be able to stop the portal from ripping a hole into the fabric of Ptheryeth...*" Baldar drifts off realizing that I am not understanding what he is saying.

"*Can you explain that a little simpler please?*"

He sighs. "*If you cannot get control of your power and complete the portal it is likely the portal will become unstable and take a lot more people out then just those in this room.*"

"*Oh.*"

The small animals sniff the air and turn towards us. Their movement causes King Demetrius and my father to look at us. My father quickly looks away, his focus intently on the gem in his hands.

Well hello to you too, father.

"Kill them!" King Demetrius roars.

As if they are in a trance, the animals all turn as one and face us. Snarls echo through the air. Then they pounce. *Here we go again.*

CHAPTER SIXTY

Portal Complete

Alaceandra

"**Y**ou need to break that gem, grab control of your energy, and complete the portal." Baldar says quickly, jumping from my shoulder and racing towards the little creatures charging at us. White light blasts through the room as Baldar vaporizes creature after creature.

I throw my fire at one of the rabid animals causing it to back up and hiss. *"How am I to do that?"*

"Get control of your power first and we can talk about it!" Baldar grunts as another white light flashes through the room.

"We need to get to that gem," I relay to the men.

"On it. Follow me," Sorin says, running into the fray.

Vines pop out of the ground, throwing the creatures left and right in order to clear a path. I follow closely at his heels and Sydon sidles up behind me, throwing a red tinted magic at the demoni close to us. I glance around to see those hit by it falling to the ground. Squinting, I realize that their chests are still rising and falling in time with their breaths.

Are they... asleep?

For some reason, a pang of happiness goes through me knowing that he is not killing them. As rabid as they might be, Baldar has made me a bit endeared to the little guys.

There has to be some way to get through this without murdering them.

Suddenly, a cyclone rips through the room, throwing the creatures traveling near us out of reach.

"Your vines are impressive, but moving things quickly out of the way is more of my specialty," the prince jokes.

"Thanks," Sorin says, an amused smile on his face.

We continue closer to the kings' dais.

Unexpectedly, pain rips through me and the prince causing us both to crumble to the ground. Through narrowed eyes, I see that King Demetrius and Mylindia both have a totem wrapped in their palms. They squeeze the figures as they sneer down at us.

"Firefly!" Sorin says, following me down to ensure that I am okay. The little creatures start to run back at us, their little faces filled with anger.

A hand touches mine. "Breathe through it, dove," Syverious grits out, he sounds almost delirious with pain. "You've got this. Show them how beautiful your wings are. Time to fly." With a deep breath, Syverious shoves wind beneath me.

I scream as I am jolted towards the dais. I make impact with King Demetrius, knocking him to the floor. The little totem he is holding falls out of his hand and rolls off the platform. Whatever spell was causing me to be wracked with pain stops immediately when his hand loses contact with the object.

Okay, not my favorite way to travel, but effective. I quickly regain my footing. Glancing down at King Demetrius, I notice that he is now out cold. Blood from a head wound starts pooling on the floor behind him.

Okay, extremely effective, looks like he knocked his head on the way down. How is that for a traumatic brain injury? I glance back over the edge to see Sorin and Sydon fighting the small creatures below me. Sam has also gotten up from the corner and has joined the fray. His black magick and Baldar's white magick creating an almost strobe-like effect throughout the room. The only one missing is the prince. He remains crouched on the ground, the look of agony straining his handsome features.

"You bitch!" The woman in pink— Mylindia — screams at me. She charges. I duck as her fist comes hurtling towards my face. Kicking at her legs, she falls to the ground, her legs getting caught up in her dress. The totem she holds tumbles out of her grip and smashes against the stone floor. The action causes the little figurine to crack in half. I look back over into the fray of creatures and bodies to see the prince is already back on his feet blowing the creatures out of melee range.

"Oh, you are going to pay for that," she growls.

Ripping at the bottom of her dress, she frees up her legs for better movement and charges me again. I dodge again, missing her attack by a mere breath. Pivoting, I throw a ball of fire in her direction. She moves out the way quickly, causing the flames to fly right past my father's head and into the back wall.

"Be careful, Alaceandra!" I hear Baldar scold me.

"Yeah, got it!" I shout back.

Would be nice if I had a weapon other than fire... Another idea strikes me and I pull the little golden pin from where it was housed in my top. *Take two, little guy.* Mylindia takes another swing at me and I use the moment of her swing to slice her with the sharp pin. She screeches in pain and jumps back. Blood wells on her forearm as she glares daggers at me. With a scream, she attacks again. I dodge her, moving just quickly enough.

"Why are you working with them?" I ask her. She kicks and I bring the little pin down letting it plunge into her skin. "Do you not know they only use people like us as pawns? I mean, look at yourself—"

She screams. "Like you could ever understand." She lands her next kick to my leg, causing me to cringe in pain. I back up quickly. Behind me, I hear my father's voice start to chant. The ground rattles as the giant creature finally fits his head through the opening into the floor. A feline creature with black fur and milky white eyes blinks slowly as it glances around the room, surveying its surroundings. The creature looks like it is straight out of a nightmare, its face covered in scabs and scars. *Guess that picture could only do you so much justice.* I think passively. I lick my lips as nervousness fills me. *Fuck, running out of time here. Okay, less chit chat.*

She punches out again and this time, I grab her arm and use her momentum to throw her over my body. She crashes into the ground next to King Demetrius. Leaning up on her forearms, she glances at him and then her eyes widen in terror at the image behind me. Turning quickly, I watch as the giant beast gets his other arm through the ground. His upper body itself almost reaches the tall ceiling. His form takes up much of the room below the dais. Fear crashes through me. Turning back around, I find that Mylindia and Demetrius have disappeared only leaving a pool of blood in their wake. *Where did they—?*

Another roar has me covering my ears. Everything in the room pauses, all eyes on the beast in the room.

"Who dares to summon me?" The beast roars.

"Me, Grantador!" My father calls. His voice strong. I creep up behind my father, noticing that his focus is now completely on the beast in front of him.

"State your purpose," the beast rumbles.

"It was told that you can grant desires," my father explains. "That unlike our energy that is tied to the land around us, yours is tied to the cosmos. Something bigger than the world we know."

The beast regards my father silently. I creep up further.

"Give it a moment," Baldar's voice whispers through my brain. *"I have a feeling you will get a clearer opportunity. You do not want to anger the grantador by causing violence with the one he is speaking to."*

Heeding Baldar's warning, I pause, readying myself.

"If that is true," my father sets the magickal gem on the floor. "Since I have summoned you, I command you to grant me power over these lands so that I may restore and control them."

The grantador blinks at my father slowly.

"Now," Baldar commands.

Darting up to my father's side, I stomp on the little gem with all my might. It shatters into a million pieces. I feel my magick release and fill the room. My father turns to me. "You insolent brat!"

"Find the thread, Alaceandra!"

Slamming my eyes closed, I find my purple thread. The energy around it is frantic, the little sparkles of purple bouncing around excitedly on the thread causing it to vibrate.

"What now Baldar?!" Panic is starting to make my hands shake.

"Calm the energy and tie a knot in the thread."

"The thread is one continuous string! How am I supposed to tie a knot on something with no end?"

Baldar does not answer. Instead, pain registers on my cheek as I feel myself slapped. I do my best to ignore the pain. Smoothing a hand over the thread, I do my best to encourage the little dots of energy to calm.

"Foolish king. How dare you turn your back on me!" The beast yells. My father's scream reaches my ears.

Ignore. Ignore. Ignore. I breathe deeply trying to calm my heart rate as wind rushes around me. Suddenly, the excited energy of the magick, lessens. Slowly, balls of energy start hurtling into the form in my mind's eye as well as the thread itself, causing the string to grow in size.

"Good. Now tie the knot," I hear Baldar whisper.

"How?" I whisper.

"I believe in you," is the only response I get.

Growling under my breath, I stare at the thread. *If there is no end, am I expected to make one? I do not have anything sharp.* The bracelet that Mandi gave me before I departed Ptheryeth starts to glow faintly and I glance down at it. With force, my body starts to move on its own accord. Grabbing onto one section, I pull it to me and pinch the now two strands at the base together. Wrapping the sectioned bit around my arm, I create a circle, and feed folded strands through the back of it.

Another roar reaches my ears along with another agonized scream and I feel moisture hit my face. Keeping my tongue firmly in my mouth, I try not to allow my curiosity get the best of me and taste the substance.

"Hurry," Baldar's voice sounds faint.

I am trying! I yell more to myself than to him. Allowing whatever magick is controlling my body to lead me, I try to secure the knot by wrapping the singular loop around the entire knot and pulling the bigger of the now two strands of thread forward creating two circular ears of thread and a secure knot at the base. The thread glows white, the purple of the thread melting into more of a lavender color.

"You did it!" Baldar cheers in my head.

I guess I did. Mandi's bracelet dims and, I look at it incredulously. I had almost forgotten I still wore the piece of jewelry. The other red band had taken so much of my attention, Mandi's bracelet had fallen to the wayside of my mind. A weird mixture of confusion and gratitude befalls me as I continue to stare at it. On one hand the bracelet could have just saved my life, on the other... On the other it just took control of my body. *Was this your plan all along, Mandi? Is this why you sent me off with it? Did you know what was going to happen?* Hoping that I will get to see my old handmaiden soon to ask these lingering questions, I refocus on the danger in front of me. Snapping my eyes open, I reveal that my father is now hovering in the air before the beast. They are speaking, but the words that they are saying are impossible to hear.

"Final step, Alaceandra. Repeat after me. Come back! Come back! The war is done. It is time to rest under your eternal sun."

Suddenly, the creature opens his mouth and my father's body gets sucked inside. A sickening crunch echoes through the room and it takes everything in me not to throw up as I realize what is happening. My heart drops as his eyes scan the room. *Probably looking for his next victim.*

I scream Baldar's words. "Come back! Come back! The war is done. It is time to rest under your eternal sun."

Everything stills for a moment and then a rush of energy fills the room. The tiny creatures that were once attacking us, now run quickly back into the portal; their bodies filling the gaps of spaces that the beast's large form does not take up. Those who do not run get sucked inside, their claws scraping against the stone floor with their refusal. Every one of the demoni seem to vanish in only a few moments. All, but one.

His body swings in my direction. I stare into the eyes of the largest beast of them all. *The Grantador.*

"You need to leave. The portal has been completed. It is time for it to be sealed." As I address the beast, time pauses and my surrounding fade to blackness. I have to hold back a scream as I am lifted up and taken to meet grantador's face. My body hanging uselessly in the air.

"No! I have been summoned. I refuse to leave without a sacrifice."

Pushing back the fear at being telepathically moved through space, I reply. *"You have consumed my father, is that not enough?"*

"It is not. He was the one foolish enough to summon me. His death was only a mere punishment. I require a sacrifice. It is your energy that brought me here."

"Energy that was stolen from me."

"The process of the ritual matters not to me. A debt is to be paid now what will it be?"

"What kind of sacrifice do you require?"

The creature's milky white eyes seem to almost stare into my very soul. *"I would like something meaningful... provide to me those you care for the most... those tied to your very existence... and I will depart."*

Those tied to my very existence? As if in answer images of Sam, Sorin, Syverious, and Sydon filter through my brain. Anger boils inside of me. *"No!"* I snap at the beast. *"If you want a sacrifice, you can take me. I will not be giving you those men."*

The beast laughs at me. *"A mere girl who has just found her powers? I am afraid that is not enough."* The beast's eyes glow. *"Goodbye, Alaceandra."*

"Goodbye?"

In the next heartbeat, I am once again able to see my surroundings. Horror fills my body as the beast crawls fully out of the portal. In response, a ferocious wind erupts from the portals depths, pulling everything within the room into its abyss. My body is frozen, suspended in the place the grantador left me as I watch Baldar, Sorin, Sam, Sydon, and Syverious try and fail to fight its pull. I scream as one by one they get sucked in. Their answering screams echoing through the room. Then I fall. Through the air. Through the portal. And into the darkness.

Epilogue

Alaceandra

I open my eyes to a new landscape entirely. I am outside. Grass tickles my skin, but the texture is far softer than anything that I have ever felt in Ptheryeth before. The sky is pitch black. Little orbs reminiscent of stars sparkle in brilliant colors of blue, purple, yellow, and pink. Despite the darkness, a blackened sun is present, providing a comforting warmth to the atmosphere.

Groggily, I sit up and look around. There are demoni. Everywhere. My eyes meet the little creatures' as they all peak at me from the tall grass.

"Lace?" I hear a voice behind me.

Spinning around, I find Sorin, Sam, Syverious, Sydon, and Baldar also littered throughout the grass.

"I am here," I answer. "W-where are we?"

It is Sam who speaks next, his voice a near whisper. "My home."

My eyes meet his in shock.

"Welcome to Unduli."

Bonus Chapter: The Brother's Reunion

Sam

After I leave the prince in the dungeons, I make my way through the palace towards the tracker that he left me to denote where Sorin is located. These last few days have been brutal. I had to travel back to Olvaria to try to pilfer any rations that I could live on and look for supplies. *All of it is worth it if we succeed.*

A ringing fills my ears and I grit my teeth against it. *My brother is nearby.* I sensed his presence in this palace when the prince and I had scouted it earlier in the week. That is why I decided to let him infiltrate first before I made my move. *There is only one person my disguises don't work against and it is him.* Since we both maintain a similar power level, our parents ensured we trained our entire childhoods to be able to overcome the other. They had to since they were uncertain who would take over the kingdom once they died. *If me and Sydon were going to fight for the throne, my parents wanted to ensure it would be a fair fight.* What they didn't realize is that I never wanted the stupid title to begin with. When I felt Alaceandra's soul sing for mine, I left Unduli. Leaving the crown to my brother. Hoping to never return.

I make it to the little tracker and peel it from the wall, pocketing it for another time. Guards stand posted outside of a door that I assume Sorin is being kept in.

"Looks like the guy woke up," one of them says. "Guess the magick on him is wearing off."

"Silence," another guard growls.

"What? No one is here. It is good for us to know what we are guarding. Whoever the guy is in there seems pretty powerful. I don't know how he got knocked out before, but he is not going back down again," the guard stretches his arms over his head. "They've tried. We had to shackle him to the bed to keep him from ripping down the fucking door!" The guard laughs. "Too bad he will be dead in a couple hours."

"We are always being watched. Watch your tongue, young one, spill too much and you are set to get us both in trouble."

The guard sighs. "Whatever."

My eyebrows fly up at this news. *Dead? These imbeciles think they can kill Sorin?* I almost snort.

I move through the shadows, careful to mask my approach. Appearing behind the two guards, I knock them out. Their bodies slouch onto the ground. Turning, I pull out a lock picking kit and get to work on the door. Before I can fully get it open footsteps sound behind me. I melt back into the shadows. The ringing in my ears increases.

"Sydon!" A man yells.

"Hmm, yes?" A male voice answers. My brother's voice. I grit my teeth.

"Demetrius and Nikoli have decided to go rogue." Another voice chimes in. The voice is familiar. I chew my bottom lip. *Is that Telvonius? What is our uncle doing here?*

"Have they?" My brother asks. "Rogue how?"

"They have captured both the princess and the prince. They are holding the prince in the dungeons. Alaceandra is tied up in the throne room."

My ears perk up at the information. *That is not good.*

"Fuck."

"They are looking to start the process of summoning the grantador."

Double fuck. Are the kings absolute idiots? Internally, I sigh knowing the answer.

"And how would they go about doing that?" Sydon growls.

"They are forcing the princess' cooperation. I heard him speaking about something with the bracelet she wears."

A low rumble fills the space. "Go. Thank you for the information."

"Of course, my king," Telvonius replies. The sound of footsteps fade. Silence spans for a moment. I keep my place in the shadows.

"Sam, I know you are there. These guards make it pretty obvious." He toes one with his shoe.

Sighing, I step out. "And? What are you going to do about it?"

His eyes flash red at me and I give him an unamused look. He blinks and the color disappears. "You heard all that?"

"I did."

"You are here to rescue her then."

"I am."

Sydon nods. He looks almost sad.

Taking that movement as confirmation he is not going to stop me, I turn to the door that I just unlocked and step into it. I feel his eyes on me, but don't acknowledge when he follows me into the room.

Sorin sits up when I enter.

"Sam!" His eyes are wild as he looks at me. "Where am I?" He looks behind me as Sydon enters and his eyes narrow. "Why is he with you?"

"He is not with me," I reply darkly. "And you are in a palace in the Dark Lands. You and Lace got captured after our fight in Olvaria."

"Lace is here," he says with certainty. "I... I felt her. She is the reason I woke up."

I nod. "Yes, well now we need to get her. The kings that captured you are trying to do a really stupid thing that can get her killed." I walk over to him and snap the shackle binding him. He stretches his hands out. "Are you well enough to be of help?"

Sorin nods. "Yes, I think so."

"Okay, let's go." I go to walk past my brother, but he grabs my arm. I glare at him.

"Why- why did you leave? Truly?" His gaze searches mine. "Why for so long?"

"It is not time to get into that right now."

"If I do not, then I fear I will never get an answer from you."

I shrug. "That might be the case, but I am not answering you now. I have to clean up your fuck up... again."

Sydon glares at me, his grip on my arm still tight, unyielding. "Then I am coming with you."

"The fuck you are—"

He holds up a hand. "You are right. It is my fuck up. Let me make it right."

We stare at each other. A powerful wave of energy surges through the room. I blow out a frustrated breath.

"Fucking fine! But stay out of my way," I yank my arm from his grip.

"No promises," he mutters.

I roll my eyes and flick my gaze back to Sorin who just stands at the edge of the bed watching the both of us. I give him a look that says I will explain later. He nods.

"Let's go."

Also by Rauri Rose

Vines and Daggers

I f even the most powerful kings can become pawns, is anyone safe?

Breaking out of castle arrest and being found in my nightdress in the middle of the forest is a surefire way to gain the infamous ire of King Nikoli. Notably more so when there is substantial evidence to prove that the man who aided my jailbreak is one of the very same men who landed me there from the start.

Alaceandra is the name, being the only heir to Tikilium land is my game, but most people just tend to call me Lace. This morning I reached the magickal age of majority at twenty-four, and my father is already set to ship me off to the prince of Helomasi. I have yet to even come into my powers, but patience has never been a virtue of King Nikoli. I always knew I would be a tool he used to gain more footing in Ptheryeth, but never did I guess that he would make his move so soon. As far as my father is concerned, I am simply the final piece that ensures his checkmate.

What he fails to realize? A king is nothing without his pawns and losing your most powerful piece too soon can lose you the game...

Vines and Daggers is Book 1 in the Powerful Pawns series by Rauri Rose. A reverse harem fantasy romance.

About the Author

Rauri loves all things romance. She have been scribbling in journals and writing stories for as long as she can remember. To her, beauty is found in allowing yourself to experience the world around you and worlds unknown from the safety of your reading nook.

Her debut novel, Vines and Daggers, spawned from a simple set of creative writing assignments that now has it's own life. She finds herself forever grateful that she gets to share Alaceandra's story with each and every one of you.

At home, she spends her time furiously writing on her laptop and keeping up with her four cats Atticus, Shadow, Midnight and Belle. She has a ton of ideas to share and hopes that you are ready to enjoy the wild ride.

Welcome to Ptheryeth!

https://www.raurirosebooks.com